REMINGTON RIDGE

The man's jaw dropped when he saw Lee Morgan, unable to move in his wonderment over how Morgan had gotten inside. When his mouth finally began to move, Lee shot him through the chest. His arms shot out to his sides and his entire torso flew backward through the window, sending blood, shattered glass, and bits of wood falling through the air.

The other man witnessed his companion's fall and turned quickly to confront their attacker. He hadn't even raised his weapon when Lee put a shot into his head, sending him flying against the wall, his hands clutching the gaping wound between his eyes. The man was oblivious to the fact that the back of his skull no longer existed.

SHOTGUN STATION

Lund Taylor heard the horses but his reflex action was directed at Lee Morgan. He fired. He probably heard the two shots, which were fired almost at the same time behind him. It was less likely that he felt them, although both hit home. Lund Taylor was dead before he hit the ground.

Taylor's shot at Morgan had been just a fraction of an inch too high. It took Morgan's hat off but the agile gunman had dropped to one knee, drawing at the same time. His skills, both inherent and practiced, once again paid dividends. Both riders tumbled from their saddles.

Other Buckskin Double Editions:

RIFLE RIVER/GUNSTOCK
HANGFIRE HILL/CROSSFIRE COUNTRY
BOLT ACTION/TRIGGER GUARD
GUNPOINT/LEVER ACTION
WINCHESTER VALLEY/GUNSMOKE GORGE

BUCKSKIN DOUBLE:

REMINGTON RIDGE

SHOTGUN STATION

KIT DALTON

LEISURE BOOKS NEW YORK CITY

A LEISURE BOOK®

March 2007

Published by

Dorchester Publishing Co., Inc.
200 Madison Avenue
New York, NY 10016

ISBN 0-8439-3171-X

The name "Leisure Books" and the stylized "L" with design are trademarks of Dorchester Publishing Co., Inc.

Printed in the United States of America.

Visit us on the web at www.dorchesterpub.com.

REMINGTON RIDGE

1

There was nothing Lee Morgan liked better than the solitary, quiet feeling of lying under the stars by a big orange fire on a cool autumn night, of being alone except for the sounds of the miles of wilderness around him and the fathomless blackness above him.

Tonight was one of those nights, except that he wasn't quite alone. In a deep sleep and curled beside him lay Lisa Anderson. Though she had known many men in her life as one of New Orleans' abundant prostitutes, at this moment she looked every bit the innocent child. Her dark brown hair was pulled back into a tight ponytail and her thin face, made pale in the moonlight, gave her an angelic appearance.

As beautiful and desirable as she was,

Lee Morgan had to wonder what had possessed him to allow her to talk him into bringing her back to Spade Bit. Though she was one of the feistiest women Lee had ever met, she had been city born and bred. And she had been educated in one of the finest schools the city had to offer. What right had he to take her away from what was a promising future? Though she had suffered a terrible setback at Madam Rosa's boarding house, Lisa would have eventually charmed her way to success and prosperity. But now, almost a thousand miles away from her home, away from every last shred of culture, Lisa looked more at home sharing Lee's bedroll than she ever had in the plush surroundings of one of New Orleans' most notorious brothels.

Lee's eyes widened at the snap of the first twig, and by the time the nearby horses had begun to stir, he was groping for the holster laying by his side. His first thought was that some small animal was prowling around the camp looking for leftovers from their sparse supper. But he wasn't taking any chances. A gun in hand was always a safe tack, especially when sleeping out in the open.

A second snap and the horses screamed almost in unison. Lee glanced to his side and saw that Lisa was still sleeping, oblivious to everything but dreams of the unbridled passion of the afternoon before. A smile still lingered on her lips. Lee eased aside the heavy woolen blanket that sheltered both of them against the night air and inched his way to his feet in a crouch. The horses were prancing nervously and would have bolted had they not been tied. Lee saw nothing else move, even in the light of the full moon. There was simply no place an intruder could hide. The nearest trees were fifty yards away, and at that distance neither he nor the horses would have heard the footsteps. Lee rubbed his eyes against sleep and the smoke from the smoldering remains of the fire that had not long before ceased to blaze.

The only other shelter was the boulder, the mammoth rock by which the two horses were tied to a lone tree. Whoever made the noise must be behind the rock, Lee figured, hidden in the moon's shadow, waiting for just the right moment to make his play. Lee was just about to lay low so as to make himself less of a target, when he saw the tracks near his bedroll, tracks that did not belong to another man.

And then he heard it, the distinct low growl of a mountain lion. Before Lee could stand again, the cougar leaped from the back of the boulder to the top, and then onto the appaloosa's back in a motion as smooth as water flowing down a river. The lion again let out a terrible cry, and Lisa sat straight up in the bedroll, trembling with the terror of the moment. The thick blanket was clutched tightly under her chin. She stared with wide eyes at Lee, unable to speak or scream.

Lee took steady aim at the wildcat and fired off a round. He saw a flash of spark as the slug hit the stone. The big cat sensed the danger but did not run. Lee guessed that the animal must have been starving for it not to run off at the sound of his warning shot. No sooner had Lee fired than the beast left the bleeding, crying horse for this new challenge. Lee barely had time to aim again before the cat was rushing toward him. Just as it leaped, Lee squeezed off another round, cursing himself for not having killed it with the first shot. As soon as the shot sounded, Lee hit the ground. If he missed, the cat would be right on top of him, and no amount of wrestling with it would save him then. He didn't even have his knife on him. And that wasn't the worst of it. Lisa would be defenseless, with no gun and no place to run. Even if she made it to one unhurt horse, their speed would be no match for the cat's.

The animal tumbled onto the ground behind him, and Lee turned just in time to see it get back to its feet, blood oozing from a torn ear, its snarling face anxious for Lee's flesh. The cat was even madder than before and Lee knew that he would not have another chance. The cat was preparing to pounce and Lee had dropped his gun in his fall. It was quiet for a moment as the two creatures stared at one another, Lee hoping desperately that he could sidestep the attack, the cat confident in its victory. It was then that Lee heard the shot, and the big cat roared and fell, writhing onto its side. Within seconds it was dead, as peaceful as Lee would have been had the cat not awakened him.

When Lee looked at Lisa, she was still holding the smoking .44 at arm's length before her. "Where'd you find the gun?" Lee asked, amazed that they were both not dead. Lisa did not answer or move, her eyes never leaving the fallen animal.

Lee walked back to the bedroll and eased the gun from the girl's shaking hand. Her eyes were still filled with terror, and Lee took her trembling body in his powerful arms, comforting her as if she were a wounded animal.

"Thank you," he said and planted a tender kiss on her forehead. She spread her arms around his naked chest and pulled him close. She shivered and Lee pulled the heavy blanket around her shoulders against her goose bumps. As the chill went through her, Lee could feel her nipples harden against his chest. Desire quickly overcame him as he tried to urge Lisa back onto the bedroll. Instead, Lisa took him in a passionate embrace. Releasing his grip, he nuzzled her neck and kissed the way down to her breasts. They were taut and white and small enough that Lee had no trouble taking the entire breast in his mouth. He slowly rolled his tongue over the nipple, sucking it, nipping it with his teeth, making it stand out even farther.

Lisa moaned as the desire she felt whenever he was near overwhelmed her once again. Despite her chill, Lisa let the coarse blanket fall from her shoulders and down her back. Her milky skin shone in the moonlight as Lee ran his hands over her lithe body, warming her with his own heat and teasing her neck and ear with his tongue. Lisa finally gave in to Lee's gentle pushes and lay on her back on the bedroll. She stretched her neck full length as Lee continued with his urgent kisses. She tore at Lee's flannel shirt until he stopped to throw it off. While Lee was still sitting, Lisa made her move for his belt buckle, not for a moment considering how vulnerable she and Lee would be should they be approached by another wild animal. There was just one wild animal Lisa had on her mind at the moment, and that was Lee Morgan.

Lisa hurriedly unfastened his belt and undid his trouser buttons with one swift tug. She pulled the pants and long johns over his hips until she was staring at the object of her desire—the magnificent organ that hung between his corded legs, the same organ that had again and again given her so much pleasure. Now she desired him in earnest. While Lee finished removing his jeans, Lisa lay back again, watching the swelling begin between Lee's legs. She unhooked the crudely fashioned buckskin skirt they had picked up for her along the road back to Spade Bit. Resting on her shoulders and lifting her buttocks high into the air, she slid the skirt over her hips and lay it neatly beside the bedroll. Lee had seated himself before her to watch the show of Lisa contorting her body to remove the last of her clothing. Lisa noticed that his cock was standing almost full length before him and, as if to coax it to the bursting point, she swung one of her legs over Lee's head and wrapped them both around his waist. The view of Lisa's slender legs holding his body and the sight of the mysterious dark patch joining them was almost too much for Lee to take. Lisa stared down her body at Lee's newly excited member. Even in the dim moonlight she could see that his organ had changed from a baby pink to a swollen purpling rod fit for a queen. And that's just what she intended to be as long as Lee would have her. And it was her one desire that that would be for as long as they lived.

With her legs still around Lee, Lisa sat up and took his cock in her fingers, sliding the loose skin back and forth until a bead of semen appeared at the tip. She dipped her finger into the drop and coated the head of his organ with a slippery film, making it ready to enter her. Lisa was already as wet as she had been since the first time they had made love three months before. The hair around her opening was drenched with her womanly juices.

Lee teased her with his fingers, gently probing her swollen opening and massaging the little bulb hidden within her folds of flesh. Then he stopped his teasing and slid one calloused finger easily inside. Lisa stiffened and fell back onto the bedroll, writhing in her passion as Lee worked one finger, then another, deep within her. With his other hand, Lee spread Lisa's legs and kneaded the inside of her thighs, feeling the muscles grow tigher with his every stroke. With one swift movement, Lee stretched his body over her and replaced his fingers with his throbbing member, feeling the heat generating in her body and the tender stroke of her fingers across his back.

From her gasps and the contortions of her body, Lee knew that it wouldn't take much to send Lisa into the throes of an orgasm. Sliding his arms under her legs, Lee lifted her thighs high into the air. Lisa lifted her ass and rode Lee's every move, sliding in closer with each thrust of his hips until the full length of him was inside her. When she reached the hilt, her moans and gasps were almost as loud as the mountain lion's screams had been.

Her orgasm was intense, drawing every ounce of strength from her soul. As frightening as her ordeal had been, all danger was forgotten as wave after wave of pleasure swept through her. All that was left was the cool autumn night and the heat of Lee Morgan's body comforting her.

Though Lisa's body was now sated and limp, Lee did not cease his savage thrusts. He was too far gone to stop for rest. There was nothing left but Lisa's smooth body and the desire to let his tightening balls release their load deep into Lisa's quivering hole. As she returned to her senses, Lisa began to respond to his desperate thrusts with small little thrusts of her own. Lee lifted his weight from her body by raising up on his elbows, and Lisa saw this as a chance to excite him even further. She ran her fingers through the thick blond hair on his chest and pinched his nipples as he had done to her. Finally, she tightened her cunt around his cock and countered Lee's every move. Lisa's attentions did not go unnoticed. Lee's load was on the verge of bursting with all the force of a fire hose. One of Lisa's hands made its way between his legs and around the sac which held his balls. All it took was a gentle squeeze and Lee hollered in ecstasy. If another wildcat had jumped on his back at that very moment, it could not have torn him away. Burst after burst of hot semen shot deep into Lisa's hole, so much that they both thought that it might overflow. Even after he came, Lee kept pumping her, savoring every second of the delicious union.

When at last he was limp again, Lee pulled out of her, causing Lisa to give a little gasp as the tip came free. Both were utterly spent and exhausted. The days of hard travel and the hours of passionate lovemaking finally caught up with them and neither said a word as they nestled in each other's arms and fell into a dreamless sleep.

High above, in the clear Idaho sky, two vultures sailed and soared on the air currents produced by the mountain passes of the Rockies. Below, Lee Morgan could almost feel their ravenous stares as they glided directly overhead. Stretched out on a lush bed of grass, Lee was wondering what had brought them out so early when he remembered the carnage of the night before. It was careless of him not to dispose of the mountain lion's carcass, and even more careless of him not to have tended to the horse's wounds. Though they were almost home and the walk would not be a great ordeal, horseflesh was more valuable than gold in Lee Morgan's mind, and if the wounded animal were severely hurt it, would be his own damn fault.

By the time he remembered the vultures, the great birds had circled down a hundred feet or so, and Lee was reminded of the times when he was a kid. He would sometimes sit still for hours in some forgotten corner of Spade Bit and watch a mountain hawk circle above with a watchful eye, and stare in awe as it swooped into dense brush and emerged with a squirming mouse held fast in its needlelike talons.

As the vultures dropped still lower, Lee roused himself and shook Lisa awake. Her groggy eyes peeled themselves open and then quickly shut again against the brilliance of the rising sun. Lisa pulled the wool blanket over her head and feigned sleep while Lee got the fire going again.

While the last of the coffee perked over the open flame, Lee grabbed one of the saddle bags and walked over to inspect the two grazing horses. From the fire, the appaloosa did not seem to be harmed, but as Lee approached, he could see several scabbing cuts on the animal's bare back. Though minor, Lee realized that he and Lisa would be walking home after all. A saddle and rider on the horse's back would only irritate the wounds and be painful for the animal. The horse shied away when Lee approached but its fright eased when it recognized the man. Lee ran his hands over the animal's smooth skin, then reached into the saddle bag for his jar of salve. The horse jumped at the renewed burning as Lee spread the salve over the cuts, but calmed again when Lee offered a sugar cube as a reward for being so tolerant. The horse gratefully crushed it with his powerful molars and went back to grazing on the sparse grass by the boulder.

As Lee moved both horses to the other side where the grass was more plentiful, he couldn't help but wonder how the rock got there in the first place. The nearest precipice was several hundred yards away, so it could not have fallen. And it certainly did not form there naturally. But he did not dwell on this. Maybe it had been rolled there many years ago to serve as some sort of Indian shrine. Though he couldn't figure it, neither did he care. There was not much on Lee Morgan's mind except getting safely back to Spade Bit and seeing how his men had fared in his absence.

Back at the camp, the smell of the fresh coffee had roused Lisa from her blissful slumber. Fully dressed now, she was sitting by the fire vainly trying to put together a quick breakfast of oatmeal and jerky. Lee had suffered several of Lisa's breakfasts and wasn't looking forward to spending the rest of the day trying to clear his throat of lumpy mush and picking burned coffee grounds from between his teeth.

"Why don't you start packing up the camp while I do the honors this morning?" Lee said, smiling while gently taking the sack of oats from Lisa's hands. "It ain't right for a lady, especially my lady, to cook on the trail. There'll be plenty of time and opportunity for cooking once we get back to the ranch. There ain't one of my boys 'cept Charlie can cook worth a damn. They'll be mightly pleased to find that there'll be a woman in the kitchen again."

Lisa gave him a queer look and sheepish smile and guessed that Lee was having a bit of fun at her expense. But she wasn't about to argue with the man who had rescued her from a miserable life of prostitution in New Orleans. After brushing off her skirt, she turned to pack up the bed roll, but not before getting in a little jab of her own. "Hope that oatmeal isn't as runny as your mouth, Mr. Morgan," she said, looking over her shoulders. Lee chuckled and threw a handful into the pot of boiling water.

"Just have to know how to measure it, ma'am," he said, mocking her tone. Then, on a more serious note, he added, "We're gonna have to eat quick this morning. I want to get back on the trail as soon as we get this place cleaned up."

"You're missing the ranch pretty bad, aren't you?" Lisa asked as she tied up the bedroll with a piece of rope.

"Missing home ain't got nothing to do with it. You looked up in the sky lately?" Lee began stirring the oatmeal as vigorously as if he were beating a cake batter.

Lisa tilted her head skyward to see what the hell he was talking about. She knew good and well there wasn't a cloud in the sky. Hadn't been for days. A gasp caught in her throat when Lisa saw the giant raptors circling above, and though Lee's back was turned, he knew she was too startled to speak.

"W-what are they?" Lisa stammered, and she scampered over to where Lee was adding more water to the already runny oatmeal. Lee saw the fear in her eyes and wished he hadn't alarmed her.

"Vultures," he said quietly. "They're after that cat you shot last night. Been up there since first light."

Lisa squeezed his arm and pulled herself even closer. "Will they attack us?" she asked.

Lee looked at her as if she were crazy, but then remembered that Lisa was city born and bred. She had no knowledge of the outdoor life at all. Every vista and every creature was new to her. Lee wondered how she would ever fit in once back on the ranch. As naive as she was, Lee had made it clear before they left New Orleans that she would have to pull her own weight once in Idaho. Women in the west were different than those back east. They worked hard, they wore practical clothes, and most important, they were a very independent lot. It wasn't without a good bit of arguing that Lee had agreed to let her return with him. He'd used every reason he could think of to convince her to stay in the east, but in the end he'd even given in to letting her stay at the ranch until she got settled. But he had vowed that if by the end of the winter she were not established on her own, she would be on a train bound for New Orleans. Surely Madam Rosa would put her up again until she found a suitable husband. Idaho might be a paradise for the strong hearted, but for a woman of weak constitution, he was convinced it would be sheer hell.

"Not unless we drop dead right here," Lee was saying. "They might look fierce, but they won't light until a while after we're gone. They like to eat in private. And don't you worry none about one of 'em swooping down on you. They're more afraid of you than you are of them. They only eat dead bodies. Scavengers is what they are."

"Maybe we should bury the cat," Lisa said sheepishly.

"What the hell for? Vultures have to eat breakfast too."

"It just seems so . . . so barbaric."

"Ha!" Lee laughed. "Barbaric! If you came out here to find manners, we might just as well turn around right now. If you think they're barbaric, wait till you meet some of the folks back in Grover. Most of them are so ornery they'd pick your pocket if you didn't keep your hands in them." Lee dipped the ladle into the steaming oatmeal broth and sloshed a serving for each of them into the bowls he had set aside. Lisa pulled herself free from Lee's side and poured them both a cup of the overdone coffee.

"Lee, are you mad at me?"

Lee looked into her eyes. "Now, what the hell gave you that idea?" But Lee knew exactly what had given her the idea. He had been short with her, and had come close to making fun of her lack of experience in matters that were second nature to him. And if there was one thing a woman hated more than anything else, that was to be made fun of by a man.

"You just seem so . . . cold this morning. Are you starting to feel sorry that you brought me along? I'll understand if you are. I know I practically begged you to bring me back with you. If you're tired of me already, I'll take the first train back."

"Now you get that idea out of your head right this minute. If I hadn't wanted you to come, you wouldn't be here now. Nothing on earth would have made me bring you if I hadn't wanted to." Lee brushed her black hair back and kissed her hard on the lips. "Now, there'll be no more talk about you taking any trains out of here. Hell, you haven't even given it a chance yet. And don't let my teasing get to you. You know I don't mean nothing by it. 'Sides, that's just a taste of what you're apt to get once we get back to the ranch." Lee picked up his spoon again and slurped down another mouthful of the watery oatmeal. "Finish up your coffee. We've still got a few hours of riding ahead of us, and with that horse hurt, most of it will have to be on foot."

Lisa smiled at him, embarrassed that she had acted like such a baby in his presence. Of course Lee was right. If she were going to make it in this rugged country, she was going to have to be stronger. Still, she couldn't help but cast nervous glances toward the sky whenever Lee was not looking.

It took less than twenty minutes to finish eating and packing. Lisa couldn't get ready fast enough. Their belongings were saddled to the one good horse, while the other was tethered to the lead horse's saddle. As Lee was cinching up the last of the packs Lisa screamed and grabbed Lee around the waist. "What is it?" Lee hollered.

Lisa covered her mouth with one hand and pointed toward the camp with the other. Lee was about to chastise her for making another of her silly outbursts when he happened to see what she was pointing at. There, not thirty paces away, the first of the vultures had lit and was slowly stalking the remains of the dead mountain lion.

Lee stood with his hands on his hips and stared bemused. "I'll be damned," he said. "Never known one of those buzzards to drop down when folks were around. Damn things must be starving to death."

"It would be just fine with me if they did," Lisa said, pulling at Lee's arm. "May we get out of here now? Call me what you like, Lee, but I don't think I can bear to watch them tear that animal apart. It's bad enough that I had to kill it in the first place."

"What!" Lee exclaimed in mock astonishment. "Now you're feeling sorry for the creature that nearly tore me to ribbons last night. Be thankful that you did kill it, darlin'. Otherwise those buzzards might be getting their fill of us this morning."

"Goodness! Lee can we please get out of here now? I don't think I can stand another minute of this."

Lee chuckled and finished cinching up the bags. Then the two of them began quickly walking north once again, Lisa looking over her shoulder every few moments to make sure none of the birds had decided that the cat didn't hit the spot.

In September the days were much shorter than they had been on that June day that Lee Morgan had decided to pack up his things for Timothy O'Sullivan's disastrous Panama expedition. His friend Sam had been right. Lee had had his fill of wild times. It was not a time to be going on crazy adventures like the one he was now returning from. Luckily he was returning with his skin intact. Though his reflexes hadn't diminished a whit, he had nearly lost his life on several occasions during his encounters with some of the fiercest Indians south of the border. Now, within a few miles of home, he was relieved to be coming back to what he had so desperately tried to escape: the drudgery of life as owner of the Spade Bit Ranch. It seemed to him odd, but the thought of managing the books, of issuing instructions, of paying tedious visits to Grover's business elite, was suddenly a welcome image. If he never saw another Indian or outlaw again, it would be too soon. If he never again tasted the life of an adventurer that would be just fine with him. Once back on Spade Bit, he would devote the rest of his life to managing the ranch. He had stuck his neck out for someone else for the last time. Perhaps he'd even get married again.

The thought of marriage brought home again the dilemma he had been wrestling with since he had agreed to bring Lisa back to Spade Bit with him; What to do about his courtship with Suzanne Clemons. Surely the poor girl must be half out of her mind with worry for him by now. He'd been gone over three months and had left without so much as saying goodbye to her. Half the town was aware that he had been sweet on her, and there wasn't a Friday night that went by that the two of them couldn't be seen walking down Main Street in their Sunday best, arm and arm and oblivious to everything and everyone around them. He knew that most had expected him to propose before he unexpectedly took off on O'Sullivan's ill-fated adventure. Now he was returning with a beautiful young woman in tow. There were bound to be rumors and enough malicious gossip to make both him and Suzanne the talk of the town once again.

He had to plan carefully if he were to live down this mistake. He was immensely attracted to Lisa, but he also had an obligation to Suzanne. If it came down to choosing between the two, he would have to choose Suzanne, so strong was his feeling for her—that is, if she would still have him. Once back at Spade Bit, Lisa would have to make her own way. Lee had made it clear that he would not marry her, no matter how much she begged. And if Lee could help it, his relationship with Lisa would never be brought to Suzanne's attention. In all likelihood, Lisa would not be able to stand up to the hardships of the Western life and would soon be on a train returning to Madam Rosa's in New Orleans. After all, the men in Grover did not come from the same cultured breeding as Lisa, and there would be few potential husbands even in Boise.

Lee quickened his gait and had to admire the fact that Lisa was not complaining about keeping up with him. She matched his progress step for step without comment, even taking her turn leading the horses. At least she's trying, Lee thought. That's more than most women of her background would do. Any other woman would have me carrying her on my back by now.

The camp was miles behind them now and the sun was as high as it could get on a September day. The terrain was rocky one moment and a flat expanse of grass the next, as they skirted foothills and slowly made their way northward. Lee figured it would be midafternoon before Spade Bit came into view, and then another hour before they crossed the range of Lee's land and reached the sturdy house Lee and his men had constructed after it had been burned by the Jack Mormons over a year before. He hoped there had been no more trouble with them while he was away. Lee was sure the ranch was in good hands. Luke was an able foreman, despite his drinking problem. And Sam was as reliable a man as he would ever find. In all likelihood, Spade Bit would be exactly as he had left it. The entire operation running with the precision of a fine Swiss timepiece.

Lisa finally broke down and said she wanted to rest and eat. After all, they had been walking for hours and the going was a far cry from a Sunday stroll. Lee couldn't agree with her more. His feet were aching so bad that nothing else had been on his mind for the last couple of miles. All he wanted to do was pull off his boots and dunk his swollen feet into a soapy tub of steaming water.

They sat in the shade of an immense fir tree that had probably been standing for a century before Lee Morgan had been born. The afternoon was far from cool, but the warmth from the sun was nothing compared to the oppressive heat Lee had faced in Panama and at the mouth of the Mississippi. Lee broke out what was left of the biscuits they had picked up the day before and then surprised Lisa with a little crock of jam he had bought to surprise her. After a feast of this, a taste of jerky, and a few swigs of the stale water from the canteens, the two lay back for a rest before hitting the trail again.

"Well, kid, we've damn near made it," Lee said, as he picked his teeth with a bit of grass he had pulled for that purpose. He glanced over to see Lisa looking at the magnificent cloud formations above—or was she looking out for vultures? "There was a time when I never wanted to see that old ranch again. Now here I am champing at the bit to get back to it. Crazy, ain't it?"

Lisa turned her distant stare directly into Lee's eyes. "If your ranch is anything like the country I've seen so far, I'd say your daddy was about the sanest man that ever lived. There's nothing in New Orleans to compare to this. I've never seen so much green in all my life."

"You think I'd bring you back here if it weren't anything close to the Garden of Eden? It took a good chunk out of my Alaska strike to buy this place back. But I figger it's worth it. It was getting to be about time I settled down and there ain't no place to do it than where my daddy raised me. I once thought settling down was about the worst thing in the world a man could do, but right now it feels just right."

The rest of the trip was relatively easy going. The hills sloped gently and the trail was well marked. At the top of a rise around three in the afternoon, Lee suddenly stopped and pointed through the thinning trees to a wisp of smoke attached to a building in the distance. "Spade Bit," he said.

"It's positively beautiful!" Lisa exclaimed. "Even more so than you said."

Suddenly Lee wasn't interested in the sight of home. What had caught his eye was the three riders patrolling the outlying border of his ranch at the bottom of the hill, three riders he did not recognize. Maybe they were just passing through, but then again, maybe they were rustlers scouting out the country. Whoever they were, Lee was not about to take any chances by giving away his presence. "Get down!" he snapped, taking Lisa by surprise.

"What? What are you talking about?" Lisa said as she was forced to the ground by Lee's heavy hand.

"I said get down, and stay down," Lee said with violence in his voice. "Don't you see those men down there?"

"Of course I see them! Aren't they your own men?"

"I don't know whose men they are, but they're sure not mine. Look how heavily armed they are. My boys would never be so loaded down with weapons 'less there was something wrong. And it's my guess that those men down there are definitely something wrong." Lee pulled out his Colt and made sure he had plenty of rounds on him. "Now, look, I want you to stay down here and mind the horses. Keep low and don't move from this spot until I get back. I'm going down there to see what this is all about. It's probably nothing, but I want to be sure before we go riding into something we don't know anything about."

"You think they might be dangerous?" Lisa looked worried now, even more so than when she first spotted the vultures.

"Anything's possible, but I'd rather be safe than sorry. I guess I'll know as soon as I show my face. If they mean us any harm, at least you'll be out of the way."

Lee backed the horses a way down the side of the hill where they had just come from and tied the lead animal to a low tree branch, hoping that he and Lisa wouldn't have to make a hasty retreat. After checking to make sure both of his Colts were fully loaded, Lee gestured again for Lisa to keep her head down and then strode down the side of the hill toward the riders. As he stepped lower, the underbrush became thicker and he was able to approach without being seen. When he was within earshot, Lee dropped into a crouch and strained to hear the bits and pieces of agitated conversation.

"What the hell we gotta spend the day snooping around the border of Morgan's land for anyway?" came the first voice. "Ain't there enough to do back on the ranch? Paxton said he wanted the place fixed up from top to bottom before that banker fellow took ownership."

Then a second voice: "Aw, quit your griping. You oughta be grateful that we're getting to go out riding instead of brushing down them goddamn horses. 'Sides, it's only for a few more days. Morgan aint' shown up yet. Everyone's given him up for dead. An' just as soon as the deed is transfered back to the bank, we get our cut, Paxton gets his share, and everyone is happy."

So that was their game! Lee couldn't believe his ears. Paxton! Billy Paxton! The very thought of the name set the hairs on the back of Lee's neck on end. So he was back . . . the son-of-a-bitch who had had his wife shot down in cold blood was back for another try at his ranch.

But he wondered where the third man had gone. He had spied three riders from the ridge above them. One of them had disappeared and might be sneaking up on him at that very moment for all he knew. Lee crouched lower, anticipating an attack and looking for an opportunity to make a move himself.

The shot in the distance resounded clearly, but Lee could not tell from which direction it came. The two riders near him at once looked startled and worried. Since these men were hirelings of Paxton's and not poachers after all, Lee figured that he had been spotted and the shot had been a warning from the missing rider to the two on horseback. Without waiting to find out the significance, Lee rose from the brush and leveled his Colt at the man he assumed was the leader of the three.

"You down there," Lee yelled. "Both of you toss down those sidearms and walk away from those horses." The two men looked at each other and then back at Lee, both with a malicious gleam in their eyes. Lee sensed that neither man knew who he was, nor did they have any intention of doing as he had commanded.

"Now!" he yelled again, gesturing with the barrel of his revolver. "Or you're both dead men."

Either the two men did not believe that one man could take on the pair of them from that distance armed with only a handgun, or they were all too willing to risk their lives for the man who had hired them, but they both unfastened the scabbards holding the rifles at the sides of their horses. Lee wasn't left with much choice. The lead man was the obvious target. Lee dropped to one knee, aimed, and pulled off a shot that caught the lead rider square in the throat. Suddenly blood was everywhere. The shot nearly severed the man's head as it exploded into his neck. His head shot back and blood spurted out onto his shirt and the fine horse he rode—one of Lee's best stallions. Then the man's head tumbled forward again and Lee saw the man's eyes staring wide as if it were the most natural thing in the world to do at the moment. With his hand still clutched to the rifle butt and one foot trapped in the stirrup, the horse began running, with the rider still attached, back toward home.

The second rider did not even have time to catch what was happening. His spooked animal reared up on its hind legs at the sound of the first shot and pawed the air as if it were trying to break out of a cage. Lee knew the animal well enough to sense that once the horse regained its footing, it would bolt wildly after the first horse, oblivious to any shooting or its rider's commands. Lee couldn't afford to let the horseman escape, even in this manner. If he got back to Spade Bit in one piece, he would tell Paxton and anyone else involved in the fight for his ranch exactly what had happened. If that happened, Paxton would have his men scouring the countryside night and day for Morgan, with orders to shoot him on sight.

So Lee aimed again, hoping to wing the man and get the information he needed to keep whatever plan Paxton had devised from working. He would decide later what to do with the man.

He lined up his shot just as the horse was coming down. He would only have time for one shot and he hoped like hell it would be better than the one he had gotten off against the wildcat the night before. As the horse hit the ground, he pulled the trigger and felt the gun buck in his hand. He knew he had shot true. The man on the horse screamed and clutched at the gaping hole in his chest as the force of the impact threw him off the back of the horse. He landed on his seat sitting up on the dirt, and as he looked at the wound, his eyes rolled slowly back into his head and he fell the rest of the way to the ground.

Lee's aim was not as true as he thought. He didn't even need to check to know that the man was dead. Lee kicked the underbrush away and emerged from the trees with his Colt still at the ready. The third rider might still be lurking about, waiting for him to come into the clearing to get a clean shot at the man who had murdered his compatriots. But Lee's concern was put at ease when he saw the cloud of dust moving rapidly away from him in the distance. Evidently, the man had seen what was happening and chose not to stick around to suffer the same fate.

Lee smiled ruefully to himself, pleased that he still had an edge on even the slickest of gunmen. It wasn't every man who could dispatch three gunmen with two shots. But his smile was quickly replaced with a scowl. Paxton had somehow managed to take his ranch, and it was going to take every bit of his cunning to get it back.

Strangely, the second rider's horse had not bolted as he had expected. Instead, it was grazing peacefully on the autumn-dried grass some yards away. Lee's sharp whistle brought its ears to erection as it recognized its long-vanished master, the same man who had broken it two years before. The horse pranced over to Lee, nosing his shoulder to make sure it was really him. Lee took the horse's reins and gave it a quick inspection. Whatever Paxton might be, at least he was taking good care of Lee's horses.

It suddenly dawned on Lee that he had forgotten all about Lisa waiting on the hill above him. She had surely heard the shots and was probably out of her mind with worry over her benefactor. Lee led the horse back through the brush and trees and began to climb the steep rise to the top of the hill. As he climbed, he glanced over his shoulder several times to make sure that the third rider had not changed his mind and returned to follow him. Lee knew that once the man reached the ranch house, it was only a matter of time before a small army of Paxton's men would be swarming toward the site of the shooting. He and Lisa would have to waste no time making plans to hide out until Lee could get to town to find out just what was going on with his ranch. If Paxton was truly involved in some sort of claim on the place, the bank was equally in on the deal.

At the top of the rise, Lee saw Lisa still laying where he had left her. At second glance he saw that the horses had been untied and wondered what had prompted Lisa to release them. Though the horses had preferred getting their fill on the thick dry grass to running off, Lee was irritated that Lisa had disobeyed him and untied their reins. Had she planned to leave him there?

"Lisa," he called. "How'd the horses get untied? You plannin' on goin' somewhere?"

When there was no answer, Lee refocused his attention on the woman lying on the ground. It suddenly dawned on him that she had not jumped up to greet him. She seemed to be gazing passively toward where the shooting had occured. "Lisa," he called again. "What are you looking at? Is there something happening down there?"

There was no answer. Could she have fallen asleep? he thought. Surely with all the excitement, that could not be possible. Lee quickly walked to her, hoping against hope that nothing had happened to her. But something had happened to her. Lisa had been very dead for at least five minutes, for as long as it had taken the third rider to shoot away the back of her head, untie the horses, and make his escape down the other side of the rise. She probably never knew what hit her. The rider must have crept up behind her and sent her to her maker before he could even yell for help. Lee sat beside her and rolled Lisa onto her side. Her face was expressionless, almost peaceful.

Lee felt his eyes well up with tears, but quickly brushed them aside and went to the horses to get his shovel.

Lee Morgan had a lot of work ahead of him.

2

"What the hell happened?" Billy Paxton was screaming at the young man who had just ridden up with the two horses and the dead man draped over the saddle of the one he was not riding. The man nervously hopped off the side of his mount and handed the reins to a smiling Luke Bransen, who was standing next to Paxton. Bransen took the reins as the man approached Paxton with his head bowed low.

"Hell if I know,"the man was saying. "Me, Billy, and Ray was down at the south end of the spread. There was a glint of something or other up on top of the rise so I went up to check it out. Weren't nothin' there but some girl and a couple of horses. She was laying down and it looked like she was spying on the boys down below. I just made sure she didn't get the chance to do no more peeping where she wasn't supposed to. Then there was some yellin' and a shot down below. I didn't know what the hell was going on. I just got out of there as quick as I could get. Back down the hill I seen Ray's horse trottin' across the meadow with Ray hangin' from the stirrup. There was another shot and I was sure Billy had caught it. I had no way of knowing how many men they were up against. Ray and Billy was good shots. They could take care of themselves in a fix. If someone had killed them, I didn't want nothin' to do with him. I ain't no coward, but I'm smart enough to know when I'm outgunned."

"What you are is a fool," Paxton chided, and slapped the man across the face. "You hear two shots and you run like the cavalry is after you. Where's your guts, man?"

The man stammered and then bowed his head once again in shame for not having pleased the man who paid his generous wages.

"You said there were two horses on the ridge with the woman," Paxton continued, "where was the other rider?"

"Hell if I know," the man answered. "I only know what I saw. He probably went down the ridge to see what was going on and ran into Ray and Billy. If it was just one of them, he was a damn good shot. Ray's got a shot clean through his neck, and that weren't done with no rifle, neither. He's sharp with a sidearm, whoever he is."

Out of the corner of his eye, Paxton saw Luke Bransen's smile get just a little bit wider. "What the hell are you grinnin' at, you goddamn jackal?" Paxton snapped at him.

Bransen immediately put on his usual poker face. "Nothin'," he mumbled, and handed Jim Johnson's ride over to the man on his left. With his hands now empty, he strode over to the horse Ray had been draped across and untied the rope around the man's belt. His form slid limply from the saddle and into the dust, and the flies that had collected on his gaping neck scattered everywhere. Jim had tried to close the wound with his handkerchief, but the blood-soaked rag had come undone and was now hanging from the man's throat by dried blood alone. Bransen thought he was going to be sick, but he knew he was going to have to take care of the body or else risk the wrath of his new keeper. Indicating for two men to get shovels and follow him to the graveyard where Lee's wife was buried, he bent and hoisted the corpse to his shoulders, and carried it quietly out of sight.

"You think it might have been Morgan out there?" Jim Johnson hesitantly asked, his eyes following Bransen and the dead man until they had passed around the corner of the ranch house.

"It don't matter what I think," Paxton said slowly, as if even the mention of Lee Morgan's name might send him into a fit of rage. "As far as you and everyone else is concerned, Morgan is dead. If he ain't, then he will be as soon as he shows his face around here. Now, if you think you're man enough to go back out to that ridge, get a half dozen men and ride back out there. Bring me the girl, the horses, and anything else you can find. And don't bother bringing that coward Billy into my sight. Just bury him where he lays. He ain't fit to have a proper burial." Paxton tore the hat off his head and clomped back indoors, a furious scowl on his face and a terrible look in his eye. Jim nodded at the command but Paxton never saw him. He was too busy trying to figure out just what he was going to do now that Morgan had returned.

Inside the house Paxton sat at the dining table pouring whiskey for the two men on either side of him. They were an unlikely trio, all uneasy with the alliance they had formed and all wary of the other mens' motivations. The man to Paxton's right had initiated the entire scheme. As the town's most powerful leading citizen, the banker Jesse Callaway was still determined to claim Spade Bit as his own and divide the land among the highest-bidding farmers. The fertile land would bring a pretty penny and make Callaway an even richer man than he already was. The man on Paxton's left was slight of build and had a thin, sallow face that bespoke his timid nature. As the town's deputy sheriff, he had built a reputation of looking the other way when gunplay was threatened, but had managed to retain his position only because there was no one else in town who would take it. Callaway had unofficially retained the man as a personal bodyguard. Not that he needed one, but Callaway felt comfortable with giving the impression of power wherever he went. Slight as he was, Chook provided the man with at least the appearance of protection.

Since their last meeting, Paxton had met with a bit of success in his adventures. Selling his services as a regulator had destroyed many lives, but made Paxton a rich man over the past year. He didn't need the money Callaway was offering for his assistance, but he still had a bone to pick with Morgan and would have done anything to see the man dragged through the mud.

"So," he said as he tossed back the first shot of aged whiskey, "it would seem that

Mr. Morgan has returned to regain his land." Callaway's eyes widened at the thought of facing the man who had come close to killing him for attempting to take over his ranch once before. Now, he was within days of taking possession of the ranch once again. If only it wasn't true, if only Morgan had not really returned, it would be his—all his.

"Are you sure?" he asked Paxton. "Couldn't it have been someone else. There's plenty of people in Grover wondering what's going on out here . . ."

"But how many are able to singlehandedly take out two of my men without picking them off from a distance with a long range?" Paxton snapped back. He had convinced himself that Morgan had indeed returned and would certainly pose a formidable threat if allowed to show his face in town.

But who had the girl been? A friend of Morgan's, perhaps? A spy enlisted by him to keep an eye on the ranch? They would soon find out. Johnson would be back in a couple of hours with the woman's body. Surely Morgan was not foolish enough to take the time to bury her. Maybe Deputy Chook or the banker would know her identity. If she was from the town, they would know for certain that Morgan had been there. But why had no one else seen him? Morgan was a striking man and not exactly a master of disguise. If anyone had seen him, it would surely have been reported.

"What do you think we ought to do?" Chook asked no one in particular. "We're already too far into this thing to back down. Half the town knows something funny's goin' on down here, and with Morgan back, all he's got to do is show his face and this whole scheme is going to be open for inspection. The whole lot of us is gonna end up behind bars. You know that, Paxton. We've already locked up Sam Lawton for no reason. Lots of folks in town's been talking about that. I ain't got the right to hold him without just cause. If the law up in Boise finds out about that they'll have my badge."

"I'll have a lot more than your badge if you don't keep him and his big mouth where folks can't hear him. Just you remember. We ain't got a thing to worry about unless Morgan shows his face and gets folks riled up. If he's got a lick of sense, he'll sneak around in town and get the word on what's going on here without showing his face to too many people. I'd be willing to bet that he's going to try to win back his ranch without making a scene. He's got a personal score to settle with me, and if I know him at all, he'll make sure I'm dead before he sees me put behind bars. He knows that if he raises too much fuss, I'll vanish before he ever gets a shot at me. Morgan's smart enough to know that the law around here ain't going to help him. If he wants his goddam ranch back, let him come here and fight for it!"

Callaway looked somewhat relieved. "It'll be him against a dozen of the best guns money can buy." Callaway sighed.

At that moment, if Lee Morgan could have kicked himself, he would have. Lisa's body was in the shallow grave he had dug for her, and now all he had left to do was fill in the hole with dirt. He was nearly in tears as he tossed the first spade full of dirt onto her lifeless form. It would seem that Spade Bit was aptly named. The spade was proving to be the most useful tool he had on the ranch. How many graves had been dug for his friends since his return two years before! He had come back to lead a quiet life as a gentleman rancher, but even when he stayed in one place death followed him like a shadow in autumn. Maybe he'd been wrong about trying to settle down. For a man like himself there was no life without looking to make sure no one was following every few moments. Once a gunman, always a gunman, he thought. There might be more and more people moving out west, but it sure as hell didn't get any safer. Not as long as men like Paxton were allowed to do as they pleased. And men like John Chook let them.

Maybe the law wouldn't do anything to keep Spade Bit from being sold off. But Lee wasn't about to give up without a fight. He never had and never would. He wasn't about to let some tough like Paxton get the best of him. He'd sooner burn the whole ranch than see it fall into Callaway's hands.

Callaway! He was the son-of-a-bitch behind the whole thing. His feud with Paxton was one thing, but knowing that Callaway was involved was quite another. How wrong he had been about the man he had so easily forgiven for trying to take his farm before. He had not even been gone all season and already the man had forgotten every promise he had made, every threat Lee had vowed should he ever try to take Spade Bit from him again.

This time it would be different. There was another girl's death to be avenged. He would show no mercy! Spade Bit would be his again. And no goddamn banker or dandy gunman was going to stand in his way.

Lee slammed the shovel down and packed the rest of the earth above the innocent girl who had lost her life because of his stupidity. It was his own damn fault that he had gone off and left the girl unguarded and unable to defend herself. Lee had vowed to avenge her death, but he hadn't the sligest idea how he was going to do it.

By now, he thought, Paxton should have found out about what had happened back at the ridge. Lee had been smart enough to take the horses and the girl away from the area Paxton's men would be searching. Though Paxton may have suspected that Lee was back, without any evidence, he would have no way of knowing for sure, and Lee would be free to move about without hindrance and without anyone knowing that he had returned.

His first thought had been to ride into Grover in plain view of everyone. But that would just scare Paxton off and though he might get his ranch back, he'd never again have the chance to finish off Paxton once and for all. Instead, Lee figured he would lay low for a couple of days and see what developed. By then Paxton might be convinced that Lee had not really returned and become emboldened once again.

In the meantime, he would pay a visit on Suzanne Clemons and try to discover precisely what was going on. That was the only good thing about Lisa's death. He could now unashamedly confront Sue without having to explain the girl. Though he mourned her passing, he knew Lisa would have been no match for the wild living that awaited her in Grover. And he would not have to face Lisa's mournful eyes every time she saw him walking through the streets with Sue.

Lee placed the crude wooden marker he had fashioned at the head of the grave and wiped his dirty hands on his jeans. The horses were still tied together in a chain of three, but did not seem to be in a hurry to start walking again. Lee made sure the ropes were secure and mounted the lead horse. He set out on a pace that would get him to town after dark and after most had retired for the evening. There would not be many people roaming the streets then and he would be able to speak to Sue in private.

Two hours later he was approaching Grover. Lee pulled the brim of his hat lower over his eyes and moved quickly along the back streets, weaving his way toward Sue Clemons' house. There was a light on in the window of what Lee Morgan knew was Sue's parlor, so she must still be awake. He tied the horses to the hitching post by the back porch and stealthily approached the window. Inside, he could see that Sue was sitting under a dim electric lamp reading a thick book. There was a wistful look in her eyes and Lee could tell that she was visibly upset about something. Maybe she would know more than he thought about what was happening at the ranch.

Lee tapped several times on the window with his fingernail and Sue nearly jumped out of her seat. At first she didn't seem to be able to tell where the sound had come from, but she was visibly frightened. Lee tapped again and Sue looked hesitantly at the window, wondering whether to investigate or run. Lee pressed his face close to the closed window so that Sue could see who was there. When she recognized his face peering inside, Sue had a horrified look as if she had just seen a ghost. Then came a look of relief and she ran to the back door, threw it open, and stared at the man still hunkered over beside her window. Lee immediately threw a finger to his lips, indicating that she should keep quiet and not give away his presence. Wordlessly, she ran to him and threw her arms around his neck. Then she broke away suddenly and indicated that they should go inside. The instant the door was shut they embraced again, Lee planting a much desired kiss on her warm lips. She pulled him onto the sofa and looked deeply into his eyes.

"What on earth happened to you?" Sue asked urgently. "You wouldn't believe what's happened since you disappeared."

"I'd believe it," Lee answered. "Fact is, I've already got a taste of some of it."

"Before I tell you anything else, Lee Morgan, you're going to tell me exactly where you've been for the last three months. Sam Lawton came to me right after you left and said you'd gone on some crazy expedition to Panama. How could you run off and leave your ranch unattended like that. What got into you, Lee?"

"I guess I ain't got an explanation that would make you forgive me for what I did. I just got an itch to do some traveling and thought it best that I leave before tears had a chance to flow. I'd planned to be back a month ago, but some folks had another idea. I'm lucky to be back at all."

"Not half as lucky as you think. Have you got any idea what's been happening out at your ranch? Rumors are flying everywhere. Everyone in town is convinced you're dead."

"I kinda figgered something like that. That's why I came here instead of riding through town this afternoon. I ran into a little trouble just south of Spade Bit and managed to hear Billy Paxton's name mentioned. You know there ain't nothin' in this world can rile me like the mention of that man's name." Lee was beginning to feel warm from the heat of the blazing fireplace and removed his jacket. Sue took the dusty garment and folded it as if it had just been freshly laundered. Lee leaned back in the couch, nearly exhausted.

"There's some leftover supper out in the kitchen. If you're hungry, I can fix you up a bite," Sue said, noticing how weathered Lee looked from his trip.

Lee's eyes brightened. "I ain't had one of your home-cooked meals since I left. I'd be grateful." Sue immediately disappeared into the kitchen. Lee thought that she had not changed at all. She was every bit as beautiful as she had been the day he left. Yet there was an odd weariness about her and her eyes looked very tired, as if she had spent long nights awake. Lee felt comfortable in her home. Sometimes even more so than he did in his own. All the feelings he had harbored for Sue suddenly came back to him in a rush. When she returned with the plateful of hot food, he came close to dropping to his knees and proposing to her on the spot. But he immediately thought better of it. Now was neither the time nor the place. Besides, after the untimely death of his first wife, Lee was going to have to think long and hard before he took another. He still was not over the pain.

Sue smiled at him as he devoured the hearty dinner. Lee had never known himself to be so hungry. He finished the meal within minutes and Sue was about to go back to the kitchen to get him a refill, when Lee swallowed the last mouthful and raised his hand for her to stop. "That's just about enough. I believe I'll have just a spot more tea to wash this down, then I want to hear all about what's been happening in town since I've been gone."

Lee could tell that Sue was not looking forward to this, but he knew he could rely on his friend to tell him everything he needed to know. Sue poured Lee another glassful of the sweet liquid, then leaned back next to him and waited for his questions.

"I've gathered that Callaway has called Paxton back in for another try at the ranch."

"It would seem that way," Sue sighed. "But to tell you the truth folks aren't quite sure just what is going on. Callaway and Deputy Chook have been making daily trips out to the ranch and that awful Paxton man and the fellows he's hired hang out at the Black Ace Saloon several times a week."

"What about my men?" Lee asked. "What's happened to all the boys runnin' the ranch? Why didn't they stop this?"

Sue didn't want to tell him, but she did anyway. "Most of them's run off, Lee. A few stopped in town on their way out. They looked like they had a good scare put into them, but there wasn't one would tell what was going on out there. Cain't say I blame them, either. Paxton's boys look like they'd kill for a glass of water on a rainy day. I imagine they intimidated a few of them into staying—at least those that didn't have no place else to go. Lee, please don't blame them. They were good men, but they weren't gunfighters. You can't expect them to lay down their lives for a man that everyone has given up for dead."

Lee felt a twinge of guilt at Sue's subtle accusation. But in his heart, he knew she was right. He should never have left the ranch, should never have gone on that fool expedition. And how could he harbor a grudge against men trained only to breed horses? "I never expected those men to look out for my welfare. I thought there was law here to do that."

"What are you talking about, Lee?" Sue chided. "You know what kind of law we have here. Did you really expect Deputy Chook to do anything? Why, he's one of the perpetrators! That young man named Sam Lawton rode into town one morning and told me he was going to Deputy Chook about the situation at the ranch. The next day he was thrown in jail for no good reason, and that's where he's been since. Chook won't let a soul in to see him and won't even explain why poor Sam is being held."

Lee looked astonished. "Sam's being held prisoner?"

"Yep. That's got folks upset more than what's going on at your ranch," Sue said.

"That boy wouldn't hurt a fly," Lee said. "Why isn't anyone doing anything about this?"

"Everyone's afraid, Lee. Paxton and his men have the whole town cowed. There's been some talk of breaking him out. But that's about all its been. Facing up to Chook is one thing, but standing up to a dozen professional gunmen is quite another."

Lee was suddenly saddened about how justice could be so corrupted even in this day and age. This was supposed to be a civilized world, yet bankers still worked their greedy schemes, gunmen still intimidated innocent citizens, and crooked lawmen still twisted the law as if the little parcel of land they watched over was their private property. Grover had been terrorized for weeks by these madmen who would own the entire town if they were able. And now that Lee Morgan was back it would seem that he was the only one able to do anything about it. And that's just what he was determined to do.

Lee took another sip of tea, then leaned back to let his supper digest. He had to think. The first thing he had to do was get Sam out of jail. That was simple enough. John Chook would be so spooked to see Lee stroll into his office that he would not only let the man out, but would probably offer to string himself up on the nearest tree. Chook would catch hell from Paxton, but what was he going to do about it? Lee figured that Paxton had guessed he was back anyway, but Paxton wouldn't admit it to anyone unless Lee showed his face to the townsfolk.

Once Sam was out, he didn't know what he would do, but whatever it was, it would be done quietly. And pretty much alone. Sam and Sue were the only people he could count on at the moment. That was like pitting two mice against a cat.

"Listen, Sue. I plan to break Sam out of jail tonight and I'm going to need your help. Seeing as my place is indisposed, how about letting the two of us hole up here for a day or two? Paxton won't risk molesting the town's leading female citizen, at least not right now. If he starts putting the pressure on, Sam and I'll hide out up in the hills. I'm going to need some time to put a plan together. It's be easy enough to ride to Boise and make sure the deed stays in my name, but if I do that, I'll never get Paxton. He'll vanish, just like last time when he ran out of tricks. You know I want him bad, and I don't intend to let him get away this time. He's going to face me, man to man."

"Oh, Lee, why do you always insist on trying to get yourself killed?" Sue said, exasperated at the thought of her man getting into another gunfight. "Can't you just inform the law up in Boise? If you tell the marshal what's going on, he'll be down here with an army of lawmen in a matter of two days."

"No!" Lee snapped. "I want Paxton for myself. He's responsible for the death of my wife, and I'm the one who has to make him pay. You can understand that, can't you?"

"I don't see the sense of it, but I can understand how you feel. I'd probably feel the same way if someone gunned you down in cold blood. Of course you and Sam are welcome to stay here as long as you like. There's plenty of room and you know I'd never pass up the chance to spend time alone with you."

"I'm obliged. Of course I'll pay you for the room and board . . ."

"Like hell you will. And don't you dare start getting formal on me, Lee Morgan. We've known each other much too long for that. Even if you did all but abandon me."

"You know I wouldn't abandon you. I just took a little . . . business trip," Lee said, almost stammering. "Now, look, I'm going over to pay Chook a little visit. I shouldn't be gone over an hour, but even if I am, I don't want you to worry. I'll leave the horses tied up around back and tap on the window again when we get back."

Sue looked wistfully at him. "Don't worry," she said. "I'll be waiting up."

Lee walked over and embraced her once again. He felt so stiff and awkward around her, but attributed this to the length of time he had been away. Being around her again would change this, he was sure. Even without his ranch he was already feeling like he was home again.

Sue opened the back door for Lee and he stepped out into the night. Immediately, he missed the warm comfort of her parlor and her soothing presence. Whatever had prompted him to leave in the first place would never overcome him again. Once he got Spade Bit back and Paxton out of the way, he was there to stay.

He checked the horses before setting out on his mission. After making sure they were secure, Lee grabbed his shotgun and loaded the barrel with two shots. Then he removed his whip and fastened it onto his belt. Lee stayed in the shadows all the way to the deputy's office, weaving in and out of alleys, avoiding the few people on the streets, wondering how he managed to get himself into these messes.

The jailhouse and Deputy Chook's office were so dark they could have been haunted. Lee approached warily, peering in windows as he moved toward the front of the building. Nothing was moving inside.

Lee stepped into the light from the gas lamps in front of the jailhouse, but stepped back into the shadows again just as quickly. There, leaning against the front door, half-asleep, was a man Lee had never seen before. One of Paxton's men, he guessed.

So, Chook was too cowardly to guard even one prisoner himself. Paxton had to assign one of his guns to do Chook's job for him.

Lee managed to slip back to the side of the building before the man could get a glimpse of him. This was going to be a little harder than he thought. There was no way Lee was going to get in to release Sam without first confronting the man at the door. But the fellow had looked half-asleep and this fact might work to Lee's advantage.

As quietly as he could, Lee removed his bullwhip from the fastening on his belt. Lee flung the woven leather weapon to its full length and watched the tip dance on the ground. This old friend had gotten him out of many a fix and now it was going to have that chance once again.

With his Colt in his left hand and the whip in his right, Lee stepped out of the shadows again and drew back the hammer on his pistol. The sudden click brought the guard out of his slumber and into action. The man responded by reaching for his gun faster than Lee had expected. Fortunately, Sue's meal and tea had pulled him out of his exhaustion. Alert as after a good night's sleep, Lee stepped forward and drew back the whip. He knew Paxton's guard had been instructed to not ask questions. He would kill any potential intruder as sure as he stood there. That way no one would dare attempt to free Sam, and Deputy Chook would keep his nose clean if there were any public outcry.

But the man fumbled with his sidearm an instant too long. Lee's whip lashed out and gripped the man's wrist like a single handcuff. In one motion, Lee jerked the man toward him and hit him in the head with the butt of his gun. The gunman opened his mouth as if to call for help, but he fell unconscious and his eyes rolled back in his head before he could make a sound. Lee was furious enough to cut the man's throat as he lay still, but decided that if he were to get his ranch back, being accused of cold-blooded murder would not look good for his case. He was going to have to do this as quietly as possible, without giving Paxton justification to do further violence.

Lee pulled a handkerchief out of his pocket and stuffed it into the unconscious man's mouth. He thought about tying the man's hands and feet, but without rope that would be impossible. Instead, he dragged the man by his feet around to the alleyway from which Lee had emerged. The man would probably remain out for a good long time, certainly long enough for him to pay a surprise visit to Chook, who by this time was in a very deep, secure sleep.

Lee returned to the front of the building and turned the door handle. He was surprised to find it unlocked until he got inside. There, on a small table beside the door was a pint of rotgut whiskey, three-quarters empty. That must have been the reason the guard had been so easily taken. Lee rested easier when he saw this. Surely the gunman would be out cold for the rest of the night.

Once fully inside, Lee gently closed the door behind him. Darkness returned to the large room as if someone had just blown out a candle. Lee waited a minute to let his eyes adjust to the dim light coming in through the few windows.

Then the thought occurred to him—what if Sam were not there? What if Paxton had gotten wind of Lee's return and had him moved back to the ranch, or worse yet, killed? Lee shuddered at the thought of what he might be moved to do to Chook and the guard outside if this were the case. Sam just had to be there, and he had to keep faith that he would be.

The jailhouse's two small cells, Lee

knew, were at the back of the building, and Chook's cot would be in an even smaller room before he got to them. Lee tucked his whip away and walked on his toes to the back, being careful not to awaken the man before he could surprise him. Lee heard a sound and stopped dead in his tracks, his gun at the ready and hoping his eyes had adjusted well enough to allow him to shoot straight. But the sound had only been snoring, and his hearing told him that the drone was coming from more than one man. So Sam Lawton was still there.

The door to Chook's quarters was ajar and Lee stepped stealthily inside. The man was laying on his back and appeared to be sleeping fitfully. Lee almost felt pity for the man. Chook didn't have an inherently evil heart, but he had chosen the wrong profession for a man of his spineless constitution. He should have stayed in New York where he had come from and taken over his overbearing father's business. But Chook could not tolerate his father's manner and customers' constant demands on him so he had fled west to make a new life for himself. He had answered an advertisement in a newspaper for a deputy to look over the town of Grover, and thought that it would be a good chance for him to make some good money and a name for himself. But things hadn't turned out quite as he had planned. Once in office, more people were making demands on him than ever. He was expected to settle disputes and keep the peace—not an easy task in a town as wild as this. No wonder the marshal had so readily hired him on. They would have taken anyone. He hadn't been sworn in two months before the banker had started requesting special favors. At first they were simple but annoying tasks, like looking over the bank while he was away on business. And those favors had soon grown into looking the other way whenever Callaway cheated someone out of a trifling amount of money. And now this . . . Chook had no idea how he had gotten involved in taking over a man's ranch, but he knew there was nothing he could do about it now, especially with Paxton and his men giving the orders.

Lee leveled his gun at the sleeping man's chest and struck a match on the sole of his shoe. Chook stirred and rolled over onto his side as Lee touched the lighted stick to the oil lamp on Chook's writing desk, and Lee guessed that he was not going to have any problem with this man at all. He could probably steal the deputy's keys, open the cell and clomp loudly out to the jailhouse without even waking the man. But he was not willing to take that chance.

The room was now filed with an eerie dim light, casting shadows of Lee onto the wall and making him appear even larger than life. With his right foot, Lee kicked the deputy's cot to wake him. Chook snorted and pulled the blanket over his head, causing his bare feet to stick out the other end. Lee kicked again and suddenly the cot was a mass of thrashing blanket.

"Who . . . What?" Chook stammered, trying to fight his way out of the binding blanket. "What's going on? What do you want?" he went on, still looking for daylight.

Lee bent down and picked up the holster laying by the cot, then placed it on the desk near the lamp. "Get up, Chook. It's time you and me had a little talk about your future in this job."

Chook recognized the voice immediately and violently flung the blanket from the cot, his eyes wide with terror at the sight of Lee Morgan standing over his bed with a gun aimed at him. "Mr. Morgan," he managed to say. "You're supposed to be . . ."

"Never you mind what I'm supposed to be. Fact is I'm here. Funny thing is, so are you. You knew good and well I'd be back and so did Paxton. I really didn't think you'd have the guts to stick around with that on your mind."

"But the guard . . ."

"Don't you worry about him. He's sleeping sounder than you were. He ain't gonna make a peep. Probably don't even know what hit 'im."

Chook sat on the edge of the cot and slumped his shoulders in defeat. He should have known Morgan would be back and should have run when he got word that he was. Now Morgan had him dead to rights and after the last fiasco with the Spade Bit ranch, he'd be lucky if Morgan let him live. "Well, kill me if you're gonna," Chook sniveled, bowing his head. Then he muttered, "I shoulda never left daddy's factory."

Lee had not planned on killing the man, but the thought had sure crossed his mind. He would have thrashed the man senseless right then if he had not felt so sorry for the coward. Instead, Lee slapped the surprised Chook across the face. "Get up and get your goddam pants on, you little shit. Look at you. You're supposed to be a lawman, but you won't lift a finger less someone's pointing a gun at your head. If I had any sense at all, I'd do you a favor and pull the trigger right now. But I'm not that nice. You're going to do some good for folks whether you like it or not. Now get dressed."

Chook had no idea what Morgan was talking about, but he stood, pulled on his pants and tucked in his night shirt.

"What do you want me to do?" he asked.

"Some cooperation, for starters. You're going to do just what I say and maybe, just maybe, you'll get the chance to redeem yourself. You screw up and Paxton's gonna be draggin' your sorry ass from the back of his horse all the way back to New York."

With a look of near panic on his face, Chook realized that he didn't have much choice at the moment. If he did as Lee asked, his name was mud as far as Paxton was concerned, Paxton would chase a man to the end of the earth to get revenge. The fact that he was back to get even with Morgan was proof. But, then, he didn't want to overestimate Morgan's kind heart either. Either way, he would probably not come out ahead, but for the moment Lee Morgan held all the cards.

Who were the riders after me on the ridge this morning?" Lee snapped at him.

"I don't know," Chook whimpered. "Couple of men Paxton sent out to patrol the border in the hills."

"Names," Lee demanded, shoving the barrel of his gun against Chook's neck.

"Honest, Morgan," Chook said, trying to twist away. "I don't rightly know. He's got over a dozen hands up there, none of them I've ever seen in these parts before. From their voices, I'd guess they were from the south but I can't be sure. The one who brought back the dead man is called John something or other. The other two I don't know."

Lee removed the gun from Chook's head. "I guess it don't matter right now," Lee said. "I'll find out soon enough. Where's your keys?"

"Keys? What keys?" Chook said, not understanding Morgan's meaning.

"The keys to the goddamn cells, you idiot! Do you think I came here to have tea and cookies with you? I want Sam Lawton out of here tonight!"

Chook looked at Morgan with admiration. The man had quietly arrived in town mere hours ago and already he knew what was happening at his ranch and that Sam Lawton was being held. Morgan was efficient if nothing else. But one thing Chook was certain Morgan didn't know was how he was going to get his ranch back from the banker who would hold the whole town hostage to get the land. And what did Morgan mean that Chook was going to have the chance to redeem himself? Did Morgan really expect him to stand up to Paxton alone? Morgan might as well kill him right out if he did.

"Look in the desk drawer," Chook said. "Your man's in the first cell down the hall."

Lee stepped to the door of the room and took a quick look down the hall. There was no sign of anyone stirring. "Open the drawer and take the keys out. Then get down the hall and open that cell."

Chook sensed that this was a test, but Lee was looking for a chance to give him what he deserved. Lee was still looking out the door while Chook walked over to the desk where the keys were tucked away, but on the top of the desk was the holster and pistol Lee had earlier placed there. Lee was giving him a chance to go for the gun, testing his willingness to do as Lee asked. Chook thought that he might have made a play and might have even gotten off a shot, but if he did, Morgan would show no mercy. It wasn't a chance he was willing to take. Morgan would be expecting him to make a move. Chook removed the keys, picked up the lamp, and walked past Lee's smirk and through the door.

Lee gestured for the man to lead the way down the dimly lit hallway, taking time to glance toward the front door, as if he expected the guard to come bursting through, guns blazing, at any moment. Lee should have felt exhilarated over having gotten this far without detection, yet he felt strangely depressed over having to go through this ordeal at all. He'd been in tight situations many a time, but for the first time he almost didn't care whether he won or lost this battle. But then he thought of Sam and Sue and how they would be depending on him. Lee was the closest thing to law and order Grover had seen since before Chook arrived.

The lamplight and the clanging keys woke Sam out of his slumber. He sat quietly up in his bunk as if he had been awake all along, expecting Paxton to come for him in the middle of the night to silence him forever. When he saw Lee Morgan step out of the shadows, a big grin covered his face and he rubbed his eyes in disbelief that his friend and employer had finally come home.

"Evenin', Mr. Morgan. I was starting to think maybe you wouldn't get back in time." But Lee could tell that Sam had never doubted that he would return to save the day.

Chook silently unlocked the door and let the bars swing open. Sam was out of bed in an instant and shaking Lee's hand with enthusiasm and gratitude. Chook just wondered what was going to happen next. Morgan couldn't very well let him go, and even Morgan wasn't ruthless enough to murder a lawman in cold blood. If he did that, he'd never see his ranch again.

"Give me them keys and go sit on the bunk," Lee demanded.

Chook did as he was told and watched as Lee locked the gate again with Chook inside. "So you're just going to leave me locked up in here all night?"

"What would you have me do? Let you go so you can run back to Paxton? If I did that, Paxton would know you helped me and I let you go. He'd kill you for sure. Like I told you, I'm giving you a chance to make good. And if I don't see you trying, I'll be the one to drag you back to New York. The keys'll be back in the drawer."

"What about me?" The voice came from the second cell. Lee looked surprised to hear Luke Bransen's voice. He looked to Sam questioningly.

"Paxton's guard brought him in this afternoon," Sam said. "Guess he figured since you were back in town he might be more trouble than he was worth. Deputy Chook here's been boasting about how Paxton has run off all your men. They kept Bransen to show them how the operation works and because he was too drunk half the time to stir things up. I came to Deputy Chook when the trouble started just like you said, Mr. Morgan. I didn't know he was involved with them or I'd have gone straight to the marshal in Boise."

The man in the cell looked sober enough. "You all right, Luke?" Lee asked. "You been hurt?"

"I'm just fine. And I'll be even finer when you let me out of this rat trap."

Sam took the keys from Lee and opened the door. Lee had gotten more than he had bargained for. As much as Bransen liked to drink, Lee valued the man's assistance. He knew every inch of the ranch—probably better than Lee himself—and that knowledge might come in awfully handy in a pinch.

"I'm forever grateful, Lee. Ain't nothing more distasteful than the inside of a jail cell." Bransen picked up the few personal belongings Paxton let him keep and hurried out of the cell, slapping Lee on the back on the way out. "Good to see you're alive, Lee. I was beginning to wonder if what everyone was saying was true."

Lee smiled at the man's spunk. Bransen was the only one of his hired men he allowed to call him by his first name. None of the others dared to address him as anything other than Mr. Morgan. Bransen hadn't changed a bit. Though several years Lee's senior, he managed to retain his youthful enthusiasm for life. That alone had gained Lee's respect. If Bransen's drinking were the cause of his self-assurance, Lee was going to have him hit the bottle at the earliest possible date.

Sam reclosed the cell door and the three men headed for the front door without so much as a goodbye to Chook. Chook, however, was too busy worrying about how he was going to explain this to Paxton to think about it. Lee took a second to toss the keys back into the drawer then followed the other two into the night. It seemed a lot colder now and from the dampness in the air Lee knew that it would not be much longer before the first snowfall dusted the range. He was worried about the well-being of his animals. Bransen would have managed the ranch without a hitch throughout the winter, but Paxton would know nothing about horses except how to ride one. Without proper attention, Lee's prize horses would be in pitiful shape come spring.

And then there was another worry. Lee had obtained Sue's permission to stay over with Sam for a night or two, but what was she going to say when he showed up with Sam and Bransen? Though harmless, Bransen was not the most couth of men. On numerous occasions Sue had commented to Lee about the man's unruly behavior in town. Bransen's drunken binges were known throughout town. Taking him to Sue's place was a chance he had no choice but to try.

There was still no one on the street to see them, but as the trio rounded the corner into the alley, Lee was stunned to see that the guard he had knocked out cold was staggering to his feet. Still without arms, Sam and Luke took a step back, not knowing that the guard had no gun either. The guard instinctively went for the gun that was no longer there, then his eyes turned white when he gripped air. Lee stepped forward with something in his hand, and the two former prisoners thought for a second that Lee was going to put the man out of his misery.

"Please . . ." the guard said, terrified, and threw his arms in front of his face to ward off his fate. "I didn't mean nothing. I was just doing a job . . ."

And then Lee shoved the whiskey bottle into his hand.

3

She was not amused. Three men in her house—and she had wanted to spend the evening alone with Lee his first night back. But she said nothing. She was even cordial and ladylike with Bransen. And he had remembered to remove his hat when he entered her home. She should be grateful, she reasoned, that Lee now had another man loyal to him in his time of need. Lee was going to need all the help he could get against Paxton's cutthroats.

After the men had eaten the snack Sue had prepared, and Lee had checked on the three horses one final time for the evening, Lee said they ought to be retiring. They would have to get up early in the morning to make plans for the recovery of the ranch. Lee still had no idea how he was going to get the ranch back and finish off Paxton, but maybe a good night's sleep would give him a brainstorm.

Sue left for her room after giving Lee a slight peck on the cheek. It was less than Lee had hoped for but more than he expected given the circumstances.

Sue had a small, but cozy home, one that most of the women in town were envious of. That was but one of the reasons she was shunned by most traditionalists, men and women alike. Headstrong and progressive minded, Sue was involved in varous causes most felt women had no place even discussing, much less participating in. And that was what had attracted Lee to her in the first place—her ability to stand up for herself, and others not as fortunate as she. Not to mention that she was the most goodhearted, most beautiful woman Lee had ever had the pleasure of knowing. She was such a stabilizing influence that Lee found himself wishing that he had met her years before.

Lee slept fitfully. The two men he had broken out of prison began snoring as soon as their heads hit their pillows. Twice he got up to throw a fresh log on the fire, and each time he went to the front window, pulling back the heavy tapestry-like curtain to get a clear view of the street.

This wouldn't do. He was so nervous Paxton would somehow find out he was staying in the Clemons house that he considered staying up to keep watch all night. But as he lay back on the cot Sue had set up for him, the heat from the hearth and the droning of the mens' snores finally lulled him off to sleep.

The next morning he awoke to the smell of bacon frying and coffee brewing. For a moment he didn't know where he was, but then he saw Sam and Luke sitting on the couch sipping the steaming coffee and remembered all the troubles awaiting him in the day ahead. He wanted a bath more than he wanted breakfast, but decided that that could wait. There were more important things on his mind than either.

The heat from the wood-burning stove in the kitchen made it warm enough so that the main hearth did not have to be relit. Yet Lee still felt a chill.

"Have some coffee, Lee," Sam said, taking another sip from the mug he held with both hands. "Sue says she'll have breakfast on in a few minutes.

Luke nodded his affirmation, wishing that he had a bit of whiskey to spice up the coffee.

Lee groggily got to his feet and rolled up his bedding, then went to the kitchen without a word to either man. He wiped the sleep from his eyes while Sue poured him a cup of hot black liquid and then went back to the main room with the two men.

Lee hardly knew what to say, but the men looked on anyways as if waiting for Lee to reveal some dark secret. Even Lee himself was wondering what he would say.

Finally, after burning his lips on the coffee, he put the mug aside and began to speak. "I know you men think I expect you to help me out of this jam. You know Paxton and Callaway have taken over my farm, and you both know I plan to get even with Paxton no matter what the cost. If you two want to scoot on out of here right now, I won't hold it against you. I didn't break you out expecting any favors, but you don't know how grateful I'd be if I could count on your assistance." Lee gave them both a long hard look and waited for their reply.

Sam and Luke could see Lee's desperation. Sure they could leave, and probably find jobs up in Boise, but Lee had always been a fair man and deserved more than that. "I'm staying," Luke said right away.

Sam hesitated a moment and then said, "Mr. Morgan, you've always done right by me. You gave me a chance when I didn't have a job, and I appreciate that more than anything."

Lee looked at the man sympathetically, knowing that he was about to bow out of

Lee's plans, but he let Sam continue.

"I don't much care for violence," Sam said, "and I know there's going to be plenty of it. But I don't care for folks throwing me into jail for obeying the law, either. You can count me into whatever you have planned. I ain't much of a match to Paxton's hired guns, but I'll do my best to help you get back your ranch."

Lee smiled at the man's devotion, and he realized that, despite his past misgivings about Luke Bransen, he had in his presence two of the finest men he could have hired. "As I understand it Paxton has about a dozen men guarding the ranch . . ."

"As of yesterday, he's got ten," Luke cut in, referring to the two scouts Lee had killed on the ridge. "Now that he knows you're back, he's likely to send for more. Paxton's a sly devil, but beneath all that he's also a coward. He wants you dead more than Callaway wants your land, but he won't stand up to you alone. He'll get all the support he can to back him up. We're going to have to make our move fast if we're to stand a chance."

"Which means we've got about two days if he's bringing in men from out of state. Even without them, the job's going to be next to impossible. Thirteen against three ain't such good odds, but I want you to know I appreciate your staying to help me." As he finished, Sue brought in the first tray of food and placed it on the dining table, and the three men wasted no time meeting her there. Fresh scrambled eggs, grits, biscuits, gravy, and crisp bacon tantalized their noses and started their mouths watering. Sue was pleased to know that her efforts were appreciated, and she hurried back to the kitchen to refill the quickly emptied trays. When she returned, she sat down to get a bit for herself before the feast vanished again.

"We've got three good horses," Lee was saying. "I've got a couple of spare side-arms and a rifle for each of us. Ammunition's no problem. Plenty of rounds in the packs I brought in last night. And thanks to Sue here, we got a place to stay for a night or two. It ain't much, but it'll have to do. I may have put enough of a scare into Chook last night to get some help from him, but I wouldn't put any money on it. Right now he's probably on his way to given Paxton the dirt on what happened last night. He'll get a good chewing out, but Paxton's smart enough not to cause any problems with the law, especially when it's working for him."

Lee went on. "The only way we're ever going to get the ranch is to split up Paxton's men, and I'd be willing to bet that's going to happen this morning. Paxton will send men in to town sometime this morning to look for us, but we're going to be on our way back to Spade with a little surprise of our own. I only hope that Paxton is there so we can get this over with fast. But even if he's not, we'll stand an even chance of reclaiming the place."

Sam looked up from his meal, excited by Lee's pep talk but with a dread that could only come from realizing that he might be riding to his death. "Even if Paxton does send half a dozen men into Grover to look for us, that's still going to leave another six at the ranch. Think the three of us can handle them?"

Lee understood Sam's concern, but stood his ground. "I'm mounting up right after breakfast. You can still back out if you want to and no one will call you a coward if you do. Six men ain't so bad if we catch them by surprise. 'Sides, if we give them a good enough scare they might run off before the shooting starts."

Now it was Sue's turn to worry. "You think Paxton will come here looking for you?"

"It's likely he'll come here right after inspecting the jail. Callaway's sure to have told him how close we are. Just make sure this place's cleaned up real good. Don't leave a trace of us out in the open. And if he starts asking questions, play dumb. Like you don't know what he's talking about. He's not likely to push you too far."

As soon as the last mouthful of breakfast was finished, Lee and his two-man army went out back to inspect, saddle up the horses and pack the few belongings they had brought inside. Lee made sure that each mount carried a rifle with plenty of spare rounds in the saddlebags. He handed both men a sidearm, which they tucked into their belts since Chook had relieved them of their holsters at the jail. Together they looked more like a band of rustlers than ranchers.

Even though he had a full night's sleep, Luke Bransen looked as if he had already fought a war. He hadn't had a drink in two full days now, and was beginning to get a bit jumpy. Lee saw the man staring vacantly and when he called out his name Luke's hand visibly twitched as if to draw. "Luke—you all right?" Lee said, more than a little concerned.

"Yeah. Just a little shaky is all. I ain't been in a fight like this since the war. Guess I've just got the jitters is all."

"You ain't got a thing to worry about," Lee reassured him. "You're the best damn horseman in these parts, and Lord knows you can shoot. Just make like those thieves back at the ranch are empty whiskey bottles and you'll be okay. Just because they've got more guns don't mean they've got more sense."

"Sure, Lee. Sure," was all Luke could say.

But Lee was beginning to worry about the man. He must have been under considerable strain since Paxton and Callaway took control of the ranch. From what Lee could gather from Sam, the two schemers had offered to let Luke stay on to manage the ranch until the deed was transfered to Callaway and the land was divided. Though Luke was still loyal to Lee, with no place else to go, he had reluctantly agreed to their proposal, all the time drinking more and slipping closer to uselessness. By the time Paxton expected that Lee had returned, there was no longer a need for Luke, Paxton had simply had Chook haul him off in a stupor to wait out the happenings in jail with Sam.

Usually Luke was a jovial, but unpredictable man. Now Lee saw within him a deep depression that only a renewed clear-headedness had allowed to show through. Luke had proved himself to be still loyal to Morgan, but it was evident that he was embarrassed that he had not done more to protect Lee's land when the trouble first started. Lee now sensed that Luke's shame was quickly being replaced by a deep-seated rage—directed both at

Paxton, for having taken advantage of him, and at himself, for not having the guts to stand up and fight when he had the chance. Now he had his second chance, and he was not going to let this opportunity to repay Paxton get away from him.

Lee considered letting his presence be known by riding down Main Street through the center of town. Luke and Sam had been released and the community's support might help along his cause. Besides, if Paxton were going to run, he would have done so at the first hint that something might go wrong with Callaway's plan. He changed his mind when he thought about how that act might lead Paxton to suspect that Sue had somehow collaborated with them. Her life might be placed in danger, and the death of another woman—especially Sue Clemons—was something he did not want resting on his shoulders.

The three men set out in full gallop, riding wordlessly, each wrapped up in his own fury over the men who would destroy their lives for a small plot of land. They headed north at first, but once well off the trail and away from Grover, they circled to the West and the well-worn road that led from town and eventually to the trail that would take them to Spade Bit and the revenge they desperately sought. They reached the trail without being recognized, and slowed to a walk so as to be alert to any approaching riders.

After his fitful night of sleep and thought, Lee was grateful for the brisk, cloudless morning. The cold air rushing past his face brought his full attention to matters at hand. He tipped his wide-brimmed hat back to get a panoramic view of the surrounding territory. It had been too long since he had taken this old trail, and the memories of those frequent trips into town to visit Sue only steeled his resolve to defend his right of property. He suddenly remembered the two sticks of dynamite in his pack. He hadn't told either Sam or Luke about them because he didn't intend to use them unless he was forced to. Still, he would not hesitate to blow up the ranch house if he thought destroying the building would destroy Paxton as well. The thought of rebuilding the ranch house a third time in as many years was not pleasant, but if he allowed Paxton to escape this time, he would never again spend a restful night.

Sam brought him out of his musings with a shout and an outstretched hand. "Mr. Morgan! Look up ahead there. Just over them trees . . ."

They had just come to the top of a rise out of a mile-long stand of pine. Ahead of them was a sloping decline that descended for another mile with no cover except for the dense grass that seemed to stretch forever down the slope on either side of the trail. Beyond that was a smaller stand of hardwoods where Lee and Sue had often picnicked. Beyond that was what had gotten Sam so feverish—a large cloud of dust swirling like a twister in the morning breeze. There were Paxton's riders, coming directly and furiously toward them. The trees and raised dust kept Lee from seeing just how many of them there were, but from the size of the cloud, he guessed there were at least the six he had expected would come to town looking for them.

From his vantage point at the top of the rise, Lee appraised the situation. The riders obviously did not expect to meet any resistance on the way to town, and it was equally evident they were very much in a hurry. Lee had seen signs that a rider had preceded them to Spade Bit earlier that morning, and had guessed that it had been either Chook or the guard Paxton had assigned to the jail. In all likelihood it was Chook who had remained in town—perhaps still locked in the cell where Lee had left him to think about his misdeeds.

At any rate, there was not much time for preparation. If Lee and his two men were still in the open when the riders broke through the trees, they would be seen for certain, and if that happened they would not stand a chance against the larger approaching party.

"Turn back," Lee said calmly to the two stunned men. Surely Lee was not running away after they had come so far. Had his trip to Panama left Morgan afraid of a fight?

The two men did as they were ordered, but understood Lee's intentions when he motioned that they should enter into the stand of pines. Far from running from a fight, Lee had strategy in mind. Dismounting, they led their horses deep into the underbrush, calmed them, and made sure they were securely tied. If any of them were to scare, Lee's position would be given away and the fight would be over before it started.

They returned to the main trail and, chancing a peek over the rise, Lee saw that the men were over half way up the side of the rise. They would be upon them within minutes. Lee could not afford to waste another moment. He took up a position behind one of the broadest pines and made sure his rifle was fully loaded. The other men followed suit. Beads of unnatural sweat popped up on Sam's forehead and Luke's damp hands shook violently.

"Keep low and keep quiet," Lee whispered in warning. "Don't shoot until they're right alongside us and you're sure you can get off a clean shot. Don't panic and we'll have them beat—or at least half of them. If Paxton's with them, he's mine."

The three crouched in the underbrush and thistle, their six eyes focused on the spot where the riders would breech the top of the hill, wide with anticipation. Then they heard the hoofbeats where it had moments before been silent. Lee prayed that the riders would not stop for a breather at the top of the hill. As fast as they were traveling, Paxton's men were not likely to spot the additional hoofprints until it was too late. But it would take only one sharp-eyed gunman to turn Lee's impromptu ambush into a disaster.

The first horseman breeched the rise like a demon from hell, the rider hunched behind the animal's neck, the horse blowing hard, steam billowing from its flaring nose. If they intended to continue riding at that pace, the horses would be dead long before they reached Grover. Lee wondered if he was so important that these men would kill their mounts to catch up to him. Then he realized that these were his own horses Paxton's men were abusing.

Renewed anger swept over him as he watched the riders come over two at a time. There were seven in all—more than he had anticipated. They were all heavily armed, but did not act as if they were expecting a fight. They were about to ride right past the trio hiding in the brush when the second horseman reined to a halt, pointed to the ground, and yelled back. It was Billy Paxton.

The regulator had spotted the maze of hoofprints Lee's men had left. Lee wasted no more time. The other riders were reining in and bunching around Paxton to see what he was pointing at. Lee took steady aim at Paxton's head as the outlaw followed the tracks with his eyes. When Lee was confident that Sam and Luke had also drawn a bead, he gently tensed his finger on the Remington's trigger and felt the gun buck solidly in his hand as the bullet left the barrel.

But Paxton's head was no longer where it had been. He had stooped to inspect the hoofprints just as Lee fired, thus fouling Lee's aim. At the sound of the shot, and the two following, Paxton's head jerked up as if someone had hit him with an uppercut. But he just as quickly turned to see the man beside him. Callaway Jones, his best man, had been hit square in the face by Lee's misplaced lead. The man was slumped over his horse, unable to scream. His hands had momentarily covered his face when he was hit, but were now hanging limp at his side, dripping warm blood on the trail. Paxton didn't have to give the man a second glance to know that he was beyond hope.

Paxton's hands immediately went to his sides and leveled with a pearl-handled pistol in each. Three of his men had fallen, one with a bullet in the side of his head and another lay on the ground dying as blood filled his punctured lung. Still, he could not see who his attackers were, or where they were shooting from. But one thing he knew for certain: Lee Morgan had fired that first shot. With only four men left, Paxton wanted to get out of there in a hurry. He had no idea how many Lee had with him, but now was no time to stand around and count heads.

With shots hitting all around him and nothing to shoot back at, Paxton did the same thing any other rational man would have done—he jumped on his horse and kicked its flanks with a spur, urging it back into a full gallop. The other three surviving members of Paxton's gang had already beat him to the idea and were several lengths in front of him, running for their lives from their unseen enemy. None of them had even bothered to fire back.

Luke broke through the brush despite Lee's call to stay put and began firing wildly at the fleeing horsemen. Paxton turned just long enough to see Bransen taking aim, then ducked as the slug whizzed past his head and into the back of the man directly in front of him. The man arched backward as the bullet tore through his body and out his chest. It was as if the man's heart had simply exploded. When the man fell from the horse, Paxton didn't even bother to look back.

Luke ran to make sure the fallen man was dead and then returned to the other three bodies where Lee and Sam were now standing, gaping at the carnage. Lee rubbed his grizzled face with the palm of his hand while he thought about what to do next. Once again he had failed to get Paxton and he was sure now that Paxton knew he was a hunted man, he was going to be more careful. For now, Paxton would have to make do in town with the two men he had left. Lee had succeeded in dividing the group. Paxton would not be able to show off his muscle in Grover now, and Lee was sure that Chook's loyalty to the man would be eroded even further once he learned of the travesty Paxton had just walked into. The men left at the ranch now had no leader, and without that to hold them together, Lee's task would be much easier.

"Luke," Lee said. "Go back up the trail and rope that miserable carcass you shot to his mount and bring him back here." Luke gave Lee a puzzled look but understood that Lee was not to be questioned. He turned immediately and backtracked to where the man lay. "And keep your eyes open," Lee reminded him. "Those fellows might make another run through here to get back to the ranch." But Lee knew that this wasn't going to happen. Paxton was probably most of the way to Grover by now.

"Sam," he went on, "help me get these bodies back on their horses. I want 'em sitting tall."

Now it was Sam's turn to give Morgan a curious look. "What do you mean to do, Mr. Morgan?" Sam asked hesitantly, hoping that Lee wouldn't snap his head off for questioning him. "We ain't gonna take them with us, is we?"

Lee's rage had not died down one bit. "Even dead, I wouldn't give this scum the pleasure of riding with me. I'm fixin' to give those boys back at the ranch a scare like they've never seen before. Just get them loaded up like I told you and you'll see what I'm blabbering about."

Together the men tied the bodies to the saddles one by one, their legs fastened to the stirrups and their wrists tied to the horn so that none of them could slip off. Then Lee tied the horses together so that they formed a chain. Sam thought for a moment he was going to be sick at the sight of the four bloody corpses mounted on the steeds. But neither man questioned

Lee's motives. They both knew the horrors Paxton had brought upon Lee in the past, and even if they didn't approve of Morgan's brutal methods of getting revenge, at least they were willing to go along with him.

Lee gave the horses a final look over, then walked to the lead horse and slapped the animal smartly on the rump. The horse shook its head violently, then took off in a trot back down the rise toward Spade Bit and home.

"You think they'll go back to the ranch?" Luke asked.

"Where else are they going to go?" Lee asked rhetorically. "Them's my animals they were riding. They know where home is, and that's where they'll go, if for no other reason than to get those bodies off their backs. And when they get there, those men are going to have something more to think about than overseeing a ranch."

"What do we do now?" Sam asked, sitting on the ground and inspecting his rifle.

"Exactly what you're doing," Lee replied. "We sit and wait. I figure it'll take about an hour for them horses to make their way back to the barn. The ones that aren't scared off ought to be easy pickins." Lee walked back to the top of the rise and surveyed the horizon. He had stood here so many times before he could point out the exact tree above which the smoke from his ranch-house chimney would rise.

Perhaps it had been profane to desecrate the men they had just killed in such a way, but it also occurred to him exactly what was at stake. It wasn't just Spade Bit that mattered, it was, in the long term, the livelihood and safety of the entire community. They had worked so hard to build civilized lives on a frontier that was even wilder now than before the white man came. If Callaway and Paxton were allowed to have their way now, they would be bolder in the future. Everyone in the county would consider that even their land might not be safe. After all, Callaway ran the bank and held all their money for safekeeping. Would he insist on calling all the shots as well?

The hour went by slowly, and the men passed the time smoking and chewing on the pieces of jerky and pemmican Sue had packed for them. Though the midmorning sun was soothing and the air invigorating, the three were none too comfortable about sitting in the middle of the trail where they might be attacked themselves. Every few minutes, one of them would go again to the top of the rise and look out to see that there were no more riders approaching. In the dense stand of pine and needles, the horses were finding little to eat and soon began giving indications that they too were ready to move on.

At length, Lee spoke: "There can't be more than four of them down on the farm. Seeing as we just killed four of 'em and three more are in town, that can't leave more than four if you counted right, Luke. Them bodies we sent down are gonna put the fear of God into them, but it's also going to keep them on their toes. They'll be looking for us. So we're going to have to circle around and approach the ranch from the west. There's a thick stand of trees there that'll provide cover and a place to leave the horses . . ."

Once again Sam had to wonder what this once sane man was getting them into. Did Morgan really think they could just walk in and take the ranch without a fight? Lee had already alerted Paxton's henchmen that something was up. Now he was going to lead them into the midst of four professional gunfighters, all of whom had every reason to want them dead.

"We're going in on foot?" was all Sam could manage to blurt out. "In broad daylight?"

"Would you rather that we ride up to the front porch and give them a few howdy-do's?" Lee joked. "Maybe we could bake them a couple of pies to show how hospitable we are. Fact is, they'd blow us off our horses before we got within a hundred yards of the place. Now, I don't know about you fellows, but I'd prefer not to get caught out in the open."

Sam silently conceded that Lee was right, especially since he was in no position to argue. It was Lee's ranch, and Sam had agreed to come along for the duration. He'd never be able to hold his head up again if he backed out now.

"If there are no more objections, we'll move out now," Lee said, rising to his feet and dusting off his trousers. The three men remounted their horses and let them trot to the bottom of the hill. Paxton had shown no sign of returning and the way seemed clear.

Once they reached the trees at the bottom, they turned north to make the long circle around to the west side of the property. Though it was still early morning, the chill had gone out of the air and the horses heated easily.

Spade Bit was only two miles away, but Lee Morgan still had a long way to go.

Once they reached the main road, Paxton and what was left of his party reined to a halt and spun around to check the trail behind them. They had run as if stampeding for well over a mile. The horses were ready to drop and the riders were not in much better shape. Paxton and his two men had managed to escape injury, but each was visibly shaken over the surprise attack.

"God damn it!" Paxton screamed, throwing his hat in the dirt and trying to keep his mount calm. "How the hell could I have been so stupid?"

The other men had dismounted to give their tired horses a deserved rest. If not for them, they would all be dead for sure.

"Bushwhacked by a son-of-a-bitch ranch hand with a rifle. I knew I should have left another guard in town." Paxton looked like a frustrated general as he sat high in his saddle and let his horse prance around the other two men. He was naturally prone to violence and could strike fear into the heart of even the bravest of men with his icy stare. Now, even his own men were beginning to wonder if he might ever turn on them in his anger.

Billy Holmes looked into Paxton's reddening face. "It wasn't just Luke shooting back there. You heard all them guns. Sounded like a damn shooting gallery. We didn't even get off a shot. I still don't know where they were shooting from."

"I wonder how long they'd been hiding in them woods," Callaway Jones added, still out of breath from the wild ride.

"You can bet Morgan and that goody-two-shoes Lawton fellow was right there with him," Paxton went on, fuming, "and now they're probably on their way to the ranch. Those boys down there better keep alert or Morgan will have them picked off one by one."

Holmes and Jones looked at the man as if he had lost all his senses. "We were going to town to find Morgan," Holmes said, "and now you know that he's heading for the ranch. Why the hell aren't we going after him? Between us and the fellows back at the ranch we can take 'em easy. What's gotten into you, Paxton?"

Paxton jumped off his horse and ran up to Holmes with his fists clenched. Holmes backed off immediately.

"Are you going to keep on questioning my decisions, or do I take your head off right now?" Paxton's eyes were bulging out and his face had become as red as his hair. "What the hell makes you think Morgan ain't still hiding out in the woods? For all we know he's got half the town with him. Morgan ain't just fast with a gun. He's smart, that Morgan is. He's got something up his sleeve, and we're not rushing into nothing without getting our advantage back."

"But what about the ranch?" Jones attempted to argue once again. "Callaway ain't going to like this."

"To hell with Callaway." Paxton said, calmer now. "You're working for me, not him. And you'll do as I say. I don't give a hoot about the ranch. It's Morgan I want, and I aim to get what will hurt him most. That's why we're still going to Grover."

There was nothing left to say. They would have to let the horses rest, but within a half hour, they would be on their way to town again. Jones and Holmes were still not sure why, but one thing was for certain, they had signed on with Paxton and it was too late to back out now.

Far from the show of bravado they had originally planned in town, the mood had turned to one of melancholy. Paxton's rage had diminished and his face was now set with a look of quiet determination. As the three men rode through the center of Grover, all heads turned their way. It was unusual for Paxton to show his face in town without a large detachment of armed rowdies. Almost everyone on the street, from playing children to proselytizing merchants, stopped what they were doing to gape at the lathered horses. Instinctively, they knew there must have been some trouble, but no one dared ask what it was. Usually when Paxton made one of his infrequent trips into town, it was to pay a call on Callaway's bank. But this time he rode right past, dismounting only when he had reached the stark jailhouse.

Paxton and his men hastily tied their

mounts to the tether and let their horses drink deep from the stale murky waters of the trough in front. They wasted no time getting inside, and the town's citizens wasted even less time going about their business.

From the cell where he had been sweeping one of the jail's stone floors, Deputy Chook heard the front door open and the sound of several sets of feet shuffling inside. With an overwhelming sense of dread he stopped what he was doing. He knew it was Paxton before he heard the man's voice. Chook had been expecting a visit all morning, and now his time had come. His first thought was to lock himself inside the cell he had been cleaning out, so that Paxton could not get at him, but that would be futile and would get Paxton even more riled.

Chook stepped out of the cell and into the hallway holding his head as high as he was able considering the circumstances. He didn't dare smile, and when he encountered the scowling faces in the front office, he could hardly hold back the tears.

"I don't even want to hear your miserable excuse for letting this happen," Paxton breathed in a voice that froze Chook in his boots. "Just tell me how many Morgan's got with him and I might just let you live."

"I-I-I don't know. J-just the three of 'em was all I saw. I was dead asleep when Morgan came in. He had a gun on me. Threatened to blow my brains out if I didn't let Lawton out. There wasn't nothin' I could do. He had the drop on me. The guard . . ."

"Shut up! I said I don't want to hear your lame excuses. I give you a simple little job to do. Just watch over two men—locked in a cell yet, and you still fuck it up. I don't know what marshal in his right mind would give you a goddam star, but I do know I ought to blow a hole through that tin badge right now. Morgan didn't have anyone with him? He just walked past the guard outside and past you, and nobody even fired a shot at him?"

All the courage Chook had tried to muster had vanished under Paxton's brutal interrogation. His head drooped and his jaw hung almost limp. "That's about how it happened," he managed to say in a voice just above a whisper. "If Morgan had someone with him, I didn't see him. He might have had some help taking out that guard, but if he did, the other fellow stayed outside."

"Help taking out the guard?" Paxton chided, looking back and forth between the two men who had come in with him. "The only thing that took out that guard was a solid punch in the jaw. He was too drunk to even know what hit him. Why the hell did you wait till near morning to come and tell me what happened?"

"Well—uh—Morgan sort of locked me in the cell before he left. I sent the guard as soon as he woke up. Looked like he'd been drinking a lot last night."

"Locked you in the cell, did he? You'll be lucky if I don't lock you in a pine box before this is over with. Do you have any idea what this has cost me?"

Chook stammered and twisted the broom handle in his sweaty hands. He braced himself for the worst. If Paxton didn't shoot him dead right then and there, he would be the most grateful man on earth.

"This whole scheme is falling apart because of your bungling. Morgan and those sorry ranch hands you were supposed to be looking out for ambushed us this morning on the way in. Four of my best men are dead, including Callaway Jones, the only man I've got besides me who could have outdrawn Morgan in a fair fight. And now he's dead with a bullet through his head. Morgan's headed for his ranch and if they don't get stopped there it's gonna be his again, and everybody in town will know what we've been up to."

Chook was stunned that Morgan had acted so fast. He didn't think Morgan still had the old fire in him. So, it was really Paxton who was lucky to be alive. Maybe it was time for Chook to rethink whose side he was really on. After all, he had been trusted with a badge and all that it stood for. Still, this was no time to make a stand for law and order. "Have you been over to tell Callaway?" Chook ventured.

"I don't give a good goddam whether Callaway gets that ranch or not. I got all the money I need. You think I came all the way back here to help out poor ol' Mr. Callaway? You must be even stupider than him. I'm back here for one reason only, and that's to put Morgan six feet under. It took me a year to build back my reputation after word got out about that last fiasco with him. There's still people saying I shot his woman in the back. I can't help it if some confound farmer gets carried away with a rifle and I can't help that she got in the way. But Morgan still blames me, and will until I make him shut up for good.

"So, Chook, should I kill you or give you another chance?" Paxton finally said. "I still aim to get Morgan. There's no way I'm runnin' now that I've come this far. 'Sides, if I did, he'd probably come after me. I'd be willing to bet he's just as determined as I am."

Chook's eyes widened at the thought of being tortured by Paxton, and he could not force himself to respond. He wished now that he were back in New York, in a nice easy job, pandering to his father's customers and staying out of trouble. What had he gotten himself into? No matter what he did, he would lose. If he did Paxton's bidding, either Morgan would kill him or he would lose his job. Even if Paxton ultimately got his revenge, the regulator would probably decide to kill him anyway. But if he stood up to Paxton, he would probably end up dead even sooner.

"Well, Chook, I'm going to count on you one last time. If you fail me, you can count your prayers. I've still got one ace left to play, and if that don't break Morgan's bank, nothing will." Paxton's eyes narrowed as his idea took form.

"Are you going back to Spade Bit?" Chook asked. If Morgan had really retaken the place, Paxton and his two sharpshooters would hardly stand a chance alone, and help was still well over a day off. He would have to try a different tack. And soon. Word would soon spread of Morgan's return, and once that happened, even the town's citizens might take up arms against Paxton.

"Spade Bit's the last place I want to see again. I aim to make Morgan come to me." Paxton was working himself into a frenzy again. He was acting more like a little kid who had just won a game of kick the can than a violent man bent on revenge. Was this man becoming unglued in his single-minded determination to kill a man everyone in town respected? And how did he intend to get at Morgan with his men dead and no one except Callaway on his side? Callaway's influence, except for what his money could buy, was nonexistent. Though respected for his position, Callaway's bank held nearly everyone's savings and the exorbitant interest he charged on loans to homesteaders certainly won him no friends.

"What do you want me to do?" Chook asked, hoping it wouldn't be much. People had been grumbling about the way he did his job, rather the way he didn't do it, for some time. Working in such close association with Callaway, and now Paxton, a known criminal, had people wondering whether their town was really safe.

"I want you to do exactly what you were doing when we came in. Just clean the offices and go about your job as if nothing were unusual. The boys and me are going over to pay our respects to Mr. Callaway and tell him what his trusty deputy let happen last night. We'll be gone about an hour, and when we get back, I'm going to want you to run a little errand for me—one that involves delivering a little message to Mr. Morgan."

Chook didn't like the sound of this. Callaway would hit the ceiling when he heard Paxton's version of how Chook ruined Callaway's last chance to claim Spade Bit. Callaway might even take up a gun himself. And what did Paxton mean about delivering a message to Morgan?

"What sort of message you got in mind, Paxton?" Chook asked nervously. He prayed that this ride out to Spade Bit was not going to be his last.

"A message that'll have Lee Morgan back in Grover before you can say Jack Robinson. I'm plannin' to be waiting for him with something he wants real bad."

"Only thing I can think of that he would want that bad is Spade Bit. And it looks like he's probably already got that," Chook said.

"You're forgetting Suzanne Clemons," Paxton said, and his broad smile revealed a golden tooth.

4

The leaves in the grove of trees to the west of Spade Bit had turned a luminescent orange in the late September sun. Winter was likely to arrive earlier than usual, for in the shade the morning's frost had not yet thawed. Still, out in the open it was as warm as a spring day, and by the time Lee and his two hands reached the cover they had shed their denim jackets and were ready for another rest.

Lee rode between the other two men through the trees, pointing the way to the stream that led to the trout-filled pond at the back of the ranch house, even though Luke and Sam probably knew where it was better than he did. The tired horses thirstily sucked up the cool, quick-moving water while the men walked around to stretch their aching legs.

The scene seemed incongruous with the task at hand. Lee reminisced in his mind about the many times his father, the famed gunfighter Frank Leslie, had taken him fishing in this stream when Lee was a boy. It had been his father's dream to retire from the limelight and raise his son in quiet seclusion, the way a son should be raised, away from the vileness of the world and in the midst of the greatest gift God ever gave to man—nature.

But like father, like son, Lee had been restless and set out with a reckless determination to make a name for himself at the first opportunity. Lee suspected that his father secretly never forgave him for this, though no harsh words were ever exchanged between them regarding Lee's hard living. At least his father had not been ashamed of him. Lee had won a reputation as a master gunfighter, but both father and son knew Lee was never in a fight unless it was for the right reason. Lee earned his notoriety, but he was no criminal, and was always as straight and strong as the oaks he was now sitting under.

Frank Leslie had worked hard in his autumn years to transform Spade Bit into the finest ranch in Idaho. People came for hundreds of miles to inspect and purchase Leslie's fine breeds, and from just as far for the chance to stud their mares with his choice stock.

But that was all very long ago. After Leslie's death, the ranch fell into disrepair, its reputation slumped, and the surrounding acreage was taken over by the hordes of sodbusters looking for the chance to find a new life in the green hills of Idaho. Spade Bit sat all but idle for years—until the day Lee Morgan found love, money, and a desire to settle down.

For him, Spade Bit was going to be a chance at a second life—a life that would not be filled with mindless killing and an endless stream of women and whiskey. Lee Morgan had changed, but the times were not changing with him—at least not fast enough. There had been one threat after another—from Wilson, from Paxton, from the farmers who coveted his land enough to kill his wife to get it. And finally from himself, as he wrestled with the idea that maybe he was not cut out for the life of a gentleman rancher. Maybe that was why he cut out for Panama without so much as a goodbye.

But now that he was back, he knew he had been wrong to leave. Paxton's threat to his property had convinced him that his father's legacy was more important to him than his freedom. And then there was Sue Clemons. That she loved him, he knew from the day they had first met, even before his wife had been killed. But until that tragic event, he never dared admit his feelings about her. She would make a fine wife, a wonderful mother. He was on the verge of asking her to marry him before he left, but now that he had returned, he was not sure that she still wanted him. The pain of being abandoned had had a grevous effect on her, and although they had not yet talked about it, he knew that it would take some time before all wounds were healed.

Right now, however, Lee Morgan had more pressing things on his mind. His home had been invaded once again and there would have to be much bloodshed before he could get it back. Even in the west, where men moved to live free from the bonds of the "civilized" east, there was still enough injustice to move an honest man to tears.

For Lee Morgan this was no time for crying. It was a time for fighting. There were four men between him and Spade Bit, and that was four men too many. He would have to take care of his unfinished business with Paxton later, there were more important matters to attend to at the moment.

"I think we've rested just about enough, fellows. This is going to be dirty work, not to mention dangerous, so let's get it over with so we can rest easy."

Sam and Luke knew what he meant. They both went to their mounts and began removing the packed gear. "Leave 'em saddled," Lee said, "just in case we have to ride outta here fast." And as soon as he said it he wished he hadn't. Losing this battle was a possibility, but he sure didn't want to give the only two men he could count on the idea that they might have to run.

Each man loaded his six-shooter and tucked a dozen more bullets in their shirt pockets so they could get at them easier should the need arise. They would have to do most of their fighting with the rifles, but there was always the chance of a close encounter. The three repeating rifles were loaded to their fullest, and boot knives were freshly honed.

They were to carry nothing more. The rest of the gear was stowed out of sight in the underbrush of the stream bank, and the horses were loosely tied to a low hanging branch of a young oak.

"By now they've gotten the message we sent down off the ridge," Lee said while cleaning the barrel of his gun. "They're gonna be expecting us, but they sure know we mean business. Before we go in I want both of you to remember, these fellows earn their livings with their guns. I don't want to give them a chance to start shooting if we can help it. You see one, you shoot to kill. Chances are that they're not as handy at long range as they are with their sidearms, and it's a good bet that once they spot us they'll all head for the ranch house. They'll have cover in there, but once they're in there, they won't be able to run anywhere but into us.

"I want you two boys to wait at the edge of the woods and cover me good. I'm going to make for the barn and let the horses out to pasture. We'll have 'em trapped then. They'll have to come out to us sooner or later, and when they do, we'll have 'em."

As they came within sight of the ranch house, Lee couldn't help but notice how quiet it was. There was no sign of any other human being. Even the birds were still—as if they had cleared out in anticipation of the upcoming bloodshed. The big red hangar of a barn stood some fifty yards off, just to their side of the house. Though anyone looking out of one of the house's upper windows would surely be able to spot him, he doubted that they would be able to do anything to stop him. He would be behind the barn before anyone inside even had time to shoulder a rifle.

Lee didn't say another word, but sprang out of the cover to the brush and sprinted toward the structure where he hoped his treasured horses would be waiting. As he hit the dirt behind the barn, he was surprised that no one had fired a shot. Perhaps they still did not know he was there.

Lee put a small door into the back of the barn when he rebuilt it the year before, after the Jack Mormons had set a torch to it. The door was intended to be a means of escape should the barn ever burn again, but right now, it would make a perfectly good means of entry. Lee gently pulled the door open a crack and peered into the dark, musty interior. There was no sound except for the easy nickering of the horses in the stalls, and the only light came from the narrow gaps and the knotholes in the planking where sunlight hesitantly streamed inside.

It was enough for Lee to see to let the horses out of their stalls and push the main door open. Lee had been expecting at least one of the men to be posted in the barn, but there had been no one. He did find, however, the four horses he had sent to the ranch with men on their backs. The bodies had been removed, but evidently, the men in the house had not wanted to take the time to remove the horse's saddles. Once Lee had opened the door, he slapped one of the horses and it bolted for the opening. The other animals followed suit, running through the yard toward the open pasture.

Then the shooting started. Lee barely had time to duck away when the first bullet bit the dirt by his feet. That was followed by another that shattered the planking of the wall Lee was hiding behind. Lee guessed that the men were firing from the upstairs window of the house. There, they would have an overview of the surrounding grounds, and a clear shot at anyone approaching the building. These men were professionals, yet they had missed him while he stood in the open. As he ran to the back of the building and the door through which he had entered, Lee couldn't help but wonder whether sending the dead men back to the ranch had made the men inside reconsider his temerity.

As he reached the back of the barn, Lee noticed that Sam and Luke had already begun returning fire to the second story window. Gesturing frantically, Lee indicated for them to stop. Firing blindly into a now empty window would do them no good. Lee was going to have to rely on his wits as much as his skill with a gun to flush the men out. And, failing that, he always had the two sticks of dynamite. He only hoped that he was right in guessing that Paxton would not return without additional help.

Instead of running back to the cover of the woods, Lee held his position by the barn. With all four men inside the house, Lee's chances were much better. At least he would know where they all were. Now he would have to position Sam and Luke on either side of the house to split up the four men inside. He waved Sam over to him and Sam sprinted the distance without incident. No more shots came from the upstairs window.

"Sam," Lee said. "I want you to get inside the barn and keep this side of the house covered. I'm going to try to position Luke behind the big oak in the front yard. That way you can keep them busy, we'll have two sides of the house covered, and they'll all stay in one room. I'm going to try to pick my way to the back of the house without being seen. There's an opening there that leads to a crawlspace under the house. From there I can come up into the kitchen and be on top of them before they even know I'm in the house."

"Whatever you say, Mr. Morgan. We're behind you all the way," Sam answered.

"All you fellows gotta do is stay out here and keep their guns busy for a few minutes. Think you can handle that?"

Sam couldn't believe that this was all Lee was asking him to do. He hoped Lee did not misunderstand his smile as he nodded his head. They might just get out of this alive yet.

"Just keep the bullets comin' till I get in there. You'll know I'm there 'cause they'll stop shooting at you and turn to me. As soon as they stop, you and Luke make for the front door. And make it quick, 'cause

I'm liable to need your help fast. Got all that?"

Sam nodded again and stepped inside the barn.

Lee whispered again, "As soon as you get into position, fire off a couple of shots so I can get back to the woods. And once I'm there, keep 'em busy till Luke can get to the tree. If he doesn't make it, we're both up the creek. Now, give me your pistol."

Sam looked at Morgan questioningly but Lee quickly explained. "You ain't going to have any need for it down here, but I'm sure as hell going to need it up there." Sam passed him the loaded weapon and emptied his pocket of shells. Lee poured them into his shirt pocket with his own. Lee caught his man's eye and for an instant he felt the unbounded admiration Sam held for him. "Good luck," Sam said shortly, shaking Lee's hand. And then he disappeared into the barn.

When Lee heard Sam's first shot, he took off as if a pack of arctic wolves were right on his heels. He was halfway to the woods when the first shot whizzed by his head, almost punching a hole through his best and only Stetson, and when he dived into the bushes with shots flying all around him, he nearly lost the thing altogether. Had Luke not joined Sam in returning fire, Lee almost surely would not have made it the rest of the way. But now was not the time to stop for thank you's. Lee joined Luke where he hid and pointed to the broad, leafless oak in the front yard. Luke knew what he was going to have to do, even before Lee explained. He frowned at the idea of having to run thirty yards in the open, but Luke knew that unless he did, there was no way Lee could get inside.

"Sam and I will cover you the best we can. Just weave in and out between the saplings and you'll make it easily," Lee said, trying to muster the most reassuring smile he could. But Luke saw through it and read the desperation etched in Lee's eyes. Without any acknowledgement of Lee's words, Luke stood and began to run with all his might straight for the tree, not even bothering to dodge bullets as Lee had suggested. He had gone almost ten yards before Lee even knew what had happened. Lee had to rush to get his rifle shouldered. He was able to get off one shot before Luke was spotted. Two men began shooting at him, firing as fast as they could cock their guns. Slugs shot up dirt and divots of grass all around him. It looked as if there had been a group of boys skipping stones in a lake of green all around him. Except these stones were made of steel and were coming with enough speed to shatter a man's leg or burst his skull.

Luke was now within the radius of the tree, with its near naked outstretched arms, but the browning leaves on the ground slowed him, making Luke lift his legs higher as he approached the trunk. The men inside were now ignoring the shots fired by Sam and Lee. They had a chance to hit a man in the open and were taking full advantage of the opportunity.

Lee saw what they were up to and also saw an opportunity. He stopped firing wildly and took careful aim at a bearded man in the window. As if an accomplished buffalo hunter, Lee took his time and gently squeezed the trigger. The gun jumped in his hands and Lee saw the man disappear from the window. He couldn't tell whether he had hit the man, but at least he had stopped shooting. When Lee turned to look for Luke, he, too, had vanished. But there had been no place to run, nowhere to hide but the tree.

Lee was just about to look *in* the tree when he saw the leaves begin to stir down below. Then Luke's head popped out of the midst of the crinkling mass. *Safe,* Lee thought. *He's made it.* But as the rest of Luke Bransen's body emerged from the pile of leaves, Lee saw the blood and saw that Luke was clutching his left arm. From the expression on Luke's face, Lee could tell that the man was in a great deal of pain. All at once Luke dropped to his knees and began thrashing about wildly, throwing leaves every which way, flailing like a mad dog. Lee thought the man had gone insane with the pain of his wound. Though Luke was still behind the tree, if he didn't get himself under control he would end up with another bullet through his chest. But the man had not gone crazy. His hands finally found the gun he had been looking for. He swept it up, made sure the barrel was not clogged with dirt, and held it up to his good shoulder. Positioning himself against the tree for support, and wincing in pain at having to use his wounded arm to steady the barrel of his rifle, Luke began firing into the open window nearest him, causing the men inside to momentarily duck out of sight. Lee didn't waste another second. He ran back into the dense cover and out of sight.

Lee hoped that Luke and Sam would be able to keep up the heavy fire while he circled around to the back of the house and put his chancy plan into action. If even one of the gunmen inside began to wonder what had happened to Lee, he could end up dead and Sam and Luke would have to flee for their lives.

The back of the ranch house seemed a different world, almost peaceful except for the gunfire coming from the front. Getting inside was going to be easier than he thought. Breaking from the cover of the trees, Lee ran to the back of the house and crawled between two rose bushes, ripping his plaid flannel shirt as his back scraped against the low thorned branches. He crawled on his elbows on the ground against the house until he reached the entrance to the crawlspace. All he had to do was open the hinged plank in the wall and crawl inside. Then he saw the lock. Someone must have anticipated someone gaining entry this way and put a padlock on the small door. It might have even been Luke or Sam trying to protect the house from intruders. And now it stood in his way of throwing the intruders out. Lee's heart sank as he looked around for another way inside. But unless he went in through the window, there was no other way. And if he broke the window he would be heard for sure.

Lee crawled past the small door and lay on his back listening to the shouting out front. He was going to have to do something soon. Sam and Luke had plenty of ammunition, but the men inside would soon realize that Lee had vanished and begin to check the other sides of the house.

With the heel of his trail-worn boot, Lee kicked at the padlock. Nothing happened. After two more sturdy kicks he thought he felt it give a little. Maybe this wasn't going to be so impossible after all. Lee drew his leg back and gave it a kick that could have knocked a horse out and the lock pulled free. Lee was able to twist the metal plate holding the lock with his bare hands and pull the door free. It opened just wide enough for him to squeeze his body inside. Once there, he pulled the door shut behind him. If someone were to look out the window, nothing would appear disturbed without closer inspection.

The dank, musty smell of moldy earth hit him immediately, the staleness of it almost forcing him to gag. It was as if he had dug his way under a cemetery. There was no light and Lee had to struggle in the confining space to reach into his pants pocket for a match. He lit the thing on his belt and held it aloft to get his bearings. Green, glowing eyes seemed to scatter everywhere as September's field mice scampered to hide from this unlikely intruder.

Lee had to crawl almost the length of the house to the kitchen entrance. Nails sticking through the door clawed at his back, forcing him to stay on his belly. The match burned low and Lee thought it best to drop it and use both arms for crawling. It fizzled into the damp earth and Lee moved on blindly, feeling his way past the support post holding up the house, stopping to wipe the spiderwebs from his face. When he had completely lost his bearings again, Lee fished out another match and struck it on one of the posts.

He had aimed himself well. There, ten feet in front of him was the square outline of light that would lead him out of this cold wet hell and into a hell of another sort—one far worse than anything Satan had ever devised.

Lee wormed the rest of the way to the opening and tilted up the trap to peek inside the once spotless kitchen. For a moment he wondered if it was his own kitchen. Spoiled food sat on every counter. Empty whiskey bottles were strewn all over the floor. Boxes of provisions were stacked up against every inch of wall space. Lee wondered whether the animals were living in the barn or in the house.

Opening the trap door to its fullest, Lee stood and pulled his body into the kitchen. His clothes were wet and filthy from the ground under the house, and his hair was coated a white mass of cobwebs. If he didn't kill the men upstairs, he would at least send them into a helpless fit of laughter.

The shooting upstairs had slowed somewhat. Lee heard commands and obscenities being shouted and there was a lot of stomping about in the room just above him. Luke and Sam had not stopped firing. For a moment Lee was tempted to put the dynamite in the rafters over his head and be done with the whole thing. Saving the house didn't matter so much now as killing the men who would take it from him. At least that way there would be no chance of his men outside being hurt.

But that might be too foolish. Lee himself could be killed and Paxton could sit in the Black Ace Saloon and gloat over his victory and over Lee's grave. Callaway would get his land and he would put his father's name to shame. There was just nothing to do but force himself up the stairs and confront the four gunmen—and pray that Sam and Luke got inside the house to back him up.

Lee checked the loads in the Colts and held them both at the ready as he inched his way on his toes to the stairs at the main entranceway. The men were in the room at the far end of the hall, and although over the gunfire and yelling they were not likely to hear him, Lee wanted to make sure they were taken completely by surprise.

Dropping low, Lee made his way up the stairs on his knees and one hand. Still holding the guns in both hands, he was careful not to take his eyes off the hallway where one of the men might come running at any time. At the top of the stairs, Lee peered around the edge of the railing he had so lovingly worked on the lathe in the barn. He had a clear view of the window facing the barn and Sam. All he had to do was shoot the two men standing on either side of it. He could have killed them from where he was, but that would have been too easy. He wanted them dead, yes, but he wanted to make sure they knew just who their killer was.

While the men were still occupied, Lee stood and walked directly to the doorway, a gun trained on each of the two men. He stood there framed like a picture for nearly a full minute until one of the men turned to reload.

The man's jaw dropped when he saw Lee Morgan, unable to move in his wonderment over how Morgan had gotten inside. When his mouth finally began to move in warning, Lee shot him through the chest. It was as if someone had suddenly come up behind the man and jerked him by the collar. His arms shot out to his sides and his entire torso flew backward through the window, sending blood, shattered glass, and bits of wood falling through the air. Lee hoped that that would be enough of an indication for Sam and Luke to make their move.

The other man in the window witnessed his companion's fall and turned quickly to confront their attacker. He hadn't even raised his weapon when Lee put a shot into his head, sending him flying against the wall, his hands clutching at the gaping wound between his eyes. The man was oblivious to the fact that the back of his skull no longer existed.

The shooting had stopped altogether. There were still two men inside the room, shielded by the door behind which Lee stood. They were staying quiet, perhaps trying to guess Lee's next move. Out of the corner of his eye, Lee saw that, aside from the man he had just killed, the four bodies he had sent down on horseback were stacked neatly in a far corner. The men he was after hadn't even taken the time to bury the corpses, preferring to hole themselves up in a room with the bodies until Paxton arrived with reinforcements—help they had not realized would never come.

Lee could hear Sam and Luke entering and then climbing the stairs. Sam ran to join him but Luke stayed at the top of the stairs. The men behind the door had not yet made a move or a sound and Lee was beginning to wonder if maybe he had miscounted them. He had just stepped back to consult with Sam when the three bullets tore through the door where he had been standing. Lee's temper snapped. In an instant he was in the room and firing round after round, not even bothering to look for his target. He was beyond caring now. If these people were going to take his father's homestead, so be it, but they were going to have to do it through a wall of gunfire.

Lee was hitting nothing—because there was nothing there to hit. A dead man lay on the floor. Lee guessed it was the same man he had shot while Luke was running to the tree. There was a gunshot wound through his gut and more blood on the floor than Lee thought a human body could hold.

The whole scene in the room was one of carnage. Blood was everywhere, broken glass was strewn all over the floor and on the bodies, and no one but Lee Morgan was breathing.

But where was the other man? Lee had been sure there were four. There was a sound outside like scraping metal, and Lee realized that the last gunman, the man who had shot at him through the door had escaped through the window. Lee ran to the shattered window and knocked out the rest of the frame. Bloody footprints marked a path to the end of the tin porch roof. The man had slid down one of the porch supports and was now running at a breakneck pace for the horses grazing a half mile away in the pasture.

Lee turned back to Sam, who was staring open-mouthed at the pile of bodies they had killed earlier. "Give me your rifle, Sam," Lee said calmly.

Sam didn't take his eyes from the dead men, but handed his rifle to Morgan. Lee snapped it out of his hands and went back to the window. He aimed and fired one shot, which shook Sam out of his trance, then tossed the gun back to Sam.

"That about does it," Lee said.

Sam fell to his knees and began to wretch. The gruesome sight had been too much for the young, inexperienced man to take. Lee left Sam in his misery and went to check on Luke's wound. Luke was sitting at the top of the stairs with his head between his knees, almost as if asleep. Lee shook him and slapped him awake. Luke had been unconscious and was still losing a lot of blood from his left arm. Sitting like a child waiting for its mother to bandage a scrape, Luke watched the blood ooze down his arm and drip to the hardwood floor from the tip of his finger.

"Sam!" Lee hollered. "Sam, quit your gagging and get over here. Luke's hurt bad." Lee lay Luke back on the floor and tore off the sleeve of his shirt, gently pulling the soaked fabric away from the wound.

In the bedroom where the gunsmoke had barely settled, Sam pulled himself together and wiped his mouth with his shirt. Wishing he had something to wash out the bad taste in his mouth, Sam got to his feet and joined Lee in the hallway. When he saw Luke's pallid face and the gaping gash in his arm, Sam thought he was going to be sick all over again.

Lee's anxious voice and a slap across the face brought Sam to matters at hand. Luke might be bleeding to death, and it was up to him and Lee to do something to save him.

"It's okay, Mr. Morgan. I'm all right now. Is he going to be . . ."

"I don't know," Lee said. Luke was unconscious again and looked as white as a two day old corpse. "Looks like he's in shock. First thing we gotta do it get him into the bedroom. Grab his legs."

Sam did as he was told and the two men carefully moved Luke's still body into the bedroom at the other end of the hall. They covered him with as many blankets as they could find, and Lee sent Sam downstairs to the kitchen to boil some water and scrounge up some clean kitchen linen.

Lee wiped as much of the blood away as he could and discovered that the injury was not as bad as it had originally seemed. There was no permanent damage to the man's arm, just a good sized chunk of flesh torn away. If Luke had had it attended to immediately after being shot, he would not be in the state he was in right now. But as the bleeding had not been checked, Luke was on the verge of death.

Lee held his handkerchief tightly against the man's arm to stop the bleeding until Sam returned with the water and cloth. Sam had also brought back part of a bottle of whiskey he had found.

"Good man," Lee said, hoping to reassure Sam that, though he had snapped at him, he was not angry.

Lee cleaned the wound as best he could and Sam uncorked the whiskey and almost took a slug for himself before handing it to Morgan. "It's a good thing he's unconscious," Lee said. "I'd sure hate to be awake and have this stuff poured into a sore. Hurts worse than salt." Lee turned the bottle over and let the contents sterilize the gash. Then he soaked a piece of cloth with it and placed it on Luke's arm. With a long section of toweling, he wrapped Luke's arm and returned it under the blanket.

"Shouldn't you tie a tourniquet," Sam questioned, remembering the first-aid manual he had been required to read in grammar school.

"He don't need it," Lee said. "He lost a lot of blood out there by the tree, but it ain't that bad. 'Sides, if I did, he'd most likely will lose that arm, and that's the hand he pours with." Lee's attempt at levity had no effect on Sam, who was still too awed by Lee's doctoring abilities to understand what was meant.

"We've got him wrapped up pretty good, but he's got to stay warm." Lee got to his feet and Sam followed him downstairs and out to the woodshed for a few logs to get a fire going in the upstairs fireplace. Once the fire was blazing, Lee went alone to the barn.

There were dozens of holes in the side of the barn and enough in the barn door itself to tell what was going on inside without opening it. Lee looked back at the house and was almost sorry he had not dynamited it. It was in such sorry repair from the month of abuse and neglect Paxton's men had put it through that Lee would not have recognized it as his own if here were not standing there looking at it with his own eyes. Shingles were coming lose on the roof, the porch steps were broken, the yard was a sea of broken bottles and trash, and finally there was the room where Lee and his men had lain siege against the four murderers holed up there. Lee had won this battle, but there was still a war to fight.

Guilt was beginning to set in. Had he been wrong to coerce Luke and Sam into helping him? This was not their ranch, and Lee had no right expecting them to help him defend it. Yet they had, and without them Lee would probably not be back home at this moment. And though Paxton's hired guns were not going to be causing anymore trouble, the cost had been Lee's nearly losing one of his best friends. If Luke did not recover, Lee would never be able to face himself again. His would be a hollow victory.

Inside the barn, Lee walked to where the tools were stored and took a spade and pick off the wall. Lee threw them over his shoulder and walked back out into the brilliant sunlight. He looked again at the pock-marked second story of the house he had rebuilt just a few short months ago, then walked slowly back to the front of the house.

"Sam," Lee shouted through the upstairs bedroom window, where Sam was sitting with Luke, "get out here. There's a lot of digging to be done."

Suzanne Clemons was worried sick. Though she knew Lee Morgan was fully capable of handling himself, she couldn't help but wonder how he would fare against the vicious gang Billy Paxton had put together. Lee had a good deal of experience in such matters, but with three men pitted against a dozen, his chances didn't seem to be very good. Sue had prayed for his safety that morning—and prayed even harder that the whole matter could be resolved without anyone getting hurt. Why didn't Paxton just go away and leave the God-fearing people of Grover alone? What had they ever done to him?

Sue had cleaned the breakfast dishes and put them away, and had moved the rest of Lee's belongings to the attic where they would not be seen should someone drop in unexpectedly. She had followed Lee's instructions perfectly, but was not sure that she could keep his secret much longer. She longed to run out into the street and tell the world that he had returned, that he had survived his trip to Panama after all. Surely the town would rally to Lee's defense if she did. They might form a posse to ride out to Spade Bit and confront Paxton's men.

Sue shrugged her shoulders and brought herself back to the real world. Who was she fooling? Sure, folks might be happy to hear that Lee was back, but this was a bustling town. People were much too busy with their own concerns now to get involved in someone else's problems. Especially if shooting might be involved.

How she wanted to march over to the bank and announce Morgan's return to Jesse Callaway in a voice loud enough for everyone to hear! She wanted to blame him, to chastise him, to force him to face the fact that his greed had been the cause of all the town's problems. Callaway wasn't good enough to make it as a banker back east, he had to come out west and use his conniving ways to swindle honest folks out of their hard-earned pay.

But that wouldn't do either. Callaway would just laugh at her, and the people in the bank would think her even more pixilated than they already did. There was nothing to do but follow her regular routine and hope that Lee returned soon.

She took a broom out of the kitchen pantry and mindlessly began sweeping the floor, angling the nonexistent dirt into the center of the room. She was so deep into her daydream about how she could help Lee that she didn't notice the strange face peering through the window at her.

Paxton and his two surviving men had walked from Callaway's bank to Sue's home so as not to attract attention in the street. As long as they seemed to be behaving themselves, people didn't care where they went or what they did. Even so, there were still a few eyes that followed them suspiciously down the main street.

Once they got near Sue's place, Paxton posted one of his men in the street in front of her house, then went around to the back with his other man. He knew that once they got inside Sue would put up little resistance. There would be no way she could fend them off, and with as few friends as she had, there would be little likelihood of any neighbors dropping in. Paxton's only problem would be getting her back to the jailhouse without arousing suspicion. If Suzanne Clemons were seen riding or walking with him, it would cause quite a stir in town.

The knock at the back of the door startled Sue out of her reverie. She wasn't expecting any visitors and no one would come around to the back door to enter, except Lee . . . She ran to the door and swung it open expecting to greet her lover's smiling tanned face. The face that greeted her was smiling and tanned, but it didn't belong to Lee Morgan.

"Good afternoon, Miz Clemons, beautiful day, ain't it?" Paxton said, the pleasant smile never leaving his face. He was dressed completely in black and seemed an imposing malevolent figure standing in her doorway with his hands poised on his hips.

Sue gasped and stepped back, taking the door in both hands to slam it in the intruder's face. Paxton took a step up and placed his foot firmly against the door, causing it to bounce back when she swung it. Another step up and Paxton was inside her house and standing just a foot away from her.

Suzanne's first thought was to run as fast and as her legs would carry her, run somewhere where she would never have to see this man again. She backed up a step and turned to make for the front door. But as she did, Paxton's massive hand clutched her wrist. There was no escape now. She wondered if he planned to kill her now or rape and torture her first. If she screamed, no one would hear her cries. Her house was set well off the main street.

"That's no way for a lady to greet a gentleman caller. Did you slam the door in Morgan's face as well?" Paxton was asking through the devil's own smile. Sue felt the blood rush from her face and her legs suddenly turned to gelatin. Even Paxton was surprised when the woman fell in a dead faint at his feet, his hand still clasping her wrist.

After Paxton carried her to the parlor couch, he sent the man who had accompanied him to the front to give the all-clear sign to the man in the street. As they entered through the back door, Paxton was hovering over the woman, waving a small bottle of smelling salts under her nose.

"Is she hurt?" Winston asked him, seeing the unconscious woman for the first time. "She ain't dead, is she?"

"No, she ain't dead," Paxton answered. "Now shut your trap and both of you search the house. Make sure there ain't no one upstairs."

Just then, Sue began tossing her head back and forth to get away from the overwhelming vapor burning her nose. Paxton removed the salts and brushed her blonde hair from her face. Suzanne's eyes shot open as if in surprise, then darted wildly about the room, trying to fathom what had happened to her. When they finally rested on Paxton's looming face, she turned pale again and her eyes rolled into her head. Paxton, who had been holding her hand, felt her grip go limp in his palm. Without trying to revive her again, he placed her hand by her side and covered her body with the afghan draped over the back of the couch. Then he replaced the cap on the bottle of salts and set it on the table beside him.

As he sat back in the easy chair to think about what to do about this new development, Wilson and Kelly came plodding down the stairs. "Ain't nothing or no one up there, boss," Kelly was saying. Then seeing Suzanne still prone on the couch. "What the hell's ailing her? She sick or something?"

Paxton stroked the grizzled stubble on his chin for a moment, never taking his eyes off the woman. "Damn!" he swore. "Just like a woman. I don't know what Morgan sees in a woman with a constitution like fine china. She just one look at me and passed out like I'd poured a bottle of liquor down her throat."

Both Wilson and Kelly snickered but their poker faces returned when Paxton shot them a malevolent glance. Paxton went on with his story. "She woke up for a second, then passed right out again when she realized what had happened." Paxton sighed and leaned forward with his elbows on his knees, his palms pressed against each other and against his lips.

Wilson and Kelly walked to the woman and stood by her side, looking hungrily at the defenseless, sleeping woman. Wilson licked his lips and reached out to place his hand on her cheek. "She looks mighty tempting, don't she? Been a long time since I had a woman this fine. Morgan sure knows how to pick 'em."

Paxton was out of his seat in an instant. Grabbing Wilson by the shoulder, he nearly threw the man across the room. "You get the hell away from her!" he shouted. Then turning to Kelly. "And don't you get any ideas in that walnut brain of yours either," he yelled.

Both Kelly and Wilson wondered what had come over their employer. Had he suddenly gone soft? He'd never denied them taking their pleasure wherever they found it before. Why was he now protecting this woman? Did he want her for himself? The two gunmen sat in the uncomfortable wooden parlor chairs, while Paxton returned to the plush chair from which he had been thinking.

Sensing that his men were waiting for an explanation for his strange behavior, Paxton began to reveal his plans. "I don't want this woman harmed in any way. We ain't got the upper hand any more," he admitted. "Folks in town are sure to be wondering why we rode in alone this morning, and if we start any trouble, they're apt to come after us. This woman is one of the town's upstanding citizens. She ain't some two dollar whore you boys can take any way you please. We're here for one reason and one reason only. And that's to use her to get Morgan. He's likely got his ranch back by now and is expecting us to come back for him. But that ain't how it's gonna be. Morgan's comin' in for us!

"But first we've gotta get this woman over to the jail without causing a scene. That means we're gonna have to sit around here till after dark. I just hope that that Chook character don't decide to up and run off. He's the one who has to deliver the message to Morgan."

"That'll get rid of him once and for all," Kelly said, chuckling. "Morgan'll kill him for sure."

Paxton looked at him sternly. "You're laughing now, but once Morgan gets the message, it's us he's gonna be out to kill. And don't you underestimate him, either. He's already got all but the three of us and once he hears that we've got his woman, he's gonna come after us with a vengeance. 'Cept he's likely as not to be half out of his mind with rage when he hears of it. He'll be even more dangerous then."

"What if the woman causes a fuss?" Wilson asked.

"Look at her." Paxton gestured with his hand. "Does this look like a woman who's gonna cause trouble?" Wilson laughed and then went into the kitchen to see what he could find to eat.

Sue had awakened a few moments before this while the men were still speaking. She had remained still and silent to hear what they were saying and what they had planned for her. She began trembling violently and finally opened her eyes when she could not control herself any longer.

Paxton saw her stirring but did not return to her side, thinking that she might faint again if she saw him again before fully regaining consciousness. Sue sat slowly on the couch, rubbing her eyes against the fog before her. When they finally cleared, she was aware of the sick feeling in her stomach.

"So, you've decided to join us," Paxton

said, loudly, to get her attention. "Not very hopsitable of you to fall asleep when guests arrive."

"You most certainly were not invited," Sue snapped, demonstrating some of the spirit that other women found so irritating.

Paxton shrugged off her remark. "I have not had the pleasure of seeing your Mr. Morgan since his return. How is he faring these days?"

Sue was about to make another cutting remark, but remembered Lee's warning about letting anyone know Morgan was back. "I wouldn't know. I had no idea Mr. Morgan was back." Sue tried to sound as cold as if she had never heard the man's name mentioned before. "I suppose that's why you're in town and not out pillaging his ranch." Sue caught herself before saying more. Her sharp tongue was going to get her in more trouble than she was already in if she wasn't careful.

"Well, Miz Clemons, you know as well as I that he has returned. But you may continue your little charade if you wish. It makes no difference to me." Paxton mocked her high-brow tone as he bit off the end of a fresh cigar. "I see you've been tidying up the house a bit. Could it be you *were* expecting company?"

"Unlike some others, I always keep myself clean. My house included. Why do you insist that I was expecting visitors?"

Paxton ignored her question. "In that case, you should work wonders over at the jail." He arched an eyebrow and waited for her response.

Sue would not give him the pleasure of seeming shocked. All she could think about was figuring out a way to get to the shotgun upstairs under her bed. Even if she could get one of them before they killed her, that would be one less man to go against Lee.

Sue and the two men sat quietly, Sue wondering just what kind of tortures they had planned for her. Wilson reentered with a tray of food, which he placed on the table in the middle of the room. "I see you've helped yourself," Sue said glumly.

Wilson returned to the chair with a sly smile spread across his face. "Not quite as much as I would have liked to," he said.

5

Chook had been pacing the floor of the old stone jailhouse nervously for almost three hours. He was beginning to feel more like a prisoner himself than a lawman. He hadn't been outside for more than five minutes since the afternoon of the day before. He'd tried reading a dime novel, playing solitare, even cleaning his firearms, but boredom and worry were getting the better of him. Where the hell was Paxton? At lunchtime he'd said he would be back within an hour or so. Now it was well after dark and there was still no sign of the man.

It had occured to Chook several times that maybe Paxton had had second thoughts about his plans for Morgan and had skipped town. Though that might have been the wisest choice for a man in Paxton's position, Chook didn't regard Paxton as a particularly rational man, especially after witnessing his burst of near-insane rage earlier that day.

At seven-o'clock, Chook couldn't stand it any longer. He had to find out for himself what had happened. He would first go over to Callaway's house to see if Paxton and his men had holed up there. After that he'd try the Black Ace. Someone in there must have seen them. Unless they stole a few horses, they must still be in town. Their own rides were still tied up outside, and getting very hungry.

Sam threw a couple of logs on the fire to keep the place warm while he was gone, then buckled on his holster and put on a light jacket, taking time to button it up to his neck. He left the light burning in his office and went to the front door, checking to make sure his gun was loaded. As an afterthought, Chook grabbed a shotgun on the way.

When he opened the front door, he was surprised to find a gun waving in his face. Without even seeing who was holding it, Chook knew it was Paxton.

"And where do you think you're going, Deputy?" Paxton demanded, pushing Chook back into the jailhouse with the barrel of the gun. "Get back in there and open this door as soon as I knock. I've got a little something out here I don't want to be seen."

Chook was too scared to respond, but closed the door again, leaving his hand on the knob so he could open it faster when Paxton returned.

Paxton went directly to the corner of the building and waved his men forward. They walked on either side of Suzanne Clemons, each leading her by an arm. Sue was dressed in her day dress, but was covered with a long flowing cape with an especially large hood that covered her face. If anyone were to see her going into the deputy's office, they would not have recognized her. As it was there was no one on the street, and Paxton was able to guide them inside without incident.

"Very good, Miz Clemons. You behaved exceedingly well out there," Paxton said as he pulled the cloak from Sue's head. Sue made her displeasure with the situation very evident. She drew back her hand to slap Paxton but stopped herself before striking him. There was no need to get him any more riled than he already was.

"Chook," Paxton said. "Please escort Miz Clemons to her new quarters, if you would. I'm sure you've tidied up the place for her."

Sue strutted through the front office to the cells at the end of the hall. For now she would cooperate—and pray that Lee was not foolish enough to fall into Paxton's trap.

She had not yet given any indication that she knew Morgan had returned, and if she could keep Paxton convinced that she was telling the truth, her demonstration of ignorance might work to her advantage. She might even make Paxton believe that she didn't care a whit for Lee Morgan.

As Chook shut the iron door and locked her in, Sue heard a knock at the front office door. Her heart sank. Surely Lee would not make such a direct approach . . . Then she heard Jesse Callaway's voice booming down the hallway.

"What's going on in here?" he demanded. "I thought you were going to get the girl. I've been watching from my office window for half the afternoon and ain't seen a blasted thing."

"Keep your damn voice down," Paxton said coldly. "The girl's locked up in the back. We had to wait till after dark to bring her in, else the whole town would know what we're up to."

Callaway lowered his voice a bit: "Well, you've certainly got 'em wondering. The town's been abuzz with rumors since you and your boys rode in this morning. Some say you're fixin' to pull out."

"I ain't pullin' out of nothin' till Morgan's dead and buried," Paxton spat.

"Like I told you this morning, I don't give a good goddam about that property out there. The whole place can burn to the ground again for all I care. I just want Morgan. And that pretty gal back there is gonna help me get him. I'd be willin' to bet that Morgan has his land back by now. But so what? Let him enjoy it for a few more hours. Come tomorrow, I'll have him planted out there forever."

"You ain't plannin' to hurt the Clemons girl, are you?" Callaway said, quietly. "Her father commands a lot of respect here in town. If folks hear that you've hurt her, you're apt to have more on your hands than you can handle."

"I ain't gonna harm a hair on her pretty little head, less she causes any trouble. Once Morgan's dead, she can go free and I'll never show my face around this two-bit town again."

She shivered, clasping her arms around herself as she sat on the cold, bare bench against the stone wall. What could Lee Morgan have possibly done to make this man hate him with such a passion? As long as she had known him, Lee had been a man who loved peace above all else. Yet he could never seem to find it. He had always lived as a hunted man—even after he had settled and decided to raise a family he was constantly on his guard.

The men's voices began dying down.

Sue resigned herself to doing what she could to make herself comfortable in the tiny cell. No one came to check on her so she blew out her lamp and crawled between the fresh sheets of the old cot fully dressed, not even bothering to remove her shoes. She lay there quietly trying to make out the men's voices but hearing only a lulling drone and the sound of bottles clanking.

She was nearly asleep when she was startled by the sound of several chairs scraping across the wooden floor. Sue guessed that she had been laying there half-awake for over two hours. That would make it after ten o'clock. It seemed that Paxton and his men hadn't drunk themselves into a stupor after all. She imagined they were preparing to leave. Callaway would of course go home. But Paxton had no place to go. Then she realized that he did. He and his men were going to her house, perhaps to sleep in her own bed. She was disgusted at the thought of it, but was powerless to keep them from her place. She prayed that it was all a dream, that tomorrow morning she would awaken in her own bed and start the day anew, with Paxton serving time in prison somewhere far away.

"Make sure you get plenty of rest," Paxton was saying to the deputy. "We'll be back before dawn tomorrow to rouse you. Then you're headin' out to Spade Bit to give Morgan our little message. If he don't show his face in town by noon, his little girl friend's body's gonna be strewn along the trail from here to Boise. You make sure he knows we mean business."

Paxton lumbered not quite drunkenly out of the building, followed by his two sharpshooters and Callaway, who looked up and down the street before stepping through the door.

Callaway was nervous, though he was not quite as downhearted as he had been earlier in the day, when Paxton had first broken the news about Morgan winning the ranch back. There was still a chance it would be his, maybe before tomorrow was over. As far as anyone knew, Morgan was lying dead in the jungles of Panama. The fact that the rumor was never proven made some question Callaway's maneuvering, especially Morgan's longtime friends, like Sue Clemon's father, one of the more vocal dissenters. Even if he didn't see Morgan as a potential son-in-law, he bought considerable amounts of Morgan's horseflesh and didn't want that business relationship disrupted.

Come tomorrow, Lee Morgan would be forced to ride into town in full view of everyone. And with Sue Clemons as security, Morgan would surely be shot dead in the street. Everyone would see it happen, and Callaway would be free to take Spade Bit with no questions asked.

Jesse Callaway began to whistle a drunken tune as he walked toward the bank. He wanted to check the vault one last time before retiring to his home across town. The banker was so governed by money that he would have lived in the bank if there had been room. Then he would never have to leave the treasures that he considered his alone. Everything of value in town, from birth registrations to family heirlooms were locked in his vault. And that one little vault made him the most powerful man in Grover.

He wiped the sweat from his fat face with an already damp handkerchief as he climbed the wooden steps to the main level of the quiet, darkened building. He inserted the key, turned it in the lock and gingerly stepped inside, as if not to wake a sleeping baby. He walked straight to the vault and stopped before the mighty steel door. But instead of opening it to examine the fortune inside, he rubbed both of his hands over the smooth surface. Callaway dropped to his knees as if in prayer before some great icon. As he bowed his head, he began to feel tired—very tired—and in a moment sleep—an alcohol-induced sleep—overcame him, enveloping all thoughts of walking home.

This was his home.

* * *

With Paxton and his two goons gone, Deputy Chook returned to the bottle the men had not quite finished. He sat in one of the stiff wooden chairs and propped his feet on another. Without the use of a glass, he began to sip the whiskey slowly, wishing that it would steel him to the task that loomed before him, at the same time hoping that it might incapacitate him to the point that Paxton would have to send one of his own men.

But after a few sips, he resigned himself to going through with Paxton's scheme. At least he would be out of Paxton's reach for a time, and dealing with Morgan was a whole lot less deadly than working under Paxton's command. At least Morgan had a conscience.

His reputation in Grover as a lawman had been on the skids for some time, and his act of treachery against the town tomorrow would be enough to get him lynched if Morgan or Paxton didn't get him first. It was his lack of leadership and guts that had gotten him into this mess and he finally admitted to himself to be overwhelmed by men more powerful, mentally and physically, than himself, and there was nothing he could do to alter that now.

At length he stood up, thinking that he would turn in and let sleep dissipate his worries—at least for a few hours. He tossed the whiskey bottle into the wastebasket, then lined the chairs back up against the wall, taking time to make sure they were straight.

Chook struck a match and lit the small lamp that always sat on the table beside the front door. Then he blew out the rest of the lamps and headed for his stark room and the cold cot that awaited him. He couldn't help but think that this would be the last night he would spend there. Tomorrow night he would probably be buried under six feet of earth in potter's field, where all the criminals in town were buried.

He had just reached his room when he thought he would check up on Sue Clemons. As he approached her cell he held the lamp high to see into the interior. Sue was sleeping fitfully, still fully dressed. If Chook had not known her situation he would have thought she was sick with fever from the way she was tossing in her sleep. Her young face was damp with perspiration and contorted as though in pain.

He felt truly sorry for the woman. She had done nothing wrong. And if she had not had the misfortune to fall in love with Lee Morgan, she would have escaped this ordeal. Why did it have to be her? Why not Mary Spots? She, too, was a friend of

Morgan's. Yet as the most prominent whore in Grover, she would not be as sorely missed as Sue. In fact, there was a good many folks in Grover who would like to see her get her due.

But Paxton had chosen Sue for the most obvious reason. Lee Morgan was in love with her. Though Lee might not be able to admit this to himself, everyone who saw the two of them together knew this to be true, and Paxton had managed to pick up on this fact. Now Sue was a pawn in this feud just as much as Chook was. And she was apt to end up just as dead if things didn't go as Paxton wanted. In fact, it would be just like Paxton to kill her even after he had gotten his revenge on Morgan, just to prove that he could humiliate Morgan even in death.

Chook stood and stared at the woman for a full five minutes. What could he do to save her? After half a bottle of whiskey, he was no longer concerned for himself. As far as he was concerned, he was already dead. It didn't matter now if it was Morgan who killed him, or Paxton, or the territorial hangman. All that mattered to him now was seeing that Sue was kept safe.

Chook walked back to the front of the building and opened the front door. He left the front door open and stepped out onto the boardwalk. It seemed unusually dark outside. The moon had not yet risen and the stars twinkled dimly. A few gas street lamps were still lit, but no one walked the streets. A thin mist seemed to hang in the air, settling the dust from the main street. There was an eerie silence, the kind that occurs after a heavy snow.

So, Paxton had not had the forethought to post a guard. *He must be damn sure of himself,* Chook thought. For a moment the deputy considered taking his horse and riding out of town. But that would only delay his death for a few days at most. Paxton would surely hunt him down like a fox, and if that happened he might not die so swiftly. Out on the trail, Paxton could torture him for weeks if he desired.

Then he thought of Sue again. He could set her free: send her to her father's house until Paxton was gone. He owed Morgan at least that much. After all, Lee had not turned him in for his involvement in Callaway's last attempt to steal Spade Bit. Morgan could have had him put away for a long time, but chose not to. And, by all rights, Lee Morgan should have killed him the night before when he discovered Chook keeping guard over Sam and Luke. Still, he had let him go free. Morgan must have thought him still worth saving. For what, even Chook did not know. He had done nothing but betray Morgan's trust since they had first met. The least he could do would be to try to keep Sue from harm.

Chook went back inside the building, thankful for the warmth of the fireplace he had kept going. He immediately went to the small office that doubled as his bedroom. He placed the lamp on the night table and sat down on the edge of his cot. The shadow of his hunched form danced on the wall and made him seem almost animated. For long moments he sat there thinking and watching the flickering lamp. At length Chook slapped his knee and stood up. He would do it. He went directly to the little table where he kept the keys to the cell. His eyes bulged and opened wide as he pulled the drawer toward him. The keys! The keys were missing. He had always kept them there. And he was sure he had replaced them after he had locked up Sue Clemons.

So that was why Paxton had not bothered to post a guard outside. Paxton had stolen the only set of keys to the cell. No wonder he had been so trusting of Chook. He shut the drawer quickly, then opened it again, thinking that the set of keys might magically appear if he wished for it hard enough. But it was not to be. The keys were gone and there was no way he could let Sue out of her prison. Chook pounded his fist on the tabletop, startling even himself.

He was powerless. Paxton had outsmarted him and stolen not only the keys, but Chook's last chance to redeem himself. He stepped back, almost dazed. When he reached the cot, Chook sat down, lay back, then fell into a deep dreamless sleep.

Lee and Sam had spent the afternoon digging a pit in which to bury the seven lifeless bodies they had killed. By nightfall, with the hole finally covered, both men were exhausted and hungry.

Luke had proven himself to be stronger than either of them had expected. Despite his loss of blood, his body temperature rose steadily, and in the early evening he regained consciousness. Lee and Sam had been cleaning the house of the filth Paxton's men had brought in, and they took turns looking in on Luke. When Lee went in to throw a new log or two on the fire, Luke was laying on his side, trying to rise. Lee dropped the logs he was carrying and ran to the man.

"Lay back down there," he said gently but curtly enough to let Luke know that he meant business. Luke stared at Lee as if he barely recognized the man, but did as he was told.

"Where am I?" he asked quietly. "Last thing I remember I was behind a tree shooting at the window." Luke moved his hand over his bad arm until he flinched at the pain in his left shoulder. He looked at

Lee curiously. "I've been shot," he said.

"Rest easy," Lee said gently, encouraging the man to lay back on the mat in front of the hearth. "You keep these blankets on and that arm still, and you'll be all right. Paxton's men are dead and you're in the house. Sam and I have been tending your wounds since this afternoon. You lost a lot of blood, so you're gonna stay right where you are until you get your senses back." Lee turned away from the man for a moment. "Sam," he called downstairs. "Bring up a big bowl of that vegetable soup you made. We have a patient up here that needs some nourishment."

"Paxton's men . . . dead?" Luke was asking through a grimace.

"We got all the ones here in the house, thanks to you and Sam. We've got the ranch back—for now. But I'd be willing to bet that Paxton and his other two goons are still in town. Ain't much I can do about that as long as you're laid up. We'll just have to wait and see what happens."

Lee turned his face to look at Luke, and realized that Luke had drifted off to sleep again. While the man was unconscious, Lee changed his dressing, all the time hoping—praying—that Luke would recover well enough to shoot again before Paxton returned with his reinforcements.

After throwing the logs into the dying

fire, Lee went down to the kitchen. "Cancel that order," he said to Sam, who was busy reheating soup over the stove.

"Is-is he all right?" Sam asked, fearing Lee meant that Luke was dead.

"He'll be okay—in time," Lee reassured him. "He woke up for a few minutes—just long enough to find out where he was. I thought he might eat something, but he was still too delirious to stay awake. Maybe he'll come around tomorrow."

It was just before dawn when Lee Morgan dragged himself out of bed. He pulled on his trousers, buckled on his gunbelt, then opened the windowshade. The air was fresh and cold from the night, but the aura of death from the day before still lingered.

It seemed so peaceful outdoors, and he recalled why he so loved sleeping under the stars. Though all the rooms of the house were built especially spaciously, Lee could not help but feel closed in, restrained from living the way God had meant for man to live. He suddenly found himself questioning his resolve to keep Spade Bit. Everything about it was confining. Owning the place was a hindrance in many ways, the most significant of which was that he could not leave it unattended. He had to be there constantly to protect his property, his horses, the men he hired; and now he was being drawn to what might be another disastrous marriage—all because he had given up the life of a drifter. And for what purpose? Because he was tired? For the sake of his dead father?

It really didn't matter. What was done was done. He wasn't about to revert to his old ways. People respected him now, and that was something he had never had as a gunman. People used to fear him. But respect was something that was even harder to come by. And he was grateful for it.

Downstairs, he got the coffee going, and after it had been perking for a few minutes he heard Sam stirring and shuffling around in the upstairs bedroom.

"Mr. Morgan," Sam called out. "Can you come up here?"

"Be right there," Lee shouted back. He wrapped a linen towel around the handle of the coffee pot and grabbed a couple of cups. With his hands full, he bounded up the stairs toward the bedroom. "What's the matter?" Lee asked before he even entered the room. It suddenly occurred to him that Paxton and his men might be launching an early attack. "We got company?"

"In a manner of speaking," Sam said as Lee passed through the door frame. Lee saw the smirk on Sam's face and was just about to cuss him out for playing games, when, out of the corner of his eye, he saw Luke. He was sitting upright on the bed, his eyes clear and alert.

A big grin of relief spread over Lee's face, as much for his own sake as for Luke's. "Well, well. Welcome back among the livin' and breathin'. How you feelin', pardner?"

"Like a freight train just ran over my arm. How about pourin' some of that coffee and gettin' me a bite to eat. I'm famished."

"Look at him," Lee said to Sam in mock seriousness. "He gets a pampering and a good night's sleep and now he's givin' orders like he owns the place."

"If you don't get me healthy enough to handle a gun again, Callaway's the one likely be owning this place." Though the remark was meant as a joke, Lee knew that Luke was right on that point.

Lee tried to keep the tone from becoming too serious. "Okay, tough guy. Breakfast coming up. And take it easy on that coffee until you get something solid in your belly."

Lee returned to the kitchen and the search for edible food. The previous tenants had left sparse provisions. It seemed that, having failed in their attempts to cook on a stove, they had left the burned pans and charred food to rot, eating only what they did not have to cook.

Lee found a few still-fresh eggs, and a big slab of salt-cured ham that had somehow been overlooked. There was flour but no milk and not enough eggs to make flapjacks. Sighing, he set to work making do with what he had. Sam had done a good job the night before of cleaning out the kitchen, but Lee still wished his housekeeper was around to do this chore. Better yet, he wished he were sitting in Sue Clemon's fine dining room, waiting to be served one of her delicious southern-style meals.

The voice came from upstairs. "Mr. Morgan, I think you better get up here again, and be quick about it." Lee moved the skillet full of solidifying eggs away from the stove and ran up the stairs two at a time. This time there was no smile on Sam's face as Lee entered the room. He had a gun drawn and was standing to the side of one of the room's tall windows.

"Paxton?" Lee managed to spit out as he duck-walked his way to the window beside Sam.

"Too far away yet to tell," Sam said. "But I don't think so. It's just one rider, and Paxton ain't got the guts to ride out here alone."

"That's no lie," Lee said, watching the dust being kicked up half a mile away. "Whoever it is looks like he's in a God-awful hurry. Better load up the rifles just in case there's more of 'em comin' up behind him."

Sam crouched down and crossed the room to where Luke was sitting. There, he loaded the three rifles, tossed one over to Lee, and handed another to Luke, who was struggling to get out of the bed.

"Stay in the bed," Sam said. "There's only one rider out there. If there's any more, you'll get your chance."

Luke stopped struggling, despite wanting to see what was going on. He leaned back against the mahogany headboard and let the rifle lay across his lap, pointed in the general direction of the bedroom door.

As the mounted man drew closer, Lee could see that the horse he rode was not one of his own. Despite the speed with which the rider came, the horse seemed uneasy, as if on unfamiliar ground. It was a horse that had not seen too many days out on the open trail.

As the rider neared the ranch house, he began to slow the horse to a walk. For a moment he even stopped and began to fumble for something in one of the saddlebags. Lee and Sam watched intently as the man unfolded a white handkerchief and held it aloft as he began to ride in again.

"Well, whoever it is, he's smart enough

to know that he's not apt to be welcome here." Lee gave out his instructions. "You stay up here and keep him covered from the window. I'm going down to see what this is all about. If there's any trouble at all, you just pull that trigger." Lee walked to the door. "And holler if you spot any more riders!" he added, as if coaching a child.

Lee's spurs clanked on the stairs as he went down. This was no neighborly visit from a farmer, and it sure wasn't Paxton. Everyone in town knew about the trouble out at Spade Bit. Why would someone venture out here?

He stepped out into the soft morning sunlight and walked to the middle of the lawn. Leaves were blown about his feet, and the cool air left his cheeks slightly numb. Lee stood with his legs apart, his arms crossed as if in defiance, and waited for the man to come nearer.

The man wore an oilskin overcoat, making him seem bigger than he actually was. Lee did not recognize the horse, but when the morning breeze blew open the coat, he did recognize the badge.

"Chook," he said aloud to himself. "What the devil is he doing out here?" He had to have started well before dawn to get here this early. Lee's look of determination changed to amusement as the sad looking man approached him.

Paxton must have put some scare into him back in Grover.

The deputy looked at Lee Morgan solemnly, then dismounted slowly. He blew his runny nose on the white handkerchief he had been waving, then tucked it into his trouser pocket.

"What's this all about, Deputy?" Lee asked the man, when it looked like Chook was going to have a hard time spitting out what he wanted to say. Water began to well up in Chook's eyes.

"Paxton sent me out here," Chook said, wiping his nose on his sleeve. "And considering the circumstances, I thought I'd better do as he wants."

"And just what are those circumstances?" Lee asked, ignoring the man's emotion. "Paxton threaten to skin you alive if you didn't?"

"That ain't it!" Chook said determinedly. "I don't care anymore what he does to me. Anything I do's gonna get me killed, so I may as well try to do something right for a change. Who knows, maybe the good Lord will have a little pity on me."

Lee began to turn angry. "Quit your babbling and sniveling and get to the point. You didn't ride out here for nothing. Spit it out, man!"

"I came out here to tell you what Paxton was planning . . ." Chook looked down at his dusty boots, and then back at Morgan.

"Well?" Morgan pressed. "Let's hear it."

"I think maybe you better be sittin' down when I tell you this. Can we go inside the house?"

"Anything you got to tell me, you can say right here and right now. Now speak up, or I'll shoot you where I stand." Lee was fuming now. "What's Paxton got on his mind? When's he ridin' in here and how many men has he got with him?"

Deputy Chook took off his hat and held it over his chest. "That's just it, Mr. Morgan. Paxton ain't planning to ride back in here. It ain't your ranch he wants, it's you. He wants you in town before noon today."

"He wants me in town before noon today," Lee repeated, almost laughing at the idea. "Did you hear that, Sam?" Lee hollered toward the upstairs window. "Paxton wants me to come in after him." Still laughing, Lee turned back to face Chook. "And just what makes him think I'm willing to oblige him?"

Chook looked toward the heavens for a moment, as if saying his final prayers, then he met Morgan's gaze with near-lifeless eyes. "Cause if you don't show, he's gonna murder Suzanne Clemons!"

The words stung Lee Morgan as if he had been slapped. He was too dazed to even respond. "Murder Sue Clemons!" Those words echoed endlessly through his head, contorting and twisting all reasoning into a violent ball of rage.

How could this happen? He had given her explicit instructions not to give any indication that she knew he had returned. Yet the worst had happened. Paxton had discovered Morgan's soft spot, and now he was as vulnerable as a newborn's skull.

He wanted to take Chook's head in his hands and twist it until the neck snapped. But Lee still had enough sense to know that this was not the deputy's fault. As much as Lee wanted to kill right then, Chook was not the man he wanted. He had to get at the man, who for the second time, was getting at him through the woman he loved. And this he would not stand for.

Chook stood shivering before him, waiting for the death blow that was sure to come. He closed his eyes and clutched his hat even closer to him. But there was no blow, nor a shot from one of Lee Morgan's infamous Colts. When he opened his eyes again, Lee was gone, as if he had never been standing there, as if none of this had really happened.

Lee was on the stoop of the year-old porch with his rifle slung over his shoulder, staring at the shell of a man in the middle of his yard. If he put a bullet through him right now, he might be doing them both a favor. Paxton would no longer have a lackey to be his gopher, and Chook would no longer be tormented by the man who had shattered his spirit. He slung the rifle to his shoulder and took aim at just the same time he came into Chook's field of vision.

His finger touched the trigger gently, testing it as if to see just how much pressure it would take before igniting the charge and sending the slug into Chook's chest. At the other end of the barrel stood Chook, passively, waiting for the inevitable.

For the first time in his life, Lee Morgan had aimed a gun at a man he intended to kill, but could not pull the trigger. It would be like shooting a puppy for misbehaving. Still, he did not lower the weapon. Chook looked at him blankly, wondering again why he was not dead.

"I ought to do it," Lee said simply.

"I didn't expect that you wouldn't," Chook responded. "I knew you'd probably kill me on the spot, but even if Paxton hadn't planned for me to come out here, I would've anyway. For your sake and for Sue Clemons."

Chook was still a weasel, but Morgan felt genuinely touched by the man's admission. Maybe there was some hope left for him after all.

Lee lowered the barrel of his rifle until it was pointed at the ground just in front of

Chook's feet. "Drop your sidearm on the ground in front of you," Lee said.

Chook did as he was asked. Could it be true that Morgan wasn't going to kill him after all?

"Now that Winchester," Lee went on. "Take it out of the holster and put it on the ground by the gun . . . and don't throw it!" Again Chook complied with what Lee said.

"Now take your horse to the barn with the others, then get your ass into the house."

Chook did not waste any time making for the barn. When he returned, his firearms were no longer laying on the front lawn and Lee Morgan had disappeared into the house. Chook stepped up to the porch and knocked on the door.

"Stop wastin' time and get in here," Morgan shouted from somewhere within. Chook pushed the door open and adjusted his eyes to the dimmer light. There was a rustling in the kitchen and Chook went to investigate. As soon as he stepped in, Lee stuck a fork in his hand and pointed him to the stove. "Make yourself useful and turn that ham. On accounta you, breakfast is getting cold."

Chook was awed by Morgan's nonchalance and seeming lack of concern for the safety of Sue Clemons. Maybe he didn't care for her as much as Paxton had suspected. Perhaps the time he had spent in Panama had distanced him from her. Neither of them passed a word as they worked in the kitchen and when Lee headed upstairs with the completed breakfast, Chook followed like an obedient sheep.

Sam was at the window, keeping a lookout over the trail leading directly from town. "You might as well sit down and have a bite," Lee said to him. "There ain't nobody else coming, least not Paxton, noways. Looks like I'm gonna have to go in after him."

Luke and Sam looked at him as if to ask, "Why bother?" Lee served everyone a helping of ham and eggs and handed the coffee pot to Chook, who poured a cup and sipped it black.

Luke ventured a first question. "What the hell's this crooked deputy doing here? That's the same jackass that had me locked up." Luke made as if to rise, then gripped his shoulder in pain. "Damn!" he said. "If I warn't so busted up, I'd kick his tail all the way to the marshal's office in Boise." Luke took an oversized bite of ham and leaned back to chew, all the while glaring at the deputy.

Chook sat quietly sipping coffee and taking small bites of food white Sam and Luke grumbled over his presence. Though Chook had resigned himself to dying, he was thankful that Lee Morgan was at least being civil to him. Considering what he had done, each man present had every reason to want to beat the man to a pulp.

"Keep your thoughts to yourself, Luke," Lee was saying. "The deputy here ain't done right by us, but I didn't hear tell of you standing up to Paxton when he rode into Spade Bit, either. Chook might not be the most honest deputy in Idaho, but everything he's done has been at the point of Paxton's gun. He ain't innocent, but he ain't as guilty as he might be either." Lee sopped the rest of his runny eggs with a hunk of ham and popped the morsel into his mouth. Then he washed the whole thing down with a gulp of cooling coffee.

"It looks like Chook here's had a change of heart about who's side he's on," Lee continued, casting a sidelong glance in the deputy's direction. "He's rode all the way out here this morning to tell me what Paxton's up to. And believe me, it don't look good." He paused for another sip.

Chook looked at Morgan curiously, wondering why Lee was lying for him, why Lee did not tell them that he had actually come out on orders from Paxton. He was certain that Morgan was developing some sort of scheme to rescue Sue, and judging from Morgan's behavior, he guessed that it involved him. Had Morgan spared his life just to send him into the jaws of the lion?

"Well . . .?" Sam urged Lee for an elaboration.

"I don't have the full story yet," Lee said, "but it seems that Paxton is getting desperate. He and the two men he has left are planning to kill Sue Clemons if I haven't shown my face in town by noon today."

Sam jumped to his feet, nearly knocking over his plate. "Miss Clemons!" he shouted in astonishment. "He's gonna kill her?"

"Looks that way," Lee said, with an unusual calmness.

"How can you just sit there and eat breakfast when she's gonna be dead in a couple of hours? We've gotta get in there and . . ."

"Sit down Sam!" Lee said, becoming irritated with Sam's outburst. "It ain't even seven yet. That gives me more than five hours. It don't take but an hour to get into Grover. The first thing we gotta do is hear out the deputy here. He's gonna tell us everything that's going on in town, aren't you, Deputy?"

All eyes were on Chook now, each man waiting for the full story, and each wondering if he would tell the truth, or concoct some lie to further ingratiate himself with Paxton.

"There ain't much more to tell than I've already told you, Lee. Paxton rode in yesterday morning snapping like a mad dog 'cause you'd killed off his best men. And he wasn't about to turn tail and run. He went over to talk to Callaway about something which he never told me. He made me stay in the jailhouse all day while he went over and kidnapped the Clemons girl."

Lee cut in: "Why didn't you come out here to tell me while he was out all day?"

"I figured if he knew I had gone to warn you last night, he would have killed her on the spot, just out of spite."

"I see," Lee said. "Well, go on."

"Anyway, he come back about seven last night with the girl all wrapped up in a cape. She didn't put up no fight neither. Came in real quiet-like. Paxton made me lock her up in one of the cells and I guess she went right off to sleep. Least we didn't hear a peep out of her anyways. After that, Paxton and the boys kicked back in the office and started celebratin' with a bottle of whiskey. They damn near finished the whole bottle, too.

"Oh, I forgot to mention that Jesse Callaway stopped in, too. Guess Paxton must have told him earlier to meet them in the office. Anyway, they all got pretty drunk toasting victory over and over again. Finally Callaway said he had to get home. Paxton and his boys cleared out too. I think they were going over to Miss Clemons' house for the night.

"After they were gone, I was fixin' to let her out and send her over to her daddy's house to hide out, but that son-of-a-bitch Paxton swiped my only set of keys. There warn't nothing I could do then. I must have passed out on my cot, 'cause the next thing I knew, Paxton was shaking me awake. That was a couple of hours ago. Within a half hour, I was on my way out here to tell you what he wanted."

Chook was honestly shaken now. He bent his head low and grasped at his thin, sandy hair with both hands. When he looked up again, his eyes were red. "If only I coulda gotten her out. Paxton woulda killed me and then probably left town without you. Then none of this would be happening."

"Was she hurt?" Lee asked. "If they touched . . ."

Chook cut Lee off before his imagination ran away with him. "She wasn't hurt as of this morning, or at least she didn't complain of it if she was. I don't doubt that those boys of Paxton's would like to do a few ungentlemanly things to her. But I don't think Paxton would let them. He ain't got no fight with the lady, Lee, and he don't intend to hurt her unless you don't show up this morning. But if it meant the difference between getting back at you and running with his tail between his legs again, I don't doubt that he'd kill her in an instant. The man's gone half mad since he got wind that you were back. He's apt to do just about anything to see you die."

Chook was quiet now, along with everyone else in the room, and the only sound came from the popping of the green logs in the fireplace. Lee had been expecting a straight fight to the finish between him and however many men Paxton could rustle up, and he had planned to spend the morning making preparations for defense around the ranch house, but Paxton's new tactic changed everything. Now he was dragging innocents into the fight as well.

"Well . . ." Sam said at length. "Are we going in or are we gonna sit here all day? Sue Clemons' life is at stake."

Lee noticed that a change had come over Sam. He seemed much bolder now than he had when Lee had first returned. Then Lee realized what it was. One day he was just a naive cowpoke trying to collect enough wages to live on, the next day he's thrown into prison, forced into a gunfight, and faced with rescuing a female prisoner —enough action to make a man out of anybody.

"*We're* not gonna do anything," Lee said. "It's me Paxton's after and it's me he's gonna get. Luke, you're too weak to be walking around, much less holding a gun. And somebody's got to stay here to look after him. That's you, Sam!"

"What!" Sam gasped. "Are you crazy? You're not thinking of riding in there alone?"

Lee smiled at the young man's enthusiasm. "No, I'm not. Deputy Chook is going to accompany me."

No one was more stunned by this than Chook himself. He would rather that Morgan had shot him dead on the lawn than return to Grover to face Paxton again. That would truly be a fate worse than death.

"You can't possibly mean that," Sam raged on. "That man is in cahoots with Paxton and Callaway. He'll probably kill you as soon as your back is turned."

"I don't intend to turn my back," Lee said. "But I'm willing to bet that he won't do it." Lee shot Chook a look that said that he'd better agree. Chook nodded in assent.

"Then at least take us with you," Sam said.

"I want you here," Lee insisted. "The two of you have done enough fighting for me. This last battle is my own. Besides, I can get into town unnoticed by myself. If we all come charging in together, we're likely to put a scare into Paxton and get Sue killed. You two stay. Agreed?"

Sam and Luke nodded, then turned their heads away from him, unable to look him in the eyes.

"Shall we ride, Deputy?" asked Lee, standing.

"Guess so," Chook said and eased himself to his feet. "Hope you know what you're doing," he mumbled, thinking that Lee had not heard.

"So do I," said Lee. "For both our sakes, so do I."

6

Lee had insisted that Chook leave the horse he had ridden in on and take one of Morgan's finest instead, the same one Luke had ridden the day before. Chook had his arms back, and though he had no intention of shooting Morgan, he wondered that Lee trusted him enough to give them back. Morgan even took the lead position on the trail giving Chook a clear shot at his back.

Lee was traveling light. He had stripped the horse of all gear except the saddle, a canteen, and the rifle, which he kept in its holster, but readily available.

Both mounts were fresh and stepped lively as they picked their way over the rocky trail. The sun was still low in the sky, and there was less than an hour of easy riding ahead of them. Lee calculated that they would reach Grover well before nine—plenty of time to scout out the situation. Once out of the trees and riding up the slope that led to the main road, Chook stepped his horse up alongside Morgan's.

After they had ridden in this fashion for a few moments, Chook ventured to speak. "Morgan, I still don't know why you didn't kill me back there when you had the chance. Just what kind of help are you expecting to get from me?"

Lee tipped his hat back but did not look Chook's way. "Deputy, I have the chance to kill you any time I want. Be thankful that you've got the chance to clear yourself in front of everyone in Grover. You won't get another. As for what I expect out of you, the answer is nothing. You can turn tail and run back to Paxton as soon as we get to town if you want, but all you're gonna get from him is a bullet, when all this is done. It's your choice."

Lee did not see the man nod, but knew that Chook would get his meaning. It was likely that they would both die today, and Lee was giving him one last chance to come out clean. If Chook could gather up the guts to stand with Morgan against Paxton, all of his past infractions would be overlooked by the townsfolk.

Chook tried Lee's patience with another question. "Have you got any kind of plan?

I mean, you can't just walk in there and call him out. He'd just haul Miss Clemons out and hold a gun to her head till his boys gunned you down. Where would that get you?"

"It wouldn't get me nowhere." Lee said without emotion. "That's why I ain't gonna do it."

"Well, what then?" Chook urged.

"Guess I'll have to think of something before we get there, won't I? 'Sides, I've got a couple of stops to make before we get down to business at hand." Chook started to drop back to a position behind Lee again, but Lee waved him back alongside him. He reached into his jacket pocket and pulled out one of the three sticks of dynamite he had the forethought to bring. Chook's eyes widened when he saw it, and nearly popped out of their sockets when Lee tossed it over to him without pause.

"Stick that in your inside jacket pocket and don't forget it's there," Lee said. Then he reached inside his shirt pocket and pulled out a pair of cigars he had picked up in New Orleans. One he stuck in his own mouth and the other he thrust toward Chook. "Have a cigar," he said.

Chook looked at it and then at Lee, wondering what was going on. "No thanks," he said. "I don't smo—"

"Start," Lee said sharply, placing the

end of the stogie into Chook's open mouth.

After that, Chook shut up, puzzled by Morgan's actions. By the time they reached the main road a mile outside Grover, Luke and Sam were already conspiring to saddle up and follow them.

It was still early enough that Lee did not have to worry about being seen by anyone on the road, and even if they did pass someone, they would be riding out of town. At the first sign of activity up ahead, however, the pair pulled off the road and headed north through the sparse trees. Despite the influx of new settlers in recent years, it was still beautiful country. Country worthy fighting and dying for, Lee reminded himself.

"Where we headed?" Chook said in an unnaturally loud whisper.

"Friend of mine's house," Lee replied. "Someone who's got just as much at stake in this as I do."

"Reckon he'll help you out?" Chook asked.

"If this man don't, he ain't fit to live," Lee answered.

They rode together for another half mile, leaves crunching under their feet, the wind in their faces. By the time they reached the little cabin just to the north of town, Chook's thin skin was nearly numb.

"That's the place," Lee said, pointing

with his arm.

Before them was a tidy little cabin with a well-attended yard. Smoke billowed from the tall stone fireplace and a fresh coat of whitewash covered the planking of the walls. Lee and Chook followed a chopping sound to the north side of the house, where wood was piled as high as the windows and a tall, lean man in his fifties was hard at work chopping more.

As the two riders came into view, the man stopped splitting wood and looked up to see who his visitors were.

"Well, I'll be! Lee Morgan, back in Grover. I'd all but given you up for dead. When did you get back?"

"Just yesterday," Lee said. He got off his mount and stretched a hand out to the man, who took it gratefully. "I been out at the ranch taking care of some business."

"Oh, yeah. I been hearing stories that there was trouble brewing out there while you were away. Hope you got it all staightened out."

"Not quite," Lee said. "Chook, get down here."

The man looked at Chook as if for the first time and asked, "What are you doing riding with the deputy, Lee? I ain't got no trouble out here. Been cuttin' a supply of timber all morning."

"Don't think I've had the pleasure, sir," Chook cut in, offering his hand and a friendly smile. The man took it and returned a nervous grin.

"Deputy, this here is Jim Clemons, Suzanne's father." Lee spoke the words as much in warning as in introduction.

The smile immediately disappeared from Chook's face and he released the grip he had on the man's hand. "Pleased to meet you," he managed to say.

Jim Clemons was more than curious now. "Lee, what's going on here? I know you didn't ride all the way out here to introduce me to the deputy. You in some kind of trouble?"

"Jim," Lee said with caution, "I think we'll need to go inside to discuss this with you."

Within fifteen minutes the house was empty again and the three men were on their way along the path from which Morgan and Chook had come. Lee led the way as they crossed the main road and into the woods on the other side, Jim cursing every step of the way, spouting in graphic detail just what he intended to do to Paxton.

"We've got one more stop to make," Lee said to the men when they were well into the woods. As they made the wide circle to the other side of the town, Chook kept looking at his pocket watch. The morning was wearing on, and still Morgan hadn't indicated what he was planning. When they finally broke the trees, the trio walked their horses along the back of the buildings facing Main Street, ignoring the stares from the people they passed.

They stopped in back of the bank building and dismounted. It wasn't an imposing structure, no bigger than most of the other stores around it, but then Grover wasn't an imposing town. Still, it was the sturdiest building in town and one of the oldest. Word had it that Jessie Callaway spent more time there than he did at home.

"Chook, I want you to stay here and mind the horses," Lee said. "Jim and I have a little business to take care of inside."

"What the hell are you wasting time for, Morgan," Chook protested. "The bank ain't even open yet, anyway."

"It ain't open for regular business," Lee said in a condescending tone, as if explaining a simple math problem to a child. "But I know Callaway comes in early to make sure all his pennies are in place, and the business I got with him ought not be done around customers."

Lee and Clemons handed Chook the reins of their horses and disappeared into the alley that led to the front of the building. The street was swarming with people, though all were too busy with their own affairs to even notice Lee and his companion mounting the bank steps. When they reached the top, Lee pounded on the door and was amazed to see it swing open at his touch.

Lee and Jim looked at one another in query. "Something ain't right here," Lee observed. "It ain't like Callaway to leave the door open before banking hours, even if he is in."

Lee pushed the door open even wider and peered inside the dark open room. There didn't seem to be anyone moving about as Lee stepped inside with Clemons close behind. A dim light filtered in through the high windows, illuminating the heavy dust in the air, and casting eerie patterns on the floor. Jim closed the door behind him, making it even harder to see.

It was Clemons who saw him first. Callaway, sprawled like a limp bag of rags by the vault door. The mystery here was becoming deeper with every passing moment.

Both men rushed to his side. Jim grabbed his wrist to check the pulse, but Lee could spell the whiskey and had already guessed what the trouble was.

"He don't seem to be hurt," Jim said.

"Course he don't," Lee said. "The fool's dead drunk." Lee bent down and took Callaway's keys from the end of the chain attached to his belt. He tossed them to

Jim, who cast Morgan a curious look. "Well, don't just stand there. Open the vault."

Jim stared at the keys in his hand. "I don't know about this," he said. "I came with you to get my daughter back, not rob no bank."

"Who said anything about robbing the bank," Lee said, bending down and slapping Callaway across the face repeatedly. "Just open the door."

Clemons tried two keys before finding the one that fit the huge door. As it turned in the lock, the door eased open quietly on well-oiled hinges. Callaway was regaining his senses, though Lee had to shake him to bring him fully awake.

"What—what is it you want? What is this?" Callaway stuttered, his eyelids fluttering, his speech still slurred and nearly incoherent.

"Get up!" Lee snapped.

Callaway's eyes suddenly focussed on the source of the voice that had so abruptly awakened him. "Lee Morgan! What the hell . . . Where did you come from? Where the hell am I?"

"Get on your feet, you drunken fool. You're in your own damn bank," Lee said.

Callaway struggled to his feet and looked around him, then began brushing off his clothes, trying to look as dignified as possible considering his predicament.

"How did you get in here?" he demanded, putting on airs.

"Just walked in the front door you left unlocked," Lee said, shoving Callaway toward the vault.

Callaway's eyes widened when he saw Clemons standing next to the open vault door, twirling the key ring on his forefinger. "What're you doing with my keys? You can't go in there." Callaway was vainly attempting to play innocent. "Who's that man?" he snapped, though he knew exactly who he was and why he was there.

Lee didn't answer but led Callaway by the arm to the inside of the vault. "Damn it, Morgan! I can't believe you'd stoop so low as to rob the same bank where you keep your money." The inside of the vault was dry and dark and uncommonly quiet, forbidding enough, but it was far from airtight: the perfect place to put Callaway for safekeeping.

"Make yourself comfortable," Lee said. "We'll be back for you just as soon as the Marshal gets here from Boise."

Callaway hung his head, knowing that his time had come. But then the life came back into his eyes when he realized what Lee meant. "But that's forty miles from here," he said. "I'll be in here all day!"

"And all night," Lee continued. "You

see, no one's gone up to get him yet."

Lee pulled the heavy door shut and Jim Clemons turned the key again. "Not a bad little trick," he said to Lee, slapping him on the back. "Shall we try for Mr. Paxton now?"

"It will be a pleasure," Lee said, taking the keys and putting them in his jacket pocket. Inside the vault, Callaway's frantic screams could almost be heard.

At the back of the building, Chook was still standing with the horses when Lee and Jim returned. Deciding it was best to do without them, they unfastened their rifles and checked the loads. Then Lee sat down on an old water bucket and explained what they would do.

Five minutes later Lee and Jim were on their way to Sue Clemons' house on Main Street. Chook was making his way to the jailhouse and his final confrontation with Billy Paxton.

The jailhouse door was locked when Chook arrived, but when he reached for his keys, he realized that Paxton still had them. He pounded on the door loud enough to wake anyone inside. Seconds later Paxton opened it, and Chook found himself staring down the barrel of Paxton's gun. He swallowed once hard, and Paxton pulled him into the building by his lapel.

"Where is he?" Paxton demanded.

"I told him you was at Sue Clemons' place, just like you said," Chook answered, not quite as frightened as he had been with Paxton in the past. "He's headed over there aimin' to gun you down all by himself. Soon as he took off, I ran over here to tell you." Chook skirted telling Paxton about the presence of Sue's father.

Paxton got a big, evil looking grin on his face. "Everything's coming together just as I planned," he said. He called to his men sitting at the table playing cards. Sue Clemons was there, too, and Chook wondered why Paxton had let her out of the cell. "Get up, you lazy sons-of-bitches. Morgan's over at the girl's house just waiting for you to come over and pick him off. Get over there and don't come back until he's dead." The two men got up and walked out the front door as if they were going to church.

"This is going to be easier than I thought," Paxton said aloud. "And even if they don't finish him off, I've still got you, Miz Clemons. You'll draw him over here like a moth to a light." He took her by the arm and threw the cell keys to Deputy Chook. "Deputy, take her in the back and lock her up. I don't want her up here gabbing and carrying on like a baby. Wilson and Kelly'll be back soon and we're getting out of town, just as soon as we collect a small fee from Callaway for getting Morgan out of the way."

Chook nodded and jingled the keys. Sue frowned at the deputy but preceeded him to the cell where she had spent the night. "You call yourself a lawman," she whispered to him on the way back. "You ought to be ashamed of yourself."

Once in her cell, Sue returned to her bunk and glared at the deputy, who was nervously fumbling with the keys. He pulled the cell door to, then fastened the keys to his belt without locking it. Then he cast a look toward the main office to see if Paxton was checking up on him. He was not. "I'm leaving the door open,' Chook whispered to Sue, who couldn't believe her ears. "If you see a chance to get out of here, take it. You won't get another." Then he turned to rejoin Paxton before she had the chance to ask questions.

"Now, it's your turn," Paxton said. "Give me those keys."

"What do you mean?" Chook asked, becoming nervous once again. Getting locked up was one thing he had not counted on. "Why are you locking me in the cell? I did what you asked."

"You'll get out," Paxton said. "The minute Morgan is dead." They walked back down the hallway to the cell next to Sue's and Chook gave her a little nod just before Paxton shoved him into the little room.

Sue understood that this was her only chance. While Paxton was concentrating on locking Chook's door, Sue grabbed the lamp next to her bed and returned to the door. Paxton hadn't even realized that she was there and would not have expected her to do what she did even if he had known. Without a word, Sue stuck her hand through the bars and hit Paxton squarely on the head with the lamp, sending shattered glass and oil spraying all over the hall and into Chook's cell. Paxton collapsed in a heap on the floor.

Sue was almost afraid to come out of her cell, for fear that something else dreadful would happen. Paxton was conscious, but barely. He rolled on the floor holding his head and moaning.

"Miss Clemons, are you there?" Chook called.

"Yes," she said, still unable to comprehend what she had just done.

"Well, what are you standing there for? Run and get help. Paxton's liable to come to any minute, and if you're here when he does, I wouldn't want to be here to see what he does to you."

Sue came out of the cell. "But what about you?" she said scanning the floor for the keys but unable to find them. "I can't just leave you here."

"Don't worry about me," Chook implored. "Just get out of here. Go get your father and Morgan. They're both at your house."

Sue didn't understand what was going on, but she did as Chook asked and ran from the building, leaving Paxton rolling on the floor in pain and the deputy there to face the consequences when he recovered. She would have to get to Lee fast.

Lee and Jim had a little surprise waiting for Wilson and Kelly when the latter two arrived at Sue's house. While Jim waited for the attack from inside the house, Lee stood across the street where he would have a commanding view of the approach to the house. Within twenty minutes, Paxton's men came lumbering down the street toward Sue's house. Both were walking as though nothing were amiss, though when they neared the house, both ducked into the alleyway and headed for the back, looking furtively for anyone that might have seen them. Lee went into action. He ran to the front door and knocked three times to alert Jim, then he drew his Colts and hugged the wall to the back of the building.

Inside, Jim made ready. He ducked behind the couch and aimed his Winchester toward the back window. There was a crash and in an instant both Wilson and Kelly were in the parlor with their guns drawn. Clemons ducked, not expecting such an abrupt entry. His sudden movement caught Wilson's eye.

"There he is, behind the couch," Wilson shouted. And both men began pumping bullets into it. Though he was laying on the floor, Clemons felt a slug tear through his leg and yelled out in pain. Now he was totally helpless. Paxton's men had him just where they wanted him—flat on the floor and unable to return fire. And when the found out he wasn't Morgan, they would have no mercy. But where was Morgan?

Kelly and Wilson had each finished the rounds in one gun and were just drawing out their other six-shooters to move in for the kill. They only had time to see Morgan's shadow stretching out on the floor before they realized that they had been set up. Both men spun around to see Lee Morgan standing in the doorway with both Colts drawn. He shot Wilson in the face before the man had even registered recognition. Wilson tore at his blood-soaked face as if trying to hold himself together, but he was dead even before he crumpled to the floor. Kelly got off one shot which flew by Morgan's head and out the door, before Morgan shot him in the stomach, sending him flying across the room and into the couch. He looked at Morgan with vacant eyes, not knowing quite what had gone wrong. Then he felt the pain and began writhing, with his hand trying to plug the gaping hole in his gut.

Lee was in no mood for mercy. Kelly had lost his gun, but Lee wasn't about to give him a chance to find it again. With a calculated aim, Lee pulled the trigger of his Colt again and took off the top of Kelly's head. The man rolled, lifeless, onto the floor and Lee ran to Clemons' side. He was unconscious, but Lee could see that he had only a flesh wound, nothing a visit to the doctor and a few stitches couldn't take care of. While he was still bent over Clemons, Lee sensed another presence in the room. He immediately drew his gun, prepared to shoot the person who had just come through the back door.

It was Sue. Lee went to her, preventing her from seeing who was lying on the floor.

"Are you all right?" she asked, staring at the carnage all over her parlor.

"Of course," Lee replied hurriedly. "Now run and get the doctor. There's men hurt here and need attention."

Sue turned to do as Lee asked, but suddenly remembered why she had come in the first place. "Paxton," she said. "I hit him over the head in the jailhouse and ran over here. The deputy is still locked in the cell over there. If that man wakes up . . . oh goodness . . . Lee you'd better get over there right away. He helped me get out and you've got to help him."

* * *

Chook was lying flat on his belly with his arm stretched through the bars, trying his best to reach Paxton's gun. But Paxton was lying on the floor just inches out of reach—and rapidly regaining consciousness. Chook gave up, resigning himself to the fate that awaited him. Even if Paxton's men didn't get Morgan, Paxton would still get his revenge on Chook for double-crossing him and then get out of town before Morgan arrived. It was ironic, Chook thought as he sat back on the edge of the bunk. To be murdered in the very office he had sworn to uphold. There was nothing left to do but wait.

Chook relit the cigar Morgan had given him on the road in, savoring the last smoke he would ever have. Paxton was on his knees now, and shaking his head to clear his senses. An angry expression contorted his face. All at once he was on his feet, and all Chook could do was stand and watch, as helpless as a zoo animal.

Paxton looked around him, still dazed and wondering what had happened. Then he saw that the girl was gone. "Son-of-a-bitch!" he screamed. "You tricked me, you goddam bastard!" Paxton was insane with rage now. All he wanted to do was kill, and Chook was the only one handy.

"You and Morgan planned this whole thing. You let the girl out and now

Morgan's got her. All my plans. Everything I worked for—ruined!" Paxton picked up the gun laying on the floor and checked the load.

"Maybe Morgan will get away again this time, but at least I can have my revenge on you before I clear out." He leveled the gun on Chook and was amazed to see that the deputy was not begging for mercy.

"Not this time," Chook said. Then he took a deep drag on the cigar and tucked it into his jacket.

Lee and Sue were still standing in her living room when the whole house shook as if wracked by a thunderstorm. Sue looked puzzled but Lee knew exactly what the noise was. When the two finally made their way to the jailhouse, they found a huge crowd gathered and the entire side of the building blown away. There was no sign of either Chook or Paxton. Chook had remembered his dynamite.

Sue's face radiated joy, as much because she was finally alone with Lee as because she was safe. Despite Lee being anxious to get back and start repairs on the ranch, Sue had insisted on having Lee over for a home cooked supper—his first in months.

Lee was glad he had decided to stay. But he wasn't the only one having a good time. He had given both Luke and Sam twenty dollars in gold and staked them to a room in the Black Ace Saloon with a couple of Mary Spots' girls. There they could tell the story of their gunfight at Spade Bit until they were too drunk to repeat it. By morning, they would be as much heroes as Morgan or Chook.

Chook! It was a pity that he had lost his life after all, but Chook had expected it all along. But in the end he had forced himself to do what was right. Though it had cost him his own life, he had stood up to the most vicious outlaw Grover had ever seen—and won. And for that he could be proud to have called himself a lawman. Lee would have to see that his family back east received a long letter expounding on his deeds. Lee had been right. Chook hadn't been the coward he might have been.

"Lee," Sue said, snapping Lee out of his musings. "What on earth are you thinking about? Have you forgotten that I'm here?" She was offering him another glass of wine. Lee took a sip while she still held the goblet and flashed her a big smile.

"Oh—you!" she said. "You haven't changed a bit. Still your old playful self." She set both glasses down on the table beside the couch, then clasped her arms around his neck and looked deep into Lee's eyes. "You know," she said, "I really wondered whether you still cared enough to come. After all, you have been away for three months. Tell me, how do the women in Panama compare?"

"I came back, didn't I?" Lee said slyly.

He slid closer to Sue and her arms tightened around him, pulling his lips toward her own. Lee knew his feelings for Sue had not changed. He was too deeply involved with her to even consider moving on and abandoning her forever. Their lips touched, furtively at first, then hungrily, as if trying to make up for all the months they had been apart.

Their lips separated and Sue buried her head in the warm, thick flesh of his neck. Her soft blonde hair brushed Lee's cheek, setting him on fire. He wanted her lips again, but when he pulled her away, he saw that her eyes were damp with tears.

"What is it?" he asked. "Why are you crying?"

Sue didn't answer immediately. The words seemed stuck in her throat. "I—I'm just so happy to be back with you," she said at length. A little smile crept onto her lips again. She wiped the wetness from her eyes with a trembling hand, and Lee stroked her silky hair with his rough palm. She shivered and massaged the back of his neck, loosening the tense muscles.

Lee returned the smile but did not speak. Sue's skin was taut beneath the soft fabric of her clothes, and Lee sensed the anticipation she was experiencing. He began to move his hands over her, remembering every inch of her back, her shoulders, her arms. His hands finally slipped under her breasts, feeling the weight of them, wanting to know the touch of them against his own flesh.

He eagerly began unbuttoning her blouse, nervously fumbling with them as if for the first time, but pretending as though he was making her wait. As he worked his way down, he discovered that she had earlier removed all of her undergarments to make things easier and hasten their lovemaking. Her blouse parted in front and Sue arched toward him, pressing her breasts hard against the rough fabric of his shirt, letting the tips become red and erect. She pulled away from him, letting Lee get a good glimpse of the beautiful, white, red-tipped orbs.

They kissed deeply once again, then Sue asked, "Are you going to stay in those clothes all night?"

Lee stood, pulled off his jacket and began to unbutton his own shirt. Sue moved to her knees before him and began working on the lower half. She worked at his belt, and then at the buttons on his trousers, and finally pulled the pants down around Lee's knees. Though they had just eaten, she looked like a starved woman.

"What about my boots?" Lee said, laughing and sitting back on the couch. "First things first."

Sue looked embarrassed in her anxiousness, but quickly began tugging off his boots. Lee chipped in and soon both boots and pants were laying in a heap on the floor. Sue stood and stepped back. Lee stared as she reached back to unfasten her skirt, which made her ample breasts seem even more prominent. She smiled slowly as Lee admired her form.

She was only a few inches shorter than Lee, and her tall frame seemed exaggerated by her long, shapely legs, joining at the vortex by a hint of fine blood hair.

Sue began to tease him by caressing her own breasts, pinching the nipples to make them stand out for him. Lee stood and came to her and she immediately tucked her hand into the waistband of his underpants and tugged them to the floor. Lee kicked them off and pulled her to him, their naked bodies burning against each other.

He kissed her with tenderness. Then as if bowing before some unknown icon, Lee bent and kissed one breast, letting his tongue linger over the fruitlike tip. She sighed deeply, then shuddered, sending a wave of gooseflesh over her body.

She fell against him and he slid a strong

arm around her waist, lifting her and carrying her, then placing her gently on the couch. The heat from the fireplace and from their own passion coated their bodies with perspiration and made them burn with anticipation.

"Oh, Lee," she said, looking up at him from the couch. "Please just stand there a moment and let me look at you. It's been so long."

Lee did as she asked, standing still in the orange glow of the fire, so she could savor every ripple of muscle, every sculpted angle of his bare flesh. His tanned body glistened with sweat, and every hair felt as if it were standing on end.

Sue's gaze began with his eyes, which radiated a brilliant blue against the ochre glow in the room. But her eyes quickly fell to his huge chest and arms, the same that had held her so close moments before. Finally there was the beautiful organ hanging in wait between his powerful legs.

Her hand reached out and touched his calf, kneading his flesh, then traced a path up his thigh until she reached the object of her desire. She cupped her hand under his balls, squeezing them gently until Lee's eyes rolled back in his head and he began to moan in pleasure. Blood was rushing into his cock, and it slowly inched its way to stiffness. Sue ran her delicate fingers along the hardening shaft, then gripped it in her fist, increasing the pressure until the tip of it mushroomed out and turned a brilliant red.

Lee placed his hands on his hips and began to pump them backward and forward until Sue picked up the rhythm with her hand. When he was fully erect, Sue leaned toward him and touched the tip of her tongue to the head, letting the drop of semen that had formed, stretch out into a long clear strand. When it broke, she licked her lips to taste him, then parted her mouth to let the entire shaft inside.

Once his entire organ was coated with saliva, she returned her hand and began pumping in earnest, sliding her hand over his foreskin with such dexterity that Lee thought he would burst. Sue knew she was getting him excited and she began to jerk him even faster. She wanted to watch him come, to shoot his load right there in front of her face. She had never seen a man come before. Not like that. Every man she had had before Lee had been on and off her in a matter of minutes. Only Lee had taken the time to really make love to her. Now she was about to watch her lover do what he had done inside her many times before. She would stroke him until his magic fluid shot out of him.

But Lee was not ready just yet. He wanted to savor their evening of lovemaking as long as he could, to enjoy much longer the pleasure she was giving him, and give her a reunion to remember as well. Lee gently removed her protesting hand. "Not just yet," he said. "We have all night for that."

Lee bent and kissed her pouting lips. Then he fell to his knees, forgetting his own pleasure and concentrating on her own. He nibbled her neck, her heaving breasts, her flat stomach, slowly working his way down to the musky scent that was unique to this woman. He placed a hand on one of her knees and urged her legs apart. He kissed his way down her thigh to the wetness that had soaked the few strands of blonde hair that curled between her legs.

With his fingers he pushed them aside to reveal the swollen pink lips, slightly parted as if inviting him to enter into the depths beyond. Without any encouragement, Sue lifted her hips toward his open mouth, and Lee slid his tongue easily inside her. Sue let out a little gasp and thrust her buttocks higher as if she were trying to fill herelf with a tiny cock. Lee darted his tongue rapidly and made her squeal, then he pursed his lips and sucked on the little button nestled within the folds of flesh.

"Oh, God, Lee. It feels so good. You couldn't know how good," she said, gasping for air. "I want you to fill me with that thing of yours." Sue pulled his head up from between her legs. Lee wiped his dripping mouth and moved over her, as Sue threw one of her legs over the back of the sofa to give him greater access to her. Lee wasted no time, but plunged his organ full length into her.

This was too much for Sue to bear. The sensation of his rod thrusting into her sent her into wave after wave of orgasm. So intense was it that she clawed at Lee's back as if to grasp onto something that would keep her from falling into oblivion. She pumped her hips and trembled under Lee Morgan's weight, begging for more, yet pleading for the uncontrollable spasms to end.

Lee was on the brink as well, nearly unable to contain himself. His cock throbbed in her viselike grip, and his balls constricted as if gathering strength for the inevitable explosion. Sue finally relaxed under him, allowing him to stroke as quickly or as slowly as he wanted.

All at once he came out of her and Sue understood just what he meant for her to do. She had wanted to see him come and now he was obliging her desire. He sat on his knees above her and Sue grasped him toward the base of his organ, immediately continuing the steady rhythm. She stared at his ripening head and watched as it swelled to even greater dimensions.

He came with a force that even she hadn't expected. The first jet of white liquid shot onto her neck and breasts. She couldn't take her eyes off of him as he spurt again and again, sending streams of hot spunk onto her belly and running down her fingers. Lee collapsed onto her, exhausted, smothering her with grateful kisses, and whispering his love for her.

The next morning over breakfast, neither spoke a word about the passion of the evening before, though Lee noticed that Sue was almost glowing with joy.

"So, what will you do now?" she asked Lee. "Do you think you might stick around a while this time, or do you plan to go off and conquer all of South America?" Her words were not mean-spirited, and Lee knew immediately what she was leading up to.

"First thing I have to do is hire some good men and get Spade Bit back into shape," he replied. "It's seen a lot of neglect this summer. The stock is in bad shape . . ."

"And what of us?" Sue cut in, getting right to the point.

Lee looked at her, sorry that he was unable to give her the answer she wanted just yet. "You know I love you dearly, Sue," he said. "But right now there are too many things I have to take care of before I can even consider marriage again. Besides, there's plenty more men like Paxton out there that could do me a lot of harm through you. Surely you understand that."

Sue didn't respond. She would let him off the hook until he had resettled. He couldn't keep giving her excuses forever. One day, in his own time, Lee would ask her. She didn't mind the wait. A man like Lee Morgan never rushed into anything that didn't involve gunplay.

With Paxton safely sleeping in potters field, Grover quickly returned to normal. The townspeople all chipped in to give Chook a hero's funeral, and everyone within an hour of the place came to see him buried.

Among the guests was Marshal Rayburn, who had come all the way from Boise for the occasion. Dressed in his finest uniform, he had first ridden out to Spade Bit to personally thank Lee Morgan for setting things straight in Grover.

As they sat in Lee's parlor discussing the events over a cup of coffee, Lee couldn't help but notice that Rayburn could not sit still, as if there was something on his mind that he was having trouble bringing up. "Something eating at you, Marshal?" Lee finally said to break the ice. "You look a mite nervous."

Rayburn sat back in his chair, glad that Morgan had prompted him. It would make what he had to say that much easier. "As a matter of fact, there is," he said. "You and I both know that despite all the hoopla in town over Chook blowing Paxton to kingdom come, Chook wasn't much of a lawman. In fact he was the most pitiful excuse for a deputy I've ever hired."

"I won't argue with that," Lee said.

"Frankly, I only gave him the job because no one else in town wanted it at the time. Ain't too many men willing to risk their necks to keep the peace in these parts. But times have changed since then. Grover's nearly doubled in size, and I don't aim to put another incompetent in Chook's seat. Lee, I came out here as much to talk to you as attend this funeral. Despite your reputation as a gunman, word's reached me even in Boise that you're just about the most honest man in these parts."

Rayburn reached into his shirt pocket, pulled out a shiny tin star and tossed it into Lee's lap. "That's why I believe you would do the town a great service to put that on your lapel beginning today. The pay ain't much, but with your name on the jailhouse door, you'd be doing a lot to keep the peace for miles around. I need a man I can count on. What do you say, Morgan?"

Lee picked up the star and looked into his reflection. He didn't have to make the marshal wait for an answer. "I'm mighty honored," he said. "And a few years ago I might have taken you up on the offer. But right now, I have a ranch that I'm determined to take care of. 'Sides, I'm not eager to be looking over my shoulder every time I walk down the street. I've made a lot of enemies in my day, and once they get wind that I'm the new Sheriff of Grover, there's apt to be folks comin' out of the woodwork to get back at me."

The marshal sighed and took a sip of coffee. "Well, I thought it might be worth a chance, comin' out to see what your feelings were on the matter. Never any harm in asking."

Lee looked at the star again and, to Rayburn's amazement, tucked it into his shirt pocket. "I just got an idea," Lee said. "Will you excuse me a moment?"

"Sure," Rayburn said, wondering what Lee was up to. "Funeral ain't till this afternoon."

Lee stood up and went out the front door to the barn. A few moments later he returned with Sam Lawton in tow. When Sam saw the marshal, he was very confused. "What's going on here, Mr. Morgan? Have I done something wrong?"

Rayburn looked over the tall young man

standing before him, suddenly knowing what was on Morgan's mind. Without Morgan saying a word, Rayburn nodded his head in assent. "Who might this be?" Rayburn asked.

"This here's Sam Lawton," he said. "I think he might be willin' to listen to your offer."

"What offer?" Sam said, trying to figure out what these two crazy men were talking and smiling about. "What are you two talking about? Why have you got me in here? I've got a lot of work to do."

Lee pulled out the star and without warning, pinned it onto Sam's jacket pocket. Sam's eyes popped open when he saw it. "The marshal here thinks you'd make a fine sheriff, and stopped by to see if I could spare you," Lee lied. "I told him you were the best man I had but he's about convinced me that the town needs a good lawman more. What do you say, Sam? I'm leaving it up to you."

"I don't know what to say," Sam said. "I ain't never really thought about nothing like this before. All I know is horses."

"And next time I come down here you'll know all about sheriffing," the marshal said, not willing to take no for an answer twice in one day.

"You'd better get your gear together," Lee instructed. "Everyone's goin' in for

Chook's funeral this afternoon, and there ain't no better time for a swearing-in ceremony. You'll ride in with us in an hour. And don't you take that badge off, either."

"I'm packin' right now," Sam said. He pushed his hat back onto his head and rushed out of the room and back to the barn.

Lee and Rayburn both shared a hearty laugh at the man's consternation. Then the marshal added on a more serious note: "Lee, do you think he can handle it? After all, he ain't much more than a boy."

"You got anyone better in mind?" Lee asked, still laughing. "Don't you worry none, Marshal. He'll do just fine. He'll be a real professional by the time you get down this way again. Everyone in town knows he's a good man. He'll have all the respect he needs. And if there's any trouble, I'll make sure he knows he can turn to me for help. But there ain't apt to be much. All Grover needs is an honest man to set a good example. And Sam's about the finest example you'll find anywhere."

"I appreciate that, Lee," the marshal said, watching Lee go to the front window and part the curtains. "I'm inclined to take your word for it."

But Lee Morgan didn't hear the marshal's thanks. He was too busy watching the young man standing by the barn door showing off his new badge, the symbol of respectability that he had earned over the last two days.

Lee saw in him everything Frank Leslie had wanted him to be when he became a man, everything that Lee Morgan had rejected in order to earn respectability the hard way—with the barrel of a gun.

SHOTGUN STATION

1

Lee Morgan had been riding, sun up to sundown, for the past ten days. He'd ridden into Texas on the fifteenth day of April, somewhere up in the panhandle. He was still in Texas and he was still a half a day's ride from his destination.

He'd bedded down with a whore named Daisy up in Amarillo. He'd lost more than he could afford in a poker game in Lubbock. A drunk half breed Apache had tried to give him a haircut in Big Spring and he heard about a job that nobody else wanted when he passed through San Angelo. He was headed for Uvalde and hating Texas more with each mile.

Uvalde was on the sun up side of the Anacacho mountain range. By Morgan's reckoning, some sixty miles from the Mexican border. The populace was two thirds Mexican with the balance made up of a mixed breed of Mexican, Indian and drifter. By the time he rode into town, he'd already decided that none of it would be worth saving should the need ever arise.

"Stall him, water him, feed him and after he's cooled down pull the burrs out of his legs and rub them down with linament."

"Si señor," the livery man replied. Simultaneously, grinning a toothless grin, he held up two short, dirty fingers. "Two pesos now an' two pesos *manana.*" Morgan frowned. "You will come then to see me. If you are not happy," the man continued, glancing at Morgan's blacksnake whip, "who knows what you will do, *señor.* It is a *jugar.*" The man shrugged. "A gamble, *señor.*"

"Yeah. And if I *am* happy?"

"Two pesos more—and he stays for as long as you like."

Morgan eyed the man. Sweat trickled from his forehead in a steady stream and finally dispersed into a number of wrinkles on his chubby, jowled face. He was balding, squinty eyed and part of his left ear was missing. His shoulders were round and held up big, powerful-looking arms. The rest of him was lard covered with coarse, black hair. He wore outsized, home sewn, denim britches. They were held up with overburdened galluses stained with sweat. He had no shirt and on his feet only sandals.

Morgan dug into his pockets and came up with four dollars. He grabbed the man's wrist, pulled his arm down and pressed the money into a sweaty palm. The man looked shocked. "All of it right now," Morgan said, "and I *will* be back tomorrow. If I'm *not* happy, you lose the *jugar.*" Their eyes met. Both then smiled and the livery man nodded, jerking free and jamming the money into his pants pocket. Morgan noted the strain the action placed on the galluses. "One more thing, *amigo*—a hotel. Uvalde got one?"

"Si, señor." He took Morgan by the upper part of his arm and led him just outside the livery barn. There, he

freed his grip and pointed toward the tallest building in sight. "The hotel—she is there." The man turned his head, looked Morgan in the eye, grinned broadly and added, *"La cucaracha!"*

The man at the livery barn hadn't lied. At least not about the cockroaches. Morgan knew he wouldn't be alone in his room. After dispatching the most daring of the disgusting insects, Morgan stripped and washed off as much of Texas as the facilities allowed. That done, he broke out his only change of clothes, dressed, strapped on his rig and went downstairs to the *cantina*. He was gratified to find an American barkeep.

"We got ice," the man said proudly. "Want a cold beer, mister?"

"Yeah." Morgan had expected a mug of beer with ice in it. The practice was common in most places if they were fortunate enough to have ice at all. Here, he found himself the recipient of a frost coated mug and beer from a keg which was surrounded by ice. It was delicious. He drank two before he spoke again.

"You want another beer, mister?"

Morgan nodded and then asked, "Where would I find Luke Masters?"

"Prob'ly down to his office." The barkeep set up the beer and then eyed Morgan. "You his new shotgun rider?"

"Word travels fast."

"Easy to figure. You don't look like a man with freight to haul and there ain't nobody else lookin' for Luke Masters 'cept for that job. Three's come in askin —an' three's rode out right after."

"Hard man to work for?"

The barkeep grinned. "Luke? Hell no. Got a disposition like a pup's—ceptin' maybe where his daughter is concerned. Mostly, though—shotgun men ridin' for Luke Masters got a mighty short life span lately."

"Know why?"

"Sure don't. Nobody else can figure it either. Up 'til about six months ago, Luke had only been robbed one time. Now all o' the sudden, his wagons been hit about a dozen times. He's lost four shotgun men an' two damn good skinners."

"Well," Morgan said, finishing his beer, "I'm not looking to end up at my own funeral but I heard the pay was pretty good."

" 'Bout the best in these parts if you live to spend it."

As Morgan took his leave, he brushed by two cowhands just coming in. One of them paused and eyed him closely. Morgan returned the stare until the cowpoke finally turned away. It appeared to Morgan that the man thought he recognized him. Morgan knew he had never seen the cowhand. It puzzled him.

The Masters' Cartage Company was housed in one of the more attractive of Uvalde's buildings. In part, that could be attributed to sharing some office space with Wells-Fargo & Co. The stage line had bought out two local firms about four years earlier and now maintained the only stage line to points west and south of Uvalde. While the railroads had forced Wells-Fargo to shrink its passenger hauling duties up north, rail transport in Texas was still begging.

The bell over the office door rang twice. Once when Morgan opened the door and again when he closed it. Neither brought anyone to the desk. Morgan's eyes scanned the photographs on the walls. Most, he reckoned, were twenty-five or thirty years old. Luke

Masters' father had founded the company and had hauled freight for some prominent clients. Among the pictures, Morgan recognized Kit Carson, Temple Houston—son of the Texas legend Sam Houston, and the fabled New Mexico lawman Pat Garrett.

"May I help you?" Morgan's head jerked toward the desk. The voice was soft—like velvet but somewhat throaty. Morgan's eyes fell upon a blonde haired, blue eyed beauty who, he guessed, was probably about twenty-five. Her hair was short and tucked up under a stetson. She wore a tight fitted buckskin shirt and britches which seemed molded to her form.

"Maybe," he said. "I'm looking for Luke Masters. I'm here about a job." The girl eyed him.

"You're no skinner."

"You're right. I sent a telegraph cable. Name's Lee Morgan."

"The shotgun." Morgan nodded. The girl came from behind the desk and extended her hand. The grip was firm. "I'm Lucy Masters. I run the office and do most of the hiring. My father is at the bank right now but you'd end up talking to me first anyhow."

"Your daddy don't make the decisions?"

"We make them together. I'm a full partner."

"The pay sounded pretty good," Morgan said, tentatively.

"It's very good but you'll earn every dime of it. We've been hit on seventeen of the last twenty-five runs. We're down to two skinners and no shotguns. You'll get expenses when you're not in Uvalde. A hundred and fifty a month wages. All the ammunition you use on the job and a bonus for every shipment that gets through." She smiled. "That's payable twice a year if you're still around to collect it."

"None of it sounds negotiable."

"None of it is."

"Maybe that's why you don't have any shotgun riders."

"No maybe about it. That's the reason, Mr. Morgan, and that's the way it stays. Take it or leave it."

"Then I'm hired," he said, adding, "*if* I take it?"

"I didn't say that. I just said that those are the rules. If you can't abide them, then there's no need to waste any more time—yours or mine."

"I can live with 'em, but I'd like to know who's out to get you."

"So would we."

"Any ideas?"

"None that I care to discuss with you, Mr. Morgan." She smiled and cocked her head. "At least not right now." She turned on her heel and went back behind the desk. She turned back. "A drink?"

"Whiskey." She poured. Morgan downed the shot and she offered another. He declined. "You said you had two drivers. They both new?"

"Only one. Sam Tanksley. He's from Amarillo. Skinned for Wells-Fargo awhile back. Comes well spoke of. Our other man has been with daddy for ten years." She grinned and shook her head. "If he was fifteen years younger we wouldn't need you. He could do both."

"Sounds like quite a man."

"He is. His name is Cimmaron Dakis but we—matter of fact most—just call him Alkali."

"I'd guess there's a story behind that," Morgan said, smiling.

"There is, but don't ask him to tell it when I'm

around. I've heard it more than my share."

The door opened and Morgan turned to see a well dressed, big man of about fifty. He had a leathery face and a friendly smile. Morgan guessed right when he concluded that the man was Luke Masters. After the proper introductions, Lucy Masters returned to her work on the company books. Morgan and the elder Masters spent more than an hour together. The conversation concluded with Masters' invite for Morgan to join them that evening for dinner. It would officially seal their bargain. Too, Masters invited Morgan to stay at the Masters' home so long as he was in their employ. It was not a practice Morgan usually indulged but two things were gnawing at him. The first was the mystery of the sudden raids on Masters' freight wagons. The second could be found at the hotel—*La Cucaracha!*

2

The Double C cattle ranch stretched out over thousands of acres of southwest Texas grassland. The main house and the center of the Double C's activities was located just a dozen miles southeast of Uvalde. West and south of the house, all the way to the Mexican border at Piedras Negras and south along the Rio Grande, Double C cattle were fattened up.

The ranch was nearly as much a part of Texas as the Alamo. Founded by Trevor and Ephram Coltrane in 1837, the operation came into its own under Trevor's son, Houston. At the birth of his daughter, Houston Coltrane lost his wife. He threw himself into raising her and expanding his empire. He did so, finally, to the exclusion of his illegitimate son, Marshall.

The day Marsh Coltrane was run off was a day still talked about in that part of Texas. Marsh decided he was man enough to handle his daddy. He was wrong. Whipped and humiliated, Marsh rode off and out of Houston Coltrane's will. He swore revenge. Three years later, the old man died and left everything to his legitimate heir, Charity Coltrane.

Charity was twenty-eight, nearly six feet tall, almond-eyed, dark of complexion and full bosomed. She could turn any man's head, dance with the best of Texas' wealthy ladies and outshoot most of the ranch hands. Save for social events, Charity Coltrane would be in denim pants, wool shirt, chaps, dogging boots and toting a pair of matched Colt's pistols. They weren't just for show.

She knew most of the Double C's ranch hands by their first names, except during the spring drives which she headed up. Once the drive was over, she turned her attention to the second of the ranch's income producing ventures—horses. Charity Coltrane could break, ride, brand and deal on cattle or horse flesh with a skill envied by the most case hardened buyer. In short, she was a woman with whom to be reckoned.

Lige Brewster, one of the ranch's top hands, pounded on the front door of the main house. The West Indian black, Kingston, responded.

"Need to see Miss Charity," Lige said, sheepishly, Kingston stepped back, eyed the hand's dirty boots and then pointed to a small rug at one side of the entryway. Lige nodded and stood on it. A few minutes later, Charity Coltrane appeared from the den.

"What is it, Lige?"

"Not real sure ma'am—but—well—I think I saw your bro—" He stopped. It was the wrong thing to call Marsh Coltrane—if it had been Marsh Coltrane he saw. Lige cleared his throat. "I think I saw Marsh Coltrane ma'am—yestiddy—at the hotel casino."

"Lige, you weren't around when Marsh was here. How can you say that?"

"I—I seen his picture, ma'am." He paused, pointing

toward the den, then he continued. "Used to hang in there—behind your poppa's desk."

Charity walked over to him. "That would take some remembering on your part."

"Yes'm—an' I said—I'm not positive but you allus tol' us—if'n we think we seen 'im—we was s'posed to say."

Charity considered him. Finally, she nodded. "Yes Lige, yes I did." She squeezed her temples between her thumb and two fingers and turned away, walking several steps before she turned back. "You fetch Li Sung and take him to town. He near raised Marsh Coltrane. If anybody would recognize him Li Sung would." Lige Brewster looked surprised. "Ma'am—I figured *you*—"

"I'll do the figuring Lige—not you. Just do what I've asked." She smiled. An order out of Charity Coltrane was never an order. Lige nodded. "When you get back send the Chinese to see me."

Lee Morgan found himself awakened to a tray of orange juice fresh squeezed, flapjacks, eggs, bacon and a pot of coffee. Lucy Masters served it up personally.

"If you'll forgive me saying so," Morgan offered, scooting up to a sitting position, "this is a hell of a way to treat a hired hand."

"Enjoy it today, Mr. Morgan. It won't happen again." She placed the tray and poured the coffee. Morgan was pleased when she produced a second empty cup and poured herself a cup. She wasn't bashful. She sat down on the edge of the bed. "Daddy likes you." They both sipped and eyed each other. "He told me you were the offspring of a pretty famous old gunman."

"Frank Leslie got around."

"Or his reputation did."

"Hmm!"

"You as good as he was supposed to be?"

Morgan chewed, swallowed and followed the mouthful with a swallow of coffee. "He wasn't *supposed* to be anything. He *was* something. I'm something too—me—Lee Morgan. I'm not Buckskin Frank Leslie."

"You sound a little resentful."

"Only of the fact that I prefer to be judged by what I do. Not who fate happened to make me."

"Fair enough." Lucy Masters poured both of them a second cup of coffee. Then, she got up and walked across the room, finally turning back. Morgan had been watching her. "You'll have a chance to prove just how good you are, Mr. Morgan. We're sending you to San Antonio to negotiate a new contract for us."

Morgan stopped eating. He considered Lucy's statement and searched her face for any sign of a joke. There was none.

"Why me? I thought I was hired on as a shotgun rider."

"You were—but if we don't land this contract—we'll have very little need of your services. Most of our clientele have either already quit us or cut down their shipments until it is difficult to make the runs pay."

"Still—why me? I'd think you or your daddy would want to handle a contract personally just to make sure you've got a more than even chance to get it."

"Usually that would be the case. On this one—well—I've got some questions about it. You're the kind of man who is supposed to be able to get the answers." She took several short sips of coffee. "Have you ever heard of Jesus Benitalde Sanchez de Lopez?"

Morgan was finishing his breakfast. He didn't answer until he was through. He eyed the girl and decided to test her mettle even further. He swung his legs from beneath the covers. She didn't even blink. He stood up, glancing back at her. Her eyes roamed over his muscular frame but she made no effort to turn away. Morgan began to dress.

"I've heard of him. Stories in the newspapers mostly." Morgan began tucking in his shirt. "Seems I recall something about a revolution."

"Uh huh—and we don't want to be mixed up in any revolution." Morgan sat on the edge of the bed and tugged on his boots. He stood up, reached for his rig and strapped it on.

"But you want the business—and the uh—*pesos* that go with it."

"That's not a *want,* Mr. Morgan. That's a *need.*"

"If you're going to dig in the dirt for your gold, Miss Masters, you're going to get your hands dirty."

She snickered. "Son of a famous gunman—no slouch himself and a philosopher in the boot. Well then, Mr. Morgan, you have a looksee at the Lopez deal and you decide just how dirty our hands are going to get."

"You still haven't answered my questions. Why me?"

"Protocol, Mr. Morgan," Lucy snapped. "Great men rarely meet face to face to negotiate." She smiled. "They dispatch emissaries."

Lee Morgan had been a lot of things in his life. He could not recall ever having been an emissary. The word grated on him. He concluded that what it really meant was simply that he was expendable. As a shotgun rider

—the same was true. Thing was, as a shotgun rider he could shoot back. Frankly, Morgan didn't know what to expect as an emissary.

Morgan was to ride out that afternoon. About noon, he left the freight office and headed for the livery barn. Half way there, he noted the cowpoke who'd stared at him as he was leaving the hotel on his first day in town. The cowpoke was in company with a Chinese man. This time they were both staring.

Morgan could feel their eyes upon him even after he'd passed them. Finally, he stopped and turned around. They were still staring but the Chinese got nervous, shook his head up and down and then turned and trotted off. The cowpoke looked back at Morgan and then he too turned and walked away. Morgan vowed, silently, that he would confront the cowpoke if he ever saw him again.

Li Sung bowed low as he entered the Double C ranch house. He stood. head bowed, while Kingston fetched the lady of the house. Charity Coltrane ushered Li Sung into the den and closed the door behind them.

"Li Sung—is Marshall in Uvalde?"

"It is many years, Missy. Li Sung's eyes not so good."

"Is it," she repeated, her voice more harsh the second time.

"I thinkee so. I thinkee master Marsh back—yes—yes."

Ten years could make quite a difference in anyone's appearance. In the case of the Coltrane clan, it was even more. Charity had gone off to a girl's school in Dallas when she was twelve. Aside from holidays and a rare visit from her father and stepbrother, she rarely saw anyone from the Double C. She had no more than returned home when the final split took place. Once that happened, her father removed all evidence of Marshall Coltrane's existence.

It had been difficult for Charity to understand how her father could have so completely reversed himself about Marsh. Once, he had done little but brag about the boy. The son he'd fathered in a single moment of passionate indiscretion. What had happened? Charity really never knew the details but the hatred between the two, or so she believed, was a major contributing factor to her father's premature death. As for Marsh, he made no secret of his intent to avenge his exile.

Charity rode, hell bent, into Uvalde and sought out Sheriff Lund Taylor. He was a big, slow, affable man who could be seen patrolling the streets with a shotgun in one hand and an axe handle in the other. Charity couldn't recall ever having heard of Lund Taylor shooting anybody.

"Miss Charity, you're a sight for sore eyes. Don't see near enough o' you these days." The sheriff had lifted his 225-pound frame out of the broken-down chair behind his desk. He stood, rather in a slouch, grinning down at Charity. He was nearly six feet, six inches tall.

"I have reason to believe that Marshall has come back. I want to know what you intend to do about it if it's true."

Lund Taylor straightened up and walked around the desk. He seated himself on its edge and then folded his arms across his chest.

"He done somethin' wrong?"

"You *know* what he did."

The sheriff was already shaking his head negatively. "No, Miss Charity," Lund said, holding up his right hand and extending his index finger into the air, "I know what he said. They's a difference. Still cain't jail a man fer talkin'."

"I've seen you pole ax a man for damn little more than just thinking."

"Yes'm. Drunk cowhands talkin' wild. Boys, most of 'em, mean no harm. Too much bad whiskey an' too long on the trail. I do that mostly fer the ramrods. They sleep it off and they's fine the next mornin'. Now, ma'am, you 're talkin' 'bout somethin' a whole heap differ'nt."

"What's he have to do? Burn down the Double C?"

Sheriff Lund Taylor grinned. "Ma'am, they ain't a man in a hunnert miles could do that. Why your boys'd have 'im strung up to a willow branch before he could git inside o' five miles from the house."

"I came here to get the law where it belongs—on my side." Charity's dark eyes flashed and she spun around, strode to the door and then turned back. "You've been *informed,* Sheriff. Anything that happens now is self defense."

"Miss Charity, the law works in both directions. Just you make sure, if anythin' does happen, that you're defendin' and not agaitatin'." The sheriff smiled and then added, "But I'll ask around. If'n it turns out to be Marsh, I'll have a little talk with 'im."

"Marsh Coltrane won't be coming back here to *talk,* Sheriff. Not even to you."

Charity was just mounting up when a feminine voice called to her. She turned and saw Lucy Masters approaching. The two of them represented about the most desirable, if not available, female element in Uvalde. Between them there was no love lost. Upon the Masters' arrival in Uvalde, Lucy's father had quickly sized up the Coltrane ranch as a likely freight customer. Charity was on a trip to the east at the time, however. By the time she returned, Lucy had replaced her as a young cowhand's favorite. Ultimately, Jack Henshaw rode out of their lives but no business dealings ever culminated between the two.

"Miss Masters," Charity said, coolly, as Lucy approached.

"I'll be both frank and brief," Lucy said. "We've been robbed a number of times lately and I've heard rumors that your own ranch has also been a target. I know your present freight arrangements are costly and we need your business. Do you still think Jack Henshaw is worth it?"

Charity considered Lucy for several seconds, mentally evaluating the assessments to which she had just alluded. Finally, Charity smiled.

"No," she said. "I don't. What do you propose?"

"A re-evaluation of our positions—a consideration of busineess between us. I'd suggest that my father come to your ranch at your convenience and discuss it."

"Very well," Charity said. "I've had some, uh, personal news with which I must deal right now. Shall we say one day next week."

"You name it."

"I'll send word to you." Lucy nodded. Just inside the office, Sheriff Lund watched the meeting with interest and concern. He had a healthy respect for most men he might have to face down. He got a cold chill down his spine when he pondered the possibilities of having to face either one or both of the hellcats he'd just been watching.

3

Morgan reined up, removed his hat and mopped his brow. He eyed a half dozen citizens who, like himself, had paused in front of the old mission called the Alamo. After a few minutes of remembering his history and mentally reciting a part of the roster of names, Morgan knew that here was Texas and here too—America. He rode on, turning onto Commerce and riding, once again, outside the city boundaries.

The Mexican *hacienda* architecture clearly marked the residence of Jesus Benitalde Sanchez de Lopez. Two sombreroed *vaqueros* stood vigil at the arched entry way. Above it, fashioned in black wrought iron were the words

La Casa de Lopez

"Pararse!" Morgan halted. *"Que habla Espanol?"*

"Some," Morgan replied, smiling and then adding, "*Poco.*"

"Como se llama?" The tallest of the *vaqueros* stepped forward as he spoke. "*Nombre?*"

"Morgan. Lee Morgan. I have come to see *Señor* de Lopez. I come from *Señorita* Masters in Uvalde."

"*Esperar.*" Morgan dismounted to wait. A few minutes later, he was escorted into the house. Its interior was plush, resplendent with the trappings of success. In what was obviously the library, Morgan was given a drink and told to make himself comfortable. A few minutes later, he turned toward the sound of the opening door and saw a tall, slim, well groomed middle aged man.

"*Señor* Morgan, I am Jesus de Lopez." The man approached, shook Morgan's hand and gestured toward a nearby overstuffed chair. Morgan got comfortable. "May I refresh your drink?"

"Yeah—uh—yes," Morgan said, "thank you."

"Now then, *señor,* I was given to understand that the Masters family harbored some reservations about contracting with us. Is that correct?"

"I think they have some questions."

"And you were sent to get the answers." The man smiled. "You look more like a *pistolero* than a business-man."

"Different business requires different skills."

"Agreed, Mr. Morgan. Some of my business requires men of your particular skill." Lopez turned toward the door. "Enrique!" Morgan looked up and a sinister looking man entered. He wore crossed *bandoleros* each of which supported a pistol. Morgan eased to his feet. Lopez turned back, smiling at Morgan. "Now," Lopez said.

Morgan's right hand became a blur but the barrel of his gun was leveled not at Enrique but squarely between

Lopez's eyes. Enrique's own guns were not yet in position.

"I don't like games," Morgan said.

"I'm impressed, Mr. Morgan. Enrique is one of my best men. Obviously you could have killed him easily." Lopez frowned. "Instead you chose me as your target."

"I doubt that I could get out of here alive," Morgan said, "even if I killed your man. I'd rather reduce the incentive than try to reduce the odds."

"I had to know just how good you are," Lopez said, extending his hands, palms upward and shrugging. "I hope you understand."

"I understand. But you still don't know, Lopez. I would have killed both of you." Enrique frowned and took a step forward. Lopez held up his hand.

"I think you could have, Mr. Morgan. Enrique, *vamos.*" The sinister *vaquero* took his leave but his eyes never strayed from Morgan's face. Morgan holstered his gun, finished his drink and sat down. This time, however, he did not lean back. Instead, he leaned forward.

"What's your deal?"

"Will you accept my hospitality for the evening, Mr. Morgan? Dinner with myself and my family? A tour of the grounds later perhaps? A good night's rest? I much prefer business talk at the start of the day. Too," Lopez said, smiling, "I would consider it a way of apologizing to you."

"I'll accept," Morgan said, "on one condition."

"Yes."

"No more games. The next man of yours who pulls a gun on me is going to die. Understood?"

"Understood," Lopez said.

Morgan's tour of the house served little more than to substantiate what he already knew. Jesus de Lopez was a wealthy man. A tour of the grounds was another matter. Once a visitor left the immediate environs of the house, the property became a compound. Morgan reckoned that more than a hundred *vaqueros* were bivouacked on the premises and there was no doubt facilities for twice that number.

"I'm impressed," Morgan said, adding, "as I assume I'm supposed to be." Lopez grinned.

"That you are is complimentary but I doubt that you have been swayed even minimally in your thinking."

"I wouldn't go quite that far," Morgan replied. "A gang of men like you've got quartered here could raise hell with hit and run raids." He considered Lopez, smiled and said, "Couldn't they?"

"They could—but they haven't. Not yet anyway."

"Revolution, *señor* Lopez? I've heard stories."

"I've heard the same ones but I too own a cattle ranch. It is, by Texas standards, rather modest but it does require *vaqueros.*"

"Yeah—sure."

Two chairs were still vacant at the dining room table when Morgan joined Lopez, Juan Diaz—Lopez's foreman, and a Mexican banker introduced as Francisco Correra. A few minutes after the formal introductions, one of the chairs was filled. Morgan could not hide his appetite.

"This is my daughter, Mr. Morgan. Madiera, come meet the *rayo veloz yanqui.*" Morgan looked quizzical. Madiera Lucia de Lopez extended her hand, backside up in anticipation of it being kissed. Morgan shook it.

"I am pleased," she said, smiling. "My father called you a lightning-fast yankee. I assume he refers to your skill with a weapon."

"It's all he's seen," Morgan said. "And meeting you is my pleasure."

"Gracias, señor."

"Bien venido, señorita."

The sixth chair at the table remained empty throughout the meal though a place had been set. Morgan glanced at it and then at Jesus de Lopez several times. He got no indication that things were not as they should be. The talk remained small. Mostly about horses, cattle and the stunning growth of Texas during the past century.

"Tell me, Morgan," de Lopez finally said, wiping the corners of his mouth as he finished his meal, "how do you perceive the acquisition of Texas by the United States?"

"If they stole it they stole too much. If they didn't they could have afforded to be generous and taken less." The reply brought laughter.

"Your quarrel then is with its size and not the fact that Mexico once owned it."

"Best I can recall, the Mexicans took it from the Indians."

"True! But is that not what you Americans did with the rest of your country?"

"It is and I guess they didn't want to show any discrimination so they showed everybody they could take from Mexicans as well."

"You seem to take all such things rather lightly," Madiera de Lopez observed.

"If you want to be serious about it, it wasn't so much

the land that the Texicans wanted as it was their freedom to live upon it. General Santa Ana had other ideas."

Morgan's eyes met those of Madiera de Lopez and they were locked in a silent exchange of desire. Madiera was beautiful. Her raven hair appeared, at times, almost blue because it was so black. Her eyes, also black, sparkled from the reflected light of crystal glassware. Her nose was slim and her lips thin, moist lines which offered a silent invitation to be kissed.

She wore a black lace *mantilla,* a high-necked, lace-collared black dress, form fitted. The form was full and equally inviting. Morgan could feel the warmth and rigidity between his thighs each time he looked at her. He suspected she sensed as much.

"The meal was excellent," Morgan finally said, pushing back from the table.

"Good! I'm pleased that you enjoyed it." The elder Lopez then silently gestured at his daughter and she stood, nodded in Morgan's direction and left the dining room. Moments later, a big, young Mexican entered the room. He was lavishly dressed and heavily armed. Everyone stood. Morgan was late but he got to his feet.

"Mr. Morgan. Please to make the acquaintance of one of my most trusted *vaqueros*.. This is Dorateo Arango." Neither man spoke but there was a silent contest of hand strength for a few moments. Finally, Arango grinned, withdrew his hand and nodded. Everyone resumed their seats.

The ensuing table talk was of the unimportant again and the newest arrival said nothing. He devoured the meal with considerable relish and then fired up a Cuban cigar. He topped off each hearty puff with a sizeable swallow of brandy. Upon completion of those treats, the young Mexican named Arango proceeded to down two jiggers of Tequila in a toast to his host.

That done, he turned to Morgan and spoke in nearly perfect English. "I hope you will deal with de Lopez. He is a good friend and an honest one. Most important however is the accomplishment itself. You would be serving both the *campensinos* and the *peons*. The peasants and the workers. Think of it well, *señor* Morgan."

Retirement in the de Lopez house came early, at least for the likes of Lee Morgan. Granted, it had been a long and busy day but ten o'clock was often the time when Morgan was getting his second wind. After several attempts at sleep, he opted to give San Antonio the once-over.

Morgan had the distinct feeling that he was being followed but he saw no one and he had not encountered any opposition to his departure. Down on Commerce Street, not too far from the Alamo, Morgan found a saloon. Its name alone prompted his entry.

The *Deguello* was far from plush but it boasted a lively casino and a variety of other forms of entertainment. The name translated to "Ask no quarter and give none"—loosely at least. It was reputed to have been the melody to which the Mexicans made their final storm of the Alamo's walls. In this setting, it brought a smile to Morgan's face.

By midnight, the steely eyed gunman had won himself about seventy-five dollars at the Keno table and decided to quit the place. He cashed in, downed a final drink and stepped into an almost deserted street.

The shot was high! It splintered the wood just inches

above and behind Morgan's head. His gun was in his hand in the flash of gunpowder which accompanied the shot and he fired toward it. He heard a grunt and the thud of a body on a wooden sidewalk.

Instinctively, when the shot had been fired, Morgan went low, drew, rolled and fired. Now, he scrambled for the meager shelter of a darkened doorway. Seconds turned to more than a minute—then two. Stealthily, Morgan eased back onto the street. It was no surprise that not a single soul had exited the saloon to investigate. Unless it was their own personal flight, few men cared to risk their necks for anyone else, much less a total stranger.

Morgan headed across the street in an attempt to find his victim. Someone who, moments before, had been his would-be killer. He was halfway across the street when he heard the voice to his right.

"Coltrane!" Again Morgan dived. This time the shot took off his hat. He fired toward its point of origin but he was certain he'd missed. A shotgun's blast ripped through the night and behind him, a body slammed into a wall. He heard a man running. He got to a crouch, stayed low until he reached his horse and then did a single stirrup ride for more than a block. Finally he pulled himself full into the saddle and rode like hell for the de Lopez spread.

Morgan nearly broke the door to the library down. He stepped inside and found himself facing five drawn guns. He didn't slow down as he walked to the desk and confronted the elder de Lopez who was just getting to his feet.

"I had nothing to do with it, Morgan. I give you my

word. It was my man who fired the shotgun—who saved your life."

"Only two other people outside of this room knew I was coming to San Antonio—and why. You're a damned unconvincing liar, Lopez." Morgan heard the gun hammers click back into position. "I'll kill you before I go down," Morgan continued, "and you know it."

"Yes, Morgan. I do know it so tell me why should I risk dying by even coming in here—by waiting for you? Hmm?" Morgan let reason back into his head. Lopez was right. Or very goddam clever.

"Then *who,* Lopez? If not you, or your men. Who?"

"Sanchez there," Lopez replied, pointing to one of his men, "he was the one with the shotgun. He said he heard a name called out."

"So did I—but it wasn't mine."

"No—it was the name Coltrane. Does that mean anything to you?"

"Not a damned thing," Morgan answered.

"The Double C ranch, Morgan. It is quite near Uvalde. It is large. Very large. Its owner is a woman. Her name is Charity Coltrane."

"Those goddamned bushwhackers didn't mistake me for any woman." Lopez held out a drink. Morgan accepted and down it in one motion. He set the glass on Lopez's desk. "And," he continued almost as though there had been no interruption, "I don't know the Coltranes and never did as far as I can recollect."

"A man of your profession meets many people under many circumstanes. Perhaps you've forgotten."

"Maybe. But not likely."

"There is another possible answer," Lopez said.

"The man you shot tonight did not die immediately. Sanchez came across him when he himself was shifting positions. He too mumbled something which included the name Coltrane and the name Marsh. It somewhat jogged my own memory. As I recall—there was a family dispute a few years ago—before the father of the Double C's present owner died. The feud centered on a son."

"Interesting, Lopez," Morgan said, "but hardly helpful."

"Perhaps this will be." Lopez handed Morgan a thick, leather-bound book. It was a history of Texas cattle ranches. "Look on page thirty-three, Morgan." Morgan considered Lopez, eyed the book and then did as he was bid. A moment later, Morgan's jaw dropped.

"Jeezus!"

"Yes—a remarkable resemblance I'd say. Your features and coloring are those of a man ten years later than that picture. I'd guess you've been mistaken for this Marshall Coltrane, and for someone his reappearance must be very disquieting."

There was no doubt that the man depicted in the book could have easily passed for Lee Morgan—or vice-versa. Side by side perhaps, the differences would be obvious but at a distance—and with several years separating the man in the photograph from his present-day enemies—Morgan made an inviting substitute.

"Seems to me you went to no small amount of trouble to prove to me that you weren't behind tonight, Lopez."

"I did, but with selfish motives. I need your approval. It means the Masters Cartage Company will haul my goods."

"Why them? There are plenty of freight outfits."

"No, Morgan, there are *not.* Those who have not shown fear at my proposal stand to lose too much American business working for me. In the case of the Masters firm they have little to lose. Unless they turn me down."

"And you want freight hauled into Mexico to supply that fancy-dressed *Generalissimo* I met last night. That right?"

"*Si, señor.* That," Lopez grinned, "*Generalissimo,* as you have called him, was born a peasant. His name is —*was* as you were told. Dorateo Arango."

"And now?"

"Francisco Villa. The people—his people have come to call him Pancho."

"He's a revolutionary. The Masters were pretty explicit about staying out of Mexican trouble."

"Pancho Villa *is* a revolutionary, but the *revolucion* is far away. Only now is he beginning to gather support, and if he is to gather enough, he must show that he can equip his army."

"That takes money," Morgan said. Almost sarcastically he added, "*Mucho dinero, señor Lopez.*"

"Quite, Mr. Morgan. The *dinero* I can supply. Villa and his men will supply the courage and the skills. Someone must haul much of both—and that will require a little of everything. Do you know of any such party?"

"I'll sleep on it." Morgan stalked out and went to his room. He sensed that he was not alone when he entered. The lamp confirmed his feeling. Madiera Lucia de Lopez was just a wisp away from naked.

"I was beginning to like your father," Morgan said, "until now. I didn't think he'd go this far."

"If my father knew I was here, *señor* Morgan, he would have you tied to a post and shot—tonight!"

"Me?"

"*Si.* He would suspect something more but he would never question me—and he wouldn't believe you."

"And I'm not too inclined to believe you, *señorita.*"

"I am here for one person—for me. My father believes I was raped when I was thirteeen. I wasn't. But that's what he believes. That is why he would not question me. Since then I've known no man. Delgado was but a boy. I am betrothed. It is the way in Mexican aristocracy, *señor* Morgan. I only wish to be a proper wife, but I know nothing of what is expected of me."

"You don't want a man. You want a teacher."

"I want both, *señor* Morgan—and I want you."

Madiera Lopez dropped the negligee and stood in the half light. It played over the supple curves of her dark skin and Morgan could feel the rise of his desire. He resisted in silence but the day's events hurtled through his thoughts. He was, he pondered, an emissary for the Masters Cartage Company of Uvalde, Texas. He was, in the eyes of the elder de Lopez, a lightning fast yankee with questionable courage. Apparently, to others, he was the spitting image of a man with whom someone had a hell of a quarrel—one Marsh Coltrane. If there was a reward for him in all of this, Madiera Lucia de Lopez might be his only chance to collect it. He stripped.

The night air and the moisture from the tip of Morgan's tongue quickly hardened Madiera's nipples. Goose bumps ran up her arms and legs and then melted away as Morgan warmed to his task. At the outset, the Mexican girl's body was limp. Morgan positioned her on the bed to suit his pleasure. In minutes she was transformed from student to participant.

She pressed against him, grinding her hips against his manhood as he manipulated the firmness of her breasts. She moaned softly and Morgan felt a twinge in his gut as his mind relayed a message of caution.

"Quietly," he whispered. She sucked in her breath and nodded. Morgan's body raised and he began an exploratory sojourn toward his ultimate destination. His tongue circled the hardened, dark brown circles which topped her breasts, skittered along her abdomen and lingered for a moment at her navel. Madiera stiffened as he went lower and, at last, he thrust home and found the center of her passion.

After what seemed a very long time, Morgan believed Madiera to be at the very peak of desire. He gently shifted her body to his left, lay down and positioned her atop him. Madiera needed little encouragement—or instruction. She now explored with lips, teeth and tongue. The exchange had brought both the gunman and the woman to the very pinnacle of human desire. They flowed into one, moving together as though they had practiced the event a hundred times before. Blood surged, breath came in short, strained gasps and then their link was welded in a gushing, breathless explosion of flesh against flesh—moisture mingling with moisture.

"Will you ask the Masters to help my father?" The question caught Morgan by surprise. They were the first words spoken by either and they aroused Morgan's original suspicions. Madiera raised to her elbows, turned toward him and kissed him, long but gently on the mouth. "I hope so. It will mean—perhaps once more for us. Maybe twice."

"You're sure as hell worth the risk," Morgan whispered.

"I think," she said, smiling, "that is a *gringo complimento.*"

"Si, si," Morgan said, pulling her close, "it sure as hell is."

Madiera departed. Morgan smoked, had a drink and dropped into the deepest and most restful sleep he'd enjoyed in weeeks.

4

"Hold your goddam horses," Morgan shouted. Ignoring the anger of the plea, Morgan's sunup visitor pounded on the door again. He opened it and came face to face with a scrubby looking gent whose belt seemed over burdened with the task of keeping his girth from spilling down the front of his pants. "Who the hell are you?"

"Sam Tanksley's the name," the man replied and handed Morgan a note.

> We got a special order from a rancher named Jessup down in Cotulla. Wants a wagon load of dynamite brought down from San Antonio. By the time you read this Sam will have the load ready. Shotgun him and then head back to Uvalde.
>
> Lucy Masters

"Shit!" Morgan looked up. "She sent me up here to do a job. I'm not through with it yet."

"You are," Jesus de Lopez said, stepping into view, "if you will tell your boss lady *yes.*" Morgan felt his face flush a little at the sight of Madiera's father. He rubbed his cheeks and eyes to cover whatever might show and then turned away.

"We were supposed to talk this morning," Morgan said, tentatively. He knew the need had been eliminated the night before.

"There is nothing which remains to be said, Mr. Morgan. Is it yes or no?"

"It's yes," Morgan answered, "but with a damned strong condition."

"*Señor?*"

"If you end up being on the wrong side of this little partnership I'll kill you." Morgan's eyes were squinty and he was staring straight into Lopez's face. He gestured behind himself with a sweep of his arms. "And all those *vaqueros* won't stop me. You got that?"

"*Si, señor* Morgan. I have it."

Morgan turned to Sam Tanksley. "You got a load ready?"

"Yep."

"Then give me two minutes and we'll move out." Tanksley nodded and left. Morgan threw his things together and as he started to leave, Jesus de Lopez grabbed his arm.

"I could spare a *vaquero* or two to ride with you."

"Thanks, but we'll be fine. If somebody still wants a piece of me I'd just as soon they'd try again and get it over with. Anyway, you'd best ready yourself for our first job."

"As you wish, *señor*. And God speed, *amigo.*" Morgan just nodded.

A hundred miles away, in the luxury of the den of the

Double C Ranch, Charity Coltrane had just finished reading a telegraph cable from San Antonio. She winced as she realized the consequences of the failed effort to eliminate the man she believed was Marsh Coltrane. Now, she knew, he was alerted and would be ever watchful of another attempt. The door opened and she saw Kingston.

"Yes, what is it?"

"Mister Railsback is heah," the tall, black man answered in his clipped, West Indian accent. Charity frowned. Jed Railsback was her ramrod. As far as she knew, he had been checking fence lines and line shacks.

"Send him in." Charity poured herself a glass of sherry and then sat down at her desk. Kingston ushered Jed into the room.

"Will there be anything else, Miss Coltrane?"

"No Kingston, not now, thank you." He nodded and took his leave, closing the door behind him.

"You look right off the trail, Jed. What's wrong?"

"Three line shacks burned out and what I figure to be forty to fifty head o' stock missin'. Horse flesh—not beef."

"Damn! It's Marsh. It's that son-of-a-bitch, Marsh!"

"Your brother?" Clearly Jed was shocked.

"He's no kin of mine, Jed—no Coltrane at all."

"Sorry ma'am. I—"

"Never mind." Charity got to her feet and walked around the desk. "You see tracks? I mean signs of riders?" He nodded. "How many?"

"More'n a dozen. Could be eighteen or twenty. Found most o' the tracks in a wallow. Hard to be accurate. They headed north as far as we trailed."

"How old?"

"Two or three days."

"North," Charity said to herself. She stared at the floor in thought and then she looked up. "Where is he taking them—toward the mountains?"

"Yes'm. Leastways that's my guess. There may be more gone too—from the west line an' mebbe south."

"There's only one pasture up along the Anacachos big enough to feed and water that much stock."

Jed Railsback nodded. "Rimfire range. Handle two—three hundred head."

"Round up the men. Leave just enough to handle the day work. Have them here in the morning." Charity noted the sudden change of expression of Jed's face. She looked quizzical. His eyes dropped. "Jed?" He shuffled his feet and twisted his hat in his hands. "Damn it, Jed! What the hell is the matter?"

He looked up and took a long, deep breath. "Ma'am. Most of 'em won't ride."

"What the hell do you mean? They won't ride? They work for me, don't they?"

"They're wranglers ma'am—not gunmen."

"They work for the Double C and by God they'll defend the Double C."

"Against a rustler or two—a squatter mebbe—but this here is a gang—paid for killers hired by your—by an outcast Coltrane. It's Coltrane business, ma'am, not the men's."

"Any business that's Double C business is theirs too—or by God they won't have work. Not here," she shouted, thrusting her finger toward the floor, "or on any goddamned ranch in the state of Texas!"

"Ma'am," Jed said, his voice calm and low in tone,

"I'll ride for you—hell—*with* you anywhere. So will a few o' the others—but not most. They won't ride against the likes o' Marsh Coltrane and them what would be sidin' with him."

"Get out!" Charity screamed. Kingston opened the door. Jed was backing toward it and Charity picked up a nearby vase. Her eyes met those of Kingston. She suddenly realized she was not being tough or a Coltrane or a ranch owner. Charity was being a woman. Granted, she was a woman angered—even scorned but this was not the time or the place or the circumstances for such actions. She replaced the vase.

"Get together as many men as you can," she said to Jed. Her voice was firm but soft. Jed smiled. Both men left. Charity sat down behind the big desk. She wanted to bawl. She didn't.

The freight run to Cotulla was uneventful. Pete Jessup and his son, Tom, met the wagon and escorted Morgan and Sam Tanksley to a shed far from the main house. Several men waited to help them unload. One of Jessup's men, inside the darkened building, looked out. His eyes got big and he turned, hurrying still deeper into the shadows. He found a second man.

Jim Kincaid looked up at the sound of Louie Howard's voice.

"Yeah Louie—the wagon here?"

"Jim—he—he's on that wagon." Kincaid looked quizzical. "Marsh Coltrane is ridin' shotgun on that freight wagon." Nearly fifteen years had passed since Marsh Coltrane had gunned down Jim Kincaid's little brother on a muddy street in Del Rio. In Kincaid's memory the act was murder and it was as fresh as this morning's breakfast biscuits.

"Git a shotgun," Kincaid said and pointed upwards. "Git in the loft. No matter what happens to me—blow that son-of-a-bitch all to hell!" Louie Howard nodded, fetched a scattergun, climbed into the loft and disappeared in the darkness. Jim Kincaid got to his feet, drew his revolver, checked it for load and walked toward the light at the end of the warehouse building.

Sam Tanksley's eyes picked up two movements almost simultaneously. The first was the appearance in the doorway of Jim Kincaid, gun drawn. The second was just above him. Sam looked up.

"Morgan—the loft!" The shotgun roared and Sam Tanksley's hat disappeared along with part of the top of his head. Morgan's actions were a blur to the half dozen onlookers. The man in the loft died instantly with a bullet through his chest. Jim Kincaid got off four shots. The first grazed Morgan's left arm. The others were fired as the result of a dying man's reflex actions and went harmlessly into the air.

"Tom—my God—no—no!" The voice was behind Morgan. He dropped and turned, firing at the sound. Tom Jessup stood between Morgan and Pete Jessup. He took Morgan's shot in the forehead.

The entire tragic scenario had unfolded in less than thirty seconds. Two of Jessup's men, his own son and old Sam Tanksley were dead. Lee Morgan didn't know why but he reasoned that there and then was neither the time or place to find out. Several of Jessup's men were making threatening gestures. Only Morgan's gun, still in his hand and still smoking, and their own testimony as to his speed, kept them from making a move. He knew there was courage—false or not—in numbers.

Morgan freed up his horse, leveled his pistol at two of Jessup's men and ordered them to load Sam's body. They complied. Morgan backed up to where he could speak to Pete Jessup.

"I don't know why your men tried to kill me," he said, "but you'd best find out and let the other ones know it was a mistake. You see to it a bank draft gets to the Masters for this load, Mr. Jessup or I'll be back."

Jessup looked up. There were tears in his eyes but Morgan could see no signs of hatred. Jessup nodded. Morgan mounted up and rode out—hard and fast.

Midway back to Uvalde, Morgan realized the possible trouble he could encounter by continuing to haul a dead man. He reined up, found a shallow arroyo and some good sized rocks. He laid Sam Tanksley out and covered him with enough, hopefully, to keep the scavengers away.

"So long, Sam, sorry I didn't get to know you better." Such was Sam Tanksley's funeral.

Uvalde's streets were deserted when Morgan rode in. It was late and it was raining. He was grateful for all the conditions. He turned into the alleyway behind the main street's businesses and worked his way toward the Masters' house. There was a single light burning. It was in the kitchen at the rear of the house. He tethered his mount, stayed to the shadows and finally rapped, lightly on the door. Lucy opened it.

"Mr. Morgan?" She squinted into the darkness in an effort to confirm her utterance. Morgan pushed her aside, entered and then closed the door. "What are you doing back so soon? I didn't expect you until tomorrow. And where's Sam?" She looked back at the door as though expecting her driver to walk through it.

"Is your father here?"

"No—I—," Morgan held up his hand. He went to the front of the house, peering out the front windows. The street was empty. The rain was falling harder. He returned to the kitchen.

"Fix a pot of coffee. It's going to be a long night."

"Damn you! What is going on?"

"Fix the coffee. When your father gets here you'll find out as much as I know. I don't intend to repeat the story anymore often than I have to, but I will tell you this much. You've got a deal with de Lopez."

"Good—I—I was beginning to wonder if there had been trouble."

"There was. Sam Tanksley is dead." Lucy's jaw dropped. "Like I said—when your dad gets here—you'll hear the rest." Morgan pointed for her to resume making the coffee. She nodded. He could see the moisture in her eyes.

Morgan had sipped coffee, smoked and made several trips back and forth to the front of the house to peer outside. He had said nothing. Nearly forty-five minutes had elapsed since his arrival. Lucy was growing increasingly impatient—even a bit angry.

"When's your dad due back?"

"Anytime now," Lucy replied, "but I told you once before, Morgan, I'm a full partner. We've been hit again, lost another driver and you obviously think someone is on your trail. I want to know right now just what the hell happened."

"To be honest about it," Morgan answered, "I was hoping you and your dad might be able to tell me. I mean not *what* happened but *why*." Both of them heard the buggy. Lucy peered through the kitchen window.

She turned back to Morgan, smiling.

"Dad's back."

"Good."

"More coffee?"

"Yeah."

"How about something to eat? Pie maybe? It's apple. I have some cookies too."

"Pie's fine," Morgan said. The back door opened and Luke Masters stepped inside. He too showed surprise at Morgan's presence but it was obvious to Lucy that he had something far more pressing on his mind that the unexpected return of one of his hired hands.

"Coffee, Dad?"

"Whiskey," he replied. "A glass full." He shed his slicker and hat. He took the whiskey, downed about half of it and then, almost ignoring Morgan's presence, he spoke to Lucy. "The last of our business is gone," he said. "Two contracts with the Del Rio Merchants' Association and the lumber deal in San Angelo."

"Dad—*why?* What happened?"

"It's what's *been* happening. I told them we had a new shotgun rider. Better protection. God," he continued, his eyes shifting from his daughter to Morgan and then down at the floor. "I even lied to them."

"About what?" Morgan asked.

"The lumber deal. I told them it was way bigger than it is—uh—*was*. I even gave the name of a banker friend of mine for verification." Luke Masters sat down now, almost as though he'd been struck a blow. "They already had a telegraph cable from Del Rio. They caught me in my own lie. He looked up. "They tore our contracts up right there in front of God and everybody and the Merchant's Association president called me a liar right to my face."

Lucy went to her father, kneeling in front of him. He turned his face away but she reached up and forced him to look at her. "It's all right, Dad. Believe me. It's all right. I understand. And we're not licked. Not yet." He frowned. Lucy turned. "Tell him, Morgan." Luke Masters looked toward the gunman.

"You've got a deal with de Lopez."

Luke grinned sardonically. "It was probably the rumors about that deal that finished us with the others. Damn! I hope it pays well."

"It will," Morgan said, "if we survive to do it."

"What do you mean?"

"Sam Tanksley and I delivered that load of dynamite down to Pete Jessup. Two of Jessup's men cut loose on me—along with Jessup's son. Sam's dead. I buried him along the trail back."

"Good God a-mighty. Why—I've known Pete Jessup for years. Long before I came to Uvalde. I don't understand it."

"It wasn't Pete," Morgan said. "Matter of fact—he tried to stop his son."

"And you—you had to—" Morgan nodded. "There's another son." Morgan saw Lucy's eyes grow large and her mouth opened as though the was about to speak. She looked at Morgan but no words came out.

"Another son?"

"Hobie. He had five years in Yuma for robbery and a shootin' I think. He's out now. Last I heard, he was in Mexico. He won't take well to this, Morgan, an' he's not likely to listen to his daddy."

"First things first," Morgan said. "I got shot at by Jessup's men—and up in San Antonio. If it hadn't been for one of Lopez's *vaqueros,* I might not have made it to Jessup's place."

"You got somethin' behind you that we don't know about?" Luke asked, pushing Lucy away and getting to his feet. Morgan could sense Masters' sudden aggression.

"Probably lots of things," Morgan said, coolly, "but none of them would have involved a couple of saddle tramps like the ones that jumped me in San Antonio."

"An' Jessup's hands?"

"Never saw 'em before—or heard tell of 'em either. That's the fact of it, Mr. Masters."

"Then *why,* Morgan?"

"Ever hear the name Coltrane?" Lucy and her father looked at each other, incredulous. Then they both stared at Morgan. "Well?"

"Of course. The Coltrane ranch is one of the biggest in Texas. The Double C." Luke Masters gestured to the southwest by poking his thumb over his right shoulder. "The house is about twelve miles from here."

Lucy suddenly stepped toward Morgan and he could see flashes of anger in her eyes as she spoke. "You saying Coltrane men jumped you?"

"No—the men who jumped me both *called* me that name."

"What?"

"They hollered it out at me just before they made their plays."

"But there are no Coltrane men. That spread is owned by Charity Coltrane—left to her lock, stock and barrel by her daddy."

"Well, Miss Masters," Morgan said, half grinning, "I don't think any of those bushwhackers mistook me for any woman ranch owner." Both Morgan and Lucy now looked to the elder Masters. He was looking toward the window, obviously deep in thought.

"I was just speaking to Charity Coltrane," Lucy continued, speaking to Morgan but still looking at her father. "She and I had, let me say, a minor disagreement awhile back. I was hoping we could bury the hatchet and do some business."

"You mentioned this woman's daddy."

"He's dead—quite a good long time now—before dad and I ever came to Uvalde."

"A brother," Luke Masters suddenly blurted out, whirling. "I remember readin' about a big family feud. I've heard tales since we been here too."

"Yes," Lucy agreed, tentatively, "I—I heard some talk."

"Best I can recollect," Luke continued, "this—brother—or whatever—well, he was an illegitimate son of the old man's. Anyways—there was a fallin' out an' the old man run 'im off."

"And when was all this?" Morgan asked.

"Got to be near a dozen years ago. We been in Uvalde for ten. Charity Coltrane owned the Double C when we got here—and still does. Runs the place by herself—hard and tough." Luke Masters looked now at his daughter. "We'll get no business out o' the Double C."

"Don't be too sure, Daddy. She didn't shoot me on the spot."

"She given to that kind of thing?" Morgan asked.

"She is," Luke replied. "Totes a pair of Colts on her hips that she's run more than one cowhand off with."

"And you're sayin' you think I'm being taken for this bastard brother?" Luke nodded. "Well—it ties in with what de Lopez told me."

Morgan went on to explain what he'd heard from the Mexican in San Antonio and, finally, about the photograph he'd seen. "I'll have to admit there was a helluva likeness. If time has treated Marsh Coltrane about the same as it's treated me—well—we could pass for kin."

"If my memory serves me at all, Morgan, any of the Double C hands that spot you will be out to gun you. Charity would kill you on sight."

"I don't take kindly to being a walking target," Morgan said. "I'd just as soon face Miss Coltrane down and show her the mistake before one of her gun hawks gets lucky."

"There's only one reasonable way to handle this," Lucy said. "I've only just spoken to Charity so I'll ride out there and invite her to come to dinner tomorrow. It'll be a switch from what we talked about—you going out there, Daddy. I don't think she'll refuse. It's certainly better to have her face Morgan here than try to get him on Double C land."

"He'd never get by that fancy, marble entryway."

"Whatever is done—and where—best get done quick. Lopez will want us soon—and when word gets back to the Double C about San Antonio, Miss Charity Coltrane may not feel so charitable."

Morgan's allusion to Charity's name brought a snicker from Lucy even under the circumstances. The evening had been one of mixed blessings and tension was high. It was Luke Masters who suggested a final drink and then a good night's sleep. No one argued against either elixir.

5

Jed Railsback had pulled together about twenty men from the Double C's contingent. He did his best to discourage Charity from riding with them. It was a futile effort. They worked north and west for three days, checking stock, riding into half a dozen box canyons and finally converging on the rolling meadow known as the Rimfire range. It was obvious there had been both cattle and horse stock there. But not for more than a week. Discouraged and seething inside, Charity ordered the search ended and the riders started back for the Double C.

"Miss Charity," Jed said, pointing to the east, "I'd guess that smoke to be the Larkin place." Charity reined up. She eyed the horizon, took her bearings and then nodded. "I could take a couple o' men and have a look-see."

"We'll all ride in. If there's trouble, at least there's enough of us to make a difference." Jed agreed and turned the men toward the ridge. They had covered less than half the distance to its crest when several shots rang out off to their left. Again, Charity called a halt. This time, they could see someone—a lone rider. The rider stood in the stirrups and was waving an upraised rifle back and forth.

"Ride down there and find out who that is and what they want," Charity ordered. Jed Railsback nodded and took the job on himself. Charity watched as Jed neared his destination. Another shot. The lone rider fell from the saddle. Two more shots and Charity saw Jed go down—but she was not certain if he'd been hit or was simply trying to save himself. A moment later, half a dozen riders appeared from the trees just beyond where the single rider had signalled. They began firing toward the Double C riders. Charity yelled for them to head for the ridge. It was exactly what they wanted.

Jed pulled himself into a firing position and began pumping shots from a Henry toward the half dozen riders. His marksmanship proved worthwhile and he forced their withdrawal. Too late, Jed turned to warn Charity of the frontal assault he knew would charge over the ridge. Indeed, it came.

If the Double C's hands were nothing else, they were not short on courage. Faced with twice their own numbers, they displayed amazing marksmanship and a collective tenacity which no doubt was a major contributing factor to such low casualties. Nonetheless, the Double C lost six good men that night and Charity Coltrane lost her favorite mount. Jed, in a dashing display of heroics, rode into heavy fire and pulled Charity from beneath her mortally wounded horse. Jed took a bullet in the back of his left leg as they galloped away.

Two reports awaited Charity Coltrane the following

morning. She had risen before sunup, dressed in the buckskins which she normally wore only at roundup time, strapped on her twin Colts and breakfasted, with Jed, in the Double C's huge library. It was Jed Railsback, his leg tender but not debilitating, who made the first report.

"The Larkins were burned out and run off and their ramrod was killed."

"The riders who hit us?"

"The same."

"Identification?"

"None at the Larkin place—but—" Jed halted, cleared his throat and started to speak again. Charity didn't wait.

"It's Marsh, isn't it?"

"Yes'm—but, well, it's worse'n we figgered."

"What do you mean?"

"He killed two hands down on the Jessup spread at Cotulla." Jed took a deep breath, held it a moment and then released it with the words, "An' Jessup's boy—Tom."

"Dear God. I know Marsh hates me—but *this*. Why others? They have nothing to do with Daddy . . . or the Double C."

"They would, Miss Charity, if'n Marsh Coltrane owned the Double C."

Charity stiffened and her eyes grew dark and her countenance sinister. "He'll kill every man-jack on this spread, all the stock and then me before that happens, Jed."

"Yes'm—I know that—an' I think he'd do it in the blink of an eye too. He's even turnin' them in town ag'in you." Charity considered the statement. She was not the most sociable ranch owner in Texas—at least with those in the town of Uvalde—but aside from a skirmish or two over something none too important, she'd never really made any dark enemies. "The sheriff's here, ma'am."

Lund Taylor removed his hat, nodded at Jed and then said, "Ma'am, I come to apologize to you and tell you that I'm callin' in deputies from Del Rio an' informin' the U.S. Marshal up in Abilene. We'll see to it that Marsh Coltrane gets his due."

"Where is he, Sheriff? You know, don't you?"

Sheriff Lund had shared a rumor he'd picked up in town with Jed. He frowned at Jed now, for it had not been his intention to share it with Charity.

"I work for the lady, Lund, an' I happen to know she was plannin' some business with them folks in a few days." Now Charity was doubly puzzled.

"I heard he's workin' with the Masters over to the freight line. He was ridin' shotgun with Sam Tanksley when the francas happened down to the Jessup place."

Charity's face paled. She had spoken to Lucy Masters only a few days ago. They had, more or less, agreed to bury the hatchet. It appeared now that Lucy's intent was to bury it to the hilt—in Charity Coltrane's back. Charity got to her feet.

"Jed. Get a horse saddled for me."

"Ma'am, I can't let you—" It was as far as Lund Taylor got. Charity had one Colt drawn and leveled at the big sheriff's belly. "You can't go keepin' your own law anymore'n anybody else."

"As of right now, Sheriff, the law has nothing to do with this. As of right now—it's Double C business—family, more or less. Don't decide that I wouldn't use this, Lund. Believe me—I will."

"I don't think you will, ma'am," Lund said. He started toward her and Jed, already starting out the door, turned, drew his pistol and brought its barrel down on the back of the sheriff's head. Lund Taylor crumpled into a heap.

"You doubt me too, Jed?"

Jed Railsback looked straight into Charity Coltrane's eyes and shook his head. "No *ma'am*—I sure didn't. That's how's come I did what I did. No need to start the shootin' any sooner'n we have to." Jed knelt and checked the sheriff's breathing and the knot on the back of his head. That done, he stood up. "He'll be hurtin' an' madder'n hell—but he'll live. I'll fetch a horse for you, Miss Charity."

As Charity prepared to ride into Uvalde and face down her family's black sheep, Lee Morgan had made a decision of his own. Several people were dead purely because he looked like someone he wasn't. Morgan was never much to ally himself with lawmen but this situation dictated unusual action. He was dressed and ready to slip out of the house when Lucy confronted him.

"You crazy, Morgan, or plannin' just to ride out and disappear?"

"I look pretty bad in either of those descriptions. But so far this has been my trouble and not yours, Granted, you've lost some business, but you've got Lopez now. If this thing is handled right, the Coltrane woman will learn the truth and nobody else needs to die."

"If you ride to the Double C you'll die."

"Didn't plan on it," Morgan replied. "That would be

the crazy part you asked me about."

Lucy eyed him. She suddenly had a twinge inside. It surprised her. She couldn't help but wonder if Morgan had somehow detected it. She identified it as *desire*. Lee Morgan was a man she *desired*. She shook off the feeling and said, "Then you're high-tailin' it?"

"That would be the other part—disappearing. Nope—neither one. Uvalde's got law. The sheriff can bring Miss Coltrane into town. We can meet. He can get verification of who I am."

"Real easy, eh? Just walk out and go see the sheriff."

Morgan looked puzzled. That was exactly what he'd planned.

"You look outside this morning?" Lucy tipped her head to the right toward the window. Morgan moved over to it, pulled the curtain aside and peered out. Five men stood just beyond the picket fence which ran along the front of the Masters' house. "There's at least two more—mebbe three—out back."

"Shit!" Morgan moved into the kitchen and got his rifle.

"What's that for?"

"That should be obvious."

"It isn't. We can't stand 'em off—not in here. You go out and you might get ten feet."

"Well then—Miss Masters—you got a plan?"

"None that really excites me. Two of those men out front work—or *did* work for Pete Jessup. I really don't think they'll give an ear to much palaver. I'm hoping they'll believe my promise to deliver you to them."

"And just when do you plan to make that promise?"

"Already have, Mr. Morgan. I got this reply." She handed him a note.

It's all up to Hobie. He'll be here by ten this morning.

Morgan read, frowned and looked up. "Hobie?"

"The other Jessup boy. Remember?" Morgan nodded. "Well, it's pretty obvious that he's not in Mexico anymore."

"Yeah." Morgan peered out again and then asked "Where's your dad?"

"Still sleeping."

"He know about this?"

"Not yet."

"If I'm figuring right—and the same way you are—those boys aren't going to let anybody out of this house until Hobie Jessup arrives."

"You're figuring right, Morgan—the same as me. Dad too—when he finds out."

"Send them another note—or whatever you did before. Tell them I'm not Coltrane. Tell them I can prove I'm not."

"Morgan—Tom Jessup is dead. If what I've heard about Hobie Jessup is true, it wouldn't make a damn if you were Jesus himself. Hobie will kill you—or try—whoever the hell you are."

"*Hobie?* Hobie Jessup?" Lucy's father came down the stairs. Morgan stayed by the window while Lucy poured the elder Masters some coffee and brought him up to date on the turn of events. Luke Masters listened, sipped his coffee and then got up and went back upstairs. He reappeared a few minutes later fully dressed and armed with a long barreled shotgun.

"Dad—put that damned thing down." Luke ignored

his daughter and started toward the door. "Dad!" Morgan turned. Luke Masters was reaching for the doorknob.

"Hold it, Mr. Masters," Morgan shouted, "there's a rider coming down the street. Could be Hobie Jessup." Luke turned the knob but he held back from opening the door. Lucy had hurried to the window and Morgan pulled back the curtain still further so that she might get a look. "Would you know Jessup on sight?"

"I doubt it. I saw his picture once or twice but that was—I don't know—several years ago." Lucy had looked at Morgan as she answered, now she turned back to look out. Her mouth opened. "My God—that's Charity Coltrane." Luke Masters now joined Lucy and Morgan at the window. Charity was still a third of a block away and two of the men had stepped into her path.

"Looks like they're squabblin'," Luke said.

"Yeah," Morgan said, laconically, "which of 'em gets to kill me."

"You think Charity Coltrane knows you're here?"

"Don't know—just seems strange—her showin' up right now."

"By God—this ain't right," Luke Masters said. "I'm a prisoner in my own home—me and mine. I'll not tolerate it a minute longer." Morgan stepped between Luke and the door. "This is *my* house, Mr. Morgan, and I'll thank you to respect them what live there and their wishes."

"I not only respect you," Morgan said, "I've come to like you. That's why I can't let you go out there—not just yet."

"Morgan! Dad! My God—they're shooting!" A shot

smashed into the window about a foot above Lucy's head. Morgan shoved both Lucy and her dad to the floor and then crouched by the window. By then, shots were being fired in both directions. Morgan saw two of Jessup's men drop. One man he guessed was a Coltrane rider got hit.

"Double C ranch men riding with Miss Coltrane."

"Morgan," Lucy screamed, "there's an attic—an access to the roof from there. Maybe you can—"

Morgan didn't need any more coaching. He took two stairs at a time. While he wasn't at all certain that Hobie Jessup wouldn't shoot first and ask questions later, the Coltrane hands had run off Jessup's men—front and back. Morgan *did* feel comfortable that Charity Coltrane would at least *ask* if the man she wanted was there before she vented her anger on the Masters. By then—if his plan held—he'd be mounted up and could draw them off the house.

By the time Morgan reached the roof, Charity Coltrane was at the front door. He heard her clearly. "Open up, Lucy, or my men will do it for you. I'm here to get Marshall Coltrane."

Morgan moved to the backside of the house and looked down. There were only two men moving about. He reckoned they were Double C hands still looking for any of the Jessup bunch. He eased down to a porch roof, edged forward until he could drop the remaining six feet, waited until the men had their backs to him and then dropped. They both turned. He'd already pulled his gun.

"Don't do it," he warned them. "I don't want to have to kill you just to prove you're wrong. But I will." One of them got his hand on the butt of his gun.

Morgan cocked his. The man's hand moved away and his arm went limp.

"You're a dead man, Coltrane, no matter what happens now."

"I'm not Coltrane, but right now, that doesn't seem to matter much. Turn around, drop the rigs, carefully and quietly. Then lie down. Face down." The men complied. By the time they had, Morgan had slipped around the corner of a woodshed and headed for the hotel casino and bar. If he was to make a stand, win, lose, or draw, that was the place to do it.

Behind him, Lucy Masters had opened the door for Charity.

"Move back," Charity ordered. She punctuated the command with a movement of the barrel of one of her Colts. Lucy backed inside. Charity saw Luke. "Put down the shotgun."

"You're wrong, Miss Coltrane. The man workin' for us is *not* Marshall Coltrane."

Charity ignored Luke Masters' statement, waited until he had complied with her command and then ordered both him and Lucy to sit.

"Jed, get in here and search the house. Bring a couple of the men with you." The back door opened. Lucy tensed. Charity moved over to her, pushed her back in the chair and leveled her pistol at the archway which led into the kitchen. Jed Railsback and two men came through the front door. One of the Coltrane men who'd been out back now entered the room.

"He's not here, Miss Charity. He came off the roof. Caught me'n Billy flat footed but he didn't git no horse. He's on foot." Charity's eyes flashed as she glanced down at Lucy. Charity holstered her gun and then back-handed Lucy, hard, across the cheek. Lucy winced and jerked back. Charity slapped her again, this time cutting her lip. Luke started to get up but the man from the back shoved him back into the chair.

"Where's Billy?"

"Tryin' to follow Marsh," came the reply. "Looked like he might have headed into town."

"Jed—take all the men you need. Get him. But I want him livin' if it's at all possible."

"Hank—you stay here and keep an eye on these two. If they so much as breath wrong—kill 'em!"

"Damn you, Charity Coltrane. You're wrong! He's not Marshall. His name is Morgan. Lee Morgan." Charity struck again. Lucy fell back into the chair, tears stinging her eyes.

There was no rear entrance to the lower level of the hotel. Morgan went to the far end of the building, eased along it until he reached the front and then checked the street in both directions.

Satisfied that he could reach the entrance unseen, Morgan made his move. Halfway there, he heard a horse, galloping hard, behind him. He stopped and turned.

"Coltrane. Marshall Coltrane. You're under arrest.' Sheriff Lund Taylor pulled up short, dropped from the saddle, freeing his Winchester in the same motion. He levered a shell into the chamber. Just then, two more men, riding hell bent for leather, rounded the corner behind the sheriff. Both had pistols drawn.

"Sheriff—behind you," Morgan yelled. Lund Taylor heard the horses but his reflex action was directed at Lee Morgan. He fired. He probably heard the two shots which were fired almost at the same time behind him. It was less likely that he felt them, although both hit home. Lund Taylor was dead before he hit the ground.

Taylor's shot at Morgan had been just a fraction of an inch too high. It took Morgan's hat off but the agile gunman had dropped to one knee, drawing at the same time. His skills, both inherent and practiced, once again paid dividends. Both riders tumbled from their saddles. Morgan got to his feet, stayed low and half dived into the hotel just below the bat wing doors.

"Everybody stand fast," he shouted. He looked around quickly, taking stock of potential trouble. About half a dozen men were inside—plus the barkeep and the man at the desk. None of them moved.

Nearly two blocks away, Charity Coltrane, Lucy and Luke Masters and Charity's men had all heard the shots. All of them moved from the house quickly and ran toward the sound of the gunfire.

"It's Hobie Jessup," a voice yelled as Charity and her men ran by. Billy Hall was emerging from between two buildings. The group halted. Billy ran to them, somewhat out of breath. "I think Marsh is in the hotel. I didn't see too much but he gunned down the sheriff and two of Jessup's men. There are a dozen or more of them at the far end of town."

"Lund Taylor's dead?" The question came from Lucy. Billy nodded. "You sure, Morgan? The man in the hotel did it?"

"Well—I—I can't say fer sure. I saw him fire. It coulda been Jessup's men. Ever'thing happened mighty fast."

Charity Coltrane turned to look for the rest of her men. They too had now moved up the street. About fifteen of them. She shouted orders to Jed Railsback.

"Take seven or eight of the men and move down Center Street. I'll take the rest and move straight ahead. We'll flush Marsh out. Try to talk to Jessup, but if he won't listen, do what you have to." Jed frowned. Luke Masters now walked up.

"You're turnin' a mistake into an all out war, Mizz Coltrane. I'm givin' you my solemn oath. That man in the hotel is not your brother. What I seen an' heard—even from him—well, he sure enough looks like Marsh Coltrane. But he's *not.*" Now, for the first time, Charity looked straight into Luke Masters' eyes. She had listened. She'd heard! She was questioning silently. Wondering.

"Miss Coltrane, I want this thing settled as much as you," Jed Railsback said, "but I got to side with Masters here. We're gettin' into a war we don't need. We oughta be sure first, *dead* sure."

"If you're lying to me," Charity said, looking first at Luke—then at Lucy, "I swear on my father's grave I'll hunt you down and kill you." She turned to Jed. "Stay put."

"Ma'am?"

"I'm going into that hotel. I'm going to find out one way or another."

"Mizz Charity, I—"

"You *what,* Masters? You lied?"

"No!"

"Then this—this man Morgan shouldn't have any reason to gun me down, should he?"

"No," came the reply, weakly.

"Miss Charity," Jed said, anxiously, "there's still Jessup."

"You and the men keep an eye on them. Warn them

off if you can, but I don't want anybody else shot who doesn't have to be."

"Please, Miss Charity, I—"

"You'll do as you're told, Jed—like always—if you're still working for me." Jed knew Charity Coltrane's mind if he didn't know much else. He knew that once it was set, there was no changing it. He nodded.

Charity kept close to the building as she walked the distance to the hotel. She reached the door without incident. She paused long enough to scan the street still ahead of her. She could see no movement, no signs of life. Her eyes trailed back along the rooftops and then down to the street. She winced when she saw the bodies of Jessup's men and that of Lund Taylor. They had often quarreled but deep within each had been a silent respect for the other. Charity looked in both directions one last time and then pushed her way into the hotel.

"I'll guess you to be Charity Coltrane of the Double C ranch." All the patrons were gathered in one corner of the room. The barkeep stood at the near end of the bar, both hands in plain sight. Midway along the bar, back toward the direction from which Charity had come, stood Lee Morgan.

"I'll be damned!" Charity stepped closer. "You're a shade too tall but outside of that I'd gun you in a minute."

"Lee Morgan. Until now I never gave a damn about bein' bigger than my dad. Taller anyway. Right now, I'm grateful for that extra two inches."

"You're a ringer for Marsh Coltrane—outside of the height. I owe you—and some other folks—an apology."

Morgan eyed the twin Colts. "You keeping those holstered is all the apology I need. I've never killed a woman. Hate to start now."

Charity smirked. "You've even got Marsh's ego. What the hell makes you so certain you *could* kill me?"

"Only that I'd take less chances with you than I would with a man—just because I'm *not* so certain."

"How about San Antonio? And the incident down on the Jessup spread? You?"

"Me."

"I guess I can't fault you for trying to stay alive."

Morgan offered up a half smile. "I appreciate that, Miss Coltrane."

"It's not over you know. Hobie Jessup isn't near as good a listener as I am, and he lost kin."

"From what I've heard, Hobie Jessup runs a mean streak—kin or no kin."

"I'll try to talk to him."

"Thanks, but I'll do my own talking. It's not your fight now."

"Maybe—maybe not. Depends on which of you killed the sheriff."

"Yeah. I was wondering when you'd get around to that question."

"What's your answer, Mr. Morgan?"

"Two two gunnies out there on the street were responsible."

"And you took them out?"

"I did. No reason except I was their ultimate target. The sheriff just happened to get in the way. He wasn't a very good listener either."

"Oh shit!" The barkeep shouted the words and then dived for the shelter of the mahogany bar. The words shifted Morgan's attention, just for a split second, to the speaker. The barkeep's eyes were upraised—the balcony above and behind Morgan.

Morgan's right hand produced his pistol even as he dived, twisting to his left and falling backwards. The last thing he saw before he was completely turned around was the blue-gray smoke belching from the barrels of Charity Coltrane's twin forty-fives. Morgan's own shots, two of them, were in proximity to Charity's and all four homed in on the two men on the balcony. One of them managed a shot of his own but it was high and harmless. Both fell forward, through the balustrade, and crashed into the tables below.

Morgan, his experience dictating continued movement until he had completely weighed the results of the confrontation, rolled clear over and came back to his feet. The bat wing doors opened and a man stepped through, drew and fired at Charity. The bullet took her down, ripping through the fleshy part of her upper left shoulder. Morgan killed the man with a single shot. He tumbled backwards and landed outside.

"Okay, Coltrane—unless you want an all out war—you face me." Morgan was already kneeling by the wounded girl.

"I'm—I'm fine. Damn!" Charity looked up. There were tears in her eyes. "It hurts. I've never been shot before."

"It hurts. Good incentive to keep from getting shot again," Morgan said, "and you're right. You're fine. Bullet went clean through."

"Coltrane!" It was the voice from outside again. "You got thirty seconds, then we start a street war."

"That would be Hobie Jessup," Charity said. "He's

good. Damned good—so I've heard."

Lee Morgan stood up and began reloading. "I'm not Marshall Coltrane, Jessup. My name is Lee Morgan. I'm sorry about your brother but he tried to kill me. I don't want to be responsible for taking two sons away from the same father. So ride out. Leave it be, Jessup."

"You got fifteen seconds left mister an' I don't give a tinker's damn *who* you are."

"Yeah," Morgan said to himself, "I figured you wouldn't."

"Watch him, Morgan," Charity warned, getting to her feet. She staggered a little but waved off Morgan's attempt to help her. "I've got some good men out there. I think they'll keep Jessup's hands busy. If you take him out it'll be over."

"I'll take him out," Morgan said.

Hobie Jessup wore a double rig, butts forward, no tie downs. Morgan had seen the style before. A practiced hand with such a rig could be among the best. Morgan figured Jessup to be practiced. He stepped through the bat wings, stopped, shifted his weight just slightly to his left leg and let his right arm hang loose. Both of Jessup's hands were poised in front of him, ready for the cross-draw move. Inside of five seconds, the two gunmen had sized each other up. Rigs, styles, weapons, general demeanor. Unlike the gentlemanly duels of mid-century, these men were merely practicing their trade. No delayed moments of honor—just sizing up the competition.

Morgan's peripheral vision had given him a summary of the situation. Both the Double C hands and Jessup's had moved to within twenty-five feet of one another. Just across the street and less than a third of a block away were Lucy and Luke Masters. Outside of seeing those things in general and eyeing Jessup's armament when he exited the hotel, Morgan's eyes were affixed to Hobie Jessup's. There would be no more talk. The odor of the shootout inside was still fresh in Morgan's nostrils. The roar of the heavy caliber weapons in the confines of so small a space still rattled around in his head. Such a sound always brought back the memory of the day Buckskin Frank Leslie faced down Kid Curry.

That shootout had been in the cookhouse at the Spade Bit Ranch. Frank Leslie died that day, but he'd outlived Kid Curry! Lee Morgan had since outlived a lot of men who'd tried him. Everyone of them had, or so they believed, a good reason for trying him. Now, Hobie Jessup had a good reason. And he tried.

Hobie cleared leather with both weapons. He aimed and fired both—as Morgan reckoned—a practiced hand. Even as he squeezed off a shot from each, however, he was firing into a fatal blast from a short barreled Smith & Wesson. The bullets from Hobie Jessup's guns went high and buried themselves in the rotting facade of the Hotel *La Cucaracha.* Hobie blinked, his jaw dropped. He glanced down at his chest. Morgan didn't know if he was still alive then or not. A moment later, he fell in the street, face down. Morgan knew then. Hobie Jessup was dead!

6

Charity woke up screaming. She winced as a sharp pain burned through the wound in her shoulder. She heard her Mexican housemaid hurrying along the hall outside the bedroom. She felt like a fool. No. More like a little girl. The pampered daughter of a well-do-do Texas cattleman and very much afraid of the things, unseen but always heard, which only seem to manifest themselves in the dark.

"*Señorita* Charity," the maid said, rapping lightly on the door. "Are you all right?"

"Yes, Maria, fine, thank you. I had a bad dream, that's all."

"Can I get you anything?" Charity started to say no but she felt wide awake and still shaky.

"Some hot cocoa, Maria, please."

"*Si señorita.* I'll bring it right up."

"Never mind. I'll be down in a few minutes." Charity threw some cold water on her face, dried it and looked in the mirror. Her eyes were red and puffy. Her shoulder hurt and she still had a lump in her throat from witnessing the scene at the Double C after she had returned three days earlier.

Four of her best ranch hands were dead. Among them Lige Brewster. While she and Jed and most of the best men were in town, on what proved to be a witch hunt, the real culprits had struck home. Stock had been butchered or run off, several out buildings burned and anyone who attempted a defense—murdered. They included, besides Lige, the Chinese cook, Li Sung, a Mexican stable hand named Sancho who was almost like a son to Maria and a Negro stable boy named Joad. Most had been shot down. Charity's nightmares, however, centered on the death of Li Sung. He was found hanging from a ceiling beam in the den. His throat had been cut.

Jed Railsback had wanted to gather every man available and move out at once to find the perpetrators —raiders who had hit more than a score of ranches in the area during the past three months. Charity was adamant. No. She feared a return of the gang to the Double C and she did not intend that it be left undefended again. Instead, she set the men to the task of cleaning up, repairing and—the most gruesome task —burial of the dead.

Charity sat alone now, sipping her cocoa. She ordered Maria back to bed. It was just past four in the morning, one of her favorite times of the day. The false dawn was near. It roused the birds and she could hear them chirping merrily. She loved the isolation. She loved the frontier life. Mostly, she loved the Double C ranch. At that moment, she was fearful for its life.

Charity finished he cocoa and returned to her room. She entertained, ever so briefly, the idea of going back to bed. She knew it would prove useless to try to sleep.

She returned to the kitchen, heated some water and went back to her room to wash up. She stood nude—eyeing herself in the mirror. Her body was lithe, curvaceous. Desirable, she thought.

The cold air hardened her nipples and, without understanding, she felt an impulse to touch them. She did. It felt good. She tweaked them gently. She sucked in her breath. She let her hands slide along her rib cage, down along her waist and then on to her thighs. "My God," she thought, "what have I come to—doing this?" Still, she couldn't stop. How long had it been since she had been with a man—any man—for any reason savc business? She couldn't remember. She closed her eyes and let her fingers touch and explore. Suddenly, in her mind's eye, she saw the face, then the form of Lee Morgan. She jerked herself back to reality. She was blushing. She didn't finish washing. She just got dressed.

Several of the townspeople had approached Luke Masters in the day or so following the biggest event in Uvalde's history. They wanted Luke to entice Lee Morgan into putting on the sheriff's badge. At least, so they said, until they could find someone permanent. Morgan and badges didn't mix. Luke tried, Morgan won out. On the third day, the morning of Charity's early awakening, Luke was scheduled to visit the Double C and talk about a freight contract. Lucy was scheduled to meet with Pete Jessup. He knew what had happened but Pete was the Jessup with brains. His two boys had always walked on trouble's edge. Now both had fallen into its chasm.

While the Masters were so engaged, Morgan, along

with Cimmaron Dakis—old Alkali, the last teamster still working for the line—had a run to make to Eagle Pass. It was southwest of Uvalde about sixty miles distant. Alkali called the run the last real heat a man had to suffer just before he went to hell.

About midway along the run, one during which neither man had spoken a word to the other, Cimmaron Dakis issued a challenge.

"Morgan, saw your shootin' t'other day. Purty good."

"Thanks."

"Saw a blacksnake draped over your saddle." Alkali turned now and looked, smiling, into Morgan's face. "Kin you use that too?"

"I've been known to."

"Good as you use that iron you tote?"

"Probably not. But good enough."

"Good 'nuff to earn yourself a quart o' sippin' liquor down to *señora* Gordo's place in the Pass?"

Morgan smiled. "*Señora* Gordo? Unless I've forgotten all my Mex *gordo* means—"

"Yep—just that—*fat.* Last I seed her she come close to weighin' in at three hunnert." Alkali guffawed. "Hot as it gits in this Godforsaken hole it could freeze a man up come nighttime. Now me—I kin enjoy a woman like the *señora*. Got some meat on her bones. Not like Miss Lucy or that there Coltrane gal. No, sir. *Señora* Gordo'll keep ya from freezin' to death."

"Or much of anything else from the sounds of it." Alkali guffawed.

"Yes sir, that'd be just about right."

"So what are you proposing, Alkali? I mean—with the blacksnake."

"Got a stretch o' trail up ahead what the skinners call Rattler Run. Snakes layin' on top o' the rocks on both sides o' the trail. Man what snaps off the most heads in two miles wins hisself a quart."

"And how will I know when we've gone two miles?" Morgan was half joking when he made the inquiry but Alkali's response told the gunman much about the tough old teamster.

"Why I'll tell you when, sonny. Made this run a hunnert times or more. It's 'xactly two miles between a big ol', half rotted stove pipe cactus an' a half dome boulder what sits on your side o' the trail."

Morgan grinned. "You've covered, Alkali." He crawled to the back of the wagon, stretched a bit to reach his horse and crawled back up front with his blacksnake whip. He hadn't used it for quite a spell and he had the distinct feeling that Alkali could part a gnat's hair with his, but it would pass the time and perhaps bring these two men closer. Morgan felt that any freight hauling to be done for de Lopez into Mexico he would want done under the direction of Alkali Dakis.

Rattlesnake Run proved to be everything Alkali had claimed. Even moving slowly, a man would have been hard pressed to count the snakes basking in the sun. They were easy prey and taking one out in no way disturbed the others. Morgan surprised even himself with his accuracy. By the end of the first mile, he was in a dead heat tie—seven snakes apiece.

"You're pretty good with that thing, sonny. How 'bout we throw in a chunk o' beef steak an' some 'taters just to sweeten the pot a mite?"

"Why not?" Morgan said. Alkali shouted, cracked his whip and the team lurched forward—adding perhaps a third again the speed. Morgan frowned and looked at the older teamster. "You making it tougher, are you?"

"Stakes is higher." Alkali turned, grinned and said, "You go first this time." A large, flat rock lay just ahead. There were three snakes on it. Morgan's whip swished through the air behind him. The wagon approached, Morgan eyed his target and snapped his wrists as his right arm arced through the air above his head. The first rattler's head came off clean. Morgan smiled, pulled back his whip and coiled it for the next time.

"Your go, Alkali." Ahead, perhaps three quarters of a mile, Morgan could see the half dome boulder—the end of the run.

"Looks like a likely target just up there on the left," Alkali said. He was pointing. Morgan looked. Three snakes were coiled on a large rock and a fourth on a smaller rock just below it. Morgan was about to ask which target Alkali would select when the old man's blacksnake cut through the air. It was a little heavier weave than Morgan's. Morgan's whip, as Alkali phrased it, was "store bought." Alkali's was hand woven. Probably, so said the old teamster, by the "Apache" he killed to get it.

Morgan's face turned ashen as he watched Dakis work the end of that whip. He'd laid it behind him only once and now controlled it with short, crisp movements of his gnarled hand. One head—two—three—the last snake head flipped into the air and Alkali's whip came to rest behind him, in the wagon box.

"You're down by three, sonny. Not too fur to go, neither. I'd reckon you'll hav to take out three at one lick an' one at another if'n you figger to win our wager."

Morgan tried. Had he been wielding a six-gun, Alkali would have already lost. Try as might, he could not do better than one head per try. The increased speed took away any chance for catching up. Morgan had been "green-horned."

"I figured you to be a lot better than you let on," Morgan said, grinning, "but I didn't plan on looking foolish."

"Best advice I can give you, sonny," Alkali replied, "is don't never take on more'n one rattler at a time an' you'll be just fine!"

Morgan dozed off in the back of the wagon for a time. Alkali was pushing the team to make the trip, deadhead, in two days. He finally pulled the team up, well after sunset, in a shallow spot just off the road.

"What did we make today?" Morgan inquired.

"Nigh on to forty mile. We can lay easy on the team tomorrow an' still make the Pass by afternoon."

"Good driving, Alkali. Damned good."

"Thanky, sonny. Allus nice to hear good words about yourself now an' ag'in."

"Damn it's hot!"

"Yes sir—that it be. Have to side with that there gen'rul what said if'n he owned Texas and hell he'd live in hell an' rent Texas out."

"To who?"

"I don't recollect he ever got that far in his figgerin'," Alkali said, grinning. "But it'd sure be to some Texican. Fella don't narry tell that story to a Texican. Li'ble to come away shy a tooth or two."

"I take it you're not a Texican. Where are you from, Alkali?" Morgan busied himself fixing coffee as he talked. Alkali unharnessed the team and prepared to tether them for the night.

"No Texas man but I can't rightly say where I'm from. Seems to me, when I turned old enough to know where I was—and who—I was here in Texas. Been here ever since."

"Your people never talked about where they came from?"

"Didn't live long enough to talk to me. Comanche' kilt 'em. Two brothers an' a sister too." Alkali walked over to the fire and poured himself a cup of coffee. He blew, touched his tongue to the liquid, nodded his approval and then sipped. He continued. "Only thing saved me was a nor'easter. Leastways, the folks on the wagon train what come on me—they tol' me that later. Folks name o' Dakis took me in. Raised me 'til I turned twelve. Started mule skinnin' 'bout then. Been to it ever since."

"How'd they know you were twelve? Find anything with your people?"

"Nothin' left. Mizz Dakis figgered from muh teeth," Alkali guffawed. "Just like a goddam horse. Actual—don't rightly know how old I am. Just as soon not. Man starts thinkin' 'bout how old he is—he starts thinkin' 'bout how little he's got done. That there grates on 'im an' he starts tryin' to make up fer lost time. Tryin' to do that, he gits right down careless. Usual, that ends up gittin' him kilt an' he goes buhfore his time."

Morgan chuckled. It was what his dad had called "pot-belly philosophizing" but there was more than a littlc truth to it. Morgan scooped himself and Alkali a plate of beans. As he handed the plate to the old teamster, Alkali's eyes fixed on Morgan's face, he kept grinning and then spoke through clenched teeth.

"Keep lookin', keep actin' simple—we got company, Morgan. On foot. Two—mebbe three of 'em. Muh rifle's still in the wagon. Seems like you'll have to count on that handgun."

"More coffee," Morgan said, more loudly than necessary.

"Yep."

"When I holler," Morgan said, softly, "go flat and roll to your left toward the wagon." Alkali nodded as he tipped his head to drain his coffee cup. *"Now!"*

Sparks flew into the darkness as bullets ripped into the fire. Alkali rolled left and then, on hands and knees, scrambled beneath the big freight wagon. Morgan rolled right, drawing and firing at the flashes of gunpowder from their would-be murderers' guns. Far off, a horse whinnied—then another. Alkali had been right. Three men. One had stayed with their mounts.

Once again, Lee Morgan's accuracy had been unfailing. One man was dead. The other would be by sunup. The vastness of the desert soon swallowed up the sounds of the gunfire. Both Morgan and Alkali remained stone dead still.

Alkali and Morgan discussed the attack well into the night and most of the next day. Their arrival in Eagle Pass, about mid-afternoon, seemed quite a surprise to the owner of the small firm with whom they had contracted. Their business done, they repaired to *señora* Gordo's in order to afford Morgan the opportunity to make good on his wager. It was not long until Alkali had fallen in with a woman about half his age.

Morgan, amused by the old teamster's audacity, whiled away his time in a poker game.

He had just completed another winning hand when Alkali suddenly appeared at the table.

"You and I had best palaver." Morgan looked up. Alkali appeared stern.

"Trouble?"

" 'Fore we left today, I poked around out there in the desert, checkin' horse tracks. Mostly, I was wantin' to know if'n them mounts was shod or not."

Morgan got to his feet, picked up his winnings and said his farewells. The two men strode toward the bar. "Indians?"

"Not hardly. Mexican ponies most likely but I found one odd track. One horse with no shoe on a right foreleg."

"Whiskey," Morgan said to the barkeep.

"Same fer me."

"And," Morgan said.

"I heard a fella talkin' upstairs—to a gal. Said he didn't have much time. Said his horse was gittin' one shot put on so she'd have to be quick about her business."

"You see this fella?"

"Nope—but I wandered down to the smithy. He's got a little chestnut mare down there. Four white stockings. She's missin' a front shoe—right foreleg."

"Stay put," Morgan said. He downed his whiskey and pushed away from the bar. "I'll introduce myself to our friend."

"Can't be sure he's still by hisself."

"That's why I want you here. If he's got friends you'll have the best chance of spotting them."

Alkali nodded. "Watch yourself."

"You too."

Morgan found the blacksmith busy. The man didn't look up when Morgan began to talk. "I'm looking for the man that owns a chestnut mare with a missing shoe on her right front leg."

"My job's shoein', mister, not keepin' track of who owns 'em."

"Just thought you might know where I could find this gent."

"Well—I don't."

"You looking for me, little man?" Morgan whirled. He saw one of the biggest men he'd ever seen. He was well over six and a half feet and must have weighed near 275 pounds. It was not fat.

"If you're one of three who shot at me last night—yeah," Morgan said, "I'm looking for you." The man grinned.

"Well, mister, you're luck's done run out—'cause you went and found me." On that word, the man lunged at Morgan. He was fast, surprisingly so for his size. He caught Morgan with a backhand swing which struck the gunman's upper shoulder but the force was enough to take Morgan off his feet. He rolled and came up in a crouch. The man swung and Morgan ducked, moving in and throwing to quick, solid punches to the man's mid-section. They were totally without effect. Morgan danced away. They circled one another, warily.

A crowd had gathered. Apparently the big man spotted Morgan, knew who he was and made one reference or another to how Morgan would end up. The blacksmith stepped between the two. He was holding a shotgun, its hammers cocked.

"I got a business here and I don't figure to have it busted up by the likes o' you two. Move outside and settle your differences." The big man moved toward him, menacingly. "Big as you are, mister—this scatter gun 'll make an awful nasty hole in your belly." The big man stopped. "And," the blacksmith added, "I'll trouble you for what you owe me just in case this gent with the fast draw rig decides to even up the fight some."

"I'll settle with you personal, smithy, when I'm finished with *him.*" The big man was pointing at Morgan with one hand and pulling money from his pocket with the other. He tossed some bills toward the blacksmith. The smithy picked up two of them, never letting his eyes leave the big man.

"I won't try you bare-handed, mister. I'll just blow your goddam head off if you come back here lookin' for trouble. Now git!"

The big man pushed several people aside so that he might block Morgan's exit and, if the gunman was so inclined, his escape route. Morgan wasn't so inclined, but he was fully aware of the trouble he faced.

"Now little man—I'm about to break you in half." The man wasn't wearing a gun or a knife or any weapon that Morgan could see. He'd learned long ago that pulling a gun on an unarmed man, no matter how outclassed he was, brought quick retaliation from the onlookers.

Morgan charged, head down, bull-like, into the man's middle. This time, there was a grunt and the man reeled backwards a few steps. But he did not go down. Instead, his huge arms encircled Morgan's chest, slipping beneath the gunman's arms. He lifted. Morgan came up. The man slammed him down and Morgan's knees buckled. Now, the hulking antagonist locked his fingers and began tightening his grip. Morgan knew the bear hug would take all the breath out of him and, once that was done, begin to crack ribs.

While the big man laughed and squeezed Morgan tried everything. First, he tried to butt the man's nose with his forehead. The big man simply turned his head sideways. Then, Morgan worked his hands up and tried to lever the man's head backwards by applying pressure under the man's chin.

"Jeezus," Morgan whispered to himself. The man's neck was like a wagon axle. "Uhhhnuh!" The man tightened the grip, lifted Morgan's feet from the ground and whirled around several times. Morgan's body felt like a rag doll. His boot toes dragged in the dirt and finally, the man stopped. Morgan was dizzy. His eyes scanned the crowd and finally fell upon Alkali. There was a man next to him—holding a pistol on him.

Morgan's breath was being forced from his body in increasingly large doses. The constriction would soon be against a rib cage with nothing inside to bolster its resistance. The man whirled Morgan again and again, the gunman could see Alkali's face. This time, the old teamster closed both hands into fists, extended his index fingers and quickly moved them to his ears. Morgan was whirled again and gasped the last of his air out.

"Now, little man, let's see what you're made of." The giant's hands slipped apart for the smallest part of a second. Then his right fingers closed around his left wrist. The crushing hold was locked into place. In a great heave, Morgan stretched his body back as far as he could. The move surprised the big man and he turned his face toward Morgan's. At that moment, Morgan's hands, fingers tight together and palms curved into little cups, shot upwards and out, away from the man's head. Like cymbals, they came back toward one another —closing finally over the man's ears.

The man howled in pain, released his grip, staggered backwards and his own hands shot up, covering his own ears as though the action would stop the pain and the ringing. Morgan was through with Marquis of Queensbury rules. His right foot lashed out, the toe of his boot landed, dead center, in the man's groin. The hulk, still holding his ears, screamed, leaned forward and then dropped to his knees. His hands came away from his ears and he flailed them, blindly, in front of him. Morgan deftly dodged his efforts, stepped inside the man's reach and, using the butt of his hand, swinging it in an upward arc, struck the base of the man's nose. He heard the bone crack. He felt the initial pressure give way. Morgan stepped back. The man's eyes rolled back in his head, blood spurted, in a needle-fine stream, from where his nose had been. His mouth opened, he teetered for just a moment and then fell, face down. He didn't move. The nose bone had been driven into the brain. The giant was dead!

"Son-of-a-bitch!" The man holding the gun on Alkali could scarcely believe what he had just witnessed. Once the realization had registered, he stepped back, raised his weapon and heard a shot. Morgan's pistol had come out of nowhere. The shot killed the man instantly.

"Clear out," Morgan shouted, uncertain as to the crowd's intentions or whether it secreted more of the big man's allies. He fired a shot into the air and another into the dirt near those closest to him. He got the desired effect and the crowd dispersed quickly. They were replaced by a U.S. marshal and a deputy.

"I'll have your gun, mister, till I can sort things out." Morgan moved back a few steps.

"Turn it over," Alkali said. "This here's a fair man an' we don't need no troubles with the law."

"Alkali—I didn't see you there. You in on this?"

"Indirect like, Marshal."

"You know this gent?"

"I know 'im." Alkali turned to Morgan. "This here is the Territorial Marshal, Cass Breymer. Cass, meet Lee Morgan."

Alkali Dakis and Lee Morgan accompanied the marshal and his deputy back to the Eagle Pass jail. There, after more than an hour, they learned the identities of the two men who had very nearly done them in. Alkali's tormentor was known to the law only as Logan. He was a sometime bounty hunter with a less than honorable reputation. The none too gentle giant who nearly ended Morgan's life was Reed Loftus.

"Now we know who," Morgan said, nodding to the marshal and smiling as he returned Morgan's gun, "but the more important question is *why*?"

"You spell trouble," Cass Breymer said, "and the answer to the first question tells me all I need to know about the second one. These trail tramps were on a Mexican payroll. I'd guess their wages came direct from Mexico City."

"Anti-revolution?"

"I'd wager on it."

Morgan didn't like what he was hearing. It spelled more trouble than he'd been led to believe by de Lopez. And it was trouble that Luke and Lucy Masters were hardly ready to handle. "How do you see this Mexican business shaping up, Marshal?"

"Bloody and long." Cass Breymer fired up a cheroot, took a long drag, let the smoke squeeze between his lips and then said, "For me—and Texas—the fella headin' up this revolution against the Mexican government is no damn better than they are. I've got a hunch that if he should win, he'd be a hell of a lot worse."

"Any move to stop him?"

"You mean from our side. From our government?" Morgan nodded. Breymer grinned and shook his head. "The last thing we'll do is interfere in the affairs of the Mexicans. Hasn't been that many years ago that we whipped 'em, Morgan. We mess into it now—we may end up havin' both bunches take into us. We won't do a thing."

Breymer got to his feet. "I got business elsewhere, Mr. Morgan, but if you'll heed a little advice, I'd stay out of the business south o' here." Breymer waggled a finger at Alkali. "That goes for you too, you old desert rat."

"I'll think on it, Marshal," Morgan said. He extended his hand and Breymer shook it. "Maybe next time we cross trails I can buy you a drink."

"I'd like that, Morgan. Maybe you could tell me a few facts about the old days—you know—set things straight for me." He smiled and held up a copy of the latest edition of "Deadwood Dick's" dime novel adventure. "Read one o' these recent about Buckskin Frank Leslie."

Morgan grinned. "Which one? Where he killed the grizzly bare handed or fought twenty Sioux to a standstill with a single shot Sharps and a Bowie knife?" Breymer laughed.

Walking back to the livery barn, Morgan was quiet. It was obvious he was deeply concerned over the commitment to de Lopez. By the time he and Alkali got there, Morgan had made a decision.

Inside, Alkali hitched up the team, all the while eyeing Morgan who was checking the bill of lading against the load. When he finished the last of the hitch work, Alkali turned to Morgan and said, "You might convince ol' man Masters to get out o' that Mexican deal, but Miss Lucy'll fight you tooth an' nail." Alkali grinned. "She'll make that Goliath you tangled with today look like a preachin' man."

"Yeah," Morgan said. "I know. They need the money. Real bad."

"I don't mind makin' the run alone," Alkali said. "Been doin' it fer more years than I care to count."

"You one o' them *seers,* Alkali, like I've heard old P.T. Barnum talk about?"

Alkali grinned. "I don't find much miracle 'bout a gent that understands another gent's thinkin'."

"You haven't known me that long."

"Saw what you did. Heard why. Heard you say what bothered you. Don't need no more'n that to make muh judgin'. Ride on out. You'll git to Uvalde by noon tomorrow if'n you don't get jumped or shot along the way. I'll be behind—an' not too far neither."

"I still owe you a steak dinner. You'd better show up and collect it," Morgan said, saddling his horse. "If you don't, you forfeit."

"Sure wouldn't want to do that. Don't figger to

sucker you into many more wagerin' contests." The two men shook hands. Morgan didn't let on just how concerned he was for Alkali's safety. It was a long, lonely and dangerous trip from Hell to Uvalde. Or, Morgan thought to himself, was it the other way 'round?

7

Morgan's hell-bent-for-leather ride back to Uvalde was uneventful save for the workings of his own imagination. He was trying to conjure up some reasonable argument to deter the Masters from honoring their contract with de Lopez. He had also reached the conclusion that whoever was raiding the area's ranches—including the big and powerful Double C—might also be responsible for crippling—or attempting to cripple—the local freight outfits. Success in these two areas would leave an open field of operation for someone.

As Alkali had predicted, Morgan arrived in Uvadle just before noon. He felt a twinge of concern when he rode up in front of the Masters' home. There were nearly a dozen mounts tethered outside. One of them he recognized. It belonged to Charity Coltrane.

"Morgan?" Lucy answered the door and registered surprise, almost shock, at seeing him. "Where's Alkali?" The question carried a tone of concern and she looked past him as she asked it.

"He's bringing the load—somewhere behind me. He'll be okay." Lucy stepped back and Morgan entered the living room. He saw many strange faces and a few he recognized.

"Morgan rode back ahead of our load from Eagle Pass, Dad," Lucy said. Then, she turned to the others. "This is Lee Morgan. He hired on as our shotgun rider." She frowned and looked back at Morgan. "Alkali is out there alone. Why?" Morgan detected a slight change in the tone of her voice. Now, Lucy Masters was playing boss lady.

"Somebody tried us on the way down. Two men tried us after we got to our destination. They're both dead. The marshal told us they were working for the Mexican government. You've got some mighty powerful enemies aligned against you, and apparently they've already heard about your contract with de Lopez." Morgan looked right at Luke Masters. "If you take my advice you'll back off. Drop that contract. It'll buy you more trouble than you can handle."

"It will leave us bankrupt if we don't take it," Lucy said, scathingly.

"It may leave you dead if you do," Morgan retorted.

"Is that why you came back ahead of Alkali? You want to talk us out of the best contract we've ever had?"

"Lucy," Luke Masters said, "I don't think Morgan is trying to undermine us." He turned to face Morgan. "I'd like to hear more. What else do you know?"

"Nothing yet."

"And with nothing you ask us to back out?"

"Look. You sent me to San Antonio to negotiate. You told me before I left that you weren't too inclined to get mixed up in a revolution. Well—I know more now than I did when I made the deal. Not much more but enough that—well, if I'd known it then—I'd have turned the deal down."

"Maybe," Lucy said. "But we know more too and with what we know I'd have taken it or ordered you to take it. Maybe you'd best hear from some of these other folks."

Charity Coltrane took the floor. As she looked at Morgan, her thoughts darted back to the privacy of her bedroom and the image of herself, nude, eyes closed and Morgan's hands on her, instead of her own. She felt her cheeks getting warm and tingly. She tried to hide the reaction, imagining it to be more obvious than it really was.

"The ranchers represented in this room have agreed to band together. They want to form a coalition for protection of one another and protection of a freight supply line in and out of Uvalde which can serve them all." Charity, as she had spoken, had turned her back on Morgan. Now, she felt under control and turned to face him. "We too have some new information. If it's accurate, it places a whole new light on the situation hereabouts."

"I'm pleased for you," Morgan said, looking first at Charity and then glancing from face to face around the room, "but I fail to see what that has to do with the Masters or their contract with the Mexicans."

"If what we know is correct, Mr. Morgan, it has everything to do with it. We have reason to believe that my—my bastard brother is back in Texas and is responsible for the recent raids." Morgan looked surprised, then quizzical. "We've had four reports in the past two days about him." She half smiled. "We know it wasn't you they saw this time."

"All right," Morgan said, walking across the room to where he could get himself a cup of coffee, "I'll admit to considering the possibility of raids on both the ranches and the freight line being done by the same gang." He poured a cup of coffee, sipped it twice, turned and then continued. "Given that it is Marshall Coltrane, what connection do you make with de Lopez or the revolution?"

"That's what we intend to find out, Mr. Morgan."

"And we want *you* to do it," Lucy interjected.

"Whoa! I hired on as a shotgun rider for a freight line. I'm not Pinkerton man."

"You have been." Morgan eye-balled the speaker. A thin faced, bearded man, wearing an expensive looking, store bought suit. "Jason Smithers, Mr. Morgan, Cattleman's Bank and Trust Company. San Antonio."

"I did some work for the Pinkertons but I'm not now —and I don't intend to."

"I didn't mean to infer that you should, sir, only that you have the kind of experience we need in this thing and you've already made some of the contacts."

"If you're what you claim and you know so damned much about me, I'd think you be pretty well up on one Mexican named de Lopez."

"I am. Frankly, it's my own opinion that Miss Coltrane's somewhat dubious kin and his cutthroats are working for the other side."

Morgan cocked his head. "The Mexican government? Anti-revolutionary?"

"Exactly!"

"What makes you think so?"

"You're a tracker of men, Mr. Morgan, and a good one as I hear it. Me? I'm a tracker of money, also a good one. I've tracked money, considerable amounts of it, through several Mexican and south Texas banks. The trail leads back to the Mexican government. The revolutionary faction, headed up by young Pancho Villa, has very few sources of funds. Right now his primary one, and his largest, is de Lopez, here in Texas, not in Mexico."

"I can add a little to the theory," Charity said. "Marsh Coltrane was always an evil man. I've no reason to think he's changed any. He's greedy, selfish, uncaring about anyone but himself and totally without principles. He was also flat broke. In spite of everything else about him, Marsh is no small thinker. He wouldn't even consider petty stage holdups—train robberies or bank jobs."

"But a revolution—that he'd go for?"

Charity smiled. "Sure, Morgan, as long as he could keep his own hide out of the line of fire. This gang of raiders is very tricky. They're good—professional. Now Marsh is a leader. But he could never have financed such an outfit on his own."

"So what we have in Marsh Coltrane—or whoever it is—is something of a poor man's Bill Quantrill—out to fill his own pocket."

"I'd say that was a fair assessment, Mr. Morgan."

"You agree, Charity?"

"I do. One more thing too. Rest assured that Marsh will keep himself right down the middle on this thing. If he comes to believe he's on the losing side, he'll jump the fence in an instant."

Morgan looked around the room. Most of the faces had shown little change in expression since his arrival. Now, each seemed a bit apprehensive. These were not gunmen or revolutionaries or political activists. These people were citizens, in business and trying to build a future, their own and that of yet unborn generations, amid a wild and dangerous environment. They had sacrificed much and asked little in return.

"All right, gentlemen and ladies," Morgan said, "you want to band together and stand against the wrongs that are being thrust upon you—very noble. Now let's look at a few facts. You have one line of supply, already strained to the limit and subject to almost total destruction with only one more raid. I give you the Masters Cartage Company of Uvalde, Texas."

Morgan returned his coffee cup to the small serving tray and moved, instead, to a nearby stand which held a variety of harder stuff. He poured a healthy measure of Tennessee mash, downed about half of it and then turned back to his audience.

"Mr. Morgan—I—" Morgan held up his hand.

"Just a moment more," he said, "please. As I was saying, the Masters here are your single supply line. Assuming they survive whoever has been striking at them, they have a questionable contract to haul goods for a known supporter of a revolution which, by its leader's own admission, is sometime off yet." Morgan finished off the Tennessee mash, walked over, refilled his glass and held up his arm in the manner of a long-winded legislator about to embark on a campaign speech. "Finally, we have a gang of professional gunmen, led by a lunatic, with loyalties in direct proportion to the fattest purse available." Morgan again downed the remainder of the whiskey in his glass, refilled it and turned back to the crowd. He hadn't eaten, he was tired and tense, a little disgusted, in part with himself, and bent on getting rip-roaring drunk, no matter the outcome of the meeting.

"Mr. Morgan, I believe, sir, you're beginning to feel the effects of that whiskey. Perhaps we should resume this meeting at some other time."

"I haven't had the pleasure, sir," Morgan said, half bowing to the speaker whose name he didn't know. "Nonetheless, a toast to your success." Morgan emptied the glass. Lucy Masters moved toward him. He glowered at her. Charity caught the look and stifled a snicker. She knew what a man had to do sometimes, and Morgan, without any doubt in her mind, was all man. Morgan downed another glass of mash. "I'll work for you," he said. "I'll find out just who is on whose side and why." He smiled. "I give you my word as a gentleman." He chuckled, "And as a gunman, scoundrel, sometimes gambler and womanizer."

He straightened to his full height, tipped his head back and drained the glass one more time. He wiped his mouth, looked at each person in the room for a moment and said, in his most serious tone, "And I will begin my duties officially, at sometime just past midday tomorrow." Lee Morgan was well on his way to one of the biggest binges he'd been on for many a year.

Lucy Masters, somewhat embarrassed, stood by the door and thanked each of the visiting ranchers. She was grateful that their wives had not accompanied them. One, John Findlay, a somewhat stiff necked, moral zealot, made the only comment about Morgan.

"I'm not certain, Miss Masters, that the man you have suggested to us is at all the man we want for the job." Charity Coltrane was within earshot and moved to rebut Findlay's observation. She found no need and gained a new and what would become lasting respect for Lucy Masters.

Lucy looked up at the straight-laced Findlay, smiled and said, "I quite agree with you, Mr. Findlay, that Morgan may not be the man we want. But having witnessed the male members of the ranchers' association here gathered today I am quite convinced he is the man we need!"

Everyone went home—everyone but Charity Coltrane. She watched Morgan make his way to the hotel saloon and casino. There, he spent more than six hours drinking and playing poker. He consumed far more whiskey than he won money, but he was surprisingly alert when he finally quit the establishment. It was nearing dark.

"Morgan!" He turned, muscles tense, obviously prepared for the worst. "You seem quite able to hold your liquor."

"It only takes one hand," he said, smiling at Charity. Then, he looked a little puzzled by her presence. "In my business you never completely drop your guard."

"Come home with me," she said.

"Why?"

"I need—to talk."

"I've had a belly full of talking since I've been in Texas and more than enough for today. Besides, I'm worried about Alkali."

"Don't be. He pulled in two hours ago. He's fine. So is the shipment. He's at the Masters' place now. If you go there you'll just have more talk." She smiled—a different smile—a woman's smile.

"And if I go home with you?"

"We'll do our talking on the way. It's near twelve miles."

"And a long ride back."

"I've got plenty of room."

The Double C ranch was everything Morgan had imagined it would be. Where Charity Coltrane herself was concerned, Morgan found his imagination lacking. The reality was breathtaking. Morgan was relaxing on the swan's down mattress and eyeing the trappings in the bedroom of a once wealthy, female Texas cattle ranch owner. Charity entered the room, moving across it on the balls of her feet. She was clad only in an unfastened, silk robe.

At the bed's edge, she dropped the robe, reached to the top of her head and removed two combs. The movement caused her breasts to sway and Morgan followed the movement, licking his lips. He was not certain that his action was prompted by his anticipation or the thirst brought about by too much Tennessee mash. He didn't care.

"You smell good," he said, as Charity leaned down and kissed him. Morgan moved over and Charity slipped beneath the covers beside him. They kissed.

Charity Coltrane conducted business with the cold calculations of a railroad president, used Colt .45's with the skill of a gunfighter, usually dressed like a wrangler and most of the time spoke like a lady. She made love like a whore.

She seemed to know every movement to make and just when to make it. She explored Morgan's body first. Fingers touched, teased and moved on. She was familiarizing herself with the terrain, becoming knowledgable enough to assure her partner's satisfaction. Lee Morgan was letting her. Then, it was his turn.

Charity's breasts were large, pendulous, somewhat pear shaped and, Morgan discovered, highly sensitive. She lapsed into a state resembling a trance each time he fondled them. His fingers kneaded and worked the pliant flesh, stroking and lightly pinching the pink, hardened tips. He slipped lower and closed his lips, gently, over one of them.

"Don't stop," she whispered. It was a breathless mandate, punctuated with a grinding of her hips into Morgan's groin. He knew he would have to concentrate to avoid a premature conclusion to their lovemaking. He did.

As their roles had reversed, Morgan found that there was barely a few square inches of Charity's flesh which was not responsive to his touch. She moaned once or twice, but most of the time only the sound of her heavy breathing and the occasional soft, sucking noises of Morgan's mouth could be heard.

When he reached the very heart of her sexual being, he mentally noted the exceptional softness of her pubic hair.

"Wait!" He was puzzled. Charity placed her hands on either side of his head and pushed him away, gently. Her hands slipped from his face and disappeared into the darkness. "Now," she said, "do it now." Morgan lowered his head. She had placed her hands in such a manner as to allow her to use her fingers to spread herself even wider. The act seemed to increase her own passion but if it did not, Morgan's movements did. His own hands free, he reached above him and began to caress her breasts again.

Thrice, Charity Coltrane's body stiffened. The third time the action was so violent she nearly bucked Morgan off. Just as suddenly, she gripped his shoulders and pushed, hard, forcing him to his knees. Nonetheless, her expertise in making requests without speaking was amazing. She led. Morgan followed. They blended as though they had enjoyed each other's desires hundreds of times.

Morgan rolled over, lay on his back and Charity straddled him. She used her hands to guide his throbbing, swollen tool into the passion soaked depths of her womanhood. Even their movements needed no rehearsal. Their timing and bodies melded into a single motion. Morgan's head was swimming with pleasure and his groin filled to the bursting point with his own passion.

"Ooh—ooh, ooh God!" Charity almost screamed when, at last, they came together in an explosive moment which drained them both. Morgan heard his own sounds. Guttural groans of total satisfaction. This was not an act of reproduction or human passion cleaned and polished by two people in love. This was raw, physical sex.

"You're the best I've ever had," Morgan said, a few minutes later. They were still side by side in the dark. He heard her little chuckle.

"I find that hard to believe. A man like you? It's nice to hear, of course, for any woman, but hard to believe."

"Yeah," Morgan agreed, "I find it hard to believe I

said it, but it doesn't change a damn thing. It's a fact."

She raised up on her elbows and looked at him. She really couldn't see him that well. It was too dark. Still, she looked. "You mean it, don't you?"

"You think I have to pay tribute to every woman I bed down? Hell—most men only do that because they think words are as important to women as actions. I give what I've got—take what there is in return and we both walk away. If we're both a little happier for it, that's reward enough. I don't have to talk about it."

Charity wanted to talk about it. She wanted to whisper in his ear how good she thought he was, and how she would want him again—soon! She didn't. Such talk from her would have ruined it. Instead, she kissed him. Then, Charity slipped from the bed, washed and put on a nightgown. By then, Lee Morgan was sound asleep.

8

Several things had to happen all at once. Even if he'd had the time, Morgan couldn't spread himself that thin, and he didn't have the time. He was no more than dressed the following morning when Charity summoned him downstairs. Jed Railsback was there. So was Jimmy Willow. He was the son of Bert and Olive Willow, two of the staunchest supporters of Charity's plan to fight back.

Morgan was still tucking in his shirttail as he came down the stairs. He could see by the look on Charity's face that something was wrong.

"Trouble?"

"Tell 'im, Jed."

"Mebbe Jimmy here could tell 'im better'n me."

"They hit our place last night, 'bout midnight. Twenty—twenty-five of 'em. Burned most o' the out buildin's an' what stock they couldn't run off they shot. Lost six men. That many more run off. They've had enough fightin'."

Morgan looked from the boy's face to Jed's and then to Charity's.

"Jimmy Willow," Charity said, pouring two cups of coffee and then pointing to a third cup while glancing at Jed. He nodded. "You met his daddy, at least briefly."

"Yeah." Morgan looked back at the boy. "Your folks make it?" He nodded. "Will they stick?"

"I don't think so. Can't without hands. Nobody'll be able to git'ny help soon. Might be too late already."

"Who were these night raiders, Jimmy?"

"You *know* damned well who they were," Charity snapped. She handed Morgan a cup of hot coffee. He looked into her eyes. Where was the Charity Coltrane of a few hours ago? The breathless, passion-filled woman? A man, he thought, just tucked his dick back between his legs like he'd holster his six-gun. Loaded and ready for use the next time. A woman seemed to change bodies. Minds, anyway.

"No, Charity," he said, "we don't know for sure and until we do, it's damned stupid to make our moves on a wrong assumption."

"What the hell difference does it make? Even if it isn't, Marsh, people are just as scared, runnin' off just as quick, or just as dead."

"You're right," Morgan agreed, shaking his head and blowing on the hot coffee, "as far as you go with it, but it makes a hell of a lot of difference in how we handle it."

"How so?"

"If it's Marshall Contrane, he won't quit 'til he's dead or he's won. Somebody else might. Too, if the gang is being grubstaked by the Mexican government—then they're going to have to show results. So far they really haven't done much, but if it's Marsh, then he could have promised the Mexicans a solid base of operations against Lopez and Villa, a base right here in Texas." Charity looked up, her eyebrows raised. She hadn't considered that possibility.

"You mean," she said, pointing at the floor, "*here*—the Double C." Morgan nodded.

"There's one way to find out—*positive,*" she said, standing up.

"How?" Morgan asked, tentatively.

"I'll put the word out that I want to talk."

"He'll kill you, Miss Charity," Jed said. " 'Bout as fast as he would me, or Morgan here."

"Faster maybe," Morgan said.

"Not the first time around he won't. After that it won't make a damn."

"The answer is *no*!"

"You don't give me orders, Morgan. And if you did I wouldn't follow them."

"Don't go emotional on me," Morgan shot back. "I need time to do some snooping and try to pull together a few men, find out who'll stand and who won't."

"An' those what will are thinnin' out ever'day," Jed said. "Ma'am, he's right."

Charity whirled and jammed her index finger into the air—right straight at Jed Railsback. "You do work for me, Jed—so you'd best remember that I give the orders on the Double C."

Morgan got his fill. He said, "Fine, lady, you do it and you damn well better enjoy it 'cause I got a gut feeling you won't have the chance very much longer."

Whether or not the meek shall inherit the earth remains a matter of conjecture, but here and now they must be credited with having already inherited their share of common sense. Young Jimmy Willow spoke up.

"Whoever's leadin' that gang out there has already got us whipped. He's got us fightin' ag'in our own-selves. All's he's gotta do is wait 'til ever'body splits up an' then move in an' kill what's left."

Eyes met. Morgan's and Charity's. Charity's and Jed's. Jed's and Morgan's. Six eyes evenly distributed, Morgan thought, among three fools and not a damned one of them could see past the end of his own nose.

"The boy is right." This from Charity. If she wasn't the first to think it, she was the first to express it. Morgan just nodded. Jed Railsback spoke up.

"Folks around here find out they got nobody to lead 'em—they'll back off fast." He turned to Morgan. "You said you needed time to snoop around an' then try to pull some men together. Way I see it—you snoop you won't get many answers. Even if'n you do, they'll prob'ly be too late to do us any good. Far as men are concerned—none hereabouts'll follow you—leastways not right now."

"Yeah, Jed, you're makin' as a good sense as young Willow here. Trouble is they're questions. Not answers. Got any of those?"

"Mebbe."

"Shoot."

"Well—thinkin' about it instead o' worryin'—Miss Charity's idea makes sense. Right now, even if it's Marshall Coltrane, they's no connection between you'n her. You're s'posed to be workin' for the Masters'."

"So far so good."

"So Miss Charity sets up a meetin'. If'n it is Marshall he'll be plumb curious. Even settin' it up could take a few days, mebbe even a week. That'd buy you some o' that time."

"And if it isn't Marshall Coltrane?"

"Then whoever it is don't seem likely to bother."

"He's right," Charity said. Morgan eyed her. There was that change in expression again. A look of confidence, hope—not hate and revenge. Those kinds of motives, Morgan knew all too well, could get you dead in a hurry. "If it is Marsh, I could even stretch the time out a little, delay by a day or two what he wants." Now she was warming to the subject. She poured more coffee. "Jed could handle things in this territory. He knows damned near every working hand in fifty miles. He could soon find out which ones got backbone."

"An' I could help too. I think my daddy might if'n he knowed there was a chance to win."

"There are a few other owners around like Jimmy's dad too. Men who are respected. Hell, with each ranch contributing even four or five guns, we could put together a small army."

"And if you're found out—whether it's Marsh or not —then what?"

"Then," Charity said, looking Morgan straight in the eye, "I'd be dead." She smiled and added, "Which I'd rather be than run off. I'm sure you can't understand that, Morgan, just how much a ranch can mean."

Morgan smiled, sardonically, at Charity's final observation. His thoughts shot back to Idaho and the burned out remnants of the Spade Bit. He shook his head to clear away the memories. He looked at Charity. He'd tell her. Sometime—somewhere—he'd tell her. Not here. Not now.

"Okay," he said. "It's Marshall Coltrane and you've

got a meeting. Then what?"

"For one thing, I can get a pretty damned good idea of just how many men he's actually got. For another, I can make him a deal with the ranch. He'll have to wait long enough to find out if I'm serious. By the time he learned the truth—well—by then we'd better be ready."

"And one way we might be ready is for me to talk to our Mexican friends again. If we can get the freight wagons moving to Mexico—and you're talking a deal with Marsh Coltrane—he'll have to keep an eye in both directions—and men."

"I'll git on to town an' start doin' some talkin'—lettin' the word spread."

" 'Scuse me fer buttin' in ag'in," Jimmy Willow said, "but it kinda seems to me that I oughta do the spreadin'. Might sound a little fishy comin' from a Double C hand. Particular the ramrod. What with our place bein' hit'n all, seems like them sidewinders would be more likely to believe what they're hearin' from somebody like me."

Morgan was just finishing his coffee. He had to swallow fast to keep from choking. Then, he laughed. "You know, Jimmy, Charity here is by far the best lookin' one of this bunch. I'd wager there aren't any better wranglers anywhere in a day's ride than Jed and I'm more than a fair hand with a six-gun. I'm damned if I know where any of us would be without your brains." Everyone looked at everyone. Soon, they were all laughing.

Jesus de Lopez listened intently to Lee Morgan's report of activities around Uvalde. Morgan didn't hold back on the details and finally got to the agreement between Lopez and the Masters Cartage Company.

"You're got your own interests to protect in this deal," Morgan said. They'd been drinking wine. Quite a lot. Morgan wasn't through. His glass was empty and he eyed the bottle.

"Help yourself, Mr. Morgan." Morgan nodded. "I can supply guards to ride with each load. Extra riders too."

"Not enough you can't," Morgan replied, sipping at his fourth glass of wine. "Besides, to be blunt about it, there are questions as to just who these raiders might be working for. Your name hasn't been taken off of the list of possible employers."

"Surely, you don't believe they work for me?"

"What *I* believe doesn't have a damn thing to do with it. You want supplies taken into Mexico for Villa, then you'll have to assure protection. That will take more than a few riders."

"I—I don't understand, *señor.*"

"Simple. Quickest way for you to protect those shipments is to help wipe out the threat to them." Morgan's proposal hadn't been a part of any plan—his or anyone else's. On the ride from Uvalde, he kept pondering the problem of manpower to combat the raiders. He knew, at best, the ranchers might come up with fifteen or twenty men like Jed Railsback. They wouldn't be as good as what they were up against and —with somebody paying them handsomely—the ranch hands sure as hell wouldn't have the incentive of their opposition.

"*Señor,* you propose that I hire gunmen to fight these men?"

"Not at all. You've already got the manpower,

Villa." Jesus de Lopez suddenly lost his composure. He was shaking his head, negatively, even as he got to his feet.

"It is out of the question, Morgan. Completely out of the question." He turned away. "It was *not* part of the agreement we had before. It—well—it cannot be done." Morgan had expected some resistance, but nothing like he was getting. He was a little puzzled.

"Your refusal won't look so hot, Lopez, to a lot of people." Lopez turned around. "And *you, señor?* How does it look to you?"

"Frankly—awful goddam fishy."

"You don't understand."

"Then clarify it for me."

Lopez paced. He sighed. He poured himself a glass of whiskey. He offered none. Again, he paced.

Lee Morgan had seen such discomfort in men before. Jesus de Lopez knew a hell of a lot more than he'd ever revealed—or something else was wrong. Morgan didn't intend to leave San Antonio until he found out what it was. He decided to wiggle the horns of the dilemma upon which Lopez was impaled.

" 'Course," he said, off-handedly, "there are other freight outfits in Texas." The comment brought unexpected results.

"You are trying to blackmail me, Morgan, and I don't like it. I could have you killed—here and now. No one would ask any questions. Even your friends in Uvalde would have to accept your death, given what happened the last time you were here."

Now Morgan was really curious. Why was this wealthy Mexican so horn-swaggled by Morgan's proposal? After all, Morgan reasoned, it was to Lopez's advantage, more than anyone's, to protect those shipments once they began.

"*Señor* Lopez, what are you afraid of?"

Lopez stopped pacing. He looked into Morgan's face. "I fear nothing," he said. "And you will leave me now. I must think. We will speak again this evening." He moved to the door, opened it and stepped aside. Morgan considered resisting, but he might go too far too soon. Instead, he went to his room.

Morgan lay on the bed, one arm resting over his eyes. He wanted to doze off but his mind was reeling, considering every possibility of which he could conceive to explain Lopez's attitude. Too, on an only slightly lesser scale of importance, Morgan wondered about the whereabouts of Madiera. She was not at the *hacienda*. Nor had she been mentioned. A knock at the door brought Morgan's gun into his hand. He felt a little silly. His mind had been miles away from his surroundings. He had acted out of years of reflex.

"It's open." Maria Correra entered the room. Morgan sat up. He frowned. She was Madiera's handmaiden by Spanish standards. She was nervous. "Close it," Morgan said. She didn't move. "It's okay. Close it." She did. Then she stood again—almost frozen. Morgan suspected the had brought a message from Madiera but the more time that passed the less he believed it. "What is it?"

The woman, pleasant enough, Morgan recalled, began rattling in Mexican. He could catch only a word or two. He finally shook his head and held up his hand. *"Ingles?"*

"Si. You're too fast—uh—*rapido."* She nodded.

"Señor Lopez, he has *mucho desgracia. Señorita*

Madiera . . . she went—taken by *el malhechor.* He—*señor* Lopez—he—he is—uh, *atemorezado. Comprende?"*

Morgan shook his head. "Barely," he mumbled. Loosely sorted out, he gathered that Madiera had gone away with someone! Morgan's head jerked up. *"El malehechor.* The evil one?" Maria nodded.

"Villa?"

"Si."

"Shit! He kidnapped her? Took her by force?" Morgan put his own hands around his own throat to demonstrate. Maria shook her head. "But," Morgan added, "she didn't want to go, and Lopez didn't want her to go."

Morgan, as best as he could, assured the frightened Maria that her tale-carrying would be safe with him. He sent her on her way and then made his own way back to the library. Now, he found the big Mexican he'd met on his first trip blocking the door.

"I need to see your boss," Morgan said, trying to remember the man's name. It finally came to him. "Enrique."

"You will not catch me as you did before, not again *señor."* He'd out-drawn the Mexican. Made him look bad in front of his boss. Now he didn't have time.

"I need to see *señor* Lopez."

"When *he* says."

Morgan smiled and shrugged, turned, spun back and let go a full fledged haymaker that took Enrique off his feet, onto the floor and into dreamland. Morgan walked over him and opened the door. Lopez was halfway to it, having heard the commotion outside. Morgan closed the door.

"Don't call for anybody," Morgan said. "You don't need more trouble and neither do I. Sit down." He gave Lopez about three seconds. "Now!"

Lopez sat, his shoulders dropped and he rubbed his face with both hands. "I think you'd better tell me everything—for both our sakes."

"It's Villa. When I first agreed to help him he was different."

"A common man with a cause." Lopez looked somewhat surprised at Morgan's rather sudden grasp of the scenario. He didn't know that Morgan had seen scores of such men over the years. Often the taste of power was far more devastating to an otherwise sound man than was either whiskey or a woman. Even gold fever seemed pale by comparison. A man with power just out of reach will often destroy everything and everyone around him to get at it.

"Did he take Madiera by force?"

"No, but force isn't always so obvious, is it, Morgan?"

"No it isn't. Where does he have her?"

"At an old mission here in San Antonio. Presumably, he wanted her to see what he has planned. Perhaps to impress her to the point where she would show interest in him as a man."

"Are you afraid he'll succeed?" Morgan asked.

"On the contrary, I'm more concerned that I know he will fail. What he will do then? I don't know." Lopez got up. He straightened. "I treated you badly before. I do need your help. I do not understand men like Villa and I do not have men to stand against him."

"And you can't stop helping him?"

"Not now, not even with Madiera's return. He has

too much influence, too many followers among the people. I can only trust to God."

"Well, mebbe we can give God a little hand," Morgan said. "Let me talk to him. Mebbe I can get some of the help I need. Villa can get closer to what he wants and we can get his mind off your daughter."

"Hiee!" Lopez slapped his forehead. "I have forgotten, *señor* Morgan. A telegraph cable for you. It came just minutes before you walked in. I was angry. I intended to read it." He picked it up and handed it to Morgan. The gunman felt a knot in his stomach when he saw the point of origin. Uvalde!

> Morgan,
> It's Marsh Coltrane. Kid put out the word and got took. Marsh left word he'd be contacting Charity. Word has it he's got 70 men riding for him. We got less than 30. Miss Charity is scared.
>
> Jed

"Bad?" Lopez asked.

Morgan folded the telegraph cable and stuffed it into his shirt pocket. "It's not good," he said. "But first things first. I'm riding out to see Villa."

"You'll need something from me. Something in writing. Without it, Villa's men will not let you pass."

"Yeah," Morgan said, "write it out." He took it but he'd already decided not to use it unless it was forced on him. Over his signature, de Lopez wrote a clearance request. Then he penned out a small map giving Morgan directions to the old mission.

Mission *Concepcion* was located about a mile and a

half from the old Alamo mission. In many ways, it resembled the original Alamo complex where Texas freedom had found its first breath of life. Morgan made the last half mile on foot.

De Lopez had not underestimated Villa's security but he had underestimated Lee Morgan. Morgan gained the outside wall using a handy tree. Once inside, he found it easy to measure the pacing of the Mexican guards. Villa fought like a guerilla in the field but had been caught up with military procedure in the barracks.

Morgan made easy work of violating Villa's security ring. It was planned to protect him against the advent of a mass attack. One man, Villa believed, was no threat. The old mission chapel was now Villa's private quarters. They included a dining room and it was there Morgan found the Mexican bandit leader. He was relieved to find Villa dining with Madiera de Lopez. Two men stood guard. One at the door and another in the anteroom which served as a kitchen.

"Buenos noches, señor Villa," Morgan said, dropping through an arched window, gun drawn. It was leveled at Villa's head. The Mexican's eyes got big but then he picked up a napkin, wiped the drooping mustache, leaned back in the high-backed chair and laughed.

"Buenos noches, señor Morgan. Congratulacion y bienvenido." He laughed again. "You have done what a hundred men could not, *mi amigo.* Come—come, join us."

"I'd just as soon make it a little more private," Morgan said, motioning with his pistol toward the guards. Villa nodded and barked orders in Spanish. The two men, both prepared to die in defense of their leader, nodded and, thought Morgan, both looked relieved. A moment later, they were gone.

"Are you comfortable, *señorita* de Lopez?" Morgan asked. She smiled and looked at Villa. "I'm fine, thank you."

"Did you come to rescue the lady, *señor* Morgan?"

"Hardly," Morgan said, holstering his gun and pulling a heavy chair from beneath the table. He accepted the wine Villa offered. He sipped at it. "I came to deal."

"I understood a bargain had already been struck between yourself and the *señorita's* papa."

"It has—for hauling freight. I want a deal with you."

"And you sneak up on me with a *pistola*?" Villa shrugged but he was still smiling. Obviously, Morgan's entrance had impressed him but he was anything but frightened.

"I did that only to prove a point."

"My *vaqueros* would have killed you even if you had killed me. It is because they too fight for Mexico—not for Villa."

"Still," Morgan said, his voice more firm now, "you'd be—uh, *muerte.*" Morgan smiled and added, *"Mi amigo!"* Villa laughed. Morgan handed him de Lopez's note.

"*Muy bueno, señor. Muy bueno!* You could have *walked* it but you did not." Now, Morgan knew, Villa was properly impressed.

"What then," Villa began, sitting back and firing up an oversized Havana, "can a humble *vaquero* do for such a famous *Americano pistolero?"*

Morgan was being patronized. Indeed, Villa was aware of what could have happened had it been

Morgan's intent to kill him. But the young revolutionary would not yet be persuaded of much else.

"Have you heard about the raiders operating between here and the border?"

"*Si.*"

"I want your help to get rid of them."

"You want Villa to risk his life and the lives of his faithful followers to rid Texas of a few *culebras*?" Morgan frowned. "*Serpientes.*"

"Snakes," Madiera offered.

"Hardly," Morgan said. "They're a little more than a few snakes. They represent an anti-revolutionary faction in this country pitted against you and financed by your enemies in Mexico." If nothing else, Morgan now had Villa's attention. He sat up straight, scooted the chair toward the table, flicked the ashes from the Havana and then leaned into Morgan.

"If you speak the truth, *Yanqui,* then I have a lieutenant who must answer for his failure. If you lie," Villa said, "I will have you shot. I have heard of a *caudrilla* raiding small ranches to the south. Are these your anti-revolutionaries?"

"They are." Morgan noted that the revelation brought a puzzled look even to Madiera's face. "There's more to their raids than stealing a few cows or horses."

"Tell me, Morgan, tell me everything."

Morgan did. He concluded with, "Simply put, if the ranchers south of here are run out and Marshal Coltrane reclaims the Double C, you've got a severed supply line and some well trained guerillas operating between you and your base of supply."

Villa grinned. "You speak like an old *hombre*

ejercito." Morgan shook his head and shrugged. "An army man, *señor.*"

"Doesn't take an army man to figure this one. Just a few facts."

"I have a good man. *My lugarteniente.*"

"Your second in command?"

"*Si.*"

"Well, he missed something."

"He has never done so before."

"There's always a first, Villa."

"Shall we see?"

"Please, let's do." Morgan turned and saw the look of concern of Madiera's face. Morgan was pushing on Villa—and on his top man. Morgan smiled to reassure Madiera but inside, he was wondering if all the information he had was accurate enough to have gone this far this fast. One little lie would be all Villa needed. He was suspicious of almost everyone outside his immediate circle of power anyway. Morgan had heard a story or two of U.S. government agents trying to infiltrate his band. They had simply disappeared. If Morgan looked like anything to Villa at this point, it was probably another Yankee spy.

Pancho Villa had a much bigger reputation than he had a physique. He was about five feet, eight inches tall and a little overweight. He looked much more like a man who should have been lounging in some *cantina* with a *señorita* and a bottle of *tequila* than leading a revolution. This, Morgan found out a few minutes later, was most definitely *not* the case with Villa's *lugarteniente*—his first lieutenant.

The man was nearly six feet four inches and his frame appeared as solid as a brick wall. Morgan thought he'd weigh about 230 pounds. He was dressed immaculately but what Morgan saw first was the man's six-shot revolver. He wore it on a hand tooled, cross-strapped shoulder rig. The holster, black leather with hand-tooled silver decor, was firmly in place high up on the man's left chest.

When he responded to Villa's summons, he entered the room, obviously surprised to see Morgan. He smiled at Madiera, instantly noted the absence of the guards and then eyed his superior with concern. He and Villa then conversed, fast and in Mexican. They spoke in tones too low for even Madiera to hear. Finally, Villa returned to his chair and the other man took up a spot at the opposite end of the long table.

"*Señor* Morgan, I would like to introduce you to Juan Miguel Delgados." Morgan pushed his chair back, stood up, fully expecting to meet the man half way and shake hands. Instead, Villa spoke an addendum. "He tells me, *señor*, that you are a *mentiroso*. A—"

"A liar," Morgan said before Villa could translate.

"Si, señor."

"Tell him for me that he's mistaken."

Villa sat down, poured himself some wine, leaned back and said, "Tell him yourself, Morgan. He was educated in your country." Villa laughed. He was playing Morgan on a string and now he'd brought the cat in to get in a few licks.

"If he speaks English," Morgan said, "then he's already been told."

"I know of this gang," Delgados said, "and I know of the man who leads it. He seeks to reclaim his own ranch and as much more land as he can. Perhaps, from what I have heard, he deserves to get it back with interest. But either way, *señor* Morgan, he has nothing to do with the revolution, Mexico or General Villa." Delgados smiled, stepped slightly to his left, away from the table and added, "That makes you very stupid, *señor*, or a liar." Madiera de Lopez was suddenly feeling frightened. She stood up. She addressed herself to Pancho Villa. "Hasn't *señor* Delgados overlooked the possibility of an honest mistake?"

Villa, enjoying the discomfort he was creating, just shrugged. "Ask him, *señorita.*"

"I've asked *you, señor* Villa. I am *your* guest, not his, and I believe I am due the proper courtesy."

"If the *señorita* expects the proper courtesy," Delgados said, sharply, "then she should conduct herself in accordance with the dictates of proper upbringing. Perhaps you have lived too long on the wrong side of the border, *señorita.* In Mexico, a lady does not interfere in the affairs of men."

"What men?" Morgan said, scathingly, gesturing first at Villa and then at Delgados himself, "an unshaven, overweight peasant boy and a fancy dan *vaquero* who happens to speak well." He'd gone all the way. He was in, Morgan thought, up to everyone's neck. The consolation, of course, lay in the fact that if he didn't pull it off, he wouldn't have to face anyone in failure. He'd be quite dead!

"Morgan!" Madiera spoke the word. Villa was on his feet. Delgados moved, cat-like, to Madiera's side, grabbed her arm and pushed her into the chair.

"You put another hand on her," Morgan said, "and I'll kill you."

"You have already earned yourself the opportunity to try, *señor* Morgan, with your insult."

"Then you did know you were being insulted. Good. That shows real progress."

"You go too far, *Yanqui,"* Villa shouted. Three doors opened and no less than three men appeared in each of them.

"Sure you've got enough men to back you, Villa, or are they here to back your fancy lieutenant there?"

"Out," Villa screamed, "get out!" Morgan had the Mexican bandit riled. Too, he could see the flush of anger on Delgado's face. "You have pushed Villa too hard."

Morgan suddenly backed up about eight steps. He did a half turn. Now he was positioned diagonally from both Mexicans.

"No, Villa, you pushed too hard and too far. I rode in here to show you you're not invulnerable and to deal honestly. I tried to remain pleasant and play your game for awhile. Game's over."

"I demand satisfaction," Delgados said. "Tomorrow morning in the courtyard."

"Bullshit! You've been reading too many dime novels, Delgados. You want me? It's here and now. You and your boss man." At last, an expression on someone's face which Morgan could recognize. Villa, who constantly wore crossed *bandoliers,* each supporting a pistol and a double holstered rig on his waist, stood, mouth agape, staring at Morgan's right hip. He had assumed the stance necessary for a gun fight. Morgan had made the last bet. Now it was Villa's turn. Morgan thought that Villa was very much aware that he would be the first to die. That Morgan would die too seemed little consolation when the chips were finally down.

"You have my honor," Delgados said. Morgan noted the tentative tone. He guessed Delgados would be fast—rattler fast. Morgan had already decided that if push came to shove, he'd take out Villa and pay the price.

"No, Delgados, I don't have the time. As to honor, by what I've seen and heard here tonight, the only one in the room deserving of any is sitting down."

"I've had enough, *señor,*" Pancho Villa said. He turned toward Delgados. "It is ended."

"I think not, General."

"It is ended. I wished only to determine the *Yanqui's* grit. I am satisfied."

"I am not."

"Delgados!"

"*Tirar, yanqui!*" Morgan did—faster perhaps than he had ever drawn his gun before, and he made a particularly exaggerated display of foolish bravado. He fired one shot a little high, blowing off the Mexican's silver-encrusted sombrero and fired a second shot right straight at the Mexican's right hand. The bullet struck the cylinder of the Mexican's gun, ripping the weapon from his hand and tearing into the flesh of his palm.

Morgan had been right. Juan Delgados, the tall, handsome and soldierly lieutenant to the would-be Mexican dictator, was fast. Lee Morgan had simply concentrated his entire being into emerging not only the victor but appearing invincible where gunplay was concerned. He knew he had the skill. Rarely did he have to use all of it in such a concentrated or showman-like form. He detested playing with guns. He'd seen a few young gunnies with their border shifts and Curly Bill spins. They were all dead. In this case, however, Morgan had determined that the situation was probably thc exception which proved the rule.

The skill he displayed left Delgados wincing in pain, still blinking at the speed with which it all happened, and Pancho Villa open mouthed. The gunsmoke was still curling into the air. Again the doors had opened and gunmen stood, weapons pointed, waiting Villa's order. Lee Morgan eyed the Mexican bandit, reckoned that he was no longer in any danger from Villa and holstered his gun. Madiera de Lopez took a table napkin and began treating Delgados' wound.

9

Morgan's climactic display to Pancho Villa was simple. After initial treatment of Delgados' wound by Madiera de Lopez, Villa's own physician took over. Morgan informed villa that he would be with the de Lopez family for one more day if he, Villa, wanted to talk further. That done, Morgan took Madiera by the arm and the two of them walked away from Villa's compound.

At just after noon on the following day, Morgan was informed that Pancho Villa was waiting for him in de Lopez's library.

"Buenos dias—rayo pistolero," Villa said, smiling. It took Morgan a few seconds to translate. Villa had called him the lightning gunman."

"Señor Villa."

"I will make my point quickly, *señor*. I can do as you have requested, help you to eliminate the gang of raiders one of two ways. The first is an agreement with you, personally. The second would be forced upon me by the circumstances—the need. It would not include you, Morgan. I would prefer the first. A deal." Villa smiled now, removed a cigar from his pocket, eyed it, took out a second and offered it to Morgan. Morgan accepted.

Both men wet the ends of the Havanas, bit off the tips, found matches, lit up the cigars and puffed several times. All the while, they were making a concerted study of each other. Villa knew what Morgan wanted. Morgan knew that Villa wanted something in return.

"If you take out the raiders, Villa, I've got what I want. Why should I deal?"

"If you do not, I will simply offer up as many men as I have to for replacement of you. They will work free for the supply wagons. I will refuse to assist anyone so long as you are involved." Villa smiled. "You will not be popular, *señor* Morgan."

"On that alone," Morgan replied sharply, "I wouldn't be losing much. I'm none too popular anywhere in Texas right now anyhow."

"Then you do not wish to hear my offer?"

"Talk's cheap, Villa. Listening is even cheaper."

"When this is over, when the raiders are finished and the supplies are flowing into my citizens' army in Mexico, you will join me. You will find nine more like yourself, *Yanqui pistoleros,* and you will join me." He held up a finger. "For one year. You will report directly to me, but we will work together. You will be special, a guerilla force to hit and run."

"I don't sell my gun for that long to anyone," Morgan said. "Besides, Villa, your threat of getting me fired doesn't wash. If the raiders are eliminated, I've no reason to stay around. The Masters family hired me to ride shotgun because of the raids."

"There is one more thing," Villa said, standing up. "If you refuse me, I'll have you hunted down and killed." He puffed on the cigar. "I will spare no effort—use as many men as it takes for as long as it takes. But I will find you, and I will have you killed."

Morgan considered the young Mexican. He knew Villa meant what he said. Here was the case in point. Villa's abuse of what little power he already wielded. He'd let the *revolucion* go to hell, Morgan thought. Delay it for as long as it took. Use whatever resources, no matter how short the supply, just to prove his point—just to kill Morgan.

"Is there a word in Mexican for sonuvabitch!"

Villa laughed. "If you wish, Morgan, you may try *bastardo* on me. It has been more widely used."

"I get the pick of the men in your outfit to use against the raiders, and I lead them—alone."

Villa frowned. "Some will not like to follow you."

"You tell 'em they will or I'll kill 'em with your blessings."

"You push me again, Morgan," Villa said. This time there was only half a smile.

"Well," Morgan said, getting to his own feet, "there is one other little thing."

Villa laughed. When he stopped, he walked over and slapped Morgan on the shoulder. "*Mi amigo,* if I turn you down, you will kill me right here, right now."

"You may end up making a good *Presidente* after all, *señor* Villa."

The deal had been cut. Neither man even considered the possible double-cross of the other. They shook hands. Just before they separated, Morgan told Villa that the first man he wanted was Delgados. Delgados, Morgan said, could select the rest of the men. Villa concluded that he would never want a man like Morgan hunting him. Both men seemed able to anticipate the other. Villa had intended to insist that Delgados be included in the selection process. Villa had reasons which were different from Morgan's for the choice. But both men knew the other's. Delgados represented the missing, written contract.

Morgan sent a telegraph cable on the morning before he rode out of San Antonio to return to Uvalde. It asked for a meeting at the Double C for that evening. In the interest of a timely delivery, he sent it to Luke Masters.

Morgan reached the five mile perimeter around the Double C about sundown. He was surprised by the increased manpower on duty and had to talk for several minutes before convincing those who stopped him that he was Lee Morgan.

He was not greeted with smiling faces when he finally entered the study at the big ranch house. Lucy Masters reached him first.

"We have a traitor in our midst," she said. "One of Charity's men took our last wagon yesterday to pick up supplies for the ranch here. She has stopped using the company in Del Rio. He got hit half way back. She sent out five men to look for him early this morning." Lucy looked down and shook her head, fighting back tears. "They found him hung from a telegraph pole. The wagon and supplies were both gone."

"Charity?"

"She and some of the other women are with the man's wife. He'd been here for many years."

"And word about Jimmy Willow or a meeting with Marsh Coltrane?"

"No."

"Where's Jed?" Morgan asked, looking around the room. "With Charity?"

"A message came into the telegraph office about half an hour ago. They sent a boy out to get somebody to pick it up. Jed went. It may be word from Marsh."

"Yeah," Morgan said. He was still looking at the long faces. The enthusiasm to make a fight was waning fast. Even his news from San Antonio might not be enough to turn the tide if things kept going sour. "Got any coffee?" Lucy nodded. "Mind gettin' me a cup?" She went to the kitchen. Morgan went on in. One or two spoke to him with a bare greeting. Most just nodded.

Lucy brought the coffee and then disappeared again. A few minutes later, she returned, this time in company with Charity Coltrane.

"Morgan, we'd best talk to these folks. Some have already said they want to pull out before Marsh hits them direct. I don't know if we can hold 'em or not. Did you get—"

"I got more than I went for," Morgan said, "but I think we'd better wait for Jed. Whatever I say needs to be last, particularly if Jed's news isn't good." Charity nodded.

"Let's give Jed a few more minutes before we get to the meeting—" She wasn't yet finished when the front door opened. It was Jed Railsback.

"Marsh wants to meet Miss Charity up at the Willuh Bend line shack. Sunup day after tomorrow. She comes in alone."

"Exactly where is it located?" Morgan asked.

Charity anticipated him. She shook her head as she replied. "Not in a spot to do what you're thinkin' about. It's on a ridge overlooking what we call the Rimfire range. Man in that shack can see for twenty miles in every direction on a clear mornin'."

"You feel any different than you did?"

"No."

Morgan turned to the gathering. "You all heard. Now let me add something. I've got men—well arms, well led professionals. Between them and you men here who have followed Jed, we can put an end to Marsh Coltrane." Morgan looked now at the Willow clan. "And we'll get Jimmy back, but we have to have a little time. Charity Coltrane is a woman you all know. You know her courage. You know her word. She can buy us that time. Then we'll have to fight. Some will have to die. Anybody that wants out—go now. No hard feelings, no effort to change your mind, no questions asked. But if you go, do it now. We have to know where we stand and with who."

Jed, Morgan, Charity and Lucy stood together, eyes scanning the group. Men shifted in their chairs. Wives looked at their faces. Some looked toward the dining room where they knew the children were gathered. It was accounting time. The books would have to be opened to all. The debits and the credits weighed against one another. Finally, each man would have to look into his own soul, and each woman into her own heart.

"Me an' muh missus—we got a boy out there somewhere. We got a lot o' work put in. Some hard, lean years, an' a few good ones as the Lord saw fit to give 'em. We'll stay with you. Least 'til we find out who an' what we're up ag'in."

"Mister Willow here speaking just for himself," Morgan asked, grasping the single opportunity he might get to pump some courage into the gatherings collective veins.

"Nobody needs to talk up for me an' mine, I'm Thad Talbert and we'll stick. We'll fight if it makes sense to do it." He looked around the room and then back at the leaders. "Heard tales about you, Mr. Morgan. Some of 'em didn't make you out to be the kind o' man I'd care to ride with, but I'm not much on talk. Action gets the job done. You said you had men. Where are they?"

"San Antonio. They're Mexican revolutionaries. They're led by a man who started out about the same as you people in a tough, lawless land, but with a dictator who collared them all. The Masters Freight Company is going to haul supplies for these men. In turn they've agreed to help clean out the raiders. After all, the Masters been hit as hard as anybody."

"I got no quarrel with ridin' with men like that if'n the Masters don't. But I'll say one more thing. Whatever happens had best happen soon. Most o' the folks sittin' here can't stand many more losses."

It was Charity who spoke up now. "Then give me time for my meeting—two more days. That's all we ask. Just two more days."

"What about the law?"

"I don't think we can count too heavy on any help from the law. It's too thin and scatterred in these parts. Still, I'll do my best to bring in some assistance from the Rangers."

The meeting broke up. Charity wanted Morgan to stay the night again. She didn't get the opportunity to ask him but he would have turned her down in any event. Lucy Masters wanted to talk to him. So did Jed Railsback.

"You're full o' surprises, Morgan," Jed said. They were walking toward Morgan's horse. "Didn't know you had any special love for Texas Rangers. Or them for you."

"I didn't say that, Jed. I just said I'd try to get them to give some help. To do that, we've got to get their attention."

"Uh huhn—'bout how I had it figured." Morgan mounted up. Lucy had already headed her carriage back toward town. She was pulling out with several of the other families, but they'd soon split up. Morgan didn't want her on the trail alone. Jed nonetheless caught hold of the harness on Morgan's mount. "One more thing, Morgan," he said, looking, Morgan thought, worried. "Luke wasn't here tonight. You know why?"

"Sure, Jed. He was feeling poorly. Stayed in town. Planned to work out some schedules for freight runs into Mexico for de Lopez."

"He warn't in town, Morgan. Leastways he wasn't at the house or the office."

Morgan looked puzzled. In Uvalde, even whore houses and saloons were in short supply if a man was of such a mind. Luke Masters wasn't. He nodded at Jed and spurred his mount.

Morgan caught up with Lucy within a mile. She stopped while he tied his mount to the rear of the buggy and then climbed up beside her. They said nothing for a ways but it was Lucy who finally set the theme.

"Morgan, what are you feelings—uh—I mean your feelings as a man about Charity Coltrane?"

Morgan didn't think there were too many surprises left in this situation. Obviously there had been one. "Whatever they might be," he said, trying to conceal his surprise, "I'd think they'd be my affair." He turned and looked into Lucy's face. "Don't you?"

"Under other circumstances—yes."

"Under *any* circumstances, Lucy, my personal feelings are just that—mine. At least 'til I'm ready to share 'em."

"Did you bed her?"

Morgan snorted. "You don't quit, do you?"

"That's no answer."

"It's none of your damned business. Hell, that situation wouldn't even be all mine to tell. Would it?"

"She'll be riding out tomorrow. She'll have to leave tomorrow to get to the line shack by sunup the next day. She wanted you to stay with her tonight."

"You don't know what the hell you're talking about."

"She's in love with you, Morgan."

"Bullshit!"

"She said so."

"To who?"

"To no one. It's in her eyes when she looks at you and in her voice when she speaks." Lucy half smiled and then looked way, straight ahead. "Even the gentleness of her touch."

"More bullshit! Female intuition."

"Or male naivete."

Morgan studied Lucy. The conversation was too far from dead center at this point to really make sense. Maybe Lucy knew that he and Charity had bedded down and maybe she didn't. Either way, Morgan thought, the depth of this conversation was a cover for something else. What?

"Where was your dad tonight?"

"Home—why?"

"No he wasn't. He wasn't at the office either." Lucy's head jerked to the left and she looked into Morgan's face. She realized his revelation was no simple ploy just to change the subject.

"Who told you that?"

Unlike Lucy, Morgan had an answer. He didn't hesitate to use it. "Jed Railsback. When he went in for the message, he stopped by."

"Why?"

"I thought maybe you could tell me. Why would Jed go to see your dad? And having gone to see him, why didn't he find him?"

"I—I don't know." Morgan considered her. He believed her. She looked shocked and puzzled.

"Let's get back," Morgan said. Lucy nodded. Morgan cracked the whip.

The cartage company's offices were locked and dark. When Morgan and Lucy finally reached the house, Lucy was scared. She hurried inside, shouting for her father. There was no answer. She began a search—room by room. Morgan joined her. Luke Masters was not there. It was nearly two o'clock in the morning.

"They've taken him—like Jimmy Willow."

"I'm riding to the office." Morgan started for the door. He turned back. "Get your coat back on. You're going with me." Lucy looked at him and nodded.

Luke Masters appeared to be asleep. He had long since moved a small cot into a back room, an old storage area at the freight company's office. He was stretched out on his back, arms folded across his chest, feet crossed at the ankles. His boots were off. His eyes were closed and he seemed to have a smile of satisfaction on his lips. The only flaw in the scene was, at first, undetectable. Luke wasn't breathing!

"Back off, Lucy."

"He's—oh God—Daddy!" Lucy covered her face, stifled a scream, which, instead, came out in short, pitiful whines. Morgan then saw the wound. Left side of Luke's head, midway between his ear and his temple. A small-caliber weapon, probably a Deringer, had inflicted it. There were black smudges on the flesh—powder burns. At first glance it appeared Luke Masters was a victim of his own hand.

Morgan covered him up and had a quick look around. He led Lucy to the front office. He sat her down. She was staring into nothingness. He searched until he found a bottle of whiskey. It was nearly full so he took a long pull for himself and then poured a smaller quantity into a water glass for Lucy. She did not protest but neither did she consume it quickly. Morgan nursed it into her a little at a time.

"I'm taking you back to the Double C." What the whiskey hadn't done, his statement did.

"No you're not. I'll not set foot on the Double C again—ever!"

Morgan frowned. "Why? No one there did this to your father."

"The hell they didn't. If Charity Coltrane had given us her freight business from the beginning—we—Dad—there would have been money enough."

"You can't stay alone." She stood up. "It's only temporary." She walked to the big rolltop on the far wall. "Charity won't even be there after tomorrow. You said so yourself." She opened the top drawer. "I'll be out there most of the time too 'til we take to the fight with Marsh."

She reached in, extracted a short barreled Allen and Wheelock revolver and turned to face Morgan. Only then did he see the gun. She cocked it. Morgan dived. Lucy fired. Morgan rolled. Lucy fired. The shot blew out the coal oil lamp, shattering the shade and spreading burning oil onto nearby papers. Morgan grabbed her, spun her toward him and let go a solid punch to the jaw. Lucy dropped. Morgan doused the flames with the whiskey—all but one shot. He downed it and slumped into a chair.

Morgan was surprised to find Jed Railsback bedded down on the floor in the main house at the ranch. Jed was equally shocked at Morgan's appearance.

"I thought Miss Charity would be sleepin' better with me right here."

"Yeah, Jed. Good idea."

"What the hell brings you—"

"Luke Masters is dead. Shot through the head. Somebody tried to make it look like he did it himself."

"Goddam! Lucy?"

"Outside. Out cold. I had to hit her."

"I'll wake Miss Charity." Morgan nodded.

Morgan related the events, how he and Lucy returned to Uvalde while Charity prepared coffee. She had furnished a sleeping draught to Morgan and he'd gotten it down Lucy's throat. Jed sat nearby, keeping an eye on the young girl.

Charity took Jed a cup of coffee and then returned to the kitchen. She spiced up Morgan's coffee with some top grade Irish whiskey. "Luke Masters was no coward. I don't give a damn. Luke wouldn't do it."

Morgan looked up. "I told you what I found. Now let

me tell you what I didn't find—a gun. Who do you know that Luke knows—who also owns a Deringer?"

"I only know one person who owns a Deringer. Thirty-two caliber." Charity sipped her coffee, looking at the floor. Morgan didn't ask the obvious question. He gave her time. She took it. She looked up. "Me. My Daddy gave it to me when I turned eighteen."

"Where is it?"

"Upstairs in a drawer in my chiffonier."

"You sure."

"There has only been two people in my bedroom recently. The gun was there two days ago. You know who the people were."

"Get it, Charity."

She wasn't gone a minute. She smiled at Jed as she went through the living room. She noticed he was not in the chair when she returned. She was moving faster. The Deringer was gone.

"It's gone," she said. Morgan had both hands on the table. His eyes shifted to the corner of the kitchen. She turned her head to follow them.

"Sit down, ma'am."

"Jed!"

"This what you're lookin' fer?" He held up the Deringer. He did it with his left hand. His right hand was full of Colt. He had it leveled at Morgan's head. "Warn this gunman not to try pullin' on a drop—leastways not on mine."

"He's one of the best pistol shots in the county, Morgan."

"I've got nothing to lose," Morgan said to Charity and then turned back to face Jed and continued, "have I, Jed? You'll have to kill us both anyway."

"Nope. Just you Morgan. And not just yet."

"Jed! Jesus! *Why?* For God's sake! You've been with me for—with the Double C—"

"More years than I care to count, Miss Charity. An' now I'm about to git paid right for 'em."

"From Marshall Coltrane," she asked, scowling at him.

"He needed somebody on the inside. He made it worthwhile. You don't have to die, ma'am. I got that worked out with him."

"You bastard! You back-shooting, low life, lying bastard!"

"Easy, ma'am, I know you're riled. But don't crowd me too much."

Morgan sensed Jed Railsback's growing anger. He intervened. "Why Luke Masters?"

"Too bad 'bout Luke—wasn't figured—just happened. He caught me fakin' that message to Miss Charity."

"Faking the—you—there isn't any meeting with Marsh?"

"There's a meetin', ma'am—just not the way you figured it."

"When Jed? Where?"

"Here. Tomorrow. The rest o' the folks in the valley will figger blood's thicker'n water when it's all over. They'll hear how you sold out to your brother."

"And Morgan?"

"He gits turned into the Rangers in place o' Marshall. Them lookin' alike an' all. Well, it kind o' takes ever'body off'n the hot part o' the stove."

"Jed." The voice was soft. It shouldn't have been there. It was. Jed's head jerked. His eyes blinked at the black smoke and red-orange flame that belched out of the end of the six-gun right straight at him. The look he assumed was so firmly established in the final seconds of his life that it locked the muscles in place in the first few seconds of his death. He had no place to fall. The force of the heavy caliber shell shoved him against the wall. He hung there a moment and then slipped into a sitting position. His arm went limp and the pistol he was holding slipped from it. Then, his head dropped to the left.

Lucy Masters slowly lowered the gun to her side and then released it. It clattered to the floor. Charity was at her side. Morgan got to his feet, checked Jed and then stood up and turned.

"The message couldn't have come from Marsh," Lucy said. Both Morgan and Charity looked puzzled and at each other before turning back to Lucy. "I hauled the material up in that country to build that line shack at Willow Bend. Jed paid me to do it out of his own pocket. Told me never to say anything to you, Charity, but he needed it built fast and the outfit from Del Rio couldn't bring the lumber in time."

"My God! Marsh wouldn't have known about the Willow Bend shack. He'd been gone for years. I—I should have thought."

"Something bothered me about it when I heard Jed's words. I didn't know what it was 'til we got home. Then it hit me. Thing was, I couldn't be sure if it was you, Charity, or Jed or maybe both. I had to get out here to find out."

"Well I'll be a sonuvabitch," Morgan said. "You were playacting that whole time. Goddam! Sarah Bernhardt herself could take a lesson from you."

Lucy smiled. Charity hugged her. Lucy looked into Charity's face. "I'm glad it wasn't you."

"She's—she's slipping, Morgan," Charity said. Indeed, Lucy Masters had faked almost everything except the sleeping draught. That, she fought off as long as she could. Between the whiskey, Luke's death, Lucy's fears and the powder—she was gone. Morgan and Charity got her bedded down. Morgan moved Jed's body out of the kitchen. Charity calmed the hired help and Morgan told the men on duty that the shot had been accidental. The story would hold until later in the day—he hoped. Charity began cleaning up. The job was nasty. Morgan helped.

"What now?" she finally asked.

"What we've been waiting for. If Jed Railsback is the only turncoat on your spread, we've got an edge. If we use it right, it ought to be enough."

"You've got a plan?"

"Yeah, but it'll keep 'til daylight. We'd best try to get some sleep." Charity was too exhausted to protest even a little bit. She nodded. Morgan bedded down on the floor near Lucy. His handgun was nearby, cocked when he fell asleep.

10

Young Jimmy Willow was more than grateful for the hard biscuit, water and plate of red beans. His captors hadn't fed him since noon of the previous day. Too, he was glad just to see another face—even the face of Ike Larraby. He didn't see it long. Ike jammed the food through the window opening, eyed Jimmy with disdain and then slammed the wooden shutter down again and locked it. Just then, Cole Larraby shouted at his brother. "Marsh wants to see you, Ike. Right now."

"Shit," Ike mumbled to himself. He was hungry. He'd planned to eat. If he got orders from Marsh, he might not get the time to eat. He shrugged and trudged off toward the old shack Marsh Coltrane had commandeered for his private quarters.

Ike and Cole Larraby represented half of Marsh Coltrane's four top guns. The other half were Larraby cousins, Lafe and Tom Caspar. Of the dubious quartet, Ike was the most disgusting. He rarely bathed. Not even his brother would sleep in the same bunkhouse with him. His stringy, matted hair and never-trimmed beard were both lice infested as was his crotch. He kept both hands busy just scratching in one place or another.

Ike Larraby was also ugly. The left side of his face dipped in toward his teeth. No hair grew along the almost inch wide scar. The scar itself ran from the corner of his mouth all the way to the base of his ear. It had come to him in a knife fight when he was fifteen. He won the fight, but there was no help for his face. The bleeding had been stopped with gunpowder. The cheek had been held together for weeks with bailing wire. The flesh grew crooked, gapped and otherwise improperly. Ike could barely stand the sight of himself. Others turned away if he looked at them head-on. Mostly he didn't. He talked out of the side of his mouth, face turned away and head cocked. It only added to the horror.

Along with his brother and their cousins, Ike Larraby was one of the most vicious, useless and totally ruthless human beings ever to sit a horse. The lot was wanted in damned near every state south of the main line of the Union Pacific. The crimes for which they were sought were as varied as their twisted minds could create. Rape, robbery, murder—downright butchery. Ike was the worst.

The four of them, given almost total license to practice their treachery by Marsh Coltrane, in turn kept the rest of Coltrane's human dung heap in line. Any complaints were handled by one of the four. Usually with a six-gun. There were damned few complaints. If nothing else could be said of them, the Larrabys and the Caspars were deadly gunhands. Too, they had one more common bond. Their numbers gave them a collective backbone. Separately, the lot had none.

* * *

Ike found Marsh just finishing his breakfast and studying a hand drawn map which rider had brought in that morning, presumably from Jed Railsback.

Marsh took the last bite of his biscuit, mopped up egg yoke, jammed it into his mouth and followed the disgusting looking blob with a swallow of coffee. He sloshed the combination back and forth between his cheeks, swallowed, sucked his teeth and then looked up.

"Jesse brought me this map. Jed stole it from old man Masters." Ike grinned. "They plan to run a dozen freight wagons south out of Uvalde loaded with men. Figure to camp between Crystal City and Carrizo Springs. Figure we'll hit 'em there and get hurt bad."

"Where they runnin' the *real* thing?"

"Right straight into our laps," Marsh said. He motioned to Ike who joined him at the table. Marsh jammed his index finger onto the map. "Twenty-five wagons will leave Uvalde two full days ahead of the decoys. Follow the Neuces River north and then west toward Rimfire Range. Then they'll cut back south to Brackettville." Ike studied the map. Scratched at himself. Marsh winkled up his nose as Ike's body odor began to reach his nostrils.

"Jeezus howdy—them wagons'll be right out in the open when they start trailin' between Salmon peak and Turkey mountain," Ike said. Then he stepped back and looked his crooked look at Marsh. "So would our boys if'n that there's a trap."

"It's no trap. The trap is south. Hell! It's right here, Ike. Right from old man Masters himself."

"You sure are mighty trustin' o' Jed Railsback."

"Right now I am," Marsh said. "When it's over, Ike,

you kill him."

"Sure Marsh—sure. Just don't forget what you promised me'n my kin for our troubles."

"I won't, Ike. Don't worry. Charity and the Masters girl are yours. I don't want to see that bitch but once, when she comes to the line shack."

"I still think that stinks. Somethin's rotten. What if she wants to deal?"

"Then we deal. Then you get her, Ike. And the girl."

"An' what about the kid out there in the shack?"

"Soon as I show Charity he's still alive and hear what she has to say—you kill him too."

"What now?"

"Take a half a dozen men and stay on that ridge behind the Willow Springs line shack 'til you see Jed and Charity coming. Make damn sure they're alone. Damn sure!"

"Yeah. Okay, Marsh, but I still think it stinks. They was s'posed to be there three days ago."

"Stop thinking, Ike. I do the thinking in this outfit, not you. Charity Coltrane is no goddam idiot. She's got to play it safe too. I figured she'd want some proof that Jimmy Willow is alive. Besides, the delay gave me the chance to get Jed involved direct. She's got anything up her sleeve—Jed's right there to kill her."

"Yeah. I guess."

"You'd best get riding."

"I'll send Lafe and Tom—" Marsh Coltrane was pouring himself another cup of coffee. He stopped, whirled and scowled at Ike Larraby.

"Did I say send Lafe and Tom? I said *you* go, Ike—*you* personal. That means what I said. It don't mean Lafe and Tom."

"I'm s'posed to be your ramrod. I'm your goddam top gun, Marsh. Not no fuckin' errand boy."

"You're what I tell you you are, Ike. Nothing more. You'd best remember that. I give you an order. I got a reason for it. You want what you've been promised. Then you do what I say when I say and how I say." Marsh turned completely now and faced the ugly gunman. "Unless you think you're good enough to run this whole show without me and good enough to take over. Is that what you think, Ike?"

Ike Larraby had often imagined himself in fine clothes, gambling at the best places in New Orleans or San Francisco. Things Marsh Coltrane had already done—briefly at least. Things he planned to do again. Sometimes, Ike fantasized about Charity Coltrane—naked—standing before him and forced to do his will. Other times, he saw her tied, spread-eagle to a big four-poster—helpless before him. Of all Ike Larraby's fantasies the one he most cherished however was drawing on Marsh Coltrane and beating him. Marsh had given Ike plenty of chances to try. Now he had another. Ike studied Marsh's face for a minute. Then he shook his head. The fantasy was still a fantasy. Ike was good. But he was scared to pull on Marsh Coltrane.

"Didn't mean nothin', Marsh. I'll ride out."

"Good. When you're sure about the situation. When you've talked to Jed himself, then you get word back here and I'll ride in."

"Yeah, Marsh. Okay."

"And one more thing, Ike. Make goddam sure Charity doesn't hear you talking to Jed or getting any ideas about Jed's loyalty. We lose him we get set back quite a spell. I set it up this way so they'd buy it. Don't fuck it up."

Marsh's words grated on Ike Larraby. No other man could have spoken to Ike that way—not and lived. The fantasy flashed through his mind again. Then it was gone. Ike nodded.

Lee Morgan, Charity, Lucy and the others would have been much more at ease had they known Marsh Coltrane's lack of trust in any judgments not his own. The reason, of course, came from Marsh's trust, once before, of his father. The total self-reliance was the chink in Marshall Coltrane's armor. The fact of it was that Ike Larraby's suspicions were worthy of considerable attention. Jed Railsback had made the worst possible kind of mistake—the kind that proved fatal.

Jed had done so out of pure greed. Faking the message to Charity to lead her to the line shack was only to insure himself a firmer grip on control of his own destiny. He didn't completely trust Marsh, and he'd hoped to use Charity as a bargaining chip. Luke Masters accidentally stumbled into the situation, which then developed too fast for Jed's thinking processes. Jed's contribution to the events had now become considerable and all of it on Morgan's side of the ledger.

In the three days since Jed's death, Charity had faked her own message. She agreed to ride with Jed, to the Willow Springs line shack. Morgan, in rummaging through Jed's belongings, learned that the line shack had been the message center between Marsh and Jed. It was no doubt why Jed used it that last time, not thinking that Marsh wasn't supposed to know anything about that line shack. Lucy Masters, a little removed from the center of the problem and knowing her father would never have taken his own life, had caught Jed's error. The offense now shifted, albeit tenuously, into Lee Morgan's hands.

Marsh Coltrane had responded to Charity's request for the meeting and agreed that one man, Jed Railsback, could accompany her. Marsh still wanted to be certain but Lee Morgan was already certain. He pulled one of the ranch hands, a man about Jed's size and build, and planned for him to pose as Jed. Morgan knew there would be lookouts. Morgan himself would ride out ahead, secret himself in an appropriate observation position and wait. He'd trail whoever rode back to Marsh Coltrane. Then, he'd have a first hand look at the enemy camp.

The plan was so simple it somewhat frightened him. Often, Morgan knew that the easiest-looking situations were those which most quickly fell apart, as Jed Railsback's had. But, with the receipt of Marsh's message, so far so good. A phony map of Masters' first shipments for the Mexicans, information about the real route, and an offer from Charity should make for a careless Marsh Coltrane. Morgan had contacted de Lopez and Pancho Villa. A single word would move their men into position. Finally, Morgan had also sent a dispatch to Texas Ranger Headquarters. He hoped its contents would bring a few additional guns into the Double C camp.

"Good morning." Charity and Morgan were drinking coffee, for the most part in silence. Lucy had been staying at the Double C since the tragic events of three days earlier. This was the earliest she had risen during those days—and the best she'd look or sounded.

"Lucy," Charity said, smiling, "you look rested for a

change."

"I feel it, for a change." Charity started to get up. "Please, let me. I've been little use lately." Charity nodded, understandingly. Lucy sat down, sipped her coffee. "I'm sorry about my outburst yesterday. Waiting on Dad's proper burial is only sensible."

"Still hurtful," Morgan said. "But we can't afford to let Marsh Coltrane know what's happened."

"I appreciate your letting them put Daddy in the ground next to your own father, Charity, even if it's just temporary. It would have been much, much harder just to see him stuck any old place."

"We'll have a proper service when he's moved. A proper tribute to him too when this is all over."

Lucy nodded. She closed her eyes and bit her lip, fighting back the urge to cry. "God! I wish it was over. How many will die before it is?"

"A damn sight fewer than before," Morgan said, "because of Luke Masters."

"I hope so. God, how I hope so." Lucy sighed. "Well then, have you decided on the first freight run for de Lopez?"

"If *he's* ready, yes," Morgan answered. "Jim Keyes, the man who's posing for Jed, and I will ride out early in the morning. If Charity's meeting with Marsh goes well, and I'm able to find their main camp, the freight will start moving two days later. A day after that—"

"It should be over."

"Yeah."

"I'm still worried about you, Charity," Lucy said. "If someone spots Jim Keyes as a fake—"

"They won't," Morgan reassured her. "All he's

doing is dropping her at the line shack and riding back south to wait."

"You don't think any of Marsh's men will want to talk to Jed personally."

"I doubt it. Stupid of Marsh if he tried. He'd run the risk of Charity spotting it and knowing she's got a turncoat working for her. No. I'm betting against that."

"Alkali told me yesterday. He's got seven more teamsters hired. By tonight he should have enough men for the wagons going in both directions. Where do Villa's men join you?"

"Just outside Laguna. Once we're sure Marsh's men are in position, Villa will provide fifty men for the wagons and another fifty to move into Rimfire Range and hit Coltrane's bunch from the rear. Any and all who get out of that ambush and make it back to the base camp will find me and the ranchers waiting for them."

"And south?"

"You take the five wagons out of here. Alkali and the real shipment will pick you up at La Pryor." Morgan grinned. "You all ought to be down in the *cantina* at Piedras Negras by the time Marsh Coltrane discovers he's been scalawagged."

Lucy Masters got to her feet. "I've got to get back to town. There's plenty to do and—" she took a deep breath, swallowed and forced a smile, "it keeps me occupied."

"I'll ride with you," Charity said.

"No. I've got business in town anyhow," Morgan said. "You get yourself ready to ride out in the morning, Charity. I'll ride with Lucy." Charity nodded.

* * *

Lucy hesitated at the front door of the Masters house. She glanced at Morgan. He felt for her. He unlocked the door and they both went in.

"You okay?" he asked. She nodded. "Then I'm going to the bank and the mercantile before I ride back to the Double C. I'll look in on you before I leave town."

"I'll be at the office by then. Stop there."

Just shy of an hour later, Lucy Masters was about to unlock the front door at the Masters Cartage Company's office when she heard a shout. Half a block away, Lee Morgan was just leaving the bank. The shout had come from one of two men positioned in the middle of the street. Even at that distance, Lucy could figure the action.

"Texas Rangers, Coltrane. You're under arrest!"

"Dear God," Lucy mumbled. She grabbed the Winchester from its saddle sheath, levered a shell into the chamber, aimed the weapon down the street and fired. She levered a second shell into place and fired again.

The shots dug up the dirt in the street short of the two rangers. They did get the men's attention, however, and Morgan took advantage of the situation. He dived behind a water trough.

One of the rangers got off a shot as Morgan dived. He missed but Morgan knew he'd not get out without a fight. The second man, armed with shotgun, fired both barrels at the trough, tearing out most of the streetside wood. The water drained out and Morgan's haven of safety was cut down to the thickness of the trough's building side edge, about two inches. Morgan rolled, came up to his knees and fired. The ranger with the shotgun dropped—hit in the leg. Morgan twisted to face the other man. He heard Lucy scream. Then—the lights went out.

Morgan thought the room was turning when he first opened his eyes. It proved to be a pinata suspended from the ceiling and gently blown by an outside breeze. He sat up. He winced. He gently felt the back of his head. The knot was good sized.

"That's as far as I'd go if I was you, mister—unless you're tryin' for another goose egg—or worse."

Morgan's eyes focused. He looked toward the voice. He saw a big man. Two hundred and fifty pounds, he thought. He was sitting in a rickety chair, its back against the wall. An adobe wall. The man had a scatter gun, both hammers locked open, leveled at Morgan's chest.

"You've made one helluva mistake," Morgan said.

"Don't think so, Coltrane. Think it's you and your lady friend what did the mistake makin'. But it's over now."

Morgan thought: Lucy! Jeezus! She'd fired too. "Where's the girl?"

"Cared for."

"Goddam it! I'm not Marshall Coltrane. My name is Lee Morgan. I sent a telegraph cable to your office from the Double C ranch. I asked for help to get Coltrane."

"Shut up!"

"Look. I can prove I'm not Coltrane. Send a rider out to the Double C. Coltrane's sister is out there. She'll tell you who I am."

The big man stood up. His vest pulled back and Morgan saw the ranger's badge. The man moved toward Morgan menacingly. "I said shut up, mister. I meant it."

Morgan scooted back on the bed. Out—he'd be no use to anyone. A quarter of an hour passed. "Mind if I smoke?"

"You ain't got the makin's. Yo ain't got nothin', mister." Morgan was about to protest again when he heard a door—then footsteps. He looked up. The big man got to his feet. The door to the room opened. One of the two rangers who'd confronted him on the street stepped into the room.

"On your feet, Coltrane, and turn around."

"I'm not Coltrane," Morgan said, standing. The ranger moved over and let go a meaty fist into Morgan's belly. The gunman, caught off guard, grunted and half doubled up. The ranger grabbed a handful of hair, twisted, turned Morgan around, jerked his arms behind him and secured his wrists in handcuffs.

Morgan recognized nothing. Once outside, he knew why. The old adobe was abandoned and nowhere near town. In fact, as Morgan was helped up on a horse—not his own—he scanned the countryside. He could not recognize any of it. Not even along the horizon. He thought: How the hell long was I out? Where did they bring me? Where to now? And where the hell is Lucy?

There were three men. The big one led Morgan's horse. By his own reckoning, they were moving south. He had to do something. What? Half an hour later, Morgan did recognize his surroundings. They were riding into La Pryor—some twenty miles south of Uvalde.

In front of the Zavala county courthouse, Morgan saw his horse and Lucy's. On the second floor of the courthouse, Morgan was taken into an office which had no sign on the door. A man was pouring himself a cup of coffee when they walked in. He had his back to them, sitting down behind an old desk. He turned and looked up.

"Hello, Coltrane." Morgan eyed the man. He remembered where he'd seen the face before. The San Antonio newspaper. This was Jute Yokley, District Deputy of the Texas Rangers. One mean sonuvabitch. Charity had told Morgan that it was rumored that Marsh had killed a man named Britt Yokley. It had happened in a whorehouse in El Paso. Thing was—young Yokley had a daddy who was—a Texas Ranger!

"I'm not Coltrane."

The man ignored Morgan. "Take his cuffs off and leave us be."

"Sir—he—"

"Do it!"

When they were alone, Jute Yokley sat down on the edge of his desk. He smiled at Morgan. "Do me a favor, Coltrane. Make a try for the window." The ranger took his gun from its holster and placed it on the desk. "Go for the gun, Coltrane. Please. Try me. Do me and Texas a big favor. You'll save the price of a hangin'."

"Goddammit, Yokley. My name is Lee Morgan. I look a little like Marsh Coltrane. But I'm not. Christ! The woman with me can tell you. So can Coltrane's sister at the Double C ranch. So can—"

Yokley back-handed Morgan. The force of the blow and the surprise sent Morgan back against the chair, nearly tipping it over.

"You cowardly, lying scum. I got two dozen people who'll witness to who you are." The big ranger grinned.

Morgan's arms were tense and his face twisted into a look of pure hatred. It was exactly what Yokley wanted. "Yeah, Coltrane. Get riled. Get *real* riled. Then I'll have an excuse to kill you." Morgan knew the man wanted one. Even a flimsy one.

"The woman. Lucy Masters. She's got nothing to do with any of this. Let her be."

"I'll take care o' the woman, Coltrane. Your worryin' days over somebody else are all over. Only one you got to worry about is you." The man stood up. He appeared as though he was going to turn around. Suddenly, he spun back and hit Morgan again—twice. Then he picked up the gun. He cocked it and placed the barrel on the bridge of Morgan's nose. "No one would know. No one would ever find out. What's saving you, Coltrane, is my desire to see you sweat and then hang."

After several seconds, the man eased the gun's hammer back down, withdrew the pistol and backed around the desk. "I'll tell you the fuckin' truth, Coltrane, I wasn't real sure I could keep from killin' you when I finally saw you. Now I want to see you at the end of a rope. But don't make any mistakes. You so much as breathe wrong and I'll kill you, Coltrane, a little at a time."

Morgan knew there was no point in continuing to deny his identity. Under no circumstances was this man going to believe him. He'd only make his situation worse and, he thought, perhaps Lucy's as well. He was also acutely aware of something else. They had refused to tell him Lucy's whereabouts. Now he knew why. As long as he didn't know where she was he wouldn't dare make a move, unless he didn't care about her. That, he thought, could be his salvation.

"You're holding all the cards," Morgan said. "What now?"

"We wait." The ranger smiled. "Don't want you to be lonely so we'll bring you some more company." Morgan frowned. "Billy!" The door opened. "Take him down with the girl. Cuff them together."

Morgan was led outside to the rear of the court building. There, he was taken into a storm cellar. A single candle burned at the bottom of the steep ladder leading into the musty room. Lucy sat huddled in a corner. Morgan saw her and considered his options. They were slim to none. He had a gun in his back and two rangers between him and freedom which, at best, might have lasted two minutes. A few moments later, he and Lucy stared at each other in the semi-darkness—handcuffed together.

"Are you all right? Did they hurt you?"

"I'm—" Lucy stopped. She looked into Morgan's face.

"What is it?"

"How would Jed Railsback have known that Charity owned a Deringer? How would he have known where she kept it? Why, my dad caught Jed by accident. Would Jed have even had the damned gun with him?"

"Jesus H. Christ," Morgan said. "Charity? It can't be! She was at the ranch the whole time."

"No she wasn't, Morgan. She left to be with the other women who were trying to give some comfort to her hired hand's wife." Morgan's brow wrinkled as he remembered. She wasn't there when he arrived. She'd been gone sometime already and she didn't come back for sometime after he arrived. She had time to go to town.

"All right, Lucy, I'll give it a maybe. You got a why?"

"She rode in to kill Jed. Dad got in the way. Jed was scared. He tried to find Dad. You told me so yourself. He even asked you about Dad. He didn't know about that back room."

"Charity did?"

"Yes. She was in it not long ago—with me."

"Lucy. Some of it makes sense, but it's pretty goddam thin in spots."

"Charity went upstairs that night for just a minute—or so it seemed. I was—well groggy—half asleep."

"Yeah. I sent her up there to look for that Deringer. It wasn't there." Morgan snapped his fingers. "Jed had it, Lucy. How'd he get it?"

"That's what I'm recollecting now. When she came back down, Jed—he—he got up. I remember them standing near the door to the kitchen. Then, Jed walked into the kitchen and Charity just stood there for a minute."

"To make it look good. Sonuvabitch! And she let *you* do what *she* rode to town to do—kill Jed Railsback."

The door to the storm cellar opened. The big ranger came down and hauled Morgan and Lucy to their feet. He took off the cuffs and stayed behind as they climbed back up the ladder. Once again, they were taken inside the courthouse and back to the second floor office. Charity Coltrane stood in the corner of the room. Jute Yokley pointed to Morgan.

"Is that man your brother?"

"Yes sir," she said.

"And the woman?"

"Lucy Masters. The one who stole the Deringer out

of my bedroom."

"And used it to kill her own father to protect this—this filth."

"Yes, sir. She killed my top wrangler too, Jed Railsback."

"And this gunman. Lee Morgan. S'posed to look like your brother here. You know anything about him?"

"Only that this woman hired him. Got him killed so the law would be off of Marsh's trail. I think he was killed up in San Antonio."

"Well," Yokley said, "I think I've heard all I need to hear." He turned, smiling at Charity, and said, "I never believed I'd see a woman with so little regard for human life and so much greed for land and power." He brought up his pistol. "But you're worse than any man I've ever come up against. You're under arrest, Miss Coltrane. We'll start with murder." Charity's jaw dropped. She looked, disbelieving, at Morgan and then at Lucy. Lucy was equally shocked. Morgan stood up.

"If we're going to keep that appointment with the real Marsh Coltrane, we'll have to ride now."

"Morgan—I—" Morgan smiled, helped Lucy up and put his finger to his lips.

"I'll explain it all on the way back to Uvalde. But you were doing a pretty good job down in that storm cellar of figuring out a few things."

"You're a dead man, Morgan," Charity screamed. Two rangers pinned her arms and forced her into a chair. Morgan and Lucy could hear her sobbing as they departed the court house. Jute Yokley caught up with them outside.

"I'll have fifteen men, the best in Texas, up there in that camp on schedule."

"We'll need 'em," Morgan said.

Morgan tied the horses to the back of Charity's buggy. She wouldn't be needing it. She was staying. The couple had gone near five miles before Lucy finally spoke.

"You've known all along, haven't you?"

"Not hardly. It came in pieces. Most of 'em you know."

"What don't I know," Lucy asked, smiling and then looking at Morgan and adding, "besides who you really are?"

"I'm Lee Morgan. On special assignment to the Texas Rangers for an old friend."

"That man Yokley?" Morgan nodded. "Did he pick you because of your friendship or because you resemble Marsh Coltrane?"

"Both. The first I owed him. He saved my hide once. The second came in handy."

"How could you be sure of getting the job with our freight line?"

"Couldn't be positive," Morgan replied, "but your dad got a little extra pushing that you didn't know about—from Jute."

"Dad—God—I—I still can't believe he's—" Morgan took Lucy's hand and squeezed hard.

"I wish to hell I could have stopped that. Everybody tried to warn your dad to back off. He was just too much a man to take their advice."

"Too damned stubborn is what Daddy was. He always was." Lucy looked up. "Today. I don't understand today. The treatment. The cellar. All that. Charity wasn't around."

"The second job for me in this little shindig is putting

the Coltrane clan out of business. The first was helping to find one Texas Ranger gone bad. Ends up he went bad by going to work for Marsh Coltrane."

"It's all so confusing. It's almost too much for me."

"It was damn near too much for me. Helluv it is—it's not over yet."

"Just who was that bad ranger?"

"The big fella with the shotgun. Remember the little detour he took comin' down from Uvalde?"

Lucy's eyes got big. "You weren't unconscious that whole trip."

"Not hardly."

"Sarah Bernhardt might do well to take a lesson from you." Suddenly Lucy frowned and looked up at Morgan. "I was bait!"

Morgan didn't respond but he raised his pant leg, reached down in his boot and extracted Charity's Deringer.

"Damn you," she said. Morgan shrugged. "Well. What now? No Charity to ride to the line shack." Morgan didn't respond. Neither did he look at her. It didn't take her long to figure it out this time. "God! Bait again?"

"Got anybody else we can send?"

"And who goes as Jed?"

"That we don't change. But you two will never reach the line shack. I'll be there by midnight with half a case of dynamite. When you're close, I'll blow it. You two fire a few shots toward the ridge. You know, make it look like you think you've been set up."

"Then?"

"Then turn around and ride like hell out of there. I'll trail whoever back to the camp." Morgan looked down at Lucy and smiled. "And that's the other change."

Lucy looked quizzical. "What?"

"The wagons will move into the area tomorrow afternoon intead of the following morning. Villa has already been notified. I'll get word to the ranchers this afternoon instead of the following morning. Villa has

"Marsh won't really have time to find out what went wrong."

"Exactly. He'll have to move on the information he last got. It'll be wrong, but by the time he finds it out, it'll also be too damned late."

"God. How I wish it was over."

"Soon," Morgan said.

"You know, I still can't figure Charity. I mean—she already had the ranch and she hated—I mean I thought she hated Marsh."

"She did, Lucy. Still does. The ranch was small stakes. Charity was the contact on the American side of the border for the anti-revolutionary faction in Mexico. She stood to get damned rich if she could knock out de Lopez and Pancho Villa."

"But I thought Marsh was being financed by the Mexican government?"

Morgan smiled and shook his head. "He was and is! Charity was their insurance. Or competition. They don't give a damn who survives, just so long as somebody stops Villa."

"My God! It's all too complicated for me."

"Yeah," Morgan said, wistfully. "In my dad's day, everything was pretty simple. He always knew who he had to face. Not anymore. I guess it'll get worse as civilization makes more demands of itself."

"I don't think I want to be around in another fifty or

seventy five years," Lucy said.

"No. Me either. Too goddamn many changes already."

Lucy smiled. She leaned up and kissed Morgan's cheek. He turned, surprised. She kissed him on the lips—gently. He felt a surge of heat in his groin. "Some things haven't changed," she said. It was a promise of things to come—literally! Morgan thought. That's one hell of an incentive to stay alive.

The buggy topped the crest of a hill. Before them, silhouetted against the gathering darkness, lay Uvalde.

11

The day matured, losing its newborn pink and taking on a bright, healthy, youthful appearance. It was just past seven o'clock and already warm enough to rouse the botflies. The horses on the ridge swished their tails to keep the pests in flight. There were five mounts. Among them Ike and Cole Larraby's.

The brothers sat atop a flat rock. Ike surveyed the sky with his crooked gaze. "Gonna be a hot sumbitch today." Cole said nothing. Instead, he elbowed his brother in the ribs. Ike looked perturbed but Cole was pointing. There were two black dots on the horizon. They slowly grew bigger.

Cole Larraby grinned, exposing short, dingy teeth. "Our booty?" He licked his scaly lips.

"More'n likely," Ike said.

Cole screwed his face into a scowl. "Goddam Marsh better not four-flush on this deal."

"He won't. He even tries," Ike said, fingering his pistol, "an I'll kill 'em."

"So when, Ike? When do we git 'er?"

"Soon, little brother. Real soon now."

The black dots had grown to the size of riders. Ike stood up and walked back to the other three men. All of them were stretched out, hats over their eyes, trying to make up for lost sleep. He kicked at their boots and they sat up, mumbling collectively.

"We got company. Soon as I ride down an' make sure, you git ready to hightail it back to camp."

"How we gonna know it's okay?"

" 'Cause I won't be shot," Ike said, kicking the man who asked the question. "Dumb sumbitch."

"Ike!" It was Cole. "They're 'bout half a mile from the shack."

"You boys mount up," Ike said, and then he walked back to where his brother stood. Above and behind these men was another rider. Lee Morgan had seen the two black dots. He also could see the trail the five riders would have to take down to the ridge. He could drop in behind them anytime. He now looked farther away. He saw nothing, but he felt certain that somewhere out there, Pancho Villa and his men, young Luke Barkley and the ranchers and Jute Yokley and the Rangers were either riding in or were ready and waiting.

Morgan unsnapped a long leather rifle scabbard. He slipped the weapon out primed and loaded it. It was an old model, .50 caliber Sharps. The famed Buffalo gun. It was accurate to a fault and had the range he needed. He tested windage. He dropped to one knee, firmed up his elbow on a flat rock, shifted the rifle's butt until it was tight but comfortable against his shoulder. He sighted.

Morgan's target was a pony keg of water at the north-east corner of the line shack. Just above it, inside the shack on a shelf was the dynamite. He eyed the riders.

They were close enough.

The roar of the Sharps would have continued echoing for several more seconds had it not been drowned out by the explosion. The shack was transformed into a ball of red-orange flame, a belch of black smoke and a shower of kindling wood in a matter of seconds.

Immediately after he fired, Morgan put the rifle aside, reached into his shirt pocket and extracted a small mirror. He stood up, positioned himself and sent two flashes in the direction of the riders. It was the pre-arranged signal to let Lucy and Jim Keyes, the Double C ranch hand, know the position of Coltrane's men. A moment later, both were firing Winchesters toward the ridge. Morgan smiled with satisfaction.

Below him, Ike couldn't believe his eyes. "Shit! We been bushwhacked." The rifle shots toward them a few moments later brought another reaction—this one from brother Cole.

"They think we did it." Both men bolted for their horses. The other riders had already mounted up—sure of an ambush. Cole shouted, "Marsh ain't gonna be too fuckin' happy about this." He spurred his mount and got a good fifteen foot lead on his heavyweight brother. In his last observation on the ridge, Cole Larraby had been right on the money.

"You goddam yellowbacks," Marsh shouted. Only Ike and Cole had to answer for the hasty retreat. "You don't know who did what. You don't know if there were fifty riders on the other side of the ridge. You don't goddam know if you got trailed comin' here."

"Marsh. Shit! I thought we better hightail it back here."

"You thought! That's your goddam trouble, Ike. Always has been. You think. Jeezus! You fuck better than you think, and from what I've heard, you ain't worth much at that."

Ike's face turned from pale to bright red. His cheeks puffed up. He began to swell like a puff adder. "Ain't no sumbitch alive kin talk me down that way." He backed up.

"Ike! goddam! don't!" Cole stepped to his left and did a half turn. Ike's gun was already out. Marsh Coltrane had already fired. Cole took the slug in the side. At that distance, it ripped through his innards like a hot poker, ripping away everything in its path. Cole's mouth was, almost instantly, filled with blood. He choked, staggered and fell face forward. Ike just stared down. He didn't see Marsh's gun barrel tip up. Marsh shot Ike Larraby right between the eyes.

"Get these bastards out of here," Marsh hollered after he pushed Ike's body aside and opened the door. Suddenly their kinship with the Larrabys seemed quite distant to Lafe and Tom Caspar. They did Marsh's bidding. Finished, the Caspar boys reported to Marsh.

"You take half the boys and you make a raid on the Double C. Don't try to take it. Hit. Ride. Hit again. Kill every son-of-a-bitch you can see. If you can get as far as the house—do it. Burn everything you can reach. Raise hell!"

"We run into more'n we kin handle, Marsh, then what?"

"Ride straight for Uvalde!"

"Uvalde?"

Marsh Coltrane smiled. "I'll be there with what's left of the town and the rest of the men." The Caspars looked at each other and grinned.

Lee Morgan's plans, at least as far as he had been able to verify them, had gone off like clockwork. Timing, movement, even the mechanical things which sometimes fail men—jammed guns, wet explosives—all of it had worked this morning. Nowhere, however, could one man completely anticipate the actions or reactions of another. War presents this scenario in epic proportions. The field troops are but extensions of the will of the generals. The generals exert that will almost solely on what they believe their enemy will do in a given set of circumstances. Victory goes to the best guesser.

If Lee Morgan had guessed wrong, it was only because he didn't really know his adversary. He had underestimated Marshall Coltrane's obsession with vengeance. Caution and common sense were discarded along with immediate and long-term goals. Marsh Coltrane had been scalawagged. He didn't even care to find out by whom. Anyone in his path was fair game. Such madness defied Morgan's cool-headed logic, and completely scrapped his well oiled plan of entrapment.

Morgan did catch up with Lucy and Jim Keyes. Neither of them looked very happy.

"A Texas Ranger just left us," Keyes said. "They won't have their men up to Coltrane's camp."

"What? Damn! Why not?"

"Morgan," Lucy said, her voice almost trembling, "Charity escaped."

"Jesus H. Christ! How?"

"She—she's a woman," Lucy said, weakly. Morgan's mind flashed to Charity's bedroom at the Double C ranch. Her body—warm, naked and smelling of perfumed talcum powder.

"Yeah. Helluva weapon."

"Jute Yokley's got ever' man available to him lookin' for her."

"She'll likely head into Mexico. That's where she's got her contacts."

"What do we do, Morgan?"

"You two get back to the ranch. Hold the ranchers from moving out yet. Damn! Hold up the wagons too. I've got to get to Villa. Hopefully this won't do anymore than delay things a little. Fifteen men shouldn't stop us, but everybody's got to know." Morgan waited until Lucy and Howie were out of sight, then he turned back north. He hadn't ridden more than half a mile when he saw the dust cloud. He reined up. He frowned. He thought: It's either one helluva big buffalo herd or—

The riders came into view. He didn't remember ever seeing just exactly that kind of sight. Eight to ten abreast and, he reckoned, five to eight deep. At least fifty men. Maybe more. They were riding hell bent for leather straight for the Double C Ranch.

He turned, spurred his horse hard, and leaned into the saddle. He wouldn't be more than five minutes ahead of them. He'd have to trust Villa's own sense and good luck. The ranchers, the wagons and their teamsters, maybe even the ranch itself would be out of luck if these men got that far. Somewhere between them and the Double C they'd have to make a fight of it.

Marshall Coltrane's anger remained almost as dangerous for other men as it had for the Larraby boys. There was one exception. In his frenzy, Marsh forgot about Jimmy Willow. Locked up and shoeless, Jimmy had no guards. In their own haste to do their leader's bidding, none of the other men thought about Jimmy either.

Less than an hour after the deaths of the Larraby boys, the raiders' camp was virtually abandoned. Marsh, riding at the head of more than forty men, cut east over a hogback ridge and then duc south on a beeline toward Uvalde. Jimmy Willow heard the commotion. He waited until he could hear it no longer. Then, he set about to free himself. He had done so in less than twenty minutes. He was startled at what he found—nothing. Nothing but two horses. The Larrabys didn't need them anymore.

Morgan, as hard and fast as he was riding, saw no signs of Lucy and Howie again. He did reach the five mile perimeter at the Double C. He had a decision to make and damned little time to make it. He scribbled out a note, affixed it to his black snake whip, removed all weapons and ammunition from his mount, slapped her on the thighs and headed her for the barn.

Morgan took up a position in a stand of trees. He hastily assembled what rounds he had for the Sharps—five of them. Loaded his pistol's sixth chamber, opened the last box of .44-.40 rifle ammunition for his Winchester and waited. He didn't have long to wait.

The first rider to die was a man next to Lafe Caspar. The Sharps round hit him in the chest and took him from his horse as though he'd been jerked from it by an unseen arm. The proximity of the riders was such that his sudden death was more a disruption than a catastrophe. Many of the second line rides reined up. Their actions resulted in similar reactions just behind them. Half a dozen men out ahead of the man who was shot didn't realize what had happened. The lot offered a skilled rifleman an inviting target and an almost stationary one.

Morgan hefted the repeater and began firing. The fusillade was devastating. Although it wasn't Morgan's intent, he hit several horses. The animals were rearing. Down they went with riders unable to dismount in time to avoid going down with them. Where no horses intervened, Morgan's deadly fire struck human targets. He killed eight men and three animals with the first twelve rounds. He shifted his position and targeted in on the first line of riders who were now aware that something was wrong. Three went down. None dead but all with wounds which would take them out of the fight.

The Caspar boys escaped Morgan's hail of fire but were forced to dismount in order to do so. They scrambled for the dubious safety of a shallow creek bed. Soon, they were joined by half a dozen of their fellow riders. None had yet seen their attacker or the direction of his fire.

Morgan shifted position again, managing to jam a round into the Sharps and completely reloading the Winchester. He singled out another target and dropped him with the Buffalo gun. It served to create as much fear among the living as it did death where it struck. Quickly, he brought the Winchester to bear again. By now, targets were becoming sparse. Nonetheless, he dropped five more men. Again, he shifted positions. This time moving south, toward the ranch. He did so amid a hail of bullets.

Almost as suddenly as Morgan had started the exchange, it ended. There was a pall of smoke amid the trees and into the open range land beyond. Morgan could no longer distinguish a clear target. Neither could his enemies.

"We best git the hell out o' here," Lafe Caspar said. His speech was a little muffled. The result of his pressing his face against the ground. "Marsh said we was s'posed to ride to Uvalde. Shit! We'll never git by here." Tom Caspar was trying to see behind him—without exposing himself. What he saw spelled big trouble. Half a dozen, perhaps as many as eight or nine men, had managed to round up their mounts—or someone's. They were getting out!

"We're losin' the boys. The goddamn yellow-bellies are skedaddlin'."

"I'll tell you fer a fact, Tom, that's what we ought do. We been hornswaggled."

"Shit, brother! Marsh'll kill us. Same as he did Ike an' Cole."

"I ain't goddam talkin' 'bout goin' back. Let's make Mexico." Tom Caspar eyed his brother. Both heard more horses behind them, men shouting to calm the animals. There were isolated shots now and again. Men firing at whatever they believed they saw. Albeit unknowingly, Lee Morgan got a vote in the Caspar's decision making process. His vote made it two against one for getting the hell out!

Morgan climbed a good sized willow tree, wedged himself into a fork in the trunk and found he could see the tops of a few heads. The Winchester removed four of them. The remaining rounds convinced the doubting Thomases. More than two thirds of the remaining riders simply panicked. Scrambling from whatever little shelter they had found, they crouched, ran, rolled or crawled back north out of range of the deadly hail of fire. First among them were Tom and Lafe Caspar.

Morgan climbed down from his perch, cast a parting glance at the disruption he'd caused, smiled and turned to head back to the ranch. He'd gone only a few hundred yards when a line of riders appeared. They were all carrying rifles at the ready, but moving cautiously. Howie Benton was at their head.

"Sounded like a damn war out here," Howie said, eyeing Morgan and looked puzzled.

"Coltrane's men. Or part of them anyhow. I turned them back. At least for the time being."

"Damn! Let's go boys. We'll finish 'em."

"Hold up, Howie," Morgan said. "We can't afford any losses. They're routed. Get every hand you can. Dig in." Morgan eyed the terrain in the direction from which the riders had just come. He pointed. "Back there. Just beyond the clearing. If they should regroup and try coming through here, you'll be in a good spot to hold 'em." Howie looked back. He also looked disappointed. He shrugged. Morgan climbed up behind him and the Double C hands rode back toward the ranch.

When Morgan reached the house, on Howie's horse, he found his own mount neatly tethered. He hurried inside, barely nodding at the two men who stood guard at the door. He was somewhat surprised to see them.

"Morgan! My God! I didn't know what to expect." Lucy Masters hugged the gunman—almost reflexively.

"Guards," he said, questioningly and gesturing with

his head toward the door.

"Howie insisted. So did Mr. Willow. I guess because of Charity."

"Yeah. Good thinking. Now you stay put. Part of Coltrane's outfit is out of action. For now at least. I've got Howie and the rest of the men about two miles out. Ready. I've got to reach Villa."

"Morgan," she swallowed. "Be careful."

Juan Miguel Delgados met his death well. No one could know how many of his enemies gave their own lives to assure the loss of his. But four at least died from wounds inflicted by Delgados' rapier.

Pancho Villa's favored *lugarteniente* was riding at the very forefront of his column. They were a dozen of Villa's best. Each a crack marksman and a veteran of almost all of Villa's earliest confrontations with *El Presidente's Federales.*

Delgados had taken these elite troops out ahead of his main column. It was one of two such columns being furnished by Villa. The young revolutionary zealot led the second column personally.

Delgados' column, by the simple process of rotten luck, cut Marsh Coltrane's trail thirty seconds before Coltrane's hell riders roared over the hillcrest. An uninformed observer would have most certainly reported that Delgados had ridden into a premeditated and well planned trap.

Both leaders and the men they led were, at the outset, shocked by the sight of the other. Coltrane's force, by weight of numbers and sheer momentum, had the advantage. That fact aside, the Mexicans inflicted serious damage to Marsh's riders and, more important, to his plan. Less a plan, really, than raw anger. Marsh realized that the Mexican riders could only represent the tip of a very dangerous iceberg.

Gathering his disrupted riders together again, along with more rational thinking processes, Marsh Coltrane ordered his men back down the ridge. There, he took stock of his remaining resources. Wiley Jenks was now Marsh's second in command, next to the Caspar boys. While Marsh paced nervously, Jenks took inventory.

"Five too bad hit to ride," Jenks reported. "Eight dead. Best I can figure, six run off."

"Fuckin' cowardly bastards!" Marsh's personal force, the men who were to have raided Uvalde, had lost almost half their number.

"Marsh, we can't." Jenks' courage floundered. "Mebbe we better figger—you know, somethin' else."

"Take two men," Marsh said, seemingly ignoring Jenks' words, "get back up on that ridge. Ride it north. Find the rest of those goddam Mexicans. I got to know what I'm up against. Send somebody south, down to the Double C. Get the Caspars back up to camp. That's where I'll take the rest of the men. Get there as soon as you can, but find me those goddam Mexicans!" Jenks nodded. He pulled two men from the ranks and was out of sight in a matter of seconds.

"Mister Coltrane. Mister Coltrane." Marsh whirled. A rider was coming in fast from the south. Several of the men nearby got to their feet. They recognized him as one of the men who'd ridden to attack the Double C. He reined up sudden and jumped from his horse. It was young Billy Eustis.

"What the hell are you doin' here?" Marsh asked, harshly.

"We got waylayed," he said. "Lost most o' the boys. Some jist run off. Lafe an' Tom too, I think."

Marsh drew his gun, raised it to forehead level and pulled the trigger. The nearby men, hard and tough as they were, recoiled in a combination of terror and anger. Almost all of them liked young Billy and he had displayed an almost puppy dog's loyalty to Marsh Coltrane.

"Mount up! We ride for camp." Twenty-four men mounted up. Those too bad hit to ride were abandoned —by Marsh's last order. He had begun his day with forty-three at his side. Fifty more had ridden with the Caspars. Marsh didn't see the seven who slowly dropped behind, slipped away and hightailed it for parts unknown. He knew only that any chance still remaining to him was valid only if he reached the fortification of the camp over looking Rimfire range.

Wiley Jenks did just as he was ordered. He found the rest of the Mexican force which Marsh Coltrane knew was out there somewhere. Jenks and the two men with him all went to the happy hunting grounds with the knowledge that they had successfully carried out their last mission in life. The Mexicans made short work of them.

Pancho Villa squatted down by his big, black stallion. He poked in the dirt with a stick. He rolled a stone about. He dropped his *sombrero* back from his head, letting it dangle by the chin strap. He waited. He got his report. Delgados had been ambushed. Villa stood.

"The *yanqui pistolero* dies." He swung into the saddle. "We ride, *mi amigos,*" he shouted, waving his arm as he turned his horse. "*Sur!*"

South!

Jimmy Willow had sense enough to stay out of the open. He'd followed the base of the rocky ridge ever since he rode out of Coltrane's camp. Now, he watched the riders gallop by him, less than a quarter of a mile away, headed back to the camp and far fewer in number. After they passed him, he spurred Ike Larraby's chestnut mare and headed for the Double C.

Above him, headed in the opposite direction, on a deadly trail toward Pancho Villa's anger, rode Lee Morgan. He reached the break in the hogback. It levelled off and sloped downward.

Morgan started down.

"*Yanqui!*" The word echoed against the rocks. Morgan reined up. He looked. Villa was standing in his stirrups, his right arm held high. He'd halted his army. Morgan waved. Villa's arm dropped, crossed in front of him and drew his pistol. He drew the other one as well. He dropped the mount's reins.

"Villa!" Morgan shouted. The Mexican bandit spurred his horse, raising the pistols in front of him. Morgan thought: The sonuvabitch is a helluva horseman. The distance was about two hundred yards and closing fast. "Shit!" Morgan would have to gamble. He dismounted, slapped the horse on the rump, reached up and unbuckled his gunbelt. He raised it above his head. Villa had halved the distance. The Mexican leaned forward slightly, gripping the pistols tighter and beginning to steady them. Morgan waggled the gunbelt back and forth and then whirled it over his head for two full circles, turning loose as it began a third.

At fifty yards, Pancho Villa fired two shots. Lee Morgan went down. Villa reined up, the black stallion rearing and Villa displaying superb ability as he kept to the saddle and holstered his guns. He brought the animal under control. It snorted. Villa high stepped the big horse up the slope. Morgan got to his feet. His left hand was clamped over his right arm. His sleeve was dark with a wetness that seeped into the material from the hole in his arm.

"You think I will not kill you, *señor*, because you beg like a dog?"

"Kill me, Villa. Or be man enough to listen."

"More of your lies. Delgados is dead. A dozen of my best *vaqueros* are dead. I have seen no wagons. No guns except those turned against me. Tell me, *yanqui,* why should Villa listen?"

"Because Villa is wrong about *why* it happened. So either listen or kill me. No one but you and I will know you shot down an unarmed man."

Villa's cross draw was a blur of speed. The pistol landed at Morgan's feet. "Pick it up. I will give you that chance. If you do not, then you die a coward—not unarmed."

"Fuck you," Morgan said. He turned his back on Villa. The angry Mexican leader nudged the stallion, ramming into Morgan's back. Morgan went down, face first, hard. Villa dismounted, picked up his gun, walked to Morgan, grabbed Morgan's arm, rolled him over and Morgan cut loose with a left. Villa reeled and landed on his back. Morgan dropped to his knees, grabbed the pistol, cocked it and leveled it at Villa's head.

"You do not frighten me, *yanqui.* My destiny is not to die in this fight. I have much to do in *Mehico.*"

"Well that's real interesting, *mi amigo,*" Morgan replied, sarcastically. "Because my destiny is not to die here either. See. I placed mine with yours for a year."

Morgan smiled, "In *Mehico!*"

"Caramba!" Villa pushed up to his elbows. "If I defy destiny, *señor,*" Villa shrugged, "who knows what would happen to my country?"

"Yeah." Morgan winced. His arm hurt like hell. "Who knows?"

"Then, Morgan, tell me your lies."

Morgan tossed the pistol to the big Mexican and sat down, hard. "To hell with you, Villa. Get me back to the ranch. I'll tell you there. *That* is my *destiny.*"

12

A full-fledged *fiesta* would have been premature. The job wasn't finished. Still, there was ample cause to be thankful. Jimmy Willow's safe return headlined the affair. The information he carried with him proved a good secondary excuse for comsumption of tequila. He'd overheard much of what Coltrane's men had been saying before they rode out. The anger of Marsh Coltrane—planned destruction of the Double C ranch and the sacking of Uvalde. So much for revenge.

Marsh's failure had been most costly to Villa, even though Marsh's rag-tag army had suffered the highest losses. The dozen Mexican *vaqueros* had been worth any twenty-five of Marsh Coltrane's saloon dregs. Lee Morgan felt much responsibility for that—his misjudgement of Marsh. So much for the best laid plans of men.

Now however, the ledger sheets again on balance, there was a respite. Villa, no less angry but directing it toward Marsh Coltrane, posted twenty men in Uvalde. Another twenty were designated to remain at the Double C. Even with his reduced force and the losses of men who rode with Delgados, Villa could still field forty veterans. At dawn, the supply wagons would leave the ranch. Bait again. If Coltrane was drawn out, Villa would be waiting. If not, he and Morgan would do it the hard way.

Morgan's wound had ripped flesh and some muscle. No bone. Cleaned and bandaged, it would heal without lingering problems. For now, he had to avoid any need for his fast draw.

The ranch was quiet now. He could hear only the occasional squeal of a *señorita.* Villa had dipped into the till and brought forth some of Uvalde's finest for his men. Morgan chuckled at Villa's attitude. Morgan had asked him what *señor* de Lopez would think of such expenditures. Villa said: "The wages of sin, *mi amigo,* are always collected at inconvenient times and unexpected places."

"Morgan." The gunman's eyes were closed. His brow wrinkled. The dream seemed real. "Morgan!" The voice was louder but still retained its softness. He blinked awake. The doorknob turned. The gun came from beneath the pillow.

Morgan sighed. "Lucy. Shout. Knock hard. Bust right in. But for God's sake, and your own, don't sneak." Morgan sat up and put his gun on the nightstand. He wasn't wearing a shirt. Lucy closed the door. "Not here," he said, suddenly realizing the purpose of her visit, "not now."

Lucy slipped from the dressing gown. The body was young, firm, unexplored. The breasts jutted upwards at their peaks and the nipples were unusually large, more flat than round on top and stood erect. The shadows played across the flesh as Lucy moved. A dark patch caught a glimmer of light, then lost it and appeared again, mysterious and inviting. The thighs were creamy, the stomach taut, the odor irresistible.

Lucy approached the bed, dropped to her knees and pulled back the top sheet. She began kissing Morgan. His wounded arm first. Then she moved it above his head and kissed his chest. She worked lower. Morgan's thumbs hooked inside the bottoms of his underdrawers and slipped them down, raising his knees only long enough to remove the drawers completely. He stretched his legs out, spreading them slightly.

Lucy's fingers began drawing nothing on his bare flesh. Her lips and then her tongue became the center of her activity. Morgan's shaft hardened and crept up to meet her advances. She slipped the knob against soft lips, bit down ever so gently and flicked her tongue, lizard like, over this most sensitive area. Morgan groaned. His legs stiffened. Lucy lowered her head and began a rhythmic series of movements which alternated between her lips, tongue and teeth.

After several minutes, Lucy's hand slipped between Morgan's legs and she fingered, stroked and tickled the flesh. The combined sensations quickly brought Morgan to the verge of release. She stopped. She stood up. Morgan's breath was coming in short, rapid gasps. She gingerly crawled over him, tugging at him to turn to face her. He did. His sudden arousal lapsed into remission as he began administering doses of passion to Lucy.

She found it difficult to remain motionless but Morgan applied more strength each time she moved until, finally, she could barely move at all. The sensations were heightened and she moaned. He worked over her breasts, concentrating on those rigid and sensitive knobs. His hands and fingers explored further down. He spread flesh and found her clitoris. It was miniscule, but it must have been all nerve endings. Lucy convulsed and climaxed immediately. He stopped. She grabbed his hands and returned them to their former positions. He resumed his ministrations.

"Take me, Morgan. My God. Take me. Make me a woman. A whole woman." He did. They reached fruition of their efforts together, bodies writhing in physical pleasure which exceeded individual pain.

Morgan's wound came open. It bled. Lucy gently washed and rebandaged it. They lay, side by side in the darkness—the quiet, the depths of their own thoughts.

"It was beautiful," Lucy said. "More than I ever imagined." She touched Morgan's arm. "Was it good for you?"

"Very good."

"As good as Charity?"

"Better," he lied. "It was selfless."

"No it wasn't. It was for me. I wanted it. I didn't care how."

"You cared." Lucy accepted what he said. What she thought was one thing but why tarnish the dream.

Marsh Coltrane had finally come to his senses. He posted men along the ridge. He charged them with staying alert at risk of their lives if they did not. He had twenty-two men who would ride with him. Two more had skulked away in the dark of the night. He sat with Wiley Jenks.

"Yesterday's events may not be as tragic as they appear. Those freight wagons are to move today. By now those people must think I'm history."

"Mebbe, but how can we be sure them wagons won't be another trap?"

"Sitting here, we can't be sure," Marsh replied. "But I intend to be sure."

Wiley frowned. "How?"

"You're riding out, Wiley. You're the only man left in this outfit I can trust. With that kid running off, we don't know anything for sure. But you're not known hereabouts. Not by anybody."

"Damn risky. An' it's my neck."

"Half our men will be moving out at sunup along the ridge, out of sight. You parallel them. If they're sending wagons out, they'll start 'em at first light. If you haven't seen any signs by an hour after sunup, join the men and come back here. There won't be any wagons, leastways not comin' in this direction."

"And if I do?"

"Approach them." Marsh grinned and reached into his shirt pocket. "I borrowed this off a marshal awhile ago. Figured it might come in hand. Pin it on."

Wiley Jenks looked at the shiny tin star.

U.S. Marshal
Texas

Jenks grinned. He liked the idea. Mostly he liked the badge.

Barely a dozen miles away, two other men were meeting.

"You risk much that is not yours to risk, *mi amigo.*" Morgan had just informed Pancho Villa that a dozen wagons carrying the real supplies for his base in Mexico would depart the Double C at sunup, going north.

"It's mine," Morgan shot back. "I'm hired to shotgun the load and deliver it. You want it now?"

Villa looked puzzled. "No," he said.

"Then it's mine 'til I make delivery."

"If you fail, Villa will kill you without the talk this time, *señor.*"

"If I fail, somebody else will have beat you to it. Now you just make sure you're in position. If Coltrane's riders are still up there and the bait draws them into that range, you'll have one chance to end it."

"And Coltrane is mine, *señor,* personally."

"I've bargained away all I'm bargaining with you, *mi amigo.* Marshall Coltrane belongs to the fella who's man enough to get him." Villa shrugged and grinned, pointing at Morgan's arm. "Perhaps it would not be so wise for you to catch up with him. I hear he is very fast."

"Can you beat him?"

"Si *señor.*"

"And I can beat you. Wound and all. Should be about right." Morgan grinned. Villa did not. He was touchy about his gun skills. In fact, the young zealot wondered if he really could beat Lee Morgan. Wound and all.

"Adios amigo. 'Til we meet in *Mehico."*

"See you, Villa," Morgan said. He turned. Villa galloped off. His men stirred up the dust as they trailed him. Morgan looked at the sky. A faint pink was bleeding up over the horizon. By daylight, Villa would be ready. He would give the Mexican half an hour. Then the wagons would follow.

He found no sign of Lucy when he entered the ranch.

He thought her still asleep. He went to the kitchen. The Chinese had prepared coffee. He poured a cup. He heard someone behind him. He turned.

"Jeezus!" Lucy stood in the doorway. She was clad in buckskins and had a Colt's .45 Peacemaker strapped on. "Who in hell do you think you are? Calamity goddam Jane?"

"Lucy Masters," came the crisp reply, "freight line owner and teamster. At least on this trip."

"The hell you are."

"Last night means nothing to me, Morgan. When it comes to business, you work for me. Remember?"

"And you stay in the office and do the bookwork."

"Uh uhn. If this load doesn't make it, there'll be no books. No office for that matter. I ride lead wagon or nothing moves out of here."

"Lucy. You're being a damned fool. What do you plan to do with that cannon on your hip?" Lucy drew, whirled, fired three times and took the wooden knobs off the corners of a cherrywood table. She breached the weapon and reloaded.

"I'll be damned!" Morgan shook his head. He couldn't help but smile. "Okay, girl, I'm convinced." He stepped over to her, leaned down, took her in his arms and kissed her. When she pulled back, Morgan said, "Just keep that pretty little head down. That's all."

She grinned. "That isn't the part I'd have thought you wanted me to protect."

"Isn't that the part that says *yes?*" Lucy laughed.

"Mornin' ma'am." Lucy halted the team. The man looked saddle weary, unkempt, and she was on her guard. So was her shotgun rider.

"G'mornin'," she replied. He eyed the line of wagons. Fifteen in all. She felt reasonably secure since there had been no signs of anyone for miles. In this particular stretch, the land undulated in gentle hills. A lone rider could be out of sight until he was almost on top of you. That had been the case. Larger numbers were easier to spot. Still, she wished Morgan was here. He was leading the second half of Villa's men and some of the ranchers whose preference it had been to see direct action.

"Heap o' freight you're haulin'. Where you bound?" Lucy noted that even as the man spoke, he was eyeing the depth of the wheel tracks.

"Del Rio," she said.

He frowned. "Little north o' the trail, aren't you?"

"Been a lot of raids lately. You must be new to the territory or you'd have known that."

"I'm new," he said, pulling back his coat and exposing the tin star. "Marshal Loving. Bert Loving. I'm down from the panhandle. Amarillo way. Man huntin'."

"I know most about. Who you runnin'?"

"Fella name o' Lathum. Charlie Lathum. Held up a stage."

"Never heard of him. But there's a lot o' ranches around where he could hire on."

"Well I'll snoop around a bit," the man said, tipping his hat. "Hope you have a good trip." Lucy nodded and snapped the reins."

"Hyah. Git up now. Hyah!"

"What do you think, ma'am?"

"I think," Lucy said, smiling, "Marsh Coltrane is

going to take the bait." She turned and looked at Willy Vestal, her shotgun rider. "Bert Loving was a deputy marshal up to San Angelo. Got killed a few months back."

"I'll be damned."

"Be alert," Lucy cautioned.

Up on the hogback, Lee Morgan, with the help of Charity Coltrane's eyeglass, had witnessed the meeting. Now, he watched the lone rider double back on his own trail, hugging the rocks along the ridge and riding hard toward Rimfire range.

"Yeah," Morgan said, "tell Coltrane he's got sitting ducks."

Wiley Jenks was back at the compound within an hour. By then, the heavily loaded wagons had only moved about five miles. Jenks downed a shot of whiskey and hurried to Marsh Coltrane's shack.

"Well," Marsh said, looking up. Jenks was smiling.

"Fifteen wagons. Deep ruts. Heavy loads. Woman. Spit of girl actual. Skinnin' the first one. Masters Cartage company it read. Out o' Uvalde."

"No escort riders?"

"Not a soul in sight. Two men to a wagon. Teamster an' a shotgun."

"That's thirty men right there."

"But they'll be in the open."

"Any of those wagons covered?"

"Nope. Not a damned one. No room in 'em fer any men. Looks to me like the real thing, Marsh. Sure."

"All right, Wiley. Good job. Now you get three or four men and scout the hogback. Stay on the sunup side. You see anything—anything at all that looks funny, you get on back—fast."

"How far south?"

"Just to the open range. If we hit those wagons—that's where we've got to do it. If anybody's laying for us—that's where *they'd* hit."

"How you goin' to do it—if'n you do it?"

"I'll take a dozen men, skirt the hogback to the south and come up behind 'em. You'll be drawing their fire. I don't want those wagons burned. If they're loaded with the real thing, they'll be ours, Wiley, and the contents will bring a pretty penny in Mexico."

"I'll ride out right now, Marsh."

"And when you come back, if everything is clear, take the men that will be left here and hit the wagons. I'm leaving now to get into position behind them. Any trouble at all—you or me—we get back here. That happens—tonight we'll split up and head for Mexico."

Pancho Villa sat beneath a willow tree by a clear, cool stream. He was puffing on a big Havana. His men lounged about in the buffalo grass, five of them posted to guard duty. He was three miles north and a mile back to the west of where Wiley Jenks would be looking. He was ready. He hoped Lee Morgan was as careful.

"Mendarez," Morgan said, pointing north and east along the ridge, "see there, where the hogback bows out to the west?"

"*Si.*"

"You take all but one man down along the ridge and into that bend. It's a box canyon. Post a man on top." Morgan pulled out his mirror. "When he tells you he's seen the flash—you ride right back here."

"*Si, señor* Morgan. I know of the canyon." Mendarez smiled. "I used it two days ago."

"Hell. For *what?*"

"To hide the *ametralladora.*"

"The—*what?*"

"How you say—*rat-tat—grande pistolero.* Canon. The gun of many bullets . . ."

"Good God! A Gatling gun?"

Mendarez grinned and shook his head. "*Si, si. Gatalino. Si!*"

"Mendarez. For Chrissake! Villa never said a word. Not a goddam word. That gun would make short work of this little war."

"It is for the *revolucion.*" Mendarez's face shed its grin and assumed a serious expression as he spoke, almost with reverence, about the *revolucion.*

"Shit! The gun won't do anybody any good if it doesn't get to Mexico, my friend. And it won't unless we use it here first."

Mendarez sighed. "It will take time, *señor.* She is *pesado.*"

"Pes—uh—yeah—heavy. Take along some help. But get that Gatling gun up here." Morgan watched Mendarez ride off. He still couldn't believe that Villa would have kept quiet about such a distinct advantage. "A goddam Gatling gun," Morgan mumbled, "and he never said a word!"

13

Wiley Jenks and ten men, riding about fifty yards apart, hell bent and firing pistols, charged toward the wagons. Jenks had ordered the men to close to a distance just out of pistol range, dismount and begin their attack in earnest with rifles. The cavalry-style charge was merely a ploy to draw the wagons' occupants' attentions. If everything was on schedule, Marsh Coltrane and the rest of the men would hit the freighters from the opposite side, unseen and unheard until it was too late. Thing was—everything wasn't on schedule.

Atop his observation point on the ridge, Lee Morgan had heard gunfire, a lot of it, a full five minutes before Jenks' men rode into view. Looking in the other direction, north, Morgan spewed a string of epithets when he saw no sign of Mendarez, the Gatling gun, and worse, no Pancho Villa. He looked back down at the engagement unfolding on Rimfire range. Coltrane's men were already at a standstill. Lucy knew the attack was coming and there were thirty men on those wagons. They would have no trouble holding off the attackers. They could not finish them however, and Morgan had no idea what had developed elsewhere. If Morgan was confused and in doubt . . . Marshall Coltrane was in shock.

As he'd planned, leading the remaining half of his men he'd worked along the ridge to the south of the open range and readied himself to attack the freighters from behind. He suddenly found himself under attack. Even more confounding to him, amid the dust and din of the gunfire, it appeared that whoever was attacking him were themselves being attacked! Marsh Coltrane, at that moment, probably enjoyed the biggest advantage of anyone in the field. He knew his dream was at an end, and he had no other reason to stay. He shot two of his own men to assure himself both a clear escape route and a horse on which to do it.

The Mexican named Mendarez found himself also confused, but more than that, scared as hell. Pancho Villa had made him personally responsible for the care and safekeeping of the precious Gatling gun. He knew his ill-tempered leader would simply have him shot when the truth was learned. Mendarez reached the box canyon to find the Gatling gun gone!

The extent of confusion and shock which stretched across the length and breadth of Rimfire range on that morning was not limited to just those men. One other man, as much angry as confused, and one woman were also players in the midst of the puzzling events. In part, they were responsible for some of them.

Charity Coltrane had, as Morgan guessed and the Texas Rangers assumed, fled into Mexico. There, using her feminine wiles and what facts she had amassed, Charity convinced Captain Luis Huerrera to lead a contingent of *Federales* into Texas and ambush Pancho Villa. Villa, she told the captain, would be totally vulnerable. Assisting *Yanqui* ranchers who were poorly armed and poorly led. Too, she assured him, he would receive unsolicited aid from Marshall Coltrane.

Charity had her facts straight. She just didn't have all of them. One of the most important, one which the good Captain would have liked to have known as well, was the loyalty of one of his lieutenants, and the man's real name. It was Francisco de Lopez! A matter of hours following Captain Huerrera's revelation of his plan to ride with Charity, young de Lopez left camp. He met with his sister, Madiera. In turn, the word reached the one man who, on this morning of mass confusion, was the one man who suffered not. Pancho Villa!

The peasant-turned-revolutionary had pulled men up from their hiding places in Mexico. They were his reserve units. Villa amassed them at a predetermined location and prepared himself with the Gatling gun to destroy Marsh Coltrane, Charity Coltrane and the northern Mexico contingent of government *Federales* in one fell swoop.

"*Prostituta! Ramera! Hija de la Diablo!*" Captain Luis Huerrera spewed the verbal venom at Charity Coltrane as Villa's hordes poured down upon the hapless *Federales* from two directions and the Gatling gun laid down a withering and fatal fusillade from a nearby ridge. Huerrara shouted the words, "Whore. Bitch. Daughter of the devil," as he reached for his handgun. Charity drew one of her Colts and shot him through the head.

At the beginning of the attack, Huerrera watched

with satisfaction as his men massacred the small band of riders who had followed Marsh Coltrane. Charity, mounted on a black stallion and attired in Mexican riding clothes, smiled at the captain, sensuously.

Certain of victory, the praise and an elevation in rank from *El Presidente,* and Charity Coltrane's favors, Huerrera was a happy man. Minutes later, his dream turned into a fatal nightmare.

Charity galloped from the field, headed for the one haven of safety closest to her. Her beloved Double C ranch. There, in a hidden wall safe, she had more than ten thousand dollars. Her dreams too had been shattered, but not her life. She would find a new one, deep in South America.

Lee Morgan was about to ride down to the wagons, flanking Coltrane's men, when more than fifty of Villa's men poured the hogback ridge to the north. Almost at the same time, Mendarez returned smiling.

"It is *acabado, señor. Terminado*—uh—"

"Over," Morgan said, frowning, "finished!"

"*Si.*" Morgan still wasn't happy. But he listened. Mendarez told him what had happened. One of Villa's lieutenants had caught Mendarez between the box canyon and the ridge.

"The sonuvabitch could have let me in on it."

"*El Generale* tells no one of such a thing. No one."

"Well he'll by God tell me from now on, or he's got no lightning-fast *Yanqui* guns."

Less than ten of Marsh Coltrane's hired guns lived to fall into Villa's hands. Nearly half of the Mexican *Federales* surrendered. Ultimately, they would transfer their loyalties to Villa. Most government soldiers were but *peons* themselves, forced into government servitude.

Morgan had just finished telling Lucy Masters of the turn of events when Villa himself rode up. He dismounted, smiled, shrugged and said, "*Siento hacer esto. Perdonar mi amigos?*"

"Shit! You're sorry. Goddam, Villa. Do you realize the risks you took?"

"Nostros area de guerra. Hay mucho. Grande riesgo."

"Goddam it, Villa, speak English. And don't give me that crap about being at war and great risks. We're not at war," Morgan said, gesturing toward Lucy, "and from now on, she gets full protection from your men or no goddam freight leaves for Mexico. At least not on any wagons run by the Masters Cartage Co." Morgan got to his feet. "You understand me, *señor* Villa?"

Lee Morgan was mad. Damned mad. Villa walked back to his horse, opened the saddlebag on one side, removed a thick envelope and brought it back. He eyed both Morgan and Lucy and then handed it to her. She glanced at Morgan and then opened it. Her thumb flipped the edges of the bills. Money. American money. More than Lucy Masters had ever seen all at one time.

"Twenty-five thousand American dollars, *señorita,*" Villa said. "That much again when these wagons reach my fortress in the hills of Mexico. From that money, you hire men, pay them as you choose. The rest, *señorita,* is yours."

"*Gracias,*" Lucy said. Morgan frowned. Lucy scowled back to him.

"Shit," Morgan mumbled.

"Muchos gracias," Lucy said.

Mendarez rode up. He looked anxious. He dismounted and hurried to Villa. He reported in Spanish. Much too fast for Morgan to translate. Villa shook his head, frowned and then turned to Lucy and Morgan.

"The woman was not among the *Federales.* Captain Huerrera's body was found among the dead. But *señorita* Coltrane was not killed or captured."

"Marshall Coltrane?"

"No, Morgan. Both, at least one of my men report, both escaped the field and rode south."

"Together?"

"No, but perhaps to the same destination?"

Lucy looked at Morgan. "The ranch?"

"Yeah."

"I'm going with you."

"Not this trip," Morgan said.

"Damn you! Stop giving me orders." Morgan's right arm moved like lightning again—wound and all. He snatched Lucy's gun from its holster. "Keep her with this train, Villa. Head for Mexico."

Villa smiled. "You ride out to face *yanqui banditos* skilled with guns and ready to kill because they are cornered, and leave me with a wildcat." Morgan couldn't help but grin.

Charity killed two of her own ranch hands coldly with deliberation and skill. Inside the house she killed her long-faithful Chinese cook. She pulled a carpetbag from a closet, hurried to the wall safe, opened it and smiled with satisfaction when she saw the money. She quickly placed it in the bag. It was then she heard the squeal of a floor board behind her. She stood and whirled around.

"Hello, little sister." Marsh had not followed

Charity. Indeed, he had not seen her on the battlefield. Pure chance and memory had dictated Marsh Coltrane's actions. He knew that there was always a sizeable cash fund secreted somewhere at the Double C.

"I'd hoped you would have been one of the first to go," Charity said. Her tone was laced with poisonous contempt. Marsh was eyeing the twin forty-fives. He smiled. Then he looked at the carpetbag and glanced down at the open safe.

"I'll relieve you of that, little sister."

"Like hell you will. I killed to get it. You think I won't kill to keep it?"

"If you were good enough. Probably. But you're not facing two men who trusted you. I saw their bodies when I rode in. And," Marsh said, "I'm not an unarmed Chinaman."

"You bastard!" Marsh grabbed the door, pulled it and jumped back into the hallway at the same time. Charity fired two shots. They were close but neither struck home. Marsh would have killed her outright but for one thing. His gun was empty!

Charity jerked the door open, fully expecting Marsh to run down the hall or try for the stairs. He was just outside, back pressed to the wall to Charity's right. The move he made caught her totally by surprise. He knocked her cold. He grabbed the carpetbag, checked its contents and then removed one of her Colts.

"Rest in peace, little sister."

"Coltrane!" Marsh turned. He fired. Morgan fired back, his bullet ripping through the carpetbag. Marsh made for the back bedroom. It led onto a roof top from which he could drop to the ground. Morgan took the stairs three at a time. He paused for only a second to glance down at Charity. He heard the window open. He ran. Marsh was already on the roof. He looked through the window, saw Morgan and fired. Morgan was forced behind the door. Marsh Coltrane dropped to the ground. Luck still riding with him. Charity's black stallion was tethered at the hitching rail. She had come through the kitchen.

Marsh heard a voice from behind him. Another of the hands. He whirled and pulled the trigger. The Colt was empty. "Damn!" Marsh mounted the stallion, jerked its head to the left, dug spurs deep into its flanks and rode out. Upstairs, Lee Morgan realized he'd delayed too long to stop Marsh Coltrane. He'd have to do it the hard way. First, he'd make certain that Charity would stay put.

"Far enough, Morgan." He turned. Charity was on her feet—her forty-five leveled at Morgan's belly. "You've seen me shoot. You want to draw against a drop?"

"You've already used up your good luck and a sizeable share of somebody else's, Charity. Give it up. You're a woman. A young woman. They won't hang you."

"What then? Twenty years? Twenty-five? No, Morgan. That's too long for Charity Coltrane."

"It's not as long as dead!"

"Charity!" The beautiful, sensuous, deadly, greedy, misguided Charity Coltrane turned. There at the foot of the stairs stood Lucy Masters. She drew against the drop. The slug smashed into Charity's sternum—the breastbone—deflected into an oblique trajectory, ripping away the top of one lung and imbedding itself in Charity's spine. Still, Charity fired. The bullet buried itself in a far wall. Charity didn't know it. She was already dead.

Morgan looked down. His expression was blank. He hadn't had time to register a feeling about Lucy's defiance. When his mind finally conjured up a thought about it, he grinned. His thought was what she must have done to escape Pancho Villa's company.

"Get after Marsh. He rode south. Be careful." Morgan was already passing her. He nodded. "Morgan. "Wait!" He frowned. He turned. "I told Villa he'd have to kill me to keep me there." She stopped.

"Yeah," Morgan said, tentatively.

"He rode back here with me." She didn't have to draw Morgan a picture.

"He saw Marsh ride out?" She nodded. "He's after him?" She nodded.

"I'll be careful," Morgan said.

Marsh Coltrane got a quarter of an hour's start on Pancho Villa, perhaps ten minutes more on Lee Morgan. The big, black stallion added to his edge. Villa's horse was a squatty animal, bred in Mexico for the *vaqueros* whose jobs often took them into rough terrain. She was the mare he used on the battlefield, not the thoroughbred he rode when he was desirous to impress someone.

Inside an hour, Villa was reduced to tracking Marsh's trail. Marsh rode almost due south out of the Double C ranch. The tracks stopped at the Frio River. Villa guessed Marsh would head for Mexico. If he stayed in the river, his speed would be cut and he would cut into the stage road about twelve miles northeast of Eagle Pass. Villa decided to gamble. He pushed the little pony hard, south to the stage road and then all out toward the border town. If Marsh once crossed into Mexico, it was a pure crap shoot as to which direction he would take. Villa had friends in Piedras Negras, just across the border. There, he could get a faster horse and, perhaps, some information.

Lee Morgan had an edge of his own. Young Jimmy Willow had overheard two of his guards discussing the possibility of a double-cross from Marsh Coltrane if plans went awry. One of them had said he'd run Marsh all the way to hell if he had to. But more likely, the gunhand said, he'd find Coltrane in the Mexican village of Hildago. Morgan opted to take his crap shoot up front.

Hildago, Coahila province, Mexico, was, in Lee Morgan's humble opinion, the world's rectum. A mile and a half west of the Rio Grande, it was a haven for whores, half-wits, men with no scruples and no country and a variety of crawling vermin which was much more preferable than its human inhabitants. A reasonably decent man who rode into Hildago and came out alive was, Morgan thought, a good candidate for his country's highest award for valor.

Morgan didn't hurry himself to get to Hildago. If he was right about Coltrane, the man would be there, taking stock of what he no longer commanded. If Morgan was wrong, it would make no difference. On the second morning after he rode away from the Double C, Morgan rode into Hildago. He reined up in front of the *Agua Negra cantina,* the Black Water saloon. He'd been told once that a visitor to Hildago could drink any liquid available in the village—including his own waste—and it would taste better than the water.

Morgan dismounted and immediately loaded the sixth

chamber on his revolver. He was already the subject of considerable scrutiny by a variety of Hildago vermin. He eyed both the spectators of his arrival and the surrounding terrain. It was a miserable collection of both. The one thing he didn't want at this point was any gunplay. He wasn't sure he could avoid it, but he intended to try. Just before he entered the *Agua Negra cantina,* Morgan loosed the tie on his black snake whip.

Morgan's thoughts were centered on the language. Inside the cantina, however, he spotted a grimy looking, overweight, underbathed, white man.

"Looking for a *yanqui.* Name's Coltrane. Marsh Coltrane. Would have ridden in on a big, black stallion. One—mebbe two days ago. You seen him?"

The man barely looked up from his fixation on a beetle which was struggling to right itself. Morgan waited. The man finally reached down and flipped the insect onto its feet. It scurried off in the direction of the bar. It was halfway there when the man produced one of two throwing knives from a waist belt, aimed and let go. He severed the beetle in half. He looked up—past Morgan.

"That's another drink you owe me," the fat man said. He got up, waddled to the knife and struggled to bend over and pick it up. He returned to the table. He sat down, poured a drink, downed it and wiped his mouth.

"I'll ask you again," Morgan said, "have you seen a *yanqui?*"

The fat man looked up. "You get pushy fast, don't you, friend?" Morgan sensed the trouble he'd walked into and decided then and there to face it down. He knew it would be tested at some point. He thought: why not now?

"Tell you what," Morgan said. "I'll stand you to what that gent owes you. Throw in a bottle of my own and buy the one you've already got against an answer to my question."

"Doing what?"

"Killing a beetle."

The man laughed. Others in the *cantina* laughed. The man asked, "What will you use, *gringo,*" the man looked down, "the fancy boots you wear?"

"I'll give you another six feet of distance. We'll use the same beetle. I'll stop your knife in mid flight and kill the beetle."

The man stopped laughing. So did the others. He considered the young blond American. He eyed Morgan's six-gun. He stood up. He was a head taller than Morgan and his girth was double. Morgan tensed—ready.

"You're a liar, *gringo.*"

"Prove it," Morgan said.

A little Mexican with a droopy moustache hurried from the bar, hands cupped. He opened them, revealing a large beetle. The fat man drew one of his knives, walked off six paces, somewhat more than six feet, scratched a mark into the rotten wood and walked back. He took the beetle, placed it on its back and then sat down. "Behind the line, *gringo.*" Morgan moved to the line and turned. The man laughed and nodded to the little Mexican. In turn, he knelt down and flipped the beetle onto its back. It scurried toward the bar.

Morgan's right arm, still sore and stiff from his wound, nonetheless tensed. Blood surged through it into his fingers. Mentally, Morgan sent messages to the arm, messages he had sent scores of times. Messages which had never yet failed him.

The knife was drawn, delicately balanced for the

smallest part of a second and then spun, a turn and a half, toward its target. Morgan's arm was a flash of motion, a blur detected by only the sharpest of onlookers. The pistol barked, the knife shattered, the barrel moved like wheat in the wind, the pistol barked. The beetle vanished. The pistol dropped into the holster.

"I repeat, my fat friend," Morgan said, coolly, "have you seen a yanqui riding a black stallion?" The fat man's mouth was open but Morgan was watching his right hand. It had eased from the table's edge, moved to his knee, edged up toward his waist and a second throwing knife.

"He's back there," the fat man said, pointing with his left hand toward the rear of the *cantina*. At the same time he spoke and pointed, his right hand moved to his waist. Morgan killed him. Whirled and put two more shots over the head of the barkeep. The mirror, already cracked, flew from its frame. Three bottles were shattered and liquid and glassware showered those nearby.

"I get an answer now or someone has bought themselves my last shot."

"The *gringo* rode in two days ago, *señor.* He stays with Conchita Ruiz in adobe six miles south, *señor.* He waits for two *pistoleros* from Torreon. They come tomorrow. Maybe the next day."

"Gracias, caballeros." Morgan backed from the *cantina.* He carefully checked the street in both directions and then mounted up. Slowly he backed his horse into the street and sidestepped the animals nearly half a block. Then, turning, he moved south with the horse at a canter.

The law in Hildago was simple. Survive. Morgan had —so far. A witness to his gun skill—a witness Morgan never saw, slipped out of the back door of the *Agua Negra cantina* and hurried along the backside of the dilapidated buildings. Inside an open barn which passed for the local livery stable, the witness, a boy of about sixteen, spoke to a surly, long-haired Mexican. The man, tall, slender and sporting a drooping moustache, smiled. He gave the boy five pesos.

A minute later, while Morgan was still backing out of the saloon, the man rode south—fast. He found Marsh Coltrane just saddling his horse.

"The *gringo* has come. He has killed *el cerdo*. He rides south." The man was smiling—a sinister smile. Marsh Coltrane knew this man would almost as soon see a contest between himself, Marsh, and the lightning fast *yanqui* as he would face the man himself for money. The choice was Marsh's.

"Three hundred dollars when you bring me the black snake whip he carried on his horse."

"I have heard of the *gringo's* speed, *señor*. I have dollars, *señor,* and I will bring the whip. But only to beetle in a single move. One thousand dollars, American dollars, *señor* and I will bring the whip. But only to show you. I keep it."

"I have friends coming," Marsh said. "Americans with guns too fast for his or yours. Perhaps I should pay them. Perhaps I will have two jobs for them."

The sinister man smiled. He eyed the window of the adobe. He could see no one, but he knew Conchita was there with a shotgun. "Perhaps, *señor,* but perhaps the *yanqui* will get here first. Perhaps your friends will come only to be at your funeral."

"Four hundred," Marsh said, "and the whip and whatever else he carries."

"Half now, *señor.*"

"Half now. You do it now on the trail between here and Hildago."

"As you wish, *señor* Coltrane." The man took the money, counted it, smiled, loaded his rifle, waved and rode off. He was barely out of sight when Marsh, joined by Conchita Ruiz, a Mexican prostitute of no more than eighteen years, mounted up and rode away from the adobe. Once again he rode south.

The Mexican gunman pulled his *sombrero* low over his eyes and slumped forward in the saddle. He gave the appearance of being drunk. He had covered nearly half the distance back to Hildago and had not encountered Lee Morgan. He had peered, carefully, from beneath his hat several times. He saw no signs of life. He cursed to himself. The *gringo* must have changed his mind or decided to wait in town for Coltrane to show. The Mexican stopped, shoved his hat back and stood up in his stirrups. Slowly, he scanned—one hundred eighty degrees. There was no rider.

The Mexican turned his horse and rode, fast, back to the adobe. He dismounted almost before the horse had come to a stop. He was barely off the animal when he looked up at the door of the crumbling building.

"You happen to be looking for me, *señor?*"

"Madre de Dios!"

The Mexican drew.

The Mexican died.

Morgan was still on a crap shoot. He was continuing to make his point. South of Hildago—so said the natives—there were two places a man could go. Hell or Laredo. If they didn't want trouble, most chose hell.

Morgan wanted Marshall Coltrane. Trouble now or trouble later. Morgan wanted it done. He chose Laredo.

The Mexican side of the Rio Grande, showing rather typical lack of imagination, was dubbed *Nuevo Laredo*. Morgan passed through this collection of whorehouses and *cantinas*. Laredo had plenty of both, but it was also a gathering point for wealthy Mexican and American businessmeen. The business, mostly, was stock. Sometimes cows, sometimes horses—usually less than above board. These businessmen didn't ask questions, rarely provided answers and had their own brand of dealing with interlopers.

Morgan hadn't been surprised to learn that Coltrane had been waiting for two gunmen. He'd been right, however, when he determined that Hildago was not the rendezvous point. The adobe had been no more than Marsh Coltrane's Mexican bank. Along with the ten thousand he'd taken from the Double C, Marsh had stashed quite a cache in Mexico in the preceding months. He'd stopped to pick it—and Conchita Ruiz up.

Morgan knew he must do what he had come to do quickly. Aside from the two gunmen Marsh was lining up, he'd have new contacts to make. Morgan had to strike first and now that would be tougher. Exactly three times tougher.

14

Morgan read the sign: *La Mujer de Oro—Cantina.*

It appealed to him. The Golden Lady saloon. He tied his horse at the single remaining spot at the hitching rail. It was summer. The peak of herding time. Friday night before many big drives north began. There would be buyers and sellers in Laredo—of almost anything.

The Golden Lady was not a sham. Its interior was an elegant display of someone's good taste. The bar, a dark, rich mahogany, ran the full length of the building—nearly half a block! The brass rail along its base was broken in continuity only by the placement of highly polished spitoons.

Saloon girls abounded. They and the male employees wore black toreador dress, save for the men's vest of gold brocade. He noted half a dozen men, posted at strategic positions, armed with shoulder rigs and shotguns. Fully half of the interior was devoted to gaming tables. There was no shortage of customers.

"Yes sir?"

"Whiskey."

"Our house whiskey is Kentucky Moon sir, unless

you have a preference."

"That's fine."

Morgan downed three shots. When the barkeep returned, Morgan asked, "I'm looking for a business associate. American. Tall. Dark haired. His name is Marshall Coltrane."

"I'm sorry, sir, I rarely learn the names of our customers. Perhaps the house manager could be of service." The barkeep pointed. Morgan looked. This man was Mexican but wearing an American suit. Finely tailored. A telltale bulge under his left arm told Morgan he was more than just a manager.

"Thanks."

"His name is Ramon Ortega."

Morgan nodded and the barkeep walked away. It was then just Morgan's eyes met those of the girl. She was very tall with raven hair which hung to her waist. Her black eyes flashed in the bright lights of the cantina. She wore a fitted gown with a flared bottom and a bodice which both issued an invitation and made a promise. Their eyes locked. The girl moved her left hand. It held a fan. She moved the fan over her face, just below her eyes. She held it there for only a moment and then lowered it. Morgan knew the signal. The Mexican woman who had once served his father at the Spade Bit Ranch had explained them all. He didn't remember all of them. He remembered this one.

"*Buenos noches, señorita.*"

"Good evening," she said. She stood up. "Will you join me for a drink, *señor?*" Her eyes rolled toward the stairway. Morgan nodded, almost unnoticibly.

The room was as immaculate, if not as large, as the casino. The woman went immcdiately to a credenza.

She didn't turn when she asked, "What is your desire, *señor*?" It wasn't a drink but that was a starting point.

"Whiskey."

"I have some excellent American stock, a Tennessee blend, I believe."

"Fine." She poured two and brought Morgan his.

"To us, *señor.*" They drank. She gestured toward two chairs at a small table in the corner. "You think me brash?"

"I think you're a very beautiful woman with an excellent command of my language and," Morgan looked around, "equally excellent tastes."

"But not too forward?"

"I'm not much on small talk, although I do like to know just who it is I'm talking to."

"They call me Hermosa."

"Beautiful. It fits."

"And you?"

"Lee Morgan."

"A buyer or seller of cattle? Or horses?"

"Neither. I'm looking for a man. An American."

"Then you are a lawman?"

"Not that either. Or a bounty hunter or a killer. I work for someone in Texas who was wronged by this man. I'd like to take him back to face my employer."

"Must you find this man tonight?"

"No."

"Then, *señor* Morgan, will you stay with me?"

Morgan got to his feet. "Don't be insulted. But no, I won't."

"Do you think me a prostitute?"

"No. At least that is not the impression you've given."

"I am not. So money can't be your reason." Morgan thought: I've got no good reason, and I'll think of myself as a damned fool later. His eyes traveled to the cleavage. The breathing only added to the desire as the woman's breasts rose and fell almost like a heartbeat.

"I've been on the trail for nearly four days. I'm damned roady. I'm even more tired. I couldn't do either of us justice."

Hermosa smiled. "I've never met a man who cared about how well he performed—or that the woman received any enjoyment at all."

Morgan's eyes had just shifted from the cleavage again when they caught sight of a dark, moving patch on the sloped side of one of the glasses. He twisted, dropped, rolled behind a love seat and heard the muffled scream as the bullet tore into Hermosa's lovely, undulating left breast. The manager's gaze froze on the woman's body. His mouth dropped open in the shock of what he'd done. Morgan killed him. The man behind him ran. Morgan had already gauged the outside front of the building. The fancy sign hung from a low, sloping roof. Access to the roof could be gained from one of six windows. He was right by one of them. He got to the roof without opening the window.

Morgan ran to the end of the roof, sat down with his feet and legs dangling over the edge, twisted, grabbing the edge and then dropping. He landed, knees bent, but upright. The man behind the manager burst through the bat wing doors. He might have saved his life if he'd kept moving. Down and in between the horses, he stopped. He looked left. He looked right. He died.

A rider galloped by, hell bent for leather. He fired twice. One bullet took Morgan's hat off and he felt the scrape against the flesh. Too close! Too goddam close. Morgan got off two shots. The man was too low in the saddle and moving too fast.

By the time Morgan had reached his own horse, the rider was out of sight, having turned the corner a block away. Morgan dug his spurs into his mount and the animal responded by throwing divots of street with her rear hooves. Morgan turned the corner. There was no sign of the rider. Morgan reined up.

Man and horse burst into view behind a fusillade of pistol fire from between two buildings. Morgan's horse whinnied. She was hit. He dismounted, slipping the Winchester into his arms as he did so. He came up from the crouch, aimed, levered, fired and saw the rider stiffen in the saddle and then tumble from it. The horse turned, slipped, and then bolted into the darkness.

If Marsh Coltrane had accomplished anything at all for himself it was limited to having bought a little more time. Morgan had gained much more from the experience. He cussed himself a score of times for having been so damned predictable. It could have caused him a very serious breathing problem!

In the daylight, *La Mujer de Oro* suddenly looked like any other whorehouse and saloon Morgan had ever been in—with just a touch more class. In daylight, the two gunnies, both Mexican, proved to be locals with more greed than skills. In daylight, Laredo was a hot, dusty, miserable Texas border town with a mean reputation and too damned many people to make it easy to find one.

Morgan was low on funds. Something he hadn't thought about when he rode out of the Double C. He was in need of a horse and some ammunition. He managed both, but there would be no rooms better than the good old *La Cucaracha* back in Uvalde.

One thing daylight did do in Laredo. It loosened some tongues. By noon, Morgan had learned from three of the Golden Lady girls and two waiters, with some encouragement from his six-gun, that the American and two mean types had spent most of an afternoon in the place. The reason for their visit and its results—were now obvious. One of the girls, however, put Morgan on a trail which, if he didn't act quickly, would grow cold fast.

There was a minor rail spur running north and east out of Laredo. Three men had stolen a hand car, blocked the rails about ten miles out, halted and robbed an incoming train. It was a payroll train which carried cattle sellers' money to the Laredo bank. The American and his two friends in the Golden Lady were overheard stating that they had to meet three friends in four days at rail terminal called Pescadito Junction.

Morgan rode out of Laredo.

And now there were six.

Pescadito Junction was a water tower, a one room railroad agent's shack, a two story whorehouse and saloon and a barn with half a roof. The latter served as the local livery. Morgan arrived at the barn at midday. The heat was stifling. There was not so much as a ripple in the air to stir a leaf had there been a tree nearby. There wasn't.

"*Buenos dias señor.*" The man at the livery barn was shirtless. Sweat poured from a balding head, ran in rivulets along every wrinkle in his face, dripped from his chin and onto a dirty, hairy chest. There, it disappeared

—maybe, Morgan thought, drowning some lice. The man was barefooted. The big toe on his left foot was black—infected from the look of it. The man couldn't see it. His gut blocked the view. "You wish me to care for your horse?"

"Can you handle a seventh?" The man looked surprised. "You do have six others here, don't you?"

"*Si!*"

"I'll keep mine. Thanks just the same. Now about the men who own the other six. Are they all in the saloon?" The fat man's eyes shifted toward the one room railroad agent's shack. Quickly. They shifted back. He smiled.

"Si, señor."

"Yeah. Now, my friend, if you've lied to me, I'll come back in a few minutes and I'll kill you. One more time. Are all the men at the saloon?" The fat man swallowed.

"I theenk, *señor—uno—*one maybe—there." He pointed to the agent's shack.

"And the others?"

The man shrugged. "I cannot say for sure." He smiled. A weak smile.

"Try saying unsure." Morgan loosed the strap holding his black snake whip in place. The fat man swallowed.

"Two upstairs. Three down."

"The one in the agent's shack. Why?"

"*Dinamita!*" He gestured with both hands, indicating an explosion. *"Estampido. Estampido."*

"They're planning to blow up a train!"

"Si, si. Blow up. *Si, si."*

"With dynamite?" The man nodded. Pleased, it seemed, that Morgan both understood and believed.

Morgan was, in fact, puzzled. What train? Why? If he'd heard right, they'd already hit the payroll train. They had ridden to Pescadito just to split up the loot.

"What train?"

"Federales, señor, they come soon. *Hoy."*

"Today."

"Si." The man looked concerned, rubbed his facial stubble in thought, trying to come up with some reasonable English. *"El tren,* she *transporter.* She carries *armas para el revolucion."*

"Jeezus! Guns! Weapons for the revolution."

"*Si si! El revolucion de Pancho Villa.*"

Morgan considered the fat man at the livery barn, but his mind was back-tracking to San Antonio. He remembered! A little map—hand drawn. It didn't amount to much. A railroad line—isolated. An X at one end. The letters P S at the other. The map was in a most unlikely place. The bedroom of Madiera Lucia de Lopez! Morgan hadn't payed much mind to it. After all, he was about to bed the bitch.

Everything came home. Morgan remembered that de Lopez had told him it was Madiera's idea to engage the little freight line from Uvalde. *Inconspicuous* she'd called it. Inconspicuous in a pig's ass! The Masters Cartage Company of Uvalde, Texas was a goddam decoy. Everything Villa did and planned was being shunted right straight to his enemies. Via de Lopez's beautiful, totally unprincipled daughter!

Marsh Coltrane's payoff would have been double. He makes a deal to keep the attention away from the actual weapons shipment. He stages raids, attacks the freight wagons, burns ranches and, in general, raises hell. Everybody is looking for him. When it's over and done,

Marsh has the Double C ranch as well as the payroll train's loot because he's tipped to when and where he can hit it and, more than likely, Madiera de Lopez.

"*Gracias,*" Morgan said. The man frowned, thinking Morgan looked strange suddenly. Preoccupied. Distant, in mind at least. The man couldn't know just how right he was. Morgan dismounted, pulled his whip and his Winchester from the horse. "Stall her." The fat man nodded. He'd no doubt been subjected to similar fear when Marsh and his gunnies rode in. The poor bastard was caught between a rock and a hard place. He had no loyalties except to himself. No goals except staying alive. There were hundreds—indeed thousands in Mexico in the same fix. In trying to change it, Pancho Villa was a hero. How much of the exposure to power would taint Villa's efforts was not for Morgan to judge. History would do that. Long after both he and Villa were supporting marble headstones. Now was now. Villa was the lesser of two evils.

A hundred yards separated the livery barn from the agent's shanty. Morgan had covered about half of it when the lone occupant of the shack appeared in the doorway. Morgan had not seen the man before. The man had not seen Morgan before. Both knew why the other was there. The man was fast—very fast. He wasn't accurate or, if so, he didn't take his time. Morgan did. And now there were five.

The exchange of shots brought predictable results. Two men charged out of the saloon. Morgan charged into the railroad shack. He spotted the plunger. He cut the wires. Bullets began ripping through the rotten wood of the building and what was left of the windows. Morgan went through one of them—on the backside.

He crossed the tracks and dropped behind the roadbed—Winchester at the ready.

There were more shots. They seemed restricted to the saloon. Someone had no doubt gotten in the way. Either that or Marsh Coltrane was displaying another fit of temper. Morgan cocked his head. Boots scraping against loose stones. Morgan rolled away from the tracks. A man appeared off to his left. The man fired. He missed. Morgan fired. He missed. He moved back toward the shack.

Half a block away, Marsh Coltrane stood outside the saloon with two men. Both white men. Both wearing two guns. Both highly skilled at using them. Toby Stiles was twenty-eight. He'd killed at least eight men in gunfights, two of them lawmen. Dave Eubanks was forty. No one was certain how many men he'd killed. But he hadn't faced all of them. Honor was not part of Dave's make-up.

"I'll send the Mexicans toward the shanty. One for each side. Morgan either shows himself or dies. If he showes himself, you be ready."

"Lemme call him out," Toby said.

"Do as you're told, Stiles. You don't know Lee Morgan." Marsh looked at his pocket watch. "Besides, we haven't the time for fancy gunplay. That train will reach the dynamite in another twenty minutes. We've got to have that shack back before that."

Toby Stiles scowled. He didn't need to know Lee Morgan. He knew Toby Stiles, and he knew he could beat anybody. He watched as Dave Eubanks talked to the Mexicans. They protested at first, but Dave told them something and one of them started in a long loop around the saloon to get to the far side of the railroad shack.

Morgan, for his part, was still trying to piece together the sudden influx of information. He was thinking about what the fat man said. *Federales*. Government soldiers. They would be here today. Why? Someone—Villa perhaps—had to pick up the weapons. An ambush. Had Villa known all along? Morgan concluded that at least Villa knew of Marsh Coltrane's plans or enough of them to want to get Marsh.

In fact, Morgan concluded, Villa's passion for wanting Marsh Coltrane wasn't a passion to kill him—but to protect him. To keep Morgan from killing him until Villa could find out what he was up to. Morgan shook his head. He could have reasoned much of this out earlier—way earlier. Maybe a few people would still be alive if he had. He heard boots in the gravel.

Morgan had completely shifted position. He'd crawled on his belly away from the shack, over the railroad bed, and along it for some twenty-five yards. He was now almost parallel with one of the Mexicans who was closing on the shack.

"*Aqui,*" Morgan shouted. The Mexican turned. Morgan killed him. He dropped into a prone position, used the roadbed for an elbow and barrel rest, tightened his grip on the Winchester, sighted in on the second Mexican who was now running away from him, judged the distance at about ninety yards and fired!

Now there were three.

Face *me* you sonuvabitch!" Toby Stiles started walking toward the shack. Dave Eubanks started to stop him. Marsh stopped Eubanks.

"Let the kid die. Get to the livery. Get a horse. Get

down to the dynamite. Stay there and blow it with a rifle shot."

"And you, Coltrane? You ridin' out with the payroll money?"

"I'll meet you, Dave. South. One day. Hell. It'll be just you and me."

"Uh uhn. If Toby dies, it'll be you, me an' Morgan. We stay 'til he dies."

Every man there heard the rider—a lone rider—coming in full bore. Morgan saw him first. He wore the uniform of a Mexican *Federale.* He rode in from the south. The sudden appearance distracted Toby Stiles. Morgan put the Winchester down.

"Stiles!" Eighty-four feet separated the men. Stiles wore a Colt's .45 Peacemaker low on his right leg. Too damned low. Still, he was greased lightning. He was no more than a tenth of a second behind Morgan's draw. But he was about two inches less accurate at that distance. He died wondering what the hell went wrong.

The *Federale* lost his footing when he dismounted. The horse kept going. The *Federale* barked Spanish too fast for either man—Marsh or Dave Eubanks. Marsh started trying to settle the man down.

"Get him, Dave. Kill Morgan. I don't care how. Kill him!" Dave considered Marsh Coltrane. He grinned and shook his head. He knew what one man, determined and skilled, could do against numbers. The lone man had nothing to lose. Every success reduced the odds and unravelled a few more nerves in his adversary. Eubanks had been there. He'd been the lone stalker. He'd also just seen a display of speed and accuracy which he knew he couldn't match.

He darted for the saloon. Marsh grabbed the Mexican

and pulled him inside as well. Morgan looked around and picked his next move. Inside the saloon, Marsh Coltrane listened to the Mexican soldier. His force, twenty-five men, had been ambushed. Forty riders, many armed with only clubs, but vicious and unafraid and led by none other than Pancho Villa himself. The plans had gone awry again.

In a typical display of a second rate leader who finally recognizes that he has lost, Marsh Coltrane killed the messenger for the message he delivered. He'd seen Dave Eubanks go upstairs. He smiled. It was time to get the hell out of Pescadito Junction. He headed for the back door.

Dave Eubanks, a high-powered Winchester fitted with a telescopic sight in his hands, peered from the saloon window. He spotted Lee Morgan's hat crown just above the edge of the railroad shack's window. He smiled. He aimed, lowering the barrel and knowing full well the bullet's capacity for piercing the two by four frame. He fired. The hat disappeared.

"Up here!" Eubanks' eyes got big and round. He leaned out, looking up and to the left toward the sound. It came from the top of the water tower. Morgan fired. Now there was one.

Pancho Villa stepped out of the livery barn. Marsh Coltrane froze in his tracks. Villa drew both his pistols, firing them alternately. Marsh, no slouch in a pinch, dived, rolled, drew and fired three times. It was all he could fire. His gun was empty. It was all he had to fire. He hit Villa in the leg. He charged the Mexican bandit, kicked the guns from his hands, and a bullet tore up the dirt near him. He turned. Morgan was coming. Marsh bolted.

Inside the livery, he backed the big, black stallion out of the stall, mounted up, spurred the animal and tore out of the barn, wheeled and rode east. Morgan knelt by Villa.

"Everything you were doing was being—" Villa was shaking his head and smiling.

"I know, *señor* Morgan." He gestured with his head. "Get Coltrane. Now you can get him, *señor.* I don't need him anymore."

"I can't catch him. Not with my mount."

"He's riding toward my men, *señor.* He will have to turn back. He has no *pistola.* Get him, Morgan."

A breeze now blew across the open country from south to north. It didn't cool things down. The wind was hot. The dust devils danced on the desert floor. The heat of the midday sun struck and ground and bounced off creating opaque, wavering barriers through which everything appeared distorted.

Morgan saw the line of riders. They appeared more distant than they were. Their horses legs looked rubbery and twisted through the heat waves. Between him and the riders, there was Marshall Coltrane.

He saw the riders. He reined up. He looked south. There were more. He looked north. The train was coming in. He turned his horse. He saw Lee Morgan. He spurred the black stallion, rode forward about fifty yards, unsheathed his rifle and held it in the air. Morgan reined up. Marsh wanted out. Morgan didn't mind obliging him.

Marsh looped the reins around the saddle horn,

leaving a little slack. The stallion pawed, seemingly aware of the imminent charge. Morgan wet his lips, tucked the reins in his mouth and bit down. He hefted the Winchester out of its scabbard. He checked it for load and levered a shell into the chamber.

Marsh Coltrane spurred the stallion and he dropped his rump, dug in and plowed forward. Morgan waited. The stallion picked up speed. Marsh leaned forward in the saddle, bringing the rifle to bear. Morgan waited. Marsh fired. Morgan heard the shell. Morgan spurred his horse.

Marsh Coltrane lifted the rifle across in front of his body to work the lever action. He'd fired the first time one handed. Morgan used both as though he was stationary. Holding reins in his mouth, he tugged or released pressure on them to signal his mount for the slightest movement. Marsh fired. Morgan winced and grunted. The bullet tore through his boot top and cut a ridge of flesh away from the inside part of his left ankle.

Morgan fired. The bullet struck Marsh's right thigh, dead center. It burrowed through tissue, muscle and finally imbedded itself in the femur. Marsh brought up his rifle to work the lever. Morgan fired. The second shot struck the saddle horn. It ripped the horn away, the reins dropped, the bullet split and a section of it buried itself in Marsh Coltrane's groin. He screamed. He dropped his weapon.

The loop in the reins dropped to the ground, the stallion's foreleg stepped through it, the animal's eyes turned fiery red in fear. It struggled to stay on its feet. It did. Marsh Coltrane, his hands cupped over his groin, went forward over the horse's head. He could not control his movement or break his fall in time. He was in a semi-ball and landed almost on the top of his head. Weight and momentum combined to break his neck. He lived for another full minute.

15

Madiera Lucia de Lopez tried to flee to Mexico. There, she would have married the son of *El Presidente.* Villa's men caught her. The beautiful Madiera would have ended her own life but for one man. Her father. He shot her through the heart.

Lee Morgan collected his money. A considerable sum from all sources. He bought a new horse, new trail gear, and new clothes. He stayed at the Double C ranch. It now belonged to Lucy Masters, purchased at auction when the county established that there were no family members to take it over. It reverted to the state for taxes.

Morgan was ready to ride out to Mexico. He still had a year of servitude and a few gun hands to round up. Villa had kept his word. Now Morgan would have to keep his.

"*Ahh. Señor Morgan. Mi Amigo.*" Morgan was just exiting the ranch house. He looked up and saw Pancho Villa. He was mounted on Marsh Coltrane's black stallion.

"You already own a black horse, Villa. Why do you want another one?"

"One for battle. One for the *parada. El grande exstasiar!*"

"Parade? Grand entrance. Into what?"

"Mehico City, mi amigo. When the lightning-fast *Yanqui* has killed all my enemies, I will ride in. *El Presidente."*

"You got a helluva vivid imagination, Villa," Morgan said.

Villa laughed. "*Si.* One day perhaps. But it is a long time yet."

"Well let's get to it."

"Manana, señor Morgan. Manana!"

"Bullshit on tomorrow. I've got nothing holding me here."

"Behind you, *mi amigo.*" Morgan frowned and turned. There stood Lucy Masters. She was supposed to have been in El Paso.

"The *revolucion.* She will keep a day or two perhaps," Villa said.

"Or a week," Morgan said. He walked over to Lucy. "What the hell are you doing here?"

"Can I go to Mexico with you?"

"Absolutely not!"

"Then whatever we do will have to be done here, won't it?"

"Uh huh." Morgan turned. "A week, Villa. That's how long the revolution will have to keep. A week. You'll just have to find something to occupy yourself."

Villa laughed. "Perhaps a few days with my *prima.*"

"Your *cousin?"*

"In *Mehico* a cousin is closer than a cousin in your

country." Villa motioned with his arm. A very young girl rode up beside him. "This is the girl of whom I spoke before, *señor* Morgan. She helped me find Coltrane and got from him the information of *señorita* de Lopez. This, *señor* Morgan, is Conchita Ruiz. *Mi prima!*"

"Well I'll be goddamned," Morgan said.